Frederic William Farrar

With the Poets

A Selection of English Poetry

Frederic William Farrar

With the Poets
A Selection of English Poetry

ISBN/EAN: 9783337275266

Printed in Europe, USA, Canada, Australia, Japan

Cover: Foto ©Andreas Hilbeck / pixelio.de

More available books at **www.hansebooks.com**

WITH THE POETS:

A SELECTION

OF

ENGLISH POETRY.

BY

F. W. FARRAR D.D.,

CANON OF WESTMINSTER.

NEW YORK:

FUNK & WAGNALLS, PUBLISHERS,

10 AND 12 DEY STREET.

1883.

PREFACE.

WHEN asked to prepare a manual of English poetry, my only hesitation arose from the number and the excellence of the collections which are already in existence. It is not long since the Archbishop of Dublin published his *Household Book of English Poetry*, and the late Mr. Emerson his *Parnassus*; and though more than twenty years have elapsed since the publication of Mr. Palgrave's *Golden Treasury*, that little volume is still exceedingly precious to all lovers of Songs and Lyrics.

My hesitation was removed when I considered that the plan here adopted differs in some respects from that which is found in most other selections; and still more when I remembered the deep pleasure which thousands of readers have derived from multitudes of different volumes of the same character with this. In my own school-days it was part of our weekly work to learn by heart a certain amount of English poetry, and an Anthology was put into our hands for this purpose. The book has probably long been out of print, nor had it any very predominant claims to attention. It admitted many poems by writers altogether unknown, or long forgotten; and while it made room for some passages of only tenth-rate excellence it excluded others of the supremest merit. Yet I can testify that the little volume gave no small amount of innocent pleasure to many boys, and that the impressions left by frequent reading of the passages there collected formed a valuable part of my own early education. The practice of learning English poetry by heart in Public Schools is not, I fear, so common as it used to be, but I am quite sure that it would with very small

expenditure of time produce more valuable results than some of
the studies in which long hours are weekly spent.

Since familiarity with the best English poetry is so desirable,
I have come to the conclusion that I can at least do no harm
by publishing the following selections. This volume is not
meant to come into competition with any existing manuals.
I have collected from our best poets in each main epoch of
English poetry such complete poems, or brief passages from
longer works, as seemed most likely to be of use in forming
the taste of young readers. No one could read or learn by
the passages here collected without being morally and mentally
the richer and better for it. "The noble mansion," says
Walter Savage Landor, "is most distinguished by the beautiful
images it retains of beings passed away ; and so is the noble
mind." The picture gallery of a pure imagination cannot be
stored with loftier or lovelier images than those which it may
derive from the writings of the true singers who are here represented. The poets, better than any other moral teachers, lead
us to "the great in conduct, and the pure in thought." No
one has better described their highest function than the poet
who so nobly fulfilled it—William Wordsworth. "I doubt
not," he wrote to a friend, "that you will share with me an invincible confidence that my writings, and among them these little
poems, will co-operate with the benign tendencies of human
nature and society, wherever found ; and that they will in
their degree, be efficacious in making men wiser and better.
. . . To console the afflicted ; to add sunlight to daylight by
making the happy happier ; to teach the young and the gracious
of every age to see, to think, to feel, and therefore to become
more actively and securely virtuous,—this is their office, which
I trust they will faithfully perform, long after we, that is, all
that is mortal of us, are mouldered in our graves." Surely this
is a lofty description of the aim of poetry ; yet, lofty as it is,
our truest poets have set before themselves no lower standard.

The first few passages are taken from Chaucer. The paucity
of them must not be taken, any more than in the case of other

poets, for a measure of Chaucer's greatness. The task of selection has been guided in every instance by special reasons, and it seemed undesirable to multiply for young readers passages which abound in archaic words and phrases. But even from the short specimens here given, it may be seen that Chaucer resembles Shakespeare in happy sprightliness and serene benignity ; that he is, as all poets should be, " simple, sensuous, passionate" ; that he knows how to awaken laughter by delicate touches of satire, and also to bring tears into the eyes by natural pathos. If he resembles Shakespeare in his cheerfulness, and power of describing character and telling a story, he resembles Wordsworth in his freedom from mere "poetic phraseology."

> And anone, as I the day espied,
> No lenger wolde I in my bed abide,
> But unto a wood that was fast by
> I went forth alone and boldely,
> And held the way downe by a brooke side,
> Til I came to a land of white and grene,
> So faire one had I never in been,
> The ground was grene y-powdrèd with daisie,
> The floures and the groves alike high
> All grene and white—was nothing else seene.

Could anything be more exquisitely true yet more absolutely simple than the little touch of simple white and green with which the poet brings a spring meadow under the sunlight before our eyes ?

Chaucer has been compared to an April day, full in itself of warmth and brightness, but followed often by rough weeks and frosty nights, which nip all the early blossoms. He died in 1400, and the whole remainder of the fifteenth century does not produce a single pre-eminent poet. The jealousy and opposition of the clergy to all novelties—a prescient intuition of the day when they should smart under the scourge of such poets as Skelton, Lindsay, and Butler—the absence of all patronage, the troubles in the civil wars of the Roses, in which, says the

chronicler, "the sound of the church bells was not heard for
drums and trumpets," may have contributed to the dearth of
prominent poets. Possibly, however, to the middle of this
century is due, in its *oldest* form, that grand old ballad of
Chevy Chase, which Sir Philip Sidney used to say "stirred his
heart like the blast of a trumpet"; and it is at least probable
that during this prosaic period many another of our great ballads
sprang from the heart of the people. These ballads form a
distinct and separate phase of literature, and are well worth
study and attention. Even the ruggedness of their antiquity,
and the uncertainty of their original form in the multitudinous
shapes they have assumed in the traditions of the people, only
make them more venerable, just as one venerates an old sword
all the more for the rust upon its scabbard and the hacks and
dents upon its blade. They deal in strong situations, and
describe with unsparing yet reverent truth the fiercest passions
of human nature. Undoubtedly they are hot, rude, graphic :
he whose mind is not strong enough to walk among scenes of
battle and murder and sudden death ; he whose "slothful loves
and dainty sympathies" are too fine spun to face the darkest and most unspoken tragedies of human life, must turn elsewhere. Yet, as Mr. Allingham observes, "All is not darkness
and tempest in this region of song ; gay stories of true love
with a happy ending are many ; and they who love enchant-
ments, and to be borne off into fairy land, may have their
wish at the turning of a leaf."

Take the well-known ballad of Helen of Kirkconnel. Her
lover is talking to Helen, when his rival aims a shot at him,
which the maiden receives into her own heart :—

> O think na ye my heart was sair,
> When my love dropt and spak na mair !
> Then did she swoon wi' meikle care
>   On fair Kirkconnel lea ;
> And I went down the water side,
> None but my foe to be my guide,
> None but my foe to be my guide
>   On fair Kirkconnel lea.

> I crossed the stream, the sword did draw,
> I hacked him into pieces sma',
> I hacked him into pieces sma',
> For her sake that died for me.

And then, after this terrific outburst of savage vengeance, mark the sudden gush of unspeakable love, tenderness, and regret, in the very next verse :—

> O Helen fair beyond compare,
> I'll mak' a garland o' your hair,
> Shall bind my heart for evermair
> Until the day I dee.
> I wad I were where Helen lies ;
> Night and day on me she cries,
> And I am weary of the skies,
> For her sake that died for me.

The same qualities come out, perhaps with yet more striking intensity, in the ballad of *Edom o' Gordon*. This traitor makes a raid upon a castle in the lord's absence, and tries to seize the person of his lady. Seeing the armed men in the distance, she thinks it is her lord returning, arrays herself in her robes, and prepares a banquet ; but when Gordon comes the gates are shut, and she mounts the tower to parley with him. He orders her to come down, on pain of being burnt in the castle with her three babes ; in reply she bids her henchman load a gun, and fires at Edom.

> She stood upon her castle wa',
>   And let twa bullets flee ;
> She missed that bloody butcher's heart,
>   And only rased his knee.

> "Set fire to the house," quo' fause Gordon,
>   Wud wi' dule and ire ;
> "Fause layde, ye sall rue that shot,
>   As ye burn in the fire."

Without a single break in the narrative, instantly, in the poet's imagination, the castle is in flames, and the thick smoke is rolling through it in choking volumes toward the chamber of the little ones.

> O then bespak her little son,
>   Sat on the nurse's knee :
> " O mither dear, gie owre this house,
>   For the reek it smothers me."
>
> " I wad gie a' my gowd, my bairn,
>   Sae wad I a' my fee,
> For ae blast of the western wind
>   To blaw the reek frae thee."
>
> O then bespak her daughter dear,
>   She was baith jimp and sma' :
> " O, row me in a pair o' sheets,
>   And throw me owre the wa'."
>
> They rowed her in a pair o' sheets,
>   And throwed her owre the wa' ;
> But on the point o' Gordon's spear
>   She gat a deadly fa'."
>
> O bonnie, bonnie was her mouth,
>   And cherry were her cheeks,
> And clear, clear was her yellow hair,
>   Whereon the red bloud dreeps.
>
> Then wi' his spear he turned her owre ;
>   O gin her face was wan !
> He said, " Ye are the first that e'er
>   I wished alive again."
>
> He cam, and lookit again at her,
>   O gin her skin was white !
> " I might hae spared that bonnie face
>   To hae been some man's delight."
>
> " Busk and boun, my merry men a', ,
>   For ill dooms I do guess :
> I canna look on that bonnie face,
>   As it lies on the grass."

Stricken with this new and wild remorse—aghast to see the sweet flower-face of the young girl, with its dew of blood upon the yellow hair—the wretch flies. Meanwhile the lord riding

back to the castle finds it in flames, and urges his men forward :—

> Then some they rade, and some they ran,
>   Out owre the grass and bent ;
> But ere the foremost could win up,
>   Baith layde and babes were brent.
>
> And after the Gordon he is gane,
>   As fast as he might dri'e ;
> And soon i' the Gordon's foul heart's bluid
>   He's wroken his fair ladye.

After reading such horrible tragedy as this, one asks, Is it a
fit subject for poetry? is it right to deal with such scenes?
The answer is simple.   It is not right, if they be told simply
to harrow our feelings with idle and fruitless emotion, which is
the vice of modern sensationalism ; but it is right, if the sin
and crime be spoken of with due gravity and rightness of feeling.   Pity and terror may be evoked, but, as was the case in
ancient tragedy, they may be evoked only for purifying purposes.   It is a sin and an error to paint the horrors of life for
the sole purpose of beguiling an idle hour ; but it is right for
the poet to gaze upon them—right for him "to see life steadily,
and see it whole," if he does so with a due sense of its solemn
and unspeakable import.

As no ballads could be given in the limited space of this
volume, I may here furnish one complete specimen, which is
very characteristic of the *intensity* and of the swift pathetic
transitions of ballad style in the midst of its simplicity—the
ballad of *Edward, or the Twa Brothers*—the ancientness and
popularity of which is best attested by the large number of
different versions in which it appears.

> There were twa brothers at the scule,
>   And when they got awa',
> It's "Will ye play at the stane-chucking,
>   Or will ye play at the ba',
> Or will ye gae up to yon hill head,
>   And there we'll wrestle a fa' ?"

"I winna play at the stane-chucking,
   I winna play at the ba',
But I'll gae up to yon bonny green hill,
   And there we'll wrestle a fa'."

They wrestled up, they wrestled down,
   Till John fell to the ground :
A dirk fell out of William's pouch,
   And gave John a deadly wound.

"O lift me up upon your back,
   Take me to yon well fair,
And wash my bluidy wounds o'er and o'er,
   And they'll ne'er bleed nae mair."

He lifted his brother upon his back,
   Ta'en him to yon well fair,
And washed his bluidy wounds o'er and o'er,
   But they bleed aye mair and mair.

"O tak ye aff my holland sark,
   And rive it gair by gair,
And bind it in my bluidy wounds,
   And they'll ne'er bleed nae mair."

He's taken aff his holland sark,
   And rived it gair by gair,
And bound it in his bluidy wounds,
   But they bled aye mair and mair.

"O tak ye aff my green sleiding,
   And row me saftly in,
And tak me up to yon kirk style,
   Where the grass grows fair and green."

He's taken aff the green sleiding,
   And rowed him saftly in,
He's laid him down by yon kirk style,
   Where the grass grows fair and green.

"O what will ye say to your father dear,
   When ye gae hame at e'en?"
"I'll say ye're lying by yon kirk style,
   Where the grass grows fair and green."

"O no, O no, my brother dear,
   O ye must not say so ;

But say that I'm gane to a foreign land,
  Where no man does me know."

When he sat in his father's chair,
  He grew baith pale and wan.
"O what bluid's that upon your brow,
  O tell to me, dear son ?"

" It is the bluid of my red roan steed,
  He wadna ride for me."
"O thy steed's bluid was ne'er sae red,
  Nor e'er sae dear to me.

" O what bluid's that upon your cheek,
  O dear son, tell to me ?"
" It is the bluid of my greyhound,
  He wadna hunt for me."

"O thy hound's bluid was ne'er sae red,
  Nor e'er sae dear to me.
  O what bluid's this upon your hand,
  O dear son tell to me ?"

"It is the bluid of my falcon gay,
  He wadna flee for me."
"O thy hawk's bluid was ne'er sae red,
  Nor e'er so dear to me."

" O what bluid's this upon your dirk,
  Dear Willie, tell to me ?"
" It is the bluid of my a'e brother,
  O dule and wae is me."

"O what will ye say to your father dear,
  Dear Willie, tell to me ?"
"I'll saddle my steed, and awa' I'll ride
  To dwell in some far countree."

" O when will ye come back hame again,
  Dear Willie, tell to me ?"
" When sun and mune leap on yon hill,
  And that will never be. "

She turned hersel' right round about,
  And her heart burst into three :
" My a'e dear son is dead and gane,
  And my t'other ane ne'er I'll see."

This ballad is truly wonderful. The picture of the gay boys
coming out of school ; the wrestle on the bonny green hill ;
the accident ; the tender care of the homicide for his brother,
and the brother's sympathizing fear of the results to him ; the
agitation as he sat in his father's chair ; the creeping chill which
comes over his mother's heart as, question after question, she
divines with more and more terrible certainty what has happened ; the boy's dread of his father's anger ; the burst of
remorse with which he makes his wild confession ; his headlong flight ; and then the terrifically powerful image, unmatched
and unmatchable save in Homer and the Niebelungen,

> She turned hersel' right round about,
> And her heart burst into three

—all these combine to give a splendid specimen of the peculiar
power and excellence of our ancient ballad literature.

Pope said that it was easy to mark the general course of
English poetry : Chaucer, Spenser, Shakespeare, Milton, Dryden, are the great landmarks of it. If we add the names of
Pope, Cowper, Wordsworth, the list of poetic epochs is complete down to the beginning of the present generation. The
dulness which I have said characterizes the whole of the fifteenth
century, lasted far on into the sixteenth. The first half indeed
of that century had the verse of Stephen Hawes and the
rugged satire of Skelton to enliven it ; but Edmund Spenser,
born in 1553, is its first epoch-making name. Ten years later
was born the poet of all time, William Shakespeare. This is
the Elizabethan age of our literature, an astonishing and
unequalled period of growth. Never again till the great
French Revolution was there such a sudden blaze of majesty,
of genius, and of strength. The decay of scholasticism, the
downfall of the feudal power, the revival of classical literature,
the discovery of America the progress of scientific invention,
above all the spread of the Reformation, and the disenthral-
ment of the national mind from the iron tyranny and super-
stition of the Dark Ages, combined to stimulate the intellect of

men, and to thrill them with such electrical flashes of eagerness and awakenment, as to account in part for the mighty result. The soil had been broken up, and the vegetation burst forth in tropical exuberance. In that day lived Shakespeare, and Bacon, and Sidney, and Spenser, and Surrey, and Hooker, and Ben Jonson, and Raleigh—and the names of poet, and soldier, and statesman, and philosopher, formed often one garland for a single brow. In poetry, however, the name of Spenser is the earliest; and in spite of the tediousness of long-continued allegory, the chivalry, the sweetness, the richness, of his *Faerie Queene* will always win him a lofty place among the lovers of true poetry. In him too, as in all our greatest, we have a steady moral purpose. His end was, he tells us, "to fashion a gentleman or noble person in virtuous and gentle discipline"; and Milton said of him, that "he dare be known to think our sage and serious poet Spenser a better teacher than Scotus or Aquinas."

But, great as Spenser was, his greatness was eclipsed by the greatest poet of that century—perhaps of any century—William Shakespeare. We cannot think of him without amazement. His works are, next to the Bible, the most precious and priceless heritage of imaginative genius. What new worlds they open to us! In one play we are in magic islands, surrounded by perilous seas, with delicate spirits singing and harping in our ears; in the next, we are sitting at the stately council-board of kings, or listening to the roar of artillery round beleaguered cities; in another our faces are reddened by the glare of the witches' caldron upon the blasted heath; in a fourth, we watch the elves, under the yellow moonlight, dancing their ringlets to the wind. And how perfect in their kind is the splendor or the loveliness of those ever-changing scenes; whether, as in the *Troilus and Cressida,*

> Upon the ringing plains of windy Troy
> We drink delight of battle with our peers;

or in *As You Like It*, we watch the wounded deer, stumbling wearily beside the rivulet under the waving boughs of the Forest

of Ardennes ; or in *Macbeth* see the " temple-haunting martlet"
flitting to and fro in the " eager air" about the Castle of Inver-
ness ; or in *Cymbeline* take shelter under the noble Briton's
cave ; or in *Romeo and Juliet* assist at the lighted masque in
the hall of the Capulets ; or with *Julius Cæsar* stand, thronged
with conspiring senators, in the Capitol of Rome. Sometimes
the electric flame of the poet's genius seems to be blazing in the
lightning, sometimes to be slumbering in the dewdrop.

In the following pages only one or two passages have been
selected from his plays—partly because they are all familiar to
us as household words, but chiefly because such passages lose
so incomparably when they are dissevered from their context.

William Shakespeare died in 1616 ; in that year Milton was
a child of eight years old. The genius of Milton dominates
throughout the seventeenth century as that of Shakespeare in
the sixteenth. It was the short and splendid period of Puritan
mastery interpolated between the Shakespeare of Elizabeth and
the Dryden of Charles II. Other poets indeed there were :
there were Donne, and Quarles, and George Herbert, and
Crashaw, and Herrick ; there were Cowley, and Marvell, and
Waller ; and a crowd of Cavalier poets before the Revolution
and after the Restoration. Side by side with these, " with his
garland and singing robes about him," stands the solitary sublime form of John Milton, perhaps the very noblest of England's
sons. Shakespeare was a more myriad-minded genius, but
Milton was the rarer and the lordlier soul. It may be his lit-
erary imperfection, but assuredly it is his moral strength, that
Milton could not have conceived such a character as Falstaff.
For that " foul gray-haired iniquity" he would have had no
bursts of inextinguishable laughter, nor any other words than
those of King Henry V.:—

> " I know thee not, old man : fall to thy prayers.
> How ill white hairs become a fool and jester !
> I have long dreamed of such a kind of man,
> So surfeit-swelled, so old, and so profane ;
> But, being awake, I do despise my dream."

A modern writer has imagined Milton appearing at the Mermaid Tavern, a pure beautiful youth, and, in answer to some burst of witty ribaldry, casting among the company that grand theory of his, "that he who would not bo frustrate of his hope to write well hereafter in laudable things, ought himself to be a true poem—that is, a composition and pattern of the best and honorablest things." "What a blush would have mounted on the old face of Ben Jonson before such a rebuke! what interruption of the jollity! what mingled uneasiness and resentment! —what forced laughter to conceal consternation! Only Shakespeare, one thinks, would have turned on the bold youth a mild and approving eye, would have looked round the room to observe the whole scene; and remembering, perhaps, some passages in his own life, would, mayhap, have had his own thoughts."

But the days of Milton's manhood were cast among men infinitely more degraded than the Elizabethan wits; and among the rhymesters of the Restoration he stands out like a being of another sphere. In the darkest days of English history, amid the loudest dissonance of Bacchus and his revellers, in days which, as Macaulay says, cannot be recalled without a blush, "the days of servitude without loyalty, and sensuality without love, of dwarfish talents and gigantic vices, the paradise of cold hearts and narrow minds, the golden age of the coward, the bigot, and the slave";—in those days, blind, detested, impoverished, deserted, Milton—

> with voice unchanged,
> To hoarse or mute, though fallen on evil days,
> On evil days though fallen, and evil tongues,
> In darkness, and with dangers compassed round
> And solitude—

still "gazed on the bright countenance of Truth in the quiet and still air of delightful studies," and gave to the world, in *Paradise Lost*, the imperishable memorial of a lofty soul. Dryden and Milton were contemporaries for more than forty years; but while Dryden was adding by numerous plays and

prologues to the corruption of the stage, Milton was speaking
in a voice which has been compared to the swell of the advancing tide, settling into the long thunder of billows, breaking
for leagues along the shore.   While the gay creatures who
fluttered in the brief sunshine of a licentious prosperity were
grating upon their "scrannel pipes" their "lean and flashy
songs," he was asserting Eternal Providence, and justifying the
ways of God to man.

There is no need to apologize for the length of the extracts
from the grand austere Puritan, who took his inspiration not
"from the heat of youth and the vapors of wine," not even
" by the invocation of Dame Memory and her siren daughters,"
but "by devout prayer to that Eternal Spirit who can enrich
with all utterance and all knowledge, and sends out his seraphim
with the hallowed fire of his altar to touch and purify the lips
of whom he will."

The next poets who mark an epoch in English literature are
Dryden and Pope.   Dryden died in the year 1700 (and here
let me remark, in passing, that three of our greatest poets died
in the first year of a century—Chaucer in 1400, Dryden in
1700, Cowper in 1800).   It is the merit of Dryden to have
brought into perfection the heroic couplet; and this is what
Gray alludes to when he says—

> Behold, where Dryden's less presumptuous car
> Wide o'er the fields of glory bear
> Two coursers of ethereal race,
> With necks in thunder clothed, and long-resounding pace.

That Dryden was a great poet is undeniable ; that he desec-
crated his high powers and burned them, like the incense of
Israel, in unhallowed shrines, is no less certain.   Happily, poetry
like most of his, "prurient yet passionless," is also ephemeral.
He was well aware of—he was even deeply penitent for—the
sin he had committed in thus polluting the vestal flames of
genius by kindling them on the altar of base passions ; and in
some of his own noblest lines he says—

O gracious God, how far have we
Profaned thy heavenly gift of poesy !
Made prostitute and profligate the Muse,
Debased to each obscene and impious use,
Whose harmony was first ordained above
For tongues of angels, and for hymns of love !—
O, wretched we, why were we hurried down
This lubrique and adulterate age . . . ?
What can we say t' excuse our second fall ?

It is not without regret that I have here omitted his famous
Alexander's Feast, and substituted for it his other less-known
Ode on St. Cecilia's Day. The latter contains however some
very majestic lines, and is in many respects better suited for
the following pages.

The impulse begun by Dryden was continued by Pope, who

Made poetry a mere mechanic art,
And every scribbler had his tune by heart.

As Milton reflects the grandeur of Puritanism in the glorious
days of Cromwell, as Dryden in his many instances of false
taste represents the decadent reign of Charles II., so Pope, in
his smooth, artificial mannerism, is the representative of the
eighteenth century. In that age critics could quote with ex-
travagant admiration a description of Night in which the
mountains are said to nod their drowsy heads, and the flowers
to sweat under the night-dews. The poet of such an age, if he
reflected the characteristics of his own time, could hardly be
expected to excel except in philosophical poetry like *The Essay
on Man,* or in such scathing satire as the lines to Addison, or
such glittering mock-heroics as *The Rape of the Lock.* In
Pope's time all affectation of "the great" in poetry was over ;
for imagination there was mere fancy ; for courageous labor and
solid study there were florid diction and *jeux d'esprits ;* for the
" leisurely ideal building up of a continuous action," there were
frivolities of which the author was half ashamed, and which
were only meant at the best to amuse the leisure of idle fine
gentlemen. So far from being born in a golden clime,

> With golden stars above,
> Dowered with the hate of hate, the scorn of scorn,
> The love of love,

the poet was "a man about town." The lofty ideal of a poet's work had fallen into utter degradation, and Pope helped its fall. Yet such was his natural genius, so correct his style, so powerful his influence, that the sixty years of vacant and regular inanity which followed are mainly due to him.

Accordingly, the next of our epoch-making poets is William Cowper, the shy, religious hypochondriac, who spent his life in remote country villages with old ladies and evangelical clergymen, and who never gave a line to the world till he was fifty years of age. His main contribution to English literature consists in the fact that by his pure simple naturalness and heartiness he was the first to break loose from those chains and swaddling-bands in which Pope had bound the English Muse, and which had produced their worst degeneracy in the vaporous follies of a multitude of writers who are now forgotten. He had indeed been preceded in this work by James Thompson, and to a certain extent by other poets, but none of these were his equals in originality and power. Joined with him in spirit were Crabbe, the homely poet of village life, Bishop Percy, the collector of the *Reliques*, and Robert Burns, the glorious Ayrshire ploughman. What they did was to turn the age from the straight-dug ditches of affected mannerism to the pure and sunny fountains of nature, simplicity, and truth. Pope, with his "mechanic art" would have despised the unvarnished truth of Crabbe's simple narratives ; he would have regarded as half barbarous the heart-stirring, passionate strains of Burns ; he would have scorned the notion of a lovely and serious poem written to an old lady's knitting-needles ; and would probably have condemned as unclassical and irregular those true and tender lines, perhaps the most pathetic poem in our language, which the recluse of Olney wrote on the receipt of his mother's picture.

Cowper is less read than he deserves to be ; but he has this

glory, that he has ever been the favorite poet of deeply religious minds ; and his history is peculiarly touching, as that of
one who, himself plunged in despair and madness, has brought
hope and consolation to a thousand other souls.

O poets, from a maniac's tongue was poured the deathless singing ;
O Christians, to your cross of hope a hopeless hand was clinging ;
O men, this man in brotherhood your weary hearts beguiling,
Groaned inly while he gave you peace, and died while ye were smiling.

He shall be strong to sanctify the poet's high vocation ;
And bow the meekest Christian down in meeker adoration ;
Nor ever shall he be in love by wise and good forsaken—
Named softly as the household name of one whom God hath taken !

Cowper died in 1800. Our own century has produced no individual names so great as those of Shakespeare or Milton ; but
it is, perhaps, richer than any which have preceded it in poetic
wealth and splendor. Poetry is no longer confined to a single
current ; but, dividing itself into a hundred channels, refreshes
every region of human intelligence and human emotion, and
like the river of bliss through the midst of heaven—

Rolls o'er Elysian flowers her amber stream.

A new spirit seems once more to have swept over the heart of
humanity. The literature of the last century has been enriched
by the works of Scott, Byron, Keats, Shelley, Moore, Wordsworth, Coleridge, Southey, Campbell, Hood, and a host of
minor poets.

Out of all these poets I select the one who most marks an
epoch—William Wordsworth. The days are not very far past
when flippant critics thought that they were crushing Wordsworth (they might, says Southey, have talked as well of crush-
Skiddaw) by quoting the two lines :

A drowsy, frowsy poem, called the Excursion,
Writ in a manner which is my aversion,

which was Byron's way of characterizing that famous poem
which Coleridge, with enthusiasm, called

> An Orphic song, indeed,
> A song divine of high and passionate thoughts,
> To their own music chanted.

Byron was long regarded as the supreme poet of his day, and he was indeed the founder, or, at any rate, the chief representative of a school. No one would question his genius or his greatness. But from his school emanated such poems as Byron's *Heaven and Earth*, Moore's *Loves of the Angels*, Shelley's *Cenci*, and Leigh Hunt's *Rimini* ; from the school of Wordsworth such poems as made men more full of admiration, hope, and love. Byron wrote much that no person of delicate feeling could read without indignation ; Wordsworth made his laurel greener by uttering nothing base. The tendency of much of Byron's verse was to make men moodier, more immoral, more egotistical, more selfish ; the tendency of all that Wordsworth wrote was "to lend ardor to virtue and confidence to truth." And therefore much of Byron's poetry and nearly all his favorite characters— his Corsairs, and Laras, and Giaours, and Selims, and Don Juans, and Manfreds—are on their way to the limbo of oblivion ; while Wordsworth has inaugurated a new epoch, and remains the greatest poet of the epoch he began. The difference between the two, as poets, may be seen in the contrast between the two as men. The one traversed all Europe in search of pleasure, and too often "his pathos is but the regret and his wisdom the languor and satiety, of the jaded voluptuary" : the other lived in a rustic cottage among the hills, and wrote with the light of heaven upon him in the bosom of a pure domestic life. One special occasion he notes, when returning home in the early morning, his whole spirit was stirred within him, as

> magnificent
> The morning rose in memorable pomp ;

and there came over him one of those crises, so marked in the history of great minds, which color the whole after-course of existence. "To the brim," he, says

> My heart was full ; I made no vows, but vows
> Were then made for me ; bond unknown to mo
> Was given, that I should be, else sinning greatly,
> A dedicated spirit : on I walked
> In thankful blessedness which yet survives.

And to this consecration—"the silent influences of the morning poured upon his head by the Invisible Hand"—he remained faithful as few priests have ever been to their calling, a priest of nature, a priest of God.

I have for many reasons excluded from the following pages the works of authors yet living. No selection of English poetry can ever be entirely satisfactory to all readers : some will wonder why one poem, which is dear to them, has been omitted, while another poem, which they fail to value, has found a place. Diversities of taste are—perhaps happily—infinite ; and unless a book be made much longer than this, much must of necessity be left out which ranks among the highest efforts of poetic genius. Many poets whose names are not represented in the following pages—such as Hawes, Sackville, Gascoigne, Daniel, Donne, Carew, Giles and Phineas Fletcher, Wither, Browne, Davenant, Philips, Parnell, Prior, Gay, Swift, Dyer, Shenstone, Young, Akenside, T. Warton, Mason, Crabbe, and others of more recent date—would furnish passages not unworthy of selection. But it is obvious that this book would have grown to an unwieldy size if many choice poems and fragments of poems had not been deliberately excluded. I can only repeat that the pretensions of this selection are very modest and humble. If, however it prove to be acceptable, if it fulfil the hopes with which it has been thrown together, it may be followed in due time by a selection from the writings of those poets, both English and American, who to our great happiness are still living among, us and "whose thoughts enrich the blood of the world."

The general plan of the work has been to arrange together the chief poets of each century, and to add selections from the Minor Poets. The term Minor Poets is not always intended as

a note of distinct inferiority.   The order in which the passages
are placed is not in every case strictly chronological.

F. W. FARRAR.

Note.—The selections in this volume from the works of Mrs. E.
Barrett Browning, Arthur Hugh Clough, Thomas Carlyle, George
Eliot, Lord Macaulay, and others, are made by the kind permission of
Mr. Robert Browning, Messrs. Macmillan and Co., Messrs. Chapman
and Hall, Mrs. C. L. Lewes, and Messrs. Longman and Co.

CONTENTS.

MINOR POETS OF THE SEVENTEENTH CENTURY.

Eighteenth Century.

Nineteenth Century.

GEOFFRY CHAUCER.

Born about 1340. Died 1400.

THE SQUIER.

WITH him ther was his sone, a yonge Squier,
A lover, and a lusty bachelor.
With lockes crull [1] as they were laide in presse.
Of twenty yere of age he was I gesse.
Of his stature he was of even lengthe,
And wonderly deliver,[2] and grete of strengthe.
And he hadde be sometime in chevachie,
In Flaundres, in Artois, and in Picardie,
And borne him wel, as of so litel space,
In hope to stonden in his ladies grace.
Embrouded was he, as it were a mede
Alle ful of freshe floures, white and rede.
Singing he was, or floyting [3] all the day,
He was as freshe as is the monthe of May.
Short was his goune, with sleves long and wide,
Wel coude he sit on hors, and fayre ride.
He coude songes make, and wel endite,
Just and eke dance, and wel pourtraie and write.
So hote he loved, that by nightertale [4]
He slep no more than doth the nightingale.
Curteis he was, lowly, and servisable,
And carf [5] before his fader at the table.

Prologue of Canterbury Tales.

[1] curled. [2] agile. [3] fluting. [4] night time.
[5] carved.

THE PERSONE.

A GOOD man ther was of religioun,
That was a poure Persone [1] of a town ;
But rich he was of holy thought and werk,
He also was a lerned man, and a clerk,
That Cristes gospel trewely wolde preche.
His parishens devoutly wolde he teche.
Benigne he was, and wonder diligent,
And in adversitie ful patient :
And such he was i-proved often sithes.[2]
Ful loth wer him to cursen for his tithes,
But rathere wolde he yeven, out of doute,
Unto his poure parishens aboute,
Of his offring, and eke of his substance.
He coude in litel thing have suffisance.
Wide was his parish, and houses fer asonder,
But he ne left nought for no rain ne thunder,
In sicknesse and in mischief to visite
The ferrest in his parish, moche and lite,[3]
Upon his fete, and in his hand a staf.
This noble ensample to his shepe he yaf,
That first he wrought, and afterward he taught.
·Out of the gospel he the wordes caught,
And this figure he added yet therto,
That if gold ruste, what shuld iren do ?
For if a preest be foule, on whom we truste,
No wonder is a lewed man to ruste :
And shame it is if that a preest take kepe,
To see a shitten shepherd, and clene shepe :
Wel ought a preest ensample for to yeve,
By his clene nesse, how his shepe shulde live.
He sette not his benifice to hire,
And lette his shepe accombred in the mire,
And ran unto London, unto Seint Poules,
To seken him a chanterie for soules,[4]
Or with a brotherhede to be withold.
But dwelt at home, and kepte well his fold,
So that the wolf ne made it not miscarie.
He was a shepherd, and no mercenarie.

[1] parson.　　　　[2] oft-times.　　　　[3] high and low.
[4] An endowment for saying masses.

And though he holy were, and virtuous,
He was to sinful men not dispitous,
Ne in his speche dangerous ne digne,[1] .
But in his teching descrete and benigne.
To drawen folk to heven, with fairenesse,
By good ensample was his bisinesse :
But it were any person obstinat,
What so he were of highe, or low estat,
Him wolde he snibben sharply for the nones.[2]
A better preest I trowe that nowher non is,
He waited after no pompe ne reverence,
He maked him no spiced [3] conscience,
But Cristes lore, and his apostles twelve,
He taught, but first he folwed it himselve.

Prologue of Canterbury Tales.

CONSTANCE AND HER CHILD.

WEPEN both yong and old in al that place,
When that the king this cursed lettre sent :
And Constance with a dedly pale face,
The fourthe day, toward the ship she wente :
But nathéless she taketh in good entente.
The will of Crist, and kneeling on the strond,
She sayde, " Lord, ay welcome be thy sond [4] !

" He that me kepte fro the false blame,
While I was in the lond amonges you,
He can me kepe fro harme and eke fro shame
In the salt see, although I se not how :
As strong as ever he was he is yet now ;
In him trust I, and in his mother dere,
That is to me my sail and eke my stere." [5]

Hire litel child lay weping in hire arm,
And, kneling, pitously to him she sayde,
" Pees, litel sone, I wol do thee no harme :"
With that hire couverchief of hire hed she braid,[6]
And over his litel eyen she it layde,
And in hire arme she lulleth it ful fast,
And into the heaven hire eyen up she cast.

---

[1] haughty.   [2] occasion.   [3] nice, fastidious.
          [4] sending, visitation,   [5] rudder.   [6] took off.

" Moder," quod she, "and mayden bright Marie.
Soth is, that thurgh woman's eggement [1]
Mankind was lorne [2] and damned ay to die,
For which thy child was on a crois yrent :
Thy blissful eyen saw al his torment ;
Than is ther no comparison betweene
Thy wo and any wo man may sustene.

" Thou saw thy child yslain before thin eyen,
And yet now liveth my litel child, parfay ! [3]
Now, lady bright, to whom all woful crien,
Thou glory of womankind, thou faire may,
Thou haven of refute, bright sterre of day,
Rew on my child, that of thy gentillnesse
Rewest on every rewful in destresse.

" O litel child, alas ! what is thy gilt,
That never wroughtest sinne as yet parde [4] ?
Why wolde thin harde father have thee spilt [5] ?
O mercy, dere constable," (quod she)
"As let my litel child dwell here with thee:
And if thou darst not saven him fro blame,
So kisse him ones in his fadres name."

Therewith she loketh backward to the lond,
And sayde ; " Farewell, housebond routheles !"
And up she rist [6] and walketh down the strond
Toward the ship, hire followeth all the prees [7].
And ever she praieth hire child to hold his pees,
And taketh hire leve, and with an holy entente,
She blesseth hire, and into the ship she wente.

Man of Lawes Tale.   Canterbury Tales.

THE LAST VERSES OF CHAUCER.

(Written on his death-bed.)

FLY from the press, and dwell with sothfastness ;
Suffice unto thy good though it be small ;
For hoard hath hate, and climbing tickleness,
Press hath envy, and weal is blent o'er all ;
Savour no more than thee behoven shall ;
Rede well thyself, that other folk canst rede,
And truth thee shall deliver 't is no drede.

---

[1] incitement.   [2] lost.   [3] by my troth.   [4] Par dieux.
    [5] killed.   [6] riseth.   [7] crowd.

Pain thee not each crooked to redress
In trust of her that turneth as a ball ;
Great rest standeth in little business ;
Beware also to spurn against a nalle ;
Strive not as doth a croche with a wall :
Deemeth thyself that deemest other's deed,
And truth thee shall deliver 't is no drede.

That thee is sent receive in buxomness ;
The wrestling of this world asketh a fall ;
Here is no home, here is but wilderness ;
Forth, pilgrim, forth ; O beast out of thy stall ;
Look up on high, and thank thy God of all ;
Waiveth thy lust and let thy ghost thee lead,
And truth thee shall deliver 't is no drede.

EDMUND SPENSER.

Born 1553. Died 1598.

UNA AND THE RED CROSS KNIGHT.

A GENTLE knight was pricking on the plain,
Yclad in mighty arms and silver shield,
Wherein old dints of deep wounds did remain,
The cruel marks of many a bloody field ;
Yet arms till that time did he never wield :
His angry steed did chide his foaming bit,
As much disdaining to the curb to yield :
Full jolly knight he seemed, and fair did sit,
As one for knightly jousts and fierce encounters fit.

And on his breast a bloody cross he bore,
The dear remembrance of his dying Lord,
For whose sweet sake that glorious badge he wore,
And dead (as living) ever him adored :
Upon his shield the like was also scored,
For sovereign hope, which in his help he had :
Right faithful true he was in deed and word ;
But of his cheer did seem too solemn sad :
Yet nothing did he dread, but ever was ydrad.

Upon a great adventure he was bound,
That glorious Gloriana to him gave,
(That greatest glorious queen of fairy lond,)
To win him worship, and her grace to have.
Which of all earthly things he most did crave ;
And ever as he rode his heart did yearn
To prove his puissance in battle brave
Upon his foe, and his new force to learn ;
Upon his foe, a dragon horrible and stern.

A lovely lady rode him fair beside,
Upon a lowly ass more white than snow ;
Yet she much whiter, but the same did hide
Under a veil that wimpled was full low,
And over all a black stole she did throw,
As one that inly mourned : so was she sad,
And heavy sat upon her palfrey slow ;
Seemed in her heart some hidden care she had,
And by her in a line a milk-white lamb she lad.

So pure and innocent, as that same lamb,
She was in life, and every virtuous lore ;
And by descent from royal lineage came
Of ancient Kings and Queens, that had of yore
Their scepters stretcht from east to western shore,
And all the world in their subjection held ;
Till that infernal fiend with foul uproar
Forwasted all their land, and them expelled ;
Whom to avenge she had this knight from far compelled.

Behind her far away a Dwarf did lag,
That lazy seemed, in being ever last,
Or wearied with bearing of her bag,
Of needments at his back. Thus as they past,
The day with clouds was sudden overcast,
And angry Jove an hideous storm of rain
Did pour into his leman's lap so fast,
That every wight to shroud it did constrain ;
And this fair couple eke to shroud themselves were fain.

Enforst to seek some cover nigh at hand,
A shady grove not far away they spied,
That promised aid the tempest to withstand ;
Whose lofty trees, yclad with summer's pride,
Did spread so broad, that heaven's light did hide
Not pierceable with power of any star :
And all within were paths and alleys wide,
With footing worn, and leading inward far.
Fair harbor that them seems, so in they entered are.

And forth they pass, with pleasure forward led,
Joying to hear the bird's sweet harmony,
Which, therein shrouded from the tempest dread,
Seemed in their song to scorn the cruel sky.

Much can they praise the trees so straight and high,
The sailing Pine, the Cedar proud and tall,
The vine-prop Elm, the Poplar never dry,
The builder Oak, sole king of forests all,
The Aspin good for staves, the Cypress funeral.

The Laurel, meed of mighty conquerors
And poets sage, the Fir that weepeth still,
The Willow worn of forlorn paramours,
The Yew obedient to the benders will,
The Birch for shafts, the Sallow for the mill,
The Myrrh sweet bleeding in the bitter wound,
The warlike Beech, the Ash for nothing ill,
The fruitful Olive, and the Plantain round,
The carver Holme, the Maple seldom inward sound.

Led with delight, they thus beguile the way,
Until the blustering storm is overblown ;
When, weening to return, whence they did stray,
They cannot find that path which first was shown,
But wander to and fro in ways unknown.
Furthest from end then, when they nearest ween,
That makes them doubt their wits be not their own :
So many paths, so many turnings seen,
That which of them to take, in divers doubt they been.

The Faerie Queen, Book I.

THE MINISTRY OF ANGELS.

AND is there care in heaven?   And is there love
In heavenly spirits to these creatures base,
That may compassion of their evils move?
There is : else much more wretched were the case
Of men than beasts.   But O ! th' exceeding grace
Of highest God that loves his creatures so,
And all his works with mercy doth embrace,
That blessed Angels he sends to and fro,
To serve to wicked man, to serve his wicked foe !

How oft do they their silver bowers leave,
To come to succour us that succour want !
How oft do they with golden pinions cleave
The flitting skies, like flying pursuivant,

Against foul fiends to aid us militant!
They for us fight, they watch and duly ward,
And their bright squadrons round about us plant;
And all for love, and nothing for reward.
O! why should heavenly God to men have such regard?

The Faerie Queen, Book II.

THE BOWER OF BLISS.

EFTSOONES they heard a most melodious sound
Of all that might delight a dainty ear,
Such as at once might not on mortal ground,
Save in this Paradise, be heard elsewhere.
Right hard it was for wight which did it hear,
To read what manner music that might be;
For all that pleasing is to living ear,
Was there consorted in one harmony;
Birds, voices, instruments, winds, waters, all agree.

The joyous birds, shrouded in cheerful shade,
Their notes unto the voice attempered sweet;
Th' angelical soft trembling voices made
To th' instruments divine respondence sweet;
The silver sounding instruments did meet
With the base murmur of the water's fall;
The water's fall with difference discreet,
Now soft, now loud, unto the wind did call,
The gentle warbling wind low answerèd to all.

The Faerie Queen, Book II.

EPITHALAMION.

WAKE now, my love, awake! for it is time;
The rosy morn long since left Tithone's bed,
All ready to her silver coach to climb:
And Phœbus 'gins to show his glorious head.
Hark! how the cheerful birds do chant their lays
And carol of Love's praise.
The merry lark her matins sings aloft;
The thrush replies; the mavis descant plays;
The ouzel shrills; the ruddock warbles soft;
So goodly all agree, with sweet consent,
To this day's merriment.

Ah ! my dear love, why do ye sleep thus long,
When meeter were that ye should now awake,
To await the coming of your joyous make,
And hearken to the birds' love-learned song,
The dewy leaves among !
For they of joy and pleasance to you sing,
That all the woods them answer, and their echo ring.

*   *   *   *   *   *

My love is now awake out of her dreams,
And her fair eyes, like stars that dimmed were
With darksome cloud, now show their goodly beams,
More bright than Hesperus his head doth rear.
Come now, ye damsels, daughters of delight,
Help quickly her to dight,
But first come ye fair hours, which were begot,
In Jove's sweet paradise of Day and Night ;
Which do the seasons of the year allot,
And all that ever in this world is fair,
Do make and still repair.
And ye three handmaids of the Cyprian Queen
The which do still adorn her beauty's pride,
Help to adorn my beautifullest bride :
And as ye her array, still throw between
Some graces to be seen ;
And, as ye use to Venus, to her sing,
The whiles the woods shall answer, and your echo ring.

*   *   *   *   *   *

Lo ! where she comes along with portly pace,
Like Phœbe, from her chamber in the East,
Arising forth to run her mighty race,
Clad all in white, that seems a virgin best.
So well it her beseems, that ye would ween
Some angel she had been.
Her long loose yellow locks like golden wire,
Sprinkled with pearl, and pearling flowers between,
Do like a golden mantle her attire.
And, being crowned with a garland green,
Seem like some maiden queen.
Her modest eyes abashed to behold,
So many gazers as on her do stare,
Upon the lowly ground affixed are ;
Nor dare lift up her countenance too bold,

But blush to hear her praises sung so loud,
So far from being proud.
Natheless do ye still loud her praises sing,
That all the woods may answer, and your echo ring.

* * * * * *

But if ye saw that which no eyes can see,
The inward beauty of her lively sprite,
Garnished with heavenly gifts of high degree,
Much more then would ye wonder at that sight,
And stand astonished like to those which read
Medusa's mazeful head.
There dwells sweet love, and constant chastity,
Unspotted faith, and comely womanhood,
Regard of honour, and high modesty ;
Where virtue reigns as queen in royal throne,
And giveth laws alone.
The which the base affections do obey,
And yield their services unto her will ;
No thought of thing uncomely ever may
Thereto approach to tempt her mind to ill.
Had ye once seen these her celestial treasures,
And unrevealed pleasures,
Then would ye wonder, and her praises sing,
That all the woods should answer, and your echo ring.

Open the temple gates unto my love,
Open them wide that she may enter in,
And all the posts adorn as doth behove,
And all the pillars deck with garlands trim,
For to receive this Saint with honour due,
That cometh in to you.
With trembling steps, and humble reverence,
She cometh in, before the Almighty's view ;
Of her, ye virgins, learn obedience,
When so ye come into these holy places,
To humble your proud faces :
Bring her up to th' high altar, that she may
The sacred ceremonies there partake,
The which do endless matrimony make ;
And let the roaring organs loudly play
The praises of the Lord in lively notes ;
The whiles with hollow throats,

The choristers the joyous anthem sing,
That all the woods may answer, and their echo ring.

Behold while she before the altar stands,
Hearing the holy priest that to her speaks,
And blesseth her with his two happy hands,
How the red roses flush up in her cheeks,
And the pure snow, with goodly vermeil stain
Like crimson dyed in grain.
That even the angels which continually
About the sacred altar do remain,
Forget their service and about her fly,
Oft peeping in her face, that seems more fair,
The more they on it stare.
But her sad eyes, still fastened on the ground,
Are governed with goodly modesty,
That suffers not one look to glance astray,
Which may let in a little thought unsound.
Why blush ye, love, to give to me your hand,
The pledge of all our band !
Sing, ye sweet angels, Alleluia sing,
That all the woods may answer, and your echo ring.

WILLIAM SHAKESPEARE.

Born 1564. Died 1616.

SPEECH OF ULYSSES TO ACHILLES.

TIME hath, my lord, a wallet at his back,
Wherein he puts alms for oblivion,
A great-sized monster of ingratitudes :
Those scraps are good deeds past ; which are devoured
As fast as they are made, forgot as soon
As done : perseverance, dear my lord,
Keeps honour bright : to have done, is to hang
Quite out of fashion, like a rusty mail
In monumental mockery.   Take the instant way ;
For honour travels in a strait so narrow,
Where one but goes abreast : keep then the path ;
For emulation hath a thousand sons,

That one by one pursue : if you give way,
Or hedge aside from the direct forthright,
Like to an entered tide, they all rush by
And leave you hindmost ;
Or, like a gallant horse fallen in first rank,
Lie there for pavement to the abject rear,
O'errun and trampled on : then what they do in present,
Though less than yours in past, must o'ertop yours ;
For time is like a fashionable host
That slightly shakes his parting guest by the hand,
And with his arms outstretched, as he would fly,
Grasps in the comer : welcome ever smiles,
And farewell goes out sighing. O, let not virtue seek
Remuneration for the thing it was ;
For beauty, wit,
High birth, vigour of bone, desert in service,
Love, friendship, charity, are subjects all
To envious and calumniating time.
One touch of nature makes the whole world kin,
That all, with one consent, praise newborn gawds,
Though they are made and moulded of things past,
And give to dust, that is a little gilt,
More laud than gilt o'erdusted.

Troilus and Cressida, Act iii. Sc. 3.

MERCY.

THE quality of mercy is not strained ;
It droppeth as the gentle rain from heaven
Upon the place beneath : it is twice blessed ;
It blesseth him that gives and him that takes :
'Tis mightiest in the mightiest : it becomes
The throned monarch better than his crown ;
His sceptre shows the force of temporal power,
The attribute to awe and majesty,
Wherein doth sit the dread and fear of kings ;
But mercy is above this sceptred sway ;
It is enthroned in the heart of kings,
It is an attribute to God himself ;
And earthly power doth then show likest God's
When mercy seasons justice. Therefore, Jew,
Though justice be thy plea, consider this—
That in the course of justice none of us

Should see salvation : we do pray for mercy.
And that same prayer doth teach us all to render
The deeds of mercy.

Merchant of Venice, Act iv. Sc. 1

MUSIC.

Lorenzo.

How sweet the moonlight sleeps upon this bank !
Here will we sit, and let the sounds of music
Creep in our ears : soft stillness and the night
Become the touches of sweet harmony.
Sit, Jessica. Look how the floor of heaven
Is thick inlaid with patines of bright gold.
There's not the smallest orb which thou behold'st
But in his motion like an angel sings,
Still quiring to the young-eyed cherubins :
Such harmony is in immortal souls ;
But whilst this muddy vesture of decay
Doth grossly close it in, we cannot hear it.

Jessica.

I am never merry, when I hear sweet music.

Lorenzo.

The reason is, your spirits are attentive :
For do but note a wild and wanton herd,
Or race of youthful and unhandled colts,
Fetching mad bounds, bellowing and neighing loud,
Which is the hot condition of their blood ;
If they but hear perchance a trumpet sound,
Or any air of music touch their ears,
You shall perceive them make a mutual stand,
Their savage eyes turn'd to a modest gaze,
By the sweet power of music : therefore the poet
Did feign that Orpheus drew trees, stones, and floods ;
Since nought so stockish, hard, and full of rage,
But music for the time doth change his nature.
The man that hath no music in himself,
Nor is not moved with concord of sweet sounds,
Is fit for treasons, stratagems, and spoils ;
The motions of his spirit are dull as night,
And his affections dark as Erebus :
Let no such man be trusted.

Merchant of Venice, Act v. Sc. 1

SLEEP.

King Henry.

How many thousand of my poorest subjects
Are at this hour asleep! O gentle Sleep,
Nature's soft nurse, how have I frighted thee,
That thou no more wilt weigh my eyelids down,
And steep my senses in forgetfulness?
Why rather, Sleep, liest thou in smoky cribs,
Upon uneasy pallets stretching thee,
And hushed with buzzing night-flies to thy slumbei ;
Than in the perfumed chambers of the great,
Under the canopies of costly state,
And lulled with sounds of sweetest melody?
O thou dull god, why liest thou with the vile
In loathsome beds, and leav'st the kingly couch
A watch-case, or a common 'larum bell?
Wilt thou upon the high and giddy mast
Seal up the ship-boy's eyes, and rock his brains
In cradle of the rude imperious surge
And in the visitation of the winds,
Who take the ruffian billows by the top,
Curling their monstrous heads, and hanging them
With deaf'ning clamours in the slippery clouds,
That, with the hurly, death itself awakes?
Canst thou, O partial Sleep, give thy repose
To the wet sea-boy in an hour so rude,
And in the calmest and most stillest night,
With all appliances and means to boot,
Deny it to a king? Then happy low, lie down
Uneasy lies the head that wears a crown.

2 *Henry IV*. Act iii. Sc. 1.

FLOWERS.

I would I had some flowers o' the spring, that might
Become your time of day ; and yours, and yours ;
That wear upon your virgin branches yet
Your maidenheads growing :—O, Proserpina,
For the flowers now, that frighted thou lett'st fall
From Dis's wagon ! daffodils,
That come before the swallow dares, and take
The winds of March with beauty ; violets, dim,
But sweeter than the lids of Juno's eyes,

Or Cytherea's breath ; pale primroses,
That die unmarried, ere they can behold
Bright Phœbus in his strength, a malady   .
Most incident to maids ; bold oxlips, and
The crown-imperial ; lilies of all kinds,
The flower-de-luce being one !   O ! these I lack,
To make you garlands of : and, my sweet friend,
To strew him o'er and o'er.

A Winter's Tale, Act iv. Sc. 3.

CLEOPATRA'S BARGE.

Enobarbus.

The barge she sat in, like a burnished throne,
Burnt on the water : the poop was beaten gold ;
Purple the sails, and so perfumed that   .
The winds were love-sick with them : the oars were silver ;
Which to the tune of flutes kept stroke, and made
The water, which they beat, to follow faster,
As amorous of their strokes.   For her own person,
It beggared all description : she did lie
In her pavilion—cloth-of-gold, of tissue—
O'er-picturing that Venus where we see
The fancy outwork nature : on each side her,
Stood pretty dimpled boys, like smiling Cupids,
With divers-colored fans, whose wind did seem
To glow the delicate cheeks which they did cool,
And what they undid, did.

Agrippa.
O, rare for Antony !

Enobarbus.

Her gentlewomen, like the Nereides,
So many mermaids, tended her i' the eyes,
And made their bends adornings : at the helm
A seeming mermaid steers ; the silken tackle
Swell with the touches of those flower-soft hands,
That yarely frame the office.   From the barge
A strange invisible perfume hits the sense
Of the adjacent wharfs.   The city cast
Her people out upon her ; and Antony,
Enthroned in the market-place, did sit alone,
Whistling to the air ; which, but for vacancy,

Had gone to gaze on Cleopatra too,
And made a gap in nature.

Antony and Cleopatra, Act ii. Sc. 2.

CUPID.

Oberon.

My gentle Puck, come hither. Thou remember'st
Since once I sat upon a promontory,
And heard a mermaid, on a dolphin's back,
Uttering such dulcet and harmonious breath,
That the rude sea grew civil at her song
And certain stars shot madly from their sphere
To hear the sea-maid's music.

Puck.

                  I remember.

Oberon.

That very time I saw, but thou couldst not,
Flying between the cold moon and the earth,
Cupid all armed : a certain aim he took
At a fair vestal throned by the west,
And loosed his love-shaft smartly from his bow,
As it should pierce a hundred thousand hearts :
But I might see young Cupid's fiery shaft
Quenched in the chaste beams of the watery moon,
And the imperial votaress passed on,
In maiden meditation, fancy-free.

A Midsummer Night's Dream, Act ii. Sc. 1.

SONNETS.

XXIX.

When, in disgrace with fortune and men's eyes,
I all alone beweep my outcast state,
And trouble deaf Heaven with my bootless cries,
And look upon myself, and curse my fate,
Wishing me like to one more rich in hope,
Featured like him, like him with friends possessed,
Desiring this man's art, and that man's scope.
With what I most enjoy contented least ;
Yet in these thoughts myself almost despising,
Haply I think on thee,—and then my state,
Like to the lark at break of day arising

From sullen earth, sings hymns at heaven's gate ;
  For thy sweet love remembered such wealth brings
  That then I scorn to change my state with kings.

XXX.

WHEN to the sessions of sweet silent thought
I summon up remembrance of things past,
I sigh the lack of many a thing I sought,
And with old woes new wail my dear time's waste :
Then can I drown an eye, unused to flow,
For precious friends hid in death's dateless night,
And weep afresh love's long since cancelled woe,
And moan the expense of many a vanished sight :
Then can I grieve at grievances foregone,
And heavily from woe to woe tell o'er
The sad account of fore-bemoaned moan,
Which I new pay as if not paid before.
  But if the while I think on thee, dear friend,
  All losses are restored and sorrows end.

XXXIII.

FULL many a glorious morning have I seen
Flatter the mountain-tops with sovereign eye,
Kissing with golden face the meadows green,
Gilding pale streams with heavenly alchymy ;
Anon permit the basest clouds to ride
With ugly rack on his celestial face,
And from the forlorn world his visage hide,
Stealing unseen to west with this disgrace :
Even so my sun one early morn did shine
With all triumphant splendor on my brow ;
But out, alack ! he was but one hour mine ;
The region cloud hath masked him from me now.
  Yet him for this my love no whit disdaineth ;
  Suns of the world may stain when heaven's sun staineth.

LX.

LIKE as the waves make toward the pebbled shore,
So do our minutes hasten to their end ;
Each changing place with that which goes before,
In sequent toil all forwards do contend.
Nativity, once in the main of light,
Crawls to maturity, wherewith being crowned,
Crooked eclipses 'gainst his glory fight,

And Time that gave, doth now his gift confound.
Time doth transfix the flourish set on youth,
And delves the parallels in beauty's brow ;
Feeds on the rarities of nature's truth,
And nothing stands but for his scythe to mow :
    And yet, to times in hope, my verse shall stand,
    Praising thy worth, despite his cruel hand.

LXVI.

TIRED with all these, for restful death I cry,—
As, to behold desert a beggar born,
And needy nothing trimmed in jollity,
And purest faith unhappily forsworn,
And gilded honour shamefully misplaced,
And maiden virtue rudely strumpeted,
And right perfection wrongfully disgraced,
And strength by limping sway disabled,
And art made tongue-tied by authority,
And folly doctor-like controlling skill,
And simple truth miscalled simplicity,
And captive good attending captain ill :
    Tired with all these, from these would I be gone,
    Save that, to die, I leave my love alone.

DIRGE.

    FEAR no more the heat o' the sun,
      Nor the furious winter's rages ;
    Thou thy worldly task hast done,
      Home art gone, and ta'en thy wages :
    Golden lads and girls all must,
    As chimney-sweepers, come to dust.

    Fear no more the frown o' the great,
      Thou art past the tyrant's stroke ;
    Care no more to clothe and eat ;
      To thee the reed is as the oak :
    The sceptre, learning, physic, must
    All follow this, and come to dust.

    Fear no more the lightning-flash,
      Nor the all-dreaded thunder-stone ,
    Fear not slander, censure rash ;
      Thou hast finished joy and moan :

All lovers young, all lovers must
Consign to thee, and come to dust.

No exorciser harm thee !
Nor no witchcraft charm thee
Ghost unlaid forbear thee !
Nothing ill come near thee !
Quiet consummation have,
And renownèd be thy grave !

Cymbeline, Act iv. Sc. 2.

MINOR POETS.

SIR PHILIP SIDNEY.

Born 1544.   Killed at the Battle of Zutphen, Sept. 22, 1586.

SONNETS.

Come Sleep ! O Sleep, that certain knot of peace,
The baiting place of wit, the balm of woe,
The poor man's wealth, the prisoner's release,
The indifferent judge between the high and low ;
With shield of proof shield me from out the prease
Of those fierce darts Despair at me doth throw.
Oh ! make in me those civil wars to cease ;
I will good tribute pay, if thou do so.
Take thou of me smooth pillows, sweetest bed,
A chamber deaf to noise, and blind of light,
A rosy garland, and a weary head :
And if these things, as being thine in right,
Move not thy heavy grace, thou shalt in me,
Livelier than elsewhere, Stella's image see.

Leave me, O Love, which reachest but to dust ;
And thou my mind, aspire to higher things ;
Grow rich in that which never taketh rust ;
Whatever fades but fading pleasure brings.
Draw in thy beams, and humble all thy might
To that sweet yoke where lasting freedoms be ;
Which breaks the clouds, and opens forth the light,
That doth both shine, and give us sight to see.

O take fast hold ; let that light be my guide
In this small course which birth draws out to death,
And think how ill becometh him to slide,
Who seeketh heaven, and comes of heavenly breath.
Then farewell, world ; thy uttermost I see :
Eternal Love, maintain thy life in me !

CHRISTOPHER MARLOWE.

Born 1564.   Died 1593.

THE PASSIONATE SHEPHERD TO HIS LOVE.

Come live with me, and be my love ;
And we will all the pleasures prove,
That hills and valleys, dales and fields,
Woods or steepy mountains yields.

And we will sit upon the rocks,
Seeing the shepherds feed their flocks
By shallow rivers, to whose falls
Melodious birds sing madrigals.

And I will make thee beds of roses,
And a thousand fragrant posies ;
A cap of flowers, and a kirtle,
Embroidered all with leaves of myrtle ;

A gown made of the finest wool,
Which from our pretty lambs we pull ;
Fair-linèd slippers for the cold,
With buckles of the purest gold ;

A belt of straw and ivy-buds,
With coral clasps and amber studs :
And if these pleasures may thee move,
Come live with me, and be my love.

Thy silver dishes for thy meat,
As precious as the gods do eat,
Shall, on an ivory table, be
Prepared each day for thee and me.

The shepherd swains shall dance and sing
For thy delight each May-morning.
If these delights thy mind may move,
Come live with me, and be my love.

SIR WALTER RALEIGH.

Born 1552. Executed 1618.

REPLY TO MARLOWE'S "THE PASSIONATE SHEPHERD TO HIS LOVE."

IF all the world and love were young,
And truth in every shepherd's tongue,
These pretty pleasures might me move
To live with thee and be thy love.

But time drives flocks from field and fold,
When rivers rage and rocks grow cold ;
And Philomel becometh dumb ;
The rest complains of cares to come.

The flowers do fade, and wanton fields
To wayward winter reckoning yields :
A honey tongue, a heart of gall,
Is fancy's spring, but sorrow's fall.

Thy gowns, thy shoes, thy beds of roses,
Thy cap, thy kirtle, and thy posies,
Soon break, soon wither, soon forgotten,-
In folly ripe, in reason rotten.

Thy belt of straw and ivy buds,
Thy coral clasps and amber studs,—
All these in me no means can move
To come to thee and be thy love.

But could youth last, and love still breed ;
Had joys no date, nor age no need ;
Then those delights my mind might move
To live with thee and be thy love.

LINES SUPPOSED TO BE WRITTEN THE NIGHT BEFORE HIS EXECUTION.

E'EN such is time ; which takes on trust
 Our youth, our joys, our all we have,
And pays us back with earth and dust ;
 Who in the dark and silent grave,
When we have wandered all our ways,
Shuts up the story of our days :
But from this earth, this grave, this dust,
My God shall raise me up, I trust.

SIR EDWARD DYER.

Born 1550. Died 1607.

MY MIND TO ME A KINGDOM IS.

My mind to me a kingdom is,
Such present joys therein I find,
That it excels all other bliss
That earth affords, or grows by kind :
Though much I want which most would have,
Yet still my mind forbids to crave.

No princely pomp, no wealthy store,
No force to win the victory,
No wily wit to salve a sore,
No shape to feed a loving eye ;
To none of these I yield as thrall :
For why? My mind doth serve for all.

I see how plenty surfeits oft,
And hasty climbers soon do fall ;
I see that those which are aloft
Mishap doth threaten most of all ;
They get with toil, they keep with fear,
Such cares my mind could never bear.

Content to live, this is my stay ;
I seek no more than may suffice ;
I press to bear no haughty sway ;
Look, what I lack my mind supplies :
Lo, thus I triumph like a king,
Content with that my mind doth bring.

Some have too much, yet still do crave ;
I little have, and seek no more.
They are but poor, though much they have,
And I am rich with little store ;
They poor, I rich ; they beg, I give ;
They lack, I leave ; they pine, I live.

I laugh not at another's loss ;
I grudge not at another's pain ;
No worldly waves my mind can toss ;
My state at one doth still remain :

I fear no foe, I fawn no friend ;
I loath not life, nor dread mine end.

Some weigh their pleasure by their lust,
Their wisdom by their rage of will ;
Their treasure is their only trust ;
A cloaked craft their store of skill :
But all the treasure that I find
Is to maintain a quiet mind.

My wealth is health and perfect ease ;
My conscience clear my chief defence ;
I neither seek by bribes to please,
Nor by deceit to breed offence :
Thus do I live ; thus will I die ;
Would all did so as well as I !

MICHAEL DRAYTON.

Born 1563. Died 1631.

THE BATTLE OF AGINCOURT.

FAIR stood the wind for France
　When we our sails advance,
Nor now to prove our chance
　Longer will tarry ;
But putting to the main,
At Kaux, the mouth of Seine,
With all his martial train,
　Landed King Harry.

And taking many a fort,
Furnished in warlike sort,
Marched towards Agincourt
　In happy hour ;
Skirmishing day by day
With those that stopped his way,
Where the French general lay
　With all his power.

Which in his height of pride,
King Henry to deride,
His ransom to provide
　To the King sending ;

Which he neglects the while,
As from a nation vile,
Yet, with an angry smile,
　Their fall portending.

And turning to his men,
Quoth our brave Henry then,
"Though they to one be ten,
　Be not amazèd.
Yet have we well begun,
Battles so bravely won
Have ever to the sun
　By fame been raisèd.

" And for myself," quoth he,
" This my full rest shall be ;
England ne'er mourn for me,
　Nor more esteem me.
Victor I will remain,
Or on this earth lie slain,
Never shall she sustain
　Loss to redeem me.

" Poictiers and Cressy tell,
When most their pride did swell,
Under our swords they fell :
  No less our skill is,
Than when our grandsire great,
Claiming the regal seat
By many a warlike feat
  Lopped the French lilies."

The Duke of York so dread
The eager vaward led,
With the main Henry sped,
  Among his henchmen.
Exeter had the rear,
A braver man not there,
O Lord ! how hot they were
  On the false Frenchmen !

They now to fight are gone,
Armour on armour shone,
Drum now to drum did groan,
  To hear was wonder ;
That with the cries they make,
The very earth did shake,
Trumpet to trumpet spake,
  Thunder to thunder.

Well it thine age became,
O noble Erpingham,
Which did the signal aim
  To our hid forces ;
When from a meadow by,
Like a storm suddenly,
The English archery
  Struck the French horses.

With Spanish yew so strong,
Arrows a cloth-yard long,
That like to serpents stung,
  Piercing the weather ;
None from his fellow starts,
But playing manly parts,
And like true English hearts,
  Stuck close together.

When down their bows they threw,
And forth their bilbows drew,
And on the French they flew ;
  Not one was tardy ;
Arms were from shoulders sent ;
Scalps to the teeth were rent,
Down the French peasants went,
  Our men were hardy.

This while our noble king,
His broad sword brandishing,
Down the French host did ding,
  As to o'erwhelm it ;
And many a deep wound lent,
His arms with blood besprent,
And many a cruel dent
  Bruisèd his helmet.

Gloucester, that duke so good,
Next of the royal blood,
For famous England stood,
  With his brave brother ;
Clarence, in steel so bright,
Though but a maiden knight,
Yet in that furious fight
  Scarce such another.

Warwick in blood did wade,
Oxford the foe invade,
And cruel slaughter made,
  Still as they ran up ;
Suffolk his axe did ply,
Beaumont and Willoughby
Bear them right doughtily,
  Ferrers and Fanhope.

Upon Saint Crispin's day
Fought was this noble fray,
Which fame did not delay
  To England to carry.
Oh, when shall Englishmen
With such acts fill a pen,
Or England breed again
  Such a King Harry !

BEAUMONT AND FLETCHER.

Beaumont born 1586 ; died 1616.   Fletcher born 1579 ; died 1625.

A SAD SONG.

WEEP no more, nor sigh, nor groan,
Sorrow calls no time that's gone:
Violets plucked, the sweetest rain
Makes not fresh nor grow again ;
Trim thy locks, look cheerfully ;
Fate's hidden ends eyes cannot see ;
Joys as wingèd dreams fly fast,
Why should sadness longer last?
Grief is but a wound to woe ;
Gentlest fair, mourn, mourn no more.

Fletcher.

FROM "AN HONEST MAN'S FORTUNE."

MAN is his own star, and the soul that can
Render an honest and a perfect man,
Commands all light, all influence, all fate ;
Nothing to him falls early or too late ;
Our acts our angels are, or good or ill,
Our fatal shadows that walk by us still.

Fletcher.

LINES ON THE TOMBS OF WESTMINSTER ABBEY.

MORTALITY, behold and fear !
What a change of flesh is here !
Think how many royal bones
Sleep within this heap of stones ;
Here they lie had realms and lands,
Who now want strength to stir their hands ;
Where from their pulpits sealed with dust
They preach "In greatness is no trust."
Here's an acre sown indeed
With the richest royall'st seed
That the earth did e'er suck in,
Since the first man died for sin ;
Here the bones of birth have cried,
"Though gods they were, as men they died."

Here are sands, ignoble things,
Dropt from the ruined sides of kings :
Here's a world of pomp and state,
Buried in dust, once dead by fate.

Beaumont.

JOSHUA SYLVESTER.

Born 1563. Died 1610.

A CONTENTED MIND.

I WEIGH not fortune's frown or smile ;
  I joy not much in earthly joys ;
I seek not state, I seek not style ;
  I am not fond of fancy's toys ;
I rest so pleased with what I have,
I wish no more, no more I crave.

I quake not at the thunder's crack ;
  I tremble not at noise of war ;
I swound not at the news of wrack ;
  I shrink not at a blazing star ;
I fear not loss, I hope not gain,
I envy none, I none disdain

I see ambition never pleased ;
  I see some Tantals starved in store ;
I see gold's dropsy seldom eased ;
  I see e'en Midas gape for more :
I neither want, nor yet abound—
Enough's a feast, content is crowned.

I feign not friendship where I hate :
  I fawn not on the great in show ;
I prize, I praise a mean estate—
  Neither too lofty nor too low :
This, this is all my choice, my cheer—
A mind content, a conscience clear.

Seventeenth Century.

JOHN MILTON.

Born 1608. Died 1674.

SOLILOQUY OF SATAN.

Is this the region, this the soil, the clime,
Said then the lost archangel, this the seat,
That we must change for heaven? this mournful gloom
For that celestial light? Be it so, since he,
Who now is Sovran, can dispose and bid
What shall be right ; farthest from him is best,
Whom reason hath equalled, force hath made supreme
Above his equals. Farewell, happy fields,
Where joy forever dwells! Hail horrors, hail
Infernal world! and thou profoundest hell,
Receive thy new possessor, one who brings
A mind not to be changed by place or time.
The mind is its own place, and in itself
Can make a heaven of hell, a hell of heaven.
What matter where, if I be still the same,
And where I should be ; all but less than he
Whom thunder hath made greater? Here at leas
We shall be free ; the Almighty hath not built
Here for his envy, will not drive us hence :
Here we may reign secure, and, in my choice,
To reign is worth ambition, though in hell,—
Better to reign in hell, than serve in heaven.
But wherefore let we then our faithful friends,
The associates and co-partners of our loss,
Lie thus astonished on the oblivious pool,
And call them not to share with us their part
In this unhappy mansion ; or once more,

With rallied arms to try what may be yet
Regained in heaven, or what more lost in hell ?
Paradise Lost, Book I.

SATAN.

HE scarce had ceased, when the superior fiend
Was moving toward the shore : his ponderous shield.
Ethereal temper, massy, large, and round,
Behind him cast ; the broad circumference
Hung on his shoulders like the moon, whose orb
Through optic glass the Tuscan artist views
At evening from the top of Fesolé,
Or in Valdarno, to descry new lands,
Rivers, or mountains, in her spotty globe.
His spear—to equal which the tallest pine
Hewn on Norwegian hills, to be the mast
Of some huge ammiral, were but a wand—
He walked with, to support uneasy steps
Over the burning marle, not like those steps
On heaven's azure ; and the torrid clime
Smote on him sore besides, vaulted with fire.
Nathless he so endured, till on the beach
Of that enflamed sea he stood, and called
His legions, angel forms, who lay entranced
Thick as autumnal leaves that strew the brooks
In Vallombrosa, where the Etrurian shades,
High overarched, embower ; or scattered sedge
Afloat, when with fierce winds Orion armed
Hath vext the Red-Sea coast, whose waves o'erthrew
Busiris and his Memphian chivalry,
While with perfidious hatred they pursued
The sojourners of Goshen, who beheld
From the safe shore their floating carcases
And broken chariot wheels : so thick bestrewn,
Abject and lost, lay these, covering the flood,
Under amazement of their hideous change.
He called so loud, that all the hollow deep
Of hell resounded :—" Princes, Potentates,
Warriors, the flower of heaven, once yours, now lost,
If such astonishment as this can seize
Eternal spirits ; or have ye chosen this place
After the toil of battle to repose

Your wearied virtue, for the ease you find
To slumber here, as in the vales of heaven ?
Or in this abject posture have ye sworn
To adore the Conqueror ? who now beholds
Cherub and seraph rolling in the flood
With scattered arms and ensigns, till anon
His swift pursuers from heaven-gates discern
The advantage, and descending, tread us down
Thus drooping, or with linkèd thunderbolts
Transfix us to the bottom of this gulf.—
Awake ! arise ! or be forever fallen !"

Paradise Lost, Book I.

ADDRESS TO LIGHT.

Hail, holy Light, offspring of heaven first born !
Or of the Eternal co-eternal beam,
May I express thee unblamed ? since God is light,
And never but in unapproached light
Dwelt from eternity, dwelt then in thee,
Bright effluence of bright essence increate.
Or hear'st thou rather pure ethereal stream,
Whose fountain who shall tell ? Before the sun,
Before the heavens thou wert, and at the voice
Of God, as with a mantle didst invest
The rising world of waters dark and deep,
Won from the void and formless infinite.
Thee I revisit now with bolder wing,
Escaped the Stygian pool, though long detained
In that obscure sojourn, while in my flight
Through utter and through middle darkness borne,
With other notes than to the Orphéan lyre,
I sung of Chaos and eternal Night ;
Taught by the heavenly Muse to venture down
The dark descent, and up to re-ascend
Though hard and rare : thee I revisit safe,
And feel thy sovran vital lamp ; but thou
Revisit'st not these eyes, that roll in vain
To find thy piercing ray, and find no dawn ;
So thick a drop serene hath quenched their orbs,
Or dim suffusion veiled. Yet not the more
Cease I to wander where the muses haunt
Clear spring, or shady grove, or sunny hill,

Smit with the love of sacred song ; but chief
Thee, Sion, and the flowery brooks beneath,
That washed thy hallowed feet, and warbling flow,
Nightly I visit : nor sometimes forget
Those other two equalled with me in fate,
So were I equalled with them in renown,
Blind Thamyris and blind Mæonides,
And Tiresias, and Phineas, prophets old :
Then feed on thoughts, that voluntary move
Harmonious numbers ; as the wakeful bird
Sings darkling, and in shadiest covert hid,
Tunes her nocturnal note.   Thus with the year
Seasons return ; but not to me returns
Day, or the sweet approach of even or morn,
Or sight of vernal gloom, or summer's rose,
Or flocks, or herds, or human face divine ;
But cloud instead, and ever-during dark
Surrounds me, from the cheerful ways of men
Cut off, and for the book of knowledge fair.

THE ADORATION OF THE ANGELS.

No sooner had the Almighty ceased, but all
The multitude of angels, with a shout,
Loud as from numbers without number, sweet
As from blest voices, uttering joy, heaven rung
With jubilee, and loud hosannas filled
The eternal regions.   Lowly reverent
Towards either throne they bow, and to the ground
With solemn adoration down they cast
Their crowns inwove with amarant and gold ;
Immortal amarant, a flower which once
In Paradise, fast by the tree of life,
Began to bloom ; but soon for man's offence
To heaven removed where first it grew, there grows,
And flowers aloft shading the fount of life,
And where the river of bliss through midst of heaven
Rolls o'er Elysian flowers her amber stream.
With these that never fade the spirits elect
Bind their resplendent locks inwreathed with beams.
Now in loose garlands thick thrown off, the bright
Pavement, that like a sea of jasper shone,
Impurpled with celestial roses smiled.

Then, crowned again, their golden harps they took,
Harps ever tuned, that glittering by their side
Like quivers hung, and with preamble sweet
Of charming symphony they introduce
Their sacred song, and waken raptures high :
No voice exempt, no voice but well could join
Melodious part, such concord is in heaven.

Paradise Lost, Book III.

THE DESCRIPTION OF ADAM AND EVE.

Two of far nobler shape, erect and tall,
Godlike erect, with native honour clad,
In naked majesty seemed lords of all,
And worthy seemed ; for in their looks divine
The image of their glorious Maker shone,
Truth, wisdom, sanctitude severe and pure
(Severe, but in true filial freedom placed),
Whence true authority in men ; though both
Not equal, as their sex not equal seemed ;
For contemplation he and valour formed ;
For softness she, and sweet attractive grace ;
He for God only, she for God in him :
His fair large front and eye sublime declared
Absolute rule ; and hyacinthine locks
Round from his parted forelock manly hung
Clustering, but not beneath his shoulders broad :
She, as a veil down to the slender waist,
Her unadorned golden tresses wore
Dishevelled, but in wanton ringlets waved.
As the vine curls her tendrils, which implied
Subjection, but required with gentle sway,
And by her yielded, by him best received,
Yielded with coy submission, modest pride,
And sweet, reluctant, amorous delay.

Paradise Lost, Book IV.

THE APPROACH OF EVENING.

Now came still Evening on, and Twilight gray
Had in her sober livery all things clad ;
Silence accompanied ; for beast and bird,
They to their grassy couch, these to their nests
Were slunk, all but the wakeful nightingale ;

She all night long her amorous descant sung ;
Silence was pleased : now glowed the firmament
With living sapphires ; Hesperus, that led
The starry host, rode brightest, till the moon,
Rising in clouded majesty, at length,
Apparent queen, unveiled her peerless light,
And o'er the dark her silver mantle threw.

Paradise Lost, Book IV.

ADAM AND EVE'S MORNING HYMN.

THESE are thy glorious works, Parent of good,
Almighty ! Thine this universal frame,
Thus wondrous fair : Thyself how wondrous then,
Unspeakable ! who sittest above these heavens,
To us invisible, or dimly seen
In these thy lowest works ; yet these declare
Thy goodness beyond thought, and power divine.
Speak, ye who best can tell, ye sons of light,
Angels ; for ye behold him, and with songs,
And choral symphonies, day without night,
Circle his throne rejoicing ; ye in heaven,
On earth join all ye creatures to extol
Him first, him last, him midst, and without end.
Fairest of stars, last in the train of night,
If better thou belong not to the dawn,
Sure pledge of day, that crown'st the smiling morn
With thy bright circlet, praise him in thy sphere,
While day arises, that sweet hour of prime.
Thou sun, of this great world both eye and soul,
Acknowledge him thy greater : sound his praise
In thy eternal course, both when thou climb'st,
And when high noon hast gained, and when thou fall'st.
Moon, that now meet'st the orient sun, now fly'st,
With the fixed stars, fixed in their orb that flies ;
And ye five other wandering fires, that move
In mystic dance not without song, resound
His praise, who out of darkness called up light.
Air, and ye elements, the eldest birth
Of Nature's womb, that in quaternion run
Perpetual circle, multiform, and mix
And nourish all things ; let your ceaseless change
Vary to our great Maker still new praise.

Ye mists and exhalations, that now rise
From hill or steaming lake, dusky or gray,
Till the sun paint your fleecy skirts with gold,
In honour to the world's great Author rise ;
Whether to deck with clouds the uncoloured sky,
Or wet the thirsty earth with falling showers,
Rising or falling, still advance his praise.
His praise, ye winds that from four quarters blow,
Breath soft or loud ; and wave your tops, ye pines,
With evrey plant, in sign of worship wave.
Fountains, and ye that warble, as ye flow,
Melodious murmurs, warbling tune his praise.
Join voices, all ye living souls : ye birds,
That singing up to heaven-gate ascend,
Bear on your wings and in your notes his praise.
Ye that in waters glide, and ye that walk
The earth, and stately tread, or lowly creep,
Witness if I be silent, morn or even,
To hill or valley, fountain or fresh shade,
Made vocal by my song, and taught his praise.
Hail, universal Lord, be bounteous still
To give us only good ; and if the night
Have gathered aught of evil or concealed,
Disperse it, as now light dispels the dark !

                                        Paradise Lost, Book V.

·ABDIEL.

He said : and, as the sound of waters deep,
Hoarse murmur echoed to his words applause
Through the infinite host : nor less for that
The flaming seraph, fearless though alone,
Encompassed round with foes, thus answered bold :
" O alienate from God ! O spirit accursed,
Forsaken of all good ! I see thy fall
Determined, and thy hapless crew involved
In this perfidious fraud, contagion spread
Both of thy crime and punishment : henceforth
No more be troubled how to quit the yoke
Of God's Messiah ; those indulgent laws
Will not be now vouchsafed ; other decrees
Against thee are gone forth without recall :
That golden sceptre which thou didst reject,
Is now an iron rod to bruise and break

Thy disobedience. Well thou didst advise ;
Yet not for thy advice or threats I fly
These wicked tents devoted, lest the wrath
Impendent, raging into sudden flame,
Distinguish not : for soon expect to feel
His thunder on thy head, devouring fire.
Then who created thee lamenting learn,
When who can uncreate thee thou shalt know.''
   So spake the seraph Abdiel, faithful found
Among the faithless, faithful only he ;
Among innumerable false, unmoved,
Unshaken, unseduced, unterrified,
His loyalty he kept, his love his zeal ;
Nor number, nor example, with him wrought
To swerve from truth, or change his constant mind,
Though single. From amidst them forth he passed,
Long way through hostile scorn, which he sustained
Superior, nor of violence feared aught ;
And, with retorted scorn, his back he turned
On those proud towers to swift destruction doomed.

                [Return of the Seraph Abdiel.]

All night the dreadless angel, unpursued,
Through heaven's wide champain held his way ; till Morn
Waked by the circling Hours, with rosy hand
Unbarred the gates of light. There is a cave
Within the mount of God, fast by his throne,
Where Light and Darkness in perpetual round
Lodge and dislodge by turns, which makes through heaven
Grateful vicissitude like day and night ;
Light issues forth, and at the other door
Obsequious Darkness enters, till her hour
To veil the heaven, though darkness there might well
Seem twilight here : and now went forth the Morn,
Such as in highest heaven, arrayed in gold
Empyreal ; from before her vanished Night
Shot through with orient beams ; when all the plain
Covered with thick embattled squadrons bright,
Chariots, and flaming arms, and fiery steeds,
Reflecting blaze on blaze, first met his view ;
War he perceived, war in procinct ; and found
Already known what he for news had thought
To have reported ; gladly then he mixed

Among those friendly powers, who him received
With joy and acclamations loud, that one,
That of so many myriads fallen yet one
Returned not lost. On to the sacred hill
They led him high applauded, and present
Before the seat supreme ; from whence a voice,
From midst a golden cloud, thus mild was heard :
"Servant of God, well done ; well hast thou fought,
The better fight, who single hast maintained
Against revolted multitudes the cause
Of truth, in word mightier than they in arms ;
And for the testimony of truth hast borne
Universal reproach, far, worse to bear
Than violence ; for this was all thy care,
To stand approved in sight of God, though worlds
Judged thee perverse : the easier conquest now
Remains thee, aided by this host of friends
Back on thy foes more glorious to return,
Than scorned thou didst depart, and to subdue
By force, who reason for their law refuse."

Paradise Lost, Books V., VI.

LYCIDAS.

YET once more, O ye laurels, and once more,
Ye myrtles brown, with ivy never-sere,
I come to pluck your berries harsh and crude ;
And, with forced fingers rude,
Shatter your leaves before the mellowing year :
Bitter constraint, and sad occasion dear,
Compels me to disturb your season due :
For Lycidas is dead, dead ere his prime,
Young Lycidas, and hath not left his peer.
Who would not sing for Lycidas ? he knew
Himself to sing, and build the lofty rime.
He must not float upon his watery bier
Unwept, and welter to the parching wind,
Without the meed of some melodious tear.
    Begin then, Sisters of the sacred well,
That from beneath the seat of Jove doth spring :
Begin, and somewhat loudly sweep the string.
Hence with denial vain, and coy excuse :
So may some gentle Muse
With lucky words favour my destined urn ;

And as he passes turn,
And bid fair peace be to my sable shroud.
For we were nursed upon the self-same hill,
Fed the same flock, by fountain, shade, and rill.
Together both, ere the high lawns appeared
Under the opening eyelids of the Morn,
We drove a-field, and both together heard
What time the gray-fly winds her sultry horn,
Battening our flocks with the fresh dews of night,
Oft till the star that rose at evening, bright,
Tow'rd heav'n's descent had sloped his westering wheel.
Meanwhile the rural ditties were not mute,
Tempered to the oaten flute ;
Rough Satyrs danced, and Fauns with cloven heel
From the glad sound would not be absent long ;
And old Damœtas loved to hear our song.
    But oh ! the heavy change now thou art gone,
Now thou art gone, and never must return !
Thee, shepherd, thee the woods and desert caves,
With wild thyme and the gadding vine o'ergrown,
And all their echoes mourn :
The willows, and the hazel copses green,
Shall now no more be seen,
Fanning their joyous leaves to thy soft lays.
As killing as the canker to the rose,
Or taint-worm to the weanling herds that graze,
Or frost to flowers, that their gay wardrobe wear,
When first the white-thorn blows ;
Such, Lycidas, thy loss to shepherd's ear.
    Where were ye, Nymphs, when the remorseless deep
Closed o'er the head of your loved Lycidas ?
For neither were ye playing on the steep,
Where your old bards, the famous Druids, lie,
Nor on the shaggy top of Mona high,
Nor yet where Deva spreads her wizard stream :
Ay me ! I fondly dream !
Had ye been there. . . for what could that have done ?
What could the Muse herself, that Orpheus bore,
The Muse herself, for her enchanting son,
Whom universal nature did lament,
When, by the rout that made the hideous roar,
His gory visage down the stream was sent,

Down the swift Hebrus to the Lesbian shore?
  Alas! what boots it with incessant care
To tend the homely, slighted, shepherd's trade,
And strictly meditate the thankless Muse?
Were it not better done, as others use,
To sport with Amaryllis in the shade,
Or with the tangles of Neæra's hair?
Fame is the spur that the clear spirit doth raise
(That last infirmity of noble mind)
To scorn delights, and live laborious days:
But the fair guerdon when we hope to find,
And think to burst out into sudden blaze,
Comes the blind Fury with the abhorrèd shears,
And slits the thin-spun life.   "But not the praise,"
Phœbus replied, and touched my trembling ears;
"Fame is no plant that grows on mortal soil,
Nor in the glistering foil
Set off to the world, nor in broad rumour lies:
But lives and spreads aloft by those pure eyes,
And perfect witness of all-judging Jove;
As he pronounces lastly on each deed,
Of so much fame in heaven expect thy meed."
  O fountain Arethuse, and thou honoured flood,
Smooth-sliding Mincius, crowned with vocal reeds!
That strain I heard was of a higher mood:
But now my oat proceeds,
And listens to the herald of the sea,
That came in Neptune's plea:
He asked the waves, and asked the felon winds,
What hard mishap had doomed this gentle swain?
And questioned every gust of rugged wings
That blows from off each beaked promontory;
They knew not of his story:
And sage Hippotades their answer brings,
That not a blast was from his dungeon strayed:
The air was calm, and on the level brine
Sleep Panope with all her sisters played.
It was that fatal and perfidious bark,
Built in the eclipse, and rigged with curses dark,
That sunk so low that sacred head of thine.
  Next Camus, reverend sire, went footing slow,
His mantle hairy, and his bonnet sedge,

Inwrought with figures dim, and on the edge,
Like to that sanguine flower inscribed with woe.
" Ah ! who hath reft," quoth he, " my dearest pledge ?"
Last came, and last did go,
The pilot of the Galilean lake ;
Two massy keys he bore of metals twain,
(The golden opes, the iron shuts amain.)
He shook his mitred locks, and stern bespake :
" How well could I have spared for thee, young swain,
Enow of such, as for their bellies' sake
Creep, and intrude, and climb into the fold !
Of other care they little reckoning make,
Than how to scramble at the shearer's feast,
And shove away the worthy bidden guest.
Blind mouths ! that scarce themselves know how to hold
A sheep-hook, or have learned aught else the least,
That to the faithful herdsman's art belongs !
What recks it them ? What need they ? They are sped ;
And, when they list, their lean and flashy songs
Grate on their scrannel pipes of wretched straw.
The hungry sheep look up, and are not fed,
But, swoln with wind, and the rank mist they draw,
Rot inwardly, and foul contagion spread :
Besides what the grim wolf with privy paw
Daily devours apace, and nothing said :
But that two-handed engine at the door
Stands ready to smite once, and smite no more."
    Return, Alpheus, the dread voice is past
That shrunk thy streams ; return Sicilian Muse,
And call the vales, and bid them hither cast
Their bells and flowerets of a thousand hues.
Ye valleys low, where the mild whispers use
Of shades, and wanton winds, and gushing brooks,
On whose fresh lap the swart star sparely looks :
Throw hither all your quaint enamelled eyes,
That on the green turf suck the honeyed showers,
And purple all the ground with vernal flowers.
Bring the rathe primrose that forsaken dies,
The tufted crow-toe, and pale jessamine,
The white pink, and the pansy freaked with jet,
The glowing violet,
The musk-rose, and the well-attired woodbine,

With cowslips wan that hang the pensive head,
And every flower that sad embroidery wears ;
Bid amaranthus all his beauty shed,
And daffodillies fill their cups with tears,
To strew the laureate hearse where Lycid lies.
For so, to interpose a little ease,
Let our frail thoughts dally with false surmise :
Ay me ! whilst thee the shores and sounding seas
Wash far away, where'er thy bones are hurled ;
Whether beyond the stormy Hebrides,
Where thou perhaps, under the whelming tide,
Visit'st the bottom of the monstrous world ;
Or whether thou, to our moist vows denied,
Sleep'st by the fable of Bellerus old,
Where the great Vision of the guarded Mount
Looks towards Namancos and Bayona's hold.
Look homeward, Angel, now, and melt with ruth :
And, O ye dolphins, waft the hapless youth.

Weep no more, woful shepherds, weep no more ;
For Lycidas, your sorrow, is not dead,
Sunk though he be beneath the watery floor ;
So sinks the day-star in the ocean-bed,
And yet anon repairs his drooping head,
And tricks his beams, and with new-spangled ore
Flames in the forehead of the morning sky :
So Lycidas sunk low, but mounted high,
Through the dear might of Him that walked the waves ;
Where, other groves and other streams along,
With nectar pure his oozy locks he laves,
And hears the unexpressive nuptial song,
In the blest kingdoms meek of joy and love.
There entertain him all the saints above,
In solemn troops and sweet societies,
That sing, and singing, in their glory move,
And wipe the tears forever from his eyes.
Now, Lycidas, the shepherds weep no more ;
Henceforth thou art the Genius of the shore,
In thy large recompense, and shalt be good
To all that wander in that perilous flood.

Thus sang the uncouth swain to the oaks and rills,
While the still Morn went out with sandals gray ;
He touched the tender stops of various quills,

With eager thought warbling his Doric lay :
And now the sun had stretched out all the hills,
And now was dropt into the western bay ;
At last he rose, and twitched his mantle blue ;
To-morrow to fresh woods and pastures new.

THE MIGHT OF INNOCENCE.

A THOUSAND fantasies
Begin to throng into my memory,
Of calling shapes, and beckoning shadows dire,
And aery tongues that syllable men's names
On sands, and shores, and desert wildernesses.
These thoughts may startle well, but not astound
The virtuous mind, that ever walks attended
By a strong siding champion, Conscience.
Oh welcome, pure-eyed Faith, white-handed Hope,
Thou hovering angel, girt with golden wings,
And thou, unblemished form of Chastity !
I see ye visibly, and now believe
That He, the Supreme Good, to whom all things ill
Are but as slavish officers of vengeance,
Would send a glistering guardian, if need were,
To keep my life and honour unassailed.

Comus.

THE LIGHT OF VIRTUE.

VIRTUE could see to do what Virtue would
By her own radiant light, though sun and moon
Were in the flat sea sunk.   And Wisdom's self
Oft seeks to sweet retired solitude ;
Where with her best nurse Contemplation,
She plumes her feathers, and lets grow her wings,
That in the various bustle of resort
Were all-to ruffled, and sometimes impaired.
He that has light within his own clear breast,
May sit in the centre, and enjoy bright day :
But he that hide a dark soul, and foul thoughts,
Benighted walks under the mid-day sun ;
Himself is his own dungeon.

Comus.

SONNETS.

ON HIS BEING ARRIVED TO THE AGE OF TWENTY-THREE.

How soon hath Time, the subtle thief of youth,
Stolen on his wing my three and twentieth year !

My hasting days fly on with full career,
But my late spring no bud or blossom shew'th.
Perhaps my semblance might deceive the truth,
That I to manhood am arrived so near ;
And inward ripeness doth much less appear,
That some more timely-happy spirits endu'th.
Yet be it less or more, or soon or slow,
It shall be still in strictest measure even
To that same lot, however mean or high,
Toward which Time leads me, and the will of heaven.
All this, if I have grace to use it so,
As ever in my great Task-master's eye.

ON THE MASSACRE LATE IN PIEMONT.

AVENGE, O Lord, thy slaughtered saints, whose bones
　Lie scattered on the Alpine mountains cold :
Even them who kept thy truth so pure of old,
When all our fathers worshipped stocks and stones.
Forget not : in thy book record their groans
Who were thy sheep, and in their ancient fold
Slain by the bloody Piemontese that rolled
Mother with infant down the rocks.　Their moans
The vales redoubled to the hills, and they
To heaven.　Their martyred blood and ashes sow
O'er all the Italian fields, where still doth sway
The triple tyrant ; that from these may grow
A hundredfold, who, having learned thy way,
Early may fly the Babylonian woe.

ON HIS BLINDNESS.

WHEN I consider how my light is spent
Ere half my days, in this dark world and wide,
And that one talent which is death to hide,
Lodged with me useless, though my soul more bent
To serve therewith my Maker, and present
My true account, lest he, returning, chide ;
"Doth God exact day-labour, light denied ? "
I fondly ask : but patience, to prevent
That murmur, soon replies, " God doth not need
Either man's work, or his own gifts ; who best
Bear his mild yoke, they serve him best : his state
Is kingly ; thousands at his bidding speed,
And post o'er land and ocean without rest :
They also serve who only stand and wait."

AT A SOLEMN MUSIC.

BLEST pair of Sirens, pledges of Heaven's joy,
Sphere-born harmonious sisters, Voice and Verse,
Wed your divine sounds, and mixed power employ,
Dead things with inbreathed sense able to pierce ;
And to our high-raised phantasy present
That undisturbèd song of pure content,
Aye sung before the sapphire-colored throne
To Him that sits thereon,
With saintly shout, and solemn jubilee ;
Where the bright Seraphim in burning row
Their loud uplifted angel-trumpets blow ;
And the Cherubic host in thousand quires
Touch their immortal harps of golden wires,
With those just spirits that wear victorious palms,
Hymns devout and holy psalms
Singing everlastingly :
While all the rounds and arches blue
Resound and echo Hallelu,
That we on earth, with undiscording voice,
May rightly answer that melodious noise ;
As once we did, till disproportioned sin
Jarred against Nature's chime, and with harsh din
Broke the fair music that all creatures made
To their great Lord, whose love their motion swayed
In perfect diapason, whilst they stood,
In first obedience, and their state of good.
O may we soon again renew that song,
And keep in tune with Heaven, till God erelong
To his celestial concert us unite,
To live with Him, and sing in endless morn of light !

ON TIME.

FLY, envious Time, till thou run out thy race ;
Call on the lazy leaden-stepping Hours,
Whose speed is but the heavy plummet's pace ;
And glut thyself with what thy womb devours,
Which is no more than what is false and vain,
And merely mortal dross ;
So little is our loss,
So little is thy gain !

For when as each thing bad thou hast entombed,
And last of all thy greedy self consumed,
Then long eternity shall greet our bliss
With an individual kiss ;
And joy shall overtake us as a flood,
When everything that is sincerely good
And perfectly divine,
With truth, and peace, and love, shall ever shine
About the supreme throne
Of Him, to whose happy-making sight alone
When once our heavenly-guided soul shall climb,
Then, all this earthly grossness quit,
Attired with stars, we shall forever sit,
Triumphing over Death, and Chance, and thee, O Time !

HYMN ON THE NATIVITY.

It was the winter wild,
While the heaven-born child
All meanly wrapt in the rude manger lies ;
Nature in awe to him
Had doffed her gaudy trim,
With her great master so to sympathize :
It was no season then for her
To wanton with the sun, her lusty paramour.

　　*　　*　　*　　*　　*　　*

No war or battle's sound
Was heard the world around :
The idle spear and shield were high uphung ;
The hookèd chariot stood
Unstained with hostile blood ;
The trumpet spake not to the armèd throng ;
And kings sat still with awful eye,
As if they surely knew their sovran lord was by.

But peaceful was the night,
Wherein the Prince of light
His reign of peace upon the earth began :
The winds, with wonder whist,
Smoothly the waters kist,
Whispering new joys to the mild ocean,
Who now hath quite forgot to rave,
While birds of calm sit brooding on the charmèd wave.

　　*　　*　　*　　*　　.　*　.　　*　　*

The oracles are dumb,
No voice or hideous hum
Runs through the archèd roof in words deceiving.
Apollo from his shrine
Can no more divine,
With hollow shriek the steep of Delphos leaving.
No nightly trance, or breathèd spell,
Inspires the pale-eyed priest from the prophetic cell.

The lonely mountains o'er
And the resounding shore,
A voice of weeping heard and loud lament ;
From haunted spring and dale,
Edged with poplar pale,
The parting genius is with sighing sent ;
With flower-inwoven tresses torn,
The nymphs in twilight shade of tangled thickets mourn.

In consecrated earth,
And on the holy hearth,
The Lars and Lemures moan with midnight plaint ;
In urns and altars round,
A drear and dying sound
Affrights the Flamens at their service quaint ;
And the chill marble seems to sweat,
While each peculiar power foregoes his wonted seat.

Peor and Baälim
Forsake their temples dim,
With that twice battered god of Palestine ;
And moonèd Astaroth,
Heaven's Queen and mother both,
Now sits not girt with taper's holy shine ;
The Libyc Hammon shrinks his horn,
In vain the Syrian maids their wounded Thammuz mourn

And sullen Moloch, fled,
Hath left in shadows dread
His burning idol all of blackest hue ;
In vain with cymbals' ring
They call the grisly king,
In dismal dance about the furnace blue ;
The brutish gods of Nile as fast,
Isis and Orus, and the dog Anubis, haste.

Nor is Osiris seen
In Memphian grove or green,
Trampling the unshowered grass with lowings loud :
Nor can he be at rest
Within his sacred chest ;
Naught but profoundest hell can be his shroud ;
In vain with timbrelled anthems dark
The sable-stolèd sorcerers bear his worshipt ark.

He feels from Judah's land
The dreaded infant's hand,
The rays of Bethlehem blind his dusky eyn ;
Nor all the gods beside
Longer dare abide,
Nor Typhon huge ending in snaky twine :
Our Babe, to show his Godhead true,
Can in his swaddling bands control the damnèd crew.

So when the sun in bed,
Curtained with cloudy red,
Pillows his chin upon an orient wave,
The flocking shadows pale
Troop to the infernal jail,
Each fettered ghost slips to his several grave ,
And the yellow-skirted fays
Fly after the night steeds, leaving their moon-loved maze.

But see, the Virgin blest
Hath laid her Babe to rest ;
Time is, our tedious song should here have ending.
Heaven's youngest-teemèd star
Hath fixed her polished car,
Her sleeping Lord, with handmaid lamp attending.
And all about the courtly stable
Bright-harnessed angels sit in order serviceable.   •

JOHN DRYDEN.

Born 1631. Died 1700.

PRIVATE JUDGMENT.

WHAT weight of ancient witness can prevail,
If private reason hold the public scale?
But, gracious God, how well dost Thou provide
For erring judgments an unerring guide !
Thy throne is darkness in the abyss of light,
A blaze of glory that forbids the sight.
O teach me to believe Thee thus concealed,
And search no farther than Thyself revealed ;
But her alone for my director take,
Whom Thou hast promised never to forsake !
My thoughtless youth was winged with vain desires ;
My manhood, long misled by wandering fires,
Followed false lights ; and when their glimpse was gone,
My pride struck out new sparkles of her own.
Such was I, such by nature still I am ;
Be Thine the glory and be mine the shame !
                                      The Hind and the Panther.

THE UNITY OF THE CATHOLIC CHURCH.

ONE in herself, not rent by schism, but sound,
Entire, one solid shining diamond,
Not sparkles shattered into sects like you :
One is the Church, and must be to be true,
One central principle of unity ;
As undivided, so from errors free ;
As one in faith, so one in sanctity.
Thus she, and none but she, the insulting rage
Of heretics opposed from age to age ;
Still when the giant-brood invades her throne,
She stoops from heaven and meets them half way down,
And with paternal thunder vindicates her crown.
But like Egyptian sorcerers you stand,
And vainly lift aloft your magic wand
To sweep away the swarms of vermin from the land.
You could like them, with like infernal force,
Produce the plague, but not arrest the course.

But when the boils and botches with disgrace
And public scandal sat upon the face,
Themselves attacked, the Magi strove no more,
They saw God's finger, and their fate deplore ;
Themselves they could not cure of the dishonest sore.
Thus one, thus pure, behold her largely spread,
Like the fair ocean from her mother-bed ;
From east to west triumphantly she rides,
All shores are watered by her wealthy tides.
The gospel-sound, diffused from pole to pole,
Where winds can carry and where waves can roll,
The self-same doctrine of the sacred page,
Conveyed to every clime, in every age.

The Hind and the Panther.

LINES PRINTED UNDER THE PORTRAIT OF MILTON.

THREE poets, in three distant ages born,
Greece, Italy, and England did adorn.
The first in loftiness of thought surpassed,
The next in majesty, in both the last.
The force of Nature could no farther go ;
To make a third she joined the former two.

ELEONORA.

THESE virtues raised her fabric to the sky ;
For that which is next heaven is charity.
But, as high turrets, for their airy steep,
Require foundations in proportion deep ;
And lofty cedars as far upward shoot,
As to the nether heavens they drive the root .
So low did her secure foundation lie,
She was not humble, but humility.
Scarcely she knew that she was great, or fair,
Or wise, beyond what other women are,
Or, which is better, knew, but never durst compare.
For, to be conscious of what all admire
And not be vain, advances virtue higher.
But still she found, or rather thought she found,
Her own worth wanting, others to abound ;
Ascribed above their due to every one,
Unjust and scanty to herself alone.
Such her devotion was, as might give rules
Of speculation to disputing schools,

And teach us equally the scales to hold
Between the two extremes of hot and cold ;
That pious heat may moderately prevail,
And we be warmed, but not be scorched by zeal.
Business might shorten, not disturb, her prayer ;
Heaven had the best, if not the greatest, share.
An active life long orisons forbids ;
Yet still she prayed, for still she prayed by deeds.
Her every day was Sabbath ; only free
From hours of prayer, for hours of charity.
Such as the Jews from servile toil released,
Where works of mercy were a part of rest ;
Such as blest angels exercise above,
Varied with sacred hymns and acts of love :
Such Sabbaths as that one she now enjoys,
E'en that perpetual one which she employs
(For such vicissitudes in heaven there are)
In praise alternate and alternate prayer.
All this she practised here ; that when she sprung
Amidst the choirs, at the first sight she sung : .
Sung, and was sung herself in angels' lays ;
For, praising her, they did her Maker praise.
All offices of heaven so well she knew,
Before she came, that nothing there was new :
And she was so familiarly received,
As one returning, not as one arrived.
* * * * * *
As precious gums are not for lasting fire,
They but perfume the temple and expire :
So was she soon exhaled, and vanished hence ;
A short sweet odour, of a vast expense.
She vanished, we can scarcely say she died,
For but a " now " did heaven and earth divide :
She passed serenely with a single breath ;
This moment perfect health, the next was death.
One sigh did her eternal bliss assure ;
So little penance needs, when souls are almost pure.
As gentle dreams our waking thoughts pursue ;
Or, one dream passed, we slide into a new ;
So close they follow, such wild order keep,
We think ourselves awake, and are asleep :
So softly death succeeded life in her :
She did but dream of heaven, and she was there.

A SONG FOR ST. CECILIA'S DAY 1687.

FROM harmony, from heavenly harmony,
This universal frame began :
When Nature underneath a heap
Of jarring atoms lay,
And could not heave her head,
The tuneful voice was heard from high,
" Arise, ye more than dead ! "

Then cold, and hot, and moist, and dry,
In order to their stations leap,
And music's power obey.
From harmony, from heavenly harmony,
This universal frame began :
From harmony to harmony
Through all the compass of the notes it ran,
The diapason closing full in man.

What passion cannot music raise and quell ?
When Jubal struck the chorded shell,
His list'ning brethren stood around,
And, wond'ring, on their faces fell,
To worship that celestial sound.
Less than a god they thought there could not dwell
Within the hollow of that shell,
That spoke so sweetly and so well.
What passion cannot music raise and quell ?

The trumpet's loud clangor
Excites us to arms,
With shrill notes of anger
And mortal alarms.

The double double double beat
Of the thundering drum,
Cries " Hark ! the foes come ;
Charge, charge ! 'tis too late to retreat."

The soft complaining flute
In dying notes discovers
The woes of hopeless lovers,
Whose dirge is whispered by the warbling lute.

Sharp violins proclaim
Their jealous pangs and desperation,

Their frantic indignation,
Depth of pains, and height of passion,
For the fair disdainful dame.

But oh! what art can teach,
What human voice can reach
The sacred organ's praise?
Notes inspiring holy love,
Notes that wing their heavenly ways
To join the choirs above.

Orpheus could lead the savage race,
And trees uprooted left their place,   ·
Sequacious of the lyre;   .
But bright Cecilia raised the wonder higher;
When to her organ, vocal breath was given;
An Angel heard, and straight appeared,
Mistaking earth for heaven.

Grand Chorus.

As from the power of sacred lays,
The spheres began to move,
And sung the great Creator's praise
To all the blessed above;
So when the last and dreadful hour
This crumbling pageant shall devour,
The trumpet shall be heard on high,
The dead shall live, the living die,
And music shall untune the sky.

JOSEPH ADDISON.

Born 1672. Died 1719.

THE BLESSINGS OF LIBERTY.

O LIBERTY, thou goddess heavenly bright,
Profuse of bliss, and pregnant with delight!
Eternal pleasures in thy presence reign,
And smiling Plenty leads thy wanton train;
Eased of her load, Subjection grows more light,
And Poverty looks cheerful in thy sight;

Thou mak'st the gloomy face of nature gay ;
Giv'st Beauty to the Sun, and pleasure to the day.
Thee, goddess, thee, Britannia's isle adores ;
How has she oft exhausted all her stores,
How oft in fields of death thy presence sought,
Nor thinks the mighty prize too dearly bought !
On foreign mountains may the Sun refine
The grape's soft juice, and mellow it to wine,
With citron groves adorn a distant soil,
And the fat olive swell with floods of oil :
We envy not the warmer clime, that lies
In ten degrees of more indulgent skies,
Nor at the coarseness of our heav'n repine,
Though o'er our heads the frozen Pleiads shine :
'Tis liberty that crowns Britannia's isle
And makes her barren rocks and her bleak mountains smile
Others with tow'ring piles may please the sight
And in their proud aspiring domes delight :
A nicer touch to the stretched canvas give,
Or teach their animated rocks to live :
'Tis Britain's care to watch o'er Europe's fate,
And hold in balance each contending state,
To threaten bold presumptuous Kings with war,
And answer her afflicted neighbours' prayer.
The Dane and Swede roused up by fierce alarms,
Bless the wise conduct of her pious arms :
Soon as her fleets appear their terrors cease,
And all the northern world lies hushed in peace.

PARAPHRASE ON PSALM XXIII.

THE Lord my pasture shall prepare,
And feed me with a shepherd's care ;
His presence shall my wants supply,
And guard me with a watchful eye ;
My noon-day walks he shall attend,
And all my midnight hours defend.

When in the sultry glebe I faint,
Or on the thirsty mountain pant ;
To fertile vales and dewy meads
My weary wandering steps he leads ;
Where peaceful rivers, soft and slow,
Amid the verdant landscape flow.

Though in the paths of death I tread,
With gloomy horrors overspread,
My steadfast heart shall fear no ill,
For Thou, O Lord, art with me still ;
Thy friendly crook shall give me aid,
And guide me through the dreadful shade.

Though in a bare and rugged way,
Through devious lonely wilds I stray,
Thy bounty shall my wants beguile :
The barren wilderness shall smile,
With sudden greens, and herbage crowned,
And streams shall murmur all around.

AN ODE.

THE spacious firmament on high,
With all the blue ethereal sky,
And spangled heavens, a shining frame,
Their great Original proclaim.
The unwearied sun, from day to day,
Does his Creator's power display,
And publishes to every land
The work of an Almighty hand.

Soon as the evening shades prevail
The moon takes up the wondrous tale,
And nightly to the listening earth
Repeats the story of her birth.
Whilst all the stars that round her burn,
And all the planets in their turn,
Confirm the tidings as they roll,
And spread the truth from pole to pole.

What though in solemn silence all
Move round this dark terrestrial ball,
What though no real voice nor sound
Amid their radiant orbs be found ;
In reason's ear they all rejoice,
And utter forth a glorious voice ;
For ever singing, as they shine,
"The Hand that made us is divine."

MINOR POETS.

BEN JONSON.

Born 1573. Died 1637.

TRUE GROWTH.

It is not growing like a tree
In bulk, doth make men better be ;
Or standing long an oak, three hundred year,
To fall a log at last, dry, bald, and sere.
    A lily of a day
    Is fairer far in May,
Although it fall and die that night,
It was the plant and flower of light.
In small proportions we just beauty see,
And in just measures life may perfect be.

EPODE FROM "THE FOREST."

Not to know vice at all, and keep true state,
Is virtue and not fate ;
Next to that virtue, is to know vice well,
And her black spite expel.
Which to effect (since no breast is so sure
Or safe, but she'll procure
Some way of entrance) we must plant a guard
Of thoughts to watch and ward ·
As the eye and ear, the ports unto the mind,
That no strange or unkind
Object arrive there, but the heart, our spy,
Give knowledge instantly
To wakeful reason, our affection's king :
Who, in th' examining,
Will quickly taste the treason, and commit
Close the close cause of it.
'Tis the securest policy we have
To make our sense our slave.
But this true course is not embraced by many—
By many ? scarce by any.
For either our affections do rebel,
Or else the sentinel,

That should ring larum to the heart, doth sleep ;
Or some great thought doth keep
Back the intelligence, and falsely swears
They are base and idle fears
Whereof the loyal conscience so complains.
Thus, by these subtle trains
Do several passions invade the mind,
And strike our reason blind.

EPITAPH ON THE COUNTESS OF PEMBROKE.

UNDERNEATH this marble hearse,
Lies the subject of all verse,
Sidney's sister, Pembroke's mother ;
Death, ere thou hast slain another,
Learned, and fair, and good as she,
Time shall throw his dart at thee !

EPITAPH ON A LADY.

UNDERNEATH this stone doth lie
As much beauty as could die :
Which in life did harbour give
To more virtue than doth live.
If at all she had a fault,
Leave it buried in this vault.

DRUMMOND OF HAWTHORNDEN.

Born 1585. Died 1649.

SONNET.

IF crost with all mishaps be my poor life,
If one short day I never spent in mirth,
If my spright with myself holds lasting strife,
If sorrow's death is but new sorrow's birth ;
If this vain world be but a sable stage
Where slave-born man plays to the scoffing stars ;
If youth be tossed with love, with weakness age,
If knowledge serve to hold our thoughts in wars ;
If time can close the hundred mouths of fame,
And make, what long since past, like that to be ;
If virtue only be an idle name,
If I, when I was born, was born to die ;
Why seek I to prolong these loathsome days ?
The fairest rose in shortest time decays.

TEARS ON THE DEATH OF MŒLIADES.[1]

REST, blessed soul, rest satiate with the sight
Of him whose beams (though dazzling) do delight ;
Life of all lives, cause of each other cause ;
The sphere and centre where the mind doth pause ;
Rest, happy soul, and wonder in that glass
Where seen is all that shall be, is, or was,
While shall be, is, or was, do pass away,
And nothing be but an eternal day.
For ever rest ; thy praise fame will enrol
In golden annals, while about the pole
The slow Boötes turns, or Sun doth rise
With scarlet scarf to cheer the mourning skies.
The virgins on thy tomb will garlands bear
Of flow'rs and with each flower let fall a tear.
Mœliades sweet courtly nymphs deplore,
From Thulè to Hydaspes' pearly shore.

Of jet,
Or porphyry,
Or that white stone
Paros affords alone,
Or these, in azure dye,
Which seem to scorn the sky ;
Here Memphis' wonders do not set,
Nor Artemisia's huge frame,
That keeps so long her lover's name,
Make no great marble Atlas stoop with gold,
To please the vulgar eye shall it behold.
The muses, Phœbus, Love, have raised of their tears
A crystal tomb to him, through which his worth appears.

FOR THE BAPTIST.

THE last and greatest herald of heaven's King,
Girt with rough skins, hies to the desert wild,
Among that savage brood the woods forth bring,
Which he than man more harmless found and mild :
His food was locusts, and what young doth spring
With honey, that from virgin hives distilled ;
Parched body, hollow eyes, some uncouth thing
Made him appear, long since from earth exiled,

[1] Prince Henry, eldest son of James I. The name is an anagram of " Miles a Deo."

There burst he forth : "All ye, whose hopes rely
On God, with me amidst these deserts mourn ;
Repent, repent, and from old errors turn."
Who listened to his voice, obeyed his cry ?
Only the echoes, which he made relent,
Rung from their marble caves, "Repent! Repent!"

MARY MAGDALEN.

"These eyes, dear Lord, once brandons of desire,
Frail scouts betraying what they had to keep,
Which their own heart, then others set on fire,
Their traitorous black before Thee here out-weep ;
These locks, of blushing deeds the fair attire,
Smooth frizzled waves, sad shelves which shadow deep,
Soul-stinging serpents in gilt curls which creep,
To touch Thy sacred feet do now aspire.
In seas of Care behold a sinking bark,
By winds of sharp remorse unto Thee driven,
O let me not exposed be ruin's mark !
My faults confest,—Lord, say they are forgiven."
Thus sighed to Jesus the Bethanian fair,
His tear-wet feet still drying with her hair.

SIR HENRY WOTTON.

Born 1568. Died 1639.

THE CHARACTER OF A HAPPY LIFE.

How happy is he born and taught,
That serveth not another's will ;
Whose armour is his honest thought,
And simple truth his utmost skill !

Whose passions not his masters are,
Whose soul is still prepared for death ;
Not tied unto the world with care
Of public fame, or private breath ;

Who envies none that chance doth raise,
Or vice ; who never understood
How deepest wounds are given by praise,
Nor rules of state, but rules of good :

Who hath his life from rumours freed,
Whose conscience is his strong retreat ;
Whose state can neither flatterers feed,
Nor ruin make accusers great :

Who God doth late and early pray
More of his grace than gifts to lend ;
And entertains the harmless day
With a religious book or friend ;

—This man is freed from servile bands
Of hope to rise, or fear to fall ;
Lord of himself, though not of lands ;
And having nothing, yet hath all.

GEORGE HERBERT.

Born 1592. Died 1634.

FROM "THE CHURCH PORCH."

Lie not ; but let thy heart be true to God,
Thy mouth to it, thy actions to them both :
Cowards tell lies, and those that fear the rod ;
The stormy working soul spits lies and froth.
Dare to be true ; nothing can need a lie ;
A fault, which needs it most, grows two thereby.

Fly idleness, which yet thou canst not fly
By dressing, mistressing and compliment.
If those take up thy day, the sun will cry
Against thee ; for his light was only lent.
God gave thy soul brave wings ; put not those feathers
Into a bed, to sleep out all ill weathers.

Restore to God his due in tithe and time :
A tithe purloined cankers the whole estate.
Sundays observe : think when the bells do chime
'Tis angels' music ; therefore come not late.
God then deals blessings : if a king did so,
Who would not haste, nay give, to see the show ?

When once thy foot enters the church, be bare ;
God is more there than thou ; for thou art there
Only by His permission. Then beware
And make thyself all reverence and fear.

Kneeling ne'er spoiled silk stocking ; quit thy state,
All equal are within the church's gate.

Resort to sermons, but to prayers most :
Praying's the end of preaching. O be drest ;
Stay not for th' other pin : why, thou hast lost
A joy for it worth worlds. Thus hell doth jest
Away thy blessings, and extremely flout thee,
Thy clothes being fast, but thy soul loose about thee.

In time of service seal up both thine eyes,
And send them to thine heart, that spying sin
They may weep out the stains by them did rise :
Those doors being shut, all by the ear comes in.
Who marks at churchtime others' symmetry
Makes all their beauty his deformity.

Let vain or busy thoughts have there no part :
Bring not thy plough, thy plots, thy pleasures hither.
Christ purged his temple ; so must thou thy heart.
All worldly thoughts are but thieves met together
To cozen thee ; look to thine actions well ;
For churches either are our heaven or hell.

Judge not the preacher, for he is thy Judge :
If thou mislike him, thou conceivest him not.
God calleth preaching folly. Do not grudge
To pick out treasures from an earthen pot.
The worst speaks something good : if all want sense,
God takes a text and preaches patience.

He that gets patience and the blessing which
Preachers conclude with, hath not lost his pains.
He that by being at church escapes the ditch
Which he might fall in by companions, gains.
He that loves God's abode, and to combine
With saints on earth, shall one day with them shine.

THE QUIP.

THE merry world did on a day
With his train-bands and mate agree
To meet together, as I lay,
And all in sport to jeer at me.

First Beauty crept into a rose,
Which when I pluckt not, "Sir," said she,
"Tell me, I pray, whose hands are those?"
But Thou shalt answer, Lord, for me.

Then Money came, and chinking still,
"What tune is this, poor man?" said he:
"I heard in music you had skill."
But Thou shalt answer, Lord, for me.

Then came brave Glory puffing by,
In silks that whistled, who but he!
He scarce allowed me half an eye;
But thou shalt answer, Lord, for me.

Then came quick Wit and Conversation,
And he would needs a comfort be,
And, to be short, made an oration:
But thou shalt answer, Lord, for me.

Yet, when the hour of Thy design
To answer these fine things shall come,
Speak not at large: say, I am Thine,
And then they have their answer home.

SIN.

Lord, with what care hast Thou begirt us round!
Parents first season us: then schoolmasters
Deliver us to laws; they send us bound
To rules of reason.   Holy messengers;
Pulpits and Sundays; sorrows dogging sin;
Afflictions sorted; anguish of all sizes;
Fine nets and stratagems to catch us in!
Bibles laid open; millions of surprises;
Blessings beforehand; ties of gratefulness;
The sound of glory ringing in our ears;
Without, our shame; within, our consciences
Angels and grace; eternal hopes and fears!
Yet all these fences and their whole array,
One cunning bosom-sin blows quite away.

VIRTUE.

Sweet day, so cool, so calm, so bright,
The bridal of the earth and sky,
Sweet dews shall weep thy fall to-night,
          For thou must die.

Sweet rose, whose hue, angry and brave,
Bids the rash gazer wipe his eye.
Thy root is ever in its grave,
   And thou must die.
Sweet spring, full of sweet days and roses,
A box where sweets compacted lie,
My music shows you have your closes,
   And all must die.
Only a sweet and virtuous soul,
Like seasoned timber, never gives ;
But when the whole world turns to coal,
   Then chiefly lives.

WILLIAM HABINGTON.

Born 1605. Died 1654.

Fix me on some bleak precipice,
Where I ten thousand years may stand :
Made now a statua of ice,
Then by the summer scorched and tanned.

Place me alone in some frail boat
'Mid th' horrors of an angry sea :
Where I, while time shall move, may float,
Despairing either land or day :

Or under earth my youth confine
To th' night and silence of a cell :
Where scorpions may my limbs entwine,
O God ! so thou forgive me Hell.

Eternity ! when I think thee,
(Which never any end must have,
Nor knew'st beginning,) and foresee
Hell is designed for sin a grave ;

My frighted flesh trembles to dust,
My blood ebbs fearfully away :
Both guilty that they did to lust
And vanity, my youth betray.

My eyes, which from such beauteous sight
Drew spider-like black venom in :
Close like the marigold at night
Oppressed with dew to bathe my sin.

My ears shut up that easy door
Which did proud fallacies admit :
And vow to hear no follies more ;
Deaf to the charms of sin and wit.

My hand (which when they touched some fair
Imagined such an excellence,
As th' ermine's skin ungentle were)
Contract themselves, and lose all sense.

But you bold sinners ! still pursue
Your valiant wickedness, and brave
Th' Almighty justice ; he'll subdue
And make you cowards in the grave.

Then when he as your judge appears,
In vain you'll tremble and lament,
And hope to soften him with tears,
To no advantage penitent.

Then you will scorn those treasures, which
So fiercely now you doat upon :
Then curse those pleasures did bewitch
You to this sad illusion.

The neighb'ring mountains which you shall
Woo too oppress you with their weight,
Disdainful will deny to fall ;
By a sad death to ease your fate.

In vain some midnight storm at sea
To swallow you, you will desire :
In vain upon the wheel you'll pray
Broken with torments to expire.

Death, at sight of which you start,
In a mad fury then you'll court :
Yet hate th' expressions of your heart,
Which only shall be sighed for sport.

No sorrow then shall enter in
With pity the great judge's ears.
This moment's ours.　Once dead, his sin
Man cannot expiate with tears.

ANONYMOUS.

Probably of the Seventeenth Century.

IT IS NOT BEAUTY I DEMAND.

It is not beauty I demand,
    A crystal brow, the moon's despair,
Nor the snow's daughter, a white hand,
    Nor mermaid's yellow pride of hair.

Tell me not of your starry eyes,
    Your lips, that seem on roses fed,
Your breasts, where Cupid tumbling lies,
    Nor sleeps for kissing of his bed,—

A bloomy pair of vermeil cheeks,
    Like Hebe's in her ruddiest hours,
A breath that softer music speaks
    Than summer winds a-wooing flowers.

These are but gauds : nay, what are lips?
    Coral beneath the ocean-stream,
Whose brink when your adventurer slips
    Full oft he perisheth on them.

And what are cheeks, but ensigns oft
    That wave hot youth to fields of blood?
Did Helen's breast, though ne'er so soft,
    Do Greece or Ilium any good?

Eyes can with baleful ardour burn ;
    Poison can breath, that erst perfumed,
There's many a white hand holds an urn,
    With lovers' hearts to dust consumed.

For crystal brows, there's nought within ;
    They are but empty cells for pride ;
He who the Siren's hair would win,
    Is mostly strangled in the tide.

Give me, instead of Beauty's bust,
    A tender heart, a loyal mind,
Which with temptation I would trust,
    Yet never linked with error find,—

One in whose gentle bosom I
  Could pour my secret heart of woes,
Like the care-burthened honey-fly,
  That hides his murmurs in the rose,—

My earthly comforter ! whose love
  So indefeasible might be,
That when my spirit wonned above,
  Hers could not stay, for sympathy.

EDMUND WALLER.

Born 1605.   Died 1687.

THE ROSE'S MESSAGE.

Go, lovely Rose !
Tell her, that wastes her time and me,
  That now she knows,
When I resemble her to thee,
How sweet and fair she seems to be.

  Tell her that's young,
And shuns to have her graces spied,
  That had'st thou sprung
In deserts where no men abide,
Thou must have uncommended died.

  Small is the worth
Of beauty from the light retired :
  Bid her come forth,
Suffer herself to be desired,
And not blush so to be admired.

  Then die ! that she
The common fate of all things rare
  · May read in thee :
How small a part of time they share,
That are so wondrous sweet and fair !

YOUTH AND AGE.

THE seas are quiet when the winds are o'er,
So calm are we when passions are no more !
For then we know how vain it was to boast
Of fleeting things, so certain to be lost.

Clouds of affection from our younger eyes
Conceal that emptiness which age descries ;
The soul's dark cottage, battered and decayed,
Lets in new light through chinks that time has made.

Stronger by weakness, wiser men become
As they draw near to their eternal home ;
Leaving the old, both worlds at once they view,
That stand upon the threshold of the new.

ROBERT HERRICK.

Born 1594. Died 1674.

A THANKSGIVING TO GOD.

Lord, thou hast given me a cell,
 Wherein to dwell ;
A little house, whose humble roof
 Is weather-proof ;
Under the spars of which I lie
 Both soft and dry ;
Where thou, my chamber for to ward,
 Hast set a guard
Of harmless thoughts, to watch and keep
 Me, while I sleep.
Low is my porch, as is my fate ;
 Both void of state ;
And yet the threshold of my door
 Is worn by the poor,
Who thither come, and freely get
 Good words, or meat.
Like as my parlour, so my hall
 And kitchen's small.
A little buttery and therein
 A little bin,
Which keeps my little loaf of bread
 Unchipt, unflead,
Some brittle sticks of thorn or briar
 Make me a fire,
Close by whose living coal I sit,
 And glow like it.
Lord, I confess too, when I dine,
 The pulse is thine,

And all those other bits that be
　　There placed by thee ;
The worts, the purslain and the mess
　　Of water-cress,
Which of thy kindness thou hast sent ;
　　And my content
Makes these and my belovèd beet
　　To be more sweet.
'Tis thou that crown'st my glittering hearth
　　With guiltless mirth,
And giv'st me wassail bowls to drink,
　　Spiced to the brink.
Lord, 'tis thy plenty-dropping hand
　　That soils my land,
And giv'st me for my bushel sown,
　　Twice ten for one ;
Thou mak'st my teeming hen to lay
　　Her egg each day ;
Besides my healthful ewes to bear
　　The twins each year ;
The while the conduits of my kine
　　Run cream for wine :
All these and better thou dost send
　　Me to this end,—
That I should render, for my part,
　　A thankful heart ;
Which, fired with incense, I resign
　　As wholly thine ;
—But the acceptance, that must be,
　　My Christ, by thee.

TO BLOSSOMS.

FAIR pledges of a fruitful tree,
　　Why do ye fall so fast ?
　　Your date is not so past,
But you may stay yet here awhile,
　　To blush and gently smile ;
　　And go at last.

What, were ye born to be
　　An hour or half's delight ;
　　And so to bid good-night ?

'Twas pity Nature brought ye forth
  Merely to show your worth,
  And lose you quite.

But you are lovely leaves, where we
  May read how soon things have
  Their end, though ne'er so brave :
And after they have shown their pride,
  Like you, a-while—they glide
  Into the grave.

RICHARD LOVELACE.

Born 1618. Died 1658.

TO ALTHEA FROM PRISON.

When Love with unconfinèd wings
  Hovers within my gates,
And my divine Althea brings
  To whisper at the grates ;
When I lie tangled in her hair,
  And fettered to her eye,
The birds that wanton in the air
  Know no such liberty.

When flowing cups run swiftly round
  With no allaying Thames,
Our careless heads with roses crowned,
  Our hearts with loyal flames ;
When thirsty grief in wine we steep,
  When healths and draughts go free,
Fishes that tipple in the deep
  Know no such liberty.

When, like committed linnets, I
  With shriller throat shall sing .
The sweetness, mercy, majesty
  And glories of my King ;
When I shall voice aloud how good
  He is, how great should be,
Enlargèd winds that curl the flood
  Know no such liberty.

Stone walls do not a prison make,
    Nor iron bars a cage ;
Minds innocent and quiet take
    That for an hermitage :
If I have freedom in my love,
    And in my soul am free,
Angels alone, that soar above,
    Enjoy such liberty.

GOING TO THE WARS.

TELL me not, sweet, I am unkind,
    That from the nunnery
Of thy chaste breast and quiet mind
    To wars and arms I fly.

True, a new mistress now I chase,
    The first foe in the field,
And with a stronger faith embrace
    A sword, a horse, a shield.

Yet this inconstancy is such
    As you too shall adore—
I could not love thee, dear, so much,
    Loved I not honour more.

JAMES SHIRLEY.

Born 1596. Died 1667.

A DIRGE.

THE glories of our blood and state
    Are shadows, not substantial things ;
There is no armour against fate ;
    Death lays his icy hand on kings,
        Sceptre and crown
        Must tumble down,
And in the dust be equal made
With the poor crooked scythe and spade.

Some men with swords may reap the field,
  . And plant fresh laurels where they kill :
But their strong nerves at last must yield ;
    They tame but one another still :

Early or late
They stoop to fate,
And must give up their murmuring breath
When they, pale captives, creep to death.

The garlands wither on your brow ;
Then boast no more your mighty deeds ;
Upon Death's purple altar now
See where the victor-victim bleeds :
Your heads must come
To the cold tomb ;
Only the actions of the just
Smell sweet, and blossom in their dust.

THOMAS DEKKER.

Born about 1590. Died 1638.

SWEET CONTENT.

ART thou poor, yet hast thou golden slumbers ?
O, sweet content !
Art thou rich, yet is thy mind perplexèd ?
O, punishment !
Dost thou laugh to see how fools are vexèd
To add to golden numbers, golden numbers ?
O, sweet content ! O sweet, O sweet content !
Work apace, apace, apace, apace ;
Honest labour bears a lovely face ;
Then hey nonny nonny, hey nonny nonny !

Canst drink the waters of the crispèd spring ?
O, sweet content !
Swimm'st thou in wealth, yet sink'st in thine own tears ?
O, punishment !
Then he that patiently want's burden bears
No burden bears, but is a king, a king !
O sweet content ! O sweet, O sweet content !
Work apace, apace, apace, apace ;
Honest labor bears a lovely face ;
Then hey nonny nonny, hey nonny nonny !

PATIENCE.

PATIENCE ! why 'tis the soul of peace :
Of all the virtues, 'tis nearest kin to heaven :
It makes men look like gods.   The best of men
That e'er wore earth about him, was a sufferer,
A soft, meek, patient, humble, tranquil spirit :
The first true gentleman that ever breathed.

RICHARD CRASHAW.

Born 1600.   Died 1650.

THE MYSTERIES OF THE INCARNATION.

THAT the great angel-blinding light should shrink
His blaze, to shine in a poor shepherd's eye ;
That the unmeasured God so low should sink,
As prisoner in a few poor rags to lie ;
That from His mother's breast He milk should drink,
Who feeds with nectar heaven's fair family ;
    That a vile manger His low bed should prove,
    Who in a throne of Stars thunders above.

That He whom the sun serves, should faintly peep
Through clouds of infant flesh ; that He, the old
Eternal Word, could be a child, and weep ;
That He who made the fire should feel the cold ;
That heaven's High Majesty His court should keep
In a clay cottage, by each blast controlled ;
    That Glory's Self should serve our griefs and fears,
    And free Eternity submit to years.

And further, that the Law's eternal Giver,
Should bleed in His own law's obedience ;
And to the circumcising knife deliver
Himself, the forfeit of His slave's offence ;
That the unblemished Lamb, blessed for ever,
Should take the mark of sin, of pain the sense :
    These are the knotty riddles, whose dark doubt
    Entangles our lost thoughts, past finding out.

SAMUEL BUTLER.

Born 1612. Died 1680.

THE WEAKNESS AND MISERY OF MAN.

Our plans are real things, and all
Our pleasures but fantastical.
Diseases of their own accord,
But cures come difficult and hard.
Our noblest piles and stateliest rooms
Are but outhouses to our tombs ;
Cities though ne'er so great and brave
But mere warehouses to the grave.
Our bravery's but a vain disguise
To hide us from the world's dull eyes,
The remedy of a defect
With which our nakedness is decked,
Yet makes us smile with pride and boast
As if we had gained by being lost.

HENRY VAUGHAN.

Born 1621. Died 1695.

BEYOND THE VEIL.

They are all gone into the world of light;
  And I alone sit lingering here ;
Their very memory is fair and bright,
  And my sad thoughts doth clear.

It glows and glitters in my cloudy breast,
  Like stars upon some gloomy grove,
Or those faint beams in which this hill is drest,
  After the sun's remove.

I see them walking in an air of glory,
  Whose light doth trample on my days :
My days, which are at best but dull and hoary,
  Mere glimmering and decays.

O holy Hope! and high Humility,
  High as the heavens above!
These are your walks, and you have showed them me,
  To kindle my cold love.

Dear, beauteous Death! the jewel of the just,
  Shining no where, but in the dark;
What mysteries do lie beyond thy dust;
  Could man outlook that mark!

        *   *   *   *   *

O Father of eternal life, and all
  Created glories under Thee!
Resume thy spirit from this world of thrall,
  Into true liberty.

Either disperse these mists, which blot and fill
  My perspective—still—as they pass:
Or else remove me hence unto that hill,
  Where I shall need no glass.

THE RETREAT.

HAPPY those early days, when I
Shined in my angel-infancy!
Before I understood this place
Appointed for my second race,
Or taught my soul to fancy aught
But a white celestial thought;
When yet I had not walked above
A mile or two from my first Love,
And looking back, at that short space,
Could see a glimpse of his bright face;
When on some gilded cloud or flower
My gazing soul would dwell an hour,
And in those weaker glories spy
Some shadows of eternity;
Before I taught my tongue to wound
My conscience with a sinful sound,
Or had the black-art to dispense
A several sin to every sense,
But felt through all this fleshly dress
Bright shoots of everlastingness.
Oh how I long to travel back,
And tread again that ancient track!

That I might once more reach that plain
Where first I left my glorious train ;
From whence the enlightened spirit sees
That shady City of palm-trees,
But ah ! my soul with too much stay
Is drunk, and staggers in the way !
Some men a forward motion love,
But I by backward steps would move ;
And when this dust falls to the urn,
In that state I came return.

ABRAHAM COWLEY.

Born 1618. Died 1667.

THE WISH.

THIS only grant me, that my means may lay
Too low for envy, for contempt too high.
    Some honour I would have
Not from great deeds, but good alone.
The unknown are better than ill known ;
    Rumour can ope the grave.
Acquaintance I would have, but when't depends
Not on the number, but the choice of friends :

Books should, not business, entertain the light,
And sleep, as undisturbed as death, the night.
    My house a cottage, more
Than palace, and should fitting be,
For all my use, not luxury.
    My garden painted o'er
With nature's hand, not art's ; and pleasures yield,
Horace might envy in his Sabine field.

Thus would I double my life's fading space,
For he that runs it well, twice runs his race.
    And in this true delight,
These unbought sports, this happy state,
I would not fear nor wish my fate,
    But boldly say each night,
To-morrow let my sun his beams display,
Or in clouds hide them ; I have liv'd to-day.

EXTRACT FROM "THE ROYAL SOCIETY."

MISCHIEF and true dishonour fall on those
Who would to laughter or to scorn expose
So virtuous and so noble a design,
So human for its use, for knowledge so divine.
The things which these proud men despise, and call
Impertinent, and vain, and small,
Those smallest things of nature let me know,
Rather than àll their greatest actions do.
Whoever would deposèd Truth advance
Into the throne usurped from it,
Must feel at first the blows of Ignorance,
And the sharp points of envious Wit.
So when, by various turns of the celestial dance,
In many thousand years
A star, so long unknown, appears,
Though heaven itself more beauteous by it grow,
It troubles and alarms the world below,
Does to the wise a star, to fools a meteor, show.

ANDREW MARVELL.

Born 1620. Died 1678.

THE BERMUDAS.

WHERE the remote Bermudas ride,
In the ocean's bosom unespied,
From a small boat, that rowed along,
The listening winds received this song. ·
" What should we do but sing His praise,
That led us through the watery maze,
Unto an isle so long unknown,
And yet far kinder than our own ?
Where He the huge sea monsters wracks,
That lift the deep upon their backs,
He lands us on a grassy stage,
Safe from the storms, and prelates' rage.
He gave us this eternal spring
Which here enamels every thing,
And sends the fowls to us in care,
On daily visits through the air ;

He hangs in shades the orange bright,
Like golden lamps in a green night,
And does in the pomegranates close
Jewels more rich than Ormus shows ;
He makes the figs our mouths to meet,
And throws the melons at our feet,
But apples plants of such a price,
No tree could ever bear them twice.
With cedars chosen by His hand
From Lebanon, He stores the land
And makes the hollow seas that roar
Proclaim the ambergrease on shore ;
He cast (of which we rather boast)
The gospel's pearl upon our coast,
And in these rocks for us did frame
A temple where to sound his fame.
Oh ! let our voice His praise exalt,
Till it arrive at heaven's vault,
Which then (perhaps) rebounding may
Echo beyond the Mexique Bay."
Thus sung they, in the English boat,
A holy and a cheerful note,
And all the way, to guide their chime,
With falling oars they kept the time.

ALEXANDER POPE.

Born 1688. Died 1744.

FROM "AN ESSAY ON MAN."

HEAVEN from all creatures hides the book of Fate,
All but the page prescribed, their present state :
From brutes what men, from men what spirits know :
Or who could suffer being here below?
The lamb thy riot dooms to bleed to-day,
Had he thy reason, would he skip and play ?
Pleased to the last, he crops the flowery food,
And licks the hand just raised to shed his blood.
O blindness to the future ! kindly given,
That each may fill the circle marked by Heaven :
Who sees with equal eye, as God of all,
A hero perish, or a sparrow fall,
Atoms or systems into ruin hurled,
And now a bubble burst, and now a world.
Hope humbly then ; with trembling pinions soar,
Wait the great teacher, Death ; and God adore,
What future bliss, he gives not thee to know,
But gives that hope, to be thy blessing now.
Hope springs eternal in the human breast :
Man never *is*, but always *to be* blest :
The soul uneasy, and confined from home,
Rests and expatiates in a world to come.
  Lo, the poor Indian ! whose untutored mind
Sees God in clouds, or hears him in the wind ;
His soul proud Science never taught to stray
Far as the solar walk, or milky way :
Yet simple nature to his hope has given,
Behind the cloud-topt hill an humbler heaven ;

Some safer world in depth of woods embraced,
Some happier island in the watery waste,
Where slaves once more their native land behold,
No fiends torment, no Christians thirst for gold.
To be, contents his natural desire,
He asks no angels wing, no seraph's fire ;
But thinks, admitted to that equal sky,
His faithful dog shall bear him company.

*   *   *   *   *   *

See some strange comfort every state attend,
And pride bestowed on all, a common friend :
See some fit passion every age supply ;
Hope travels through, nor quits us when we die.
Behold the child, by Nature's kindly law,
Pleased with a rattle, tickled with a straw :
Some livelier plaything gives his youth delight,
A little louder, but as empty quite.
Scarfs, garters, gold, amuse his riper stage,
And beads and prayer-books are the toys of age.
Pleased with this bauble still, as that before ;
'Till tired he sleeps, and Life's poor play is o'er.
Meanwhile opinion gilds with varying rays
Those painted clouds that beautify our days :
Each want of happiness by Hope supplied,
And each vacuity of sense by Pride :
These build as fast as knowledge can destroy ;
In Folly's cup still laughs the bubble, Joy ;
One prospect lost, another still we gain ;
And not a vanity is given in vain ;
Even mean Self-love becomes, by force divine,
The scale to measure others' wants by thine.
See ! and confess, one comfort still must rise ;
'Tis this, Though man's a fool, yet God is wise.

ON THE CHARACTER OF ADDISON.

PEACE to all such ! but were there one whose fires
True genius kindles, and fair fame inspires ;
Blest with each talent and each art to please,
And born to write, converse, and live with ease :
Should such a man, too fond to live alone,
Bear, like the Turk, no brother near the throne,

View him with scornful, yet with jealous eyes,
And hate for arts that caused himself to rise ;
Damn with faint praise, assent with civil leer,
And, without sneering, teach the rest to sneer ;
Willing to wound, and yet afraid to strike,
Just hint a fault, and hesitate dislike ;
Alike reserved to blame or to commend,
A timorous foe, and a suspicious friend ;
Dreading even fools, by flatterers besieged,
And so obliging, that he ne'er obliged ;
Like Cato, give his little senate laws,
And sit attentive to his own applause ;
While wits and templars every sentence raise,
And wonder with a foolish face of praise—
Who but must laugh, if such a man there be !
Who would not weep, if Atticus were he !

FROM "AN ELEGY ON AN UNFORTUNATE LADY."

What can atone (O ever injured shade !)
Thy fate unpitied, and thy rites unpaid ?
No friend's complaint, no kind domestic tear,
Pleased thy pale ghost, or graced thy mournful bier :
By foreign hands thy dying eyes were closed,
By foreign hands thy decent limbs composed,
By foreign hands thy humble grave adorned,
By strangers honoured, and by strangers mourned !
What though no friends in sable weeds appear ;
Grieve for an hour, perhaps, then mourn a year,
And bear about the mockery of woe
To midnight dances, and the public show ?
What though no weeping Loves thy ashes grace,
Nor polished marble emulate thy face ?
What though no sacred earth allow thee room,
Nor hallowed dirge be muttered o'er thy tomb ?
Yet shall thy grave with rising flowers be drest,
And the green turf lie lightly on thy breast :
There shall the Morn her earliest tears bestow,
There the first roses of the year shall blow ;
While angels with their silver wings o'ershade
The ground now sacred by thy relics made.
So, peaceful rests, without a stone, a name,
What once had beauty, titles, wealth, and fame.

How loved, how honoured once, avails thee not,
To whom related, or by whom begot ;
A heap of dust alone remains of thee ;
'Tis all thou art, and all the proud shall be !

THE UNIVERSAL PRAYER.

FATHER of all ! in every age,
   In every clime ador'd,
By saint, by savage, and by sage,
   Jehovah, Jove, or Lord !

Thou Great First Cause, least understood,
   Who all my sense confined
To know but this, that thou art good,
   And that myself am blind :

Yet gave me in this dark estate,
   To see the good from ill ;
And, binding nature fast in fate,
   Left free the human will.

What conscience dictates to be done,
   Or warns me not to do,
This teach me more than hell to shun,
   That more than heaven pursue.

What blessings thy free bounty gives
   Let me not cast away ;
For God is paid when man receives :
   To enjoy is to obey.

Yet not to earth's contracted span
   Thy goodness let me bound,
Or think thee Lord alone of man,
   When thousand worlds are round.

Let not this weak unknowing hand
   Presume thy bolts to throw,
And deal damnation round the land
   On each I judge thy foe.

If I am right, thy grace impart
   Still in the right to stay ;
If I am wrong, oh ! teach my heart
   To find that better way.

Save me alike from foolish pride,
 Or impious discontent,
At aught thy wisdom has denied,
 Or aught thy goodness lent.

Teach me to feel another's woe,
 To hide the fault I see ;
That mercy I to others show,
 That mercy show to me.

Mean though I am, not wholly so,
 Since quickened by thy breath ;
O lead me, wheresoe'er I go,
 Through this day's life or death.

This day be bread and peace my lot ;
 All else beneath the sun
Thou know'st if best bestowed or not,
 And let thy will be done.

To thee, whose temple is all space ;
 Whose altar, earth, sea, skies ;
One chorus let all being raise !
 All nature's incense rise !

ODE ON SOLITUDE.

HAPPY the man, whose wish and care
A few paternal acres bound,
Content to breathe his native air,
   In his own ground.

Whose herds with milk, whose fields with bread,
 Whose flocks supply him with attire ;
Whose trees in summer yield him shade,
   In winter fire.

Blest, who can unconcern'dly find
 Hours, days, and years slide soft away,
In health of body, peace of mind,
   Quiet by day,

Sound sleep by night ; study and ease,
 Together mixed ; sweet recreation,
And innocence, which most does please,
   With meditation.

Thus let me live, unseen, unknown ;
Thus unlamented let me die,
Steal from the world, and not a stone
Tell where I lie.

EPITAPH ON MRS. ELIZABETH CORBETT. [1]

HERE rests a Woman, Good without pretence,
Blest with plain Reason, and with sober Sense ;
No Conquests she, but o'er her Self, desir'd,
No Arts essay'd, but not to be admir'd :
Passion and Pride were to her Soul unknown ;
Convinc'd that Virtue only is our own.
So unaffected, so compos'd a Mind,
So firm, yet soft, so strong, yet so refined,
Heaven, as its purest Gold, by Tortures tried ;
The Saint sustain'd it, but the Woman died.

JAMES THOMSON.

Born 1700. Died 1748.

FROM "THE SEASONS."

A SNOW SCENE.

THE keener tempests come : and fuming dun
From all the livid east, or piercing north,
Thick clouds ascend—in whose capacious womb
A vapory deluge lies, to snow congealed.
Heavy they roll their fleecy world along ;
And the sky saddens with the gathered storm.
Through the hushed air the whitening shower descends,
At first thin wavering ; till at last the flakes
Fall broad, and wide, and fast, dimming the day
With a continual flow. The cherished fields
Put on their winter-robe of purest white.
'Tis brightness all ; save where the new snow melts
Along the mazy current. Low the woods
Bow their hoar head ; and, ere the languid sun
Fain from the west emits his evening ray,
Earth's universal face, deep-hid and chill,

[1] In St. Margaret's Church, Westminster.

Is one wide dazzling waste, that buries wide
The works of man.   Drooping, the laborer-ox
Stands covered o'er with snow, and then demands
The fruit of all his toil.   The fowls of heaven,
Tamed by the cruel season, crowd around
The winnowing store, and claim the little boon
Which Providence assigns them.   One alone,
The redbreast, sacred to the household gods,
Wisely regardful of the embroiling sky,
In joyless fields and thorny thickets leaves
His shivering mates, and pays to trusted man
His annual visit.   Half-afraid, he first
Against the window beats ; then brisk alights
On the warm hearth ; then, hopping o'er the floor,
Eyes all the smiling family askance,
And pecks, and starts, and wonders where he is—
Till, more familiar grown, the table crumbs
Attract his slender feet.   The foodless wilds
Pour forth their brown inhabitants.   The hare,
Though timorous of heart, and hard beset
By death in various forms, dark snares, and dogs,
And more unpitying men, the garden seeks,
Urged on by fearless want.   The bleating kind
Eye the black heaven, and next the glistening earth,
With looks of dumb despair ; then, sad dispersed,
Dig for the withered herb through heaps of snow.

A HYMN ON THE SEASONS.

These as they change, Almighty Father, these
Are but the varied God.   The rolling year
Is full of thee.   Forth in the pleasing Spring
Thy beauty walks, thy tenderness and love.
Wide flush the fields ; the softening air is balm ;
Echo the mountains round ; the forest smiles ;
And every sense, and every heart, is joy.
Then comes thy glory in the Summer-months
With light and heat refulgent.   Then thy sun
Shoots full perfection through the swelling year.
And oft thy voice in dreadful thunder speaks ;
And oft at dawn, deep noon, or falling eve,
By brooks and groves, in hollow-whispering gales.
Thy bounty shines in Autumn unconfined,

And spreads a common feast for all that lives.
In Winter awful thou ! with clouds and storms
Around thee thrown, tempest o'er tempest rolled,
Majestic darkness ! on the whirlwind's wing,
Riding sublime thou bidst the world adore,
And humblest nature with thy northern blast.

SAMUEL JOHNSON.

Born 1700.   Died 1784.

THE FALL OF GREATNESS.

In full-blown dignity see Wolsey stand,
Law in his voice, and fortune in his hand :
To him the church, the realm, their powers consign,
Through him the rays of regal bounty shine :
Turned by his nod the stream of honour flows,
His smile alone security bestows :
Still to new heights his restless wishes tower,
Claim leads to claim, and power advances power ;
Till conquest unresisted ceased to please,
And rights submitted left him none to seize :
At length his sovereign frowns—the train of state
Mark the keen glance, and watch the sign to hate.
Where'er he turns, he meets a stranger's eye,
His suppliants scorn him, and his followers fly ;
Now drops at once the pride of awful state,
The golden canopy, the glittering plate,
The regal palace, the luxurious board,
The liveried army, and the menial lord.
With age, with cares, with maladies oppressed,
He seeks the refuge of monastic rest.
Grief aids disease, remembered folly stings,
And his last sighs reproach the faith of kings.
Speak thou whose thoughts at humble peace repine,
Shall Wolsey's wealth with Wolsey's end be thine ?
Or liv'st thou now, with safer pride content,
The wisest justice on the banks of Trent?
For, why did Wolsey, near the steeps of fate,
On weak foundations raise th' enormous weight ?

Why but to sink beneath misfortune's blow,
With louder ruin to the gulphs below.
   What gave great Villiers to th' assassin's knife,
And fixed disease on Harley's closing life?
What murdered Wentworth, and what exiled Hyde,
By kings protected, and to kings allied?
What but their wish indulged in courts to shine,
And power too great to keep, or to resign.
When first the college rolls receives his name,
The young enthusiast quits his ease for fame ;
Resistless burns the fever of renown,
Caught from the strong contagion of the gown :
O'er Bodley's dome his future labours spread,
And Bacon's mansion trembles o'er his head.[1]
Are these thy views?   Proceed, illustrious youth,
And Virtue guard thee to the throne of Truth !
Yet should thy soul indulge the generous heat
Till captive Science yields her last retreat ;
Should Reason guide thee with her brightest ray,
And pour on misty doubt resistless day ;
Should no false kindness lure to loose delight,
Nor praise relax, nor difficulty fright ,
Should tempting Novelty thy cell refrain,
And Sloth effuse her opiate fumes in vain ;
Should Beauty blunt on fops her fatal dart,
Nor claim the triumphs of a lettered heart ;
Should no disease thy torpid veins invade,
Nor Melancholy's phantoms haunt thy shade ;
Yet hope not life from grief or danger free,
Nor think the doom of man reversed for thee :
Deign on the passing world to turn thine eyes,
And pause awhile from letters to be wise ;
There mark what ills the scholar's life assail,
Toil, envy, want, the patron, and the jail.
See nations, slowly wise and meanly just,
To buried merit raise the tardy bust.
If dreams yet flatter, once again attend,
Hear Lydiat's life, and Galileo's end.

    *   *   *   *   *   *

[1] There is a tradition that the study of Friar Bacon, built on an arch over the bridge, will fall when a man greater than Bacon shall pass under it. To prevent such an accident it was pulled down many years since.

On what foundation stands the warrior's pride,
How just his hopes, let Swedish Charles decide ;
A frame of adamant, a soul of fire,
No dangers fright him, and no labours tire ;
O'er love, o'er fear, extends his wide domain,
Unconquered lord of pleasure and of pain ;
No joys to him pacific sceptres yield,
War sounds the trump, he rushes to the field ;
Behold surrounding kings their powers combine,
And one capitulate, and one resign ;
Peace courts his hand, but spreads her charms in vain,
" Think nothing gained," he cries, " till nought remain,
On Moscow's walls till Gothic standards fly,
And all be mine beneath the polar sky."
The march begins in military state,
And nations on his eye suspended wait,
Stern Famine guards the solitary coast,
And Winter barricades the realms of Frost ;
He comes, nor want nor cold his course delay ;—
Hide, blushing Glory, hide Pultowa's day :
The vanquished hero leaves his broken bands,
And shows his miseries in distant lands ;
Condemned a needy suppliant to wait,
While ladies interpose, and slaves debate.
But did not Chance at length her error mend ?
Did no subverted empire mark his end ?
Did rival monarchs give the fatal wound ?
Or hostile millions press him to the ground ?
His fall was destined to a barren strand,
A petty fortress, and a dubious hand ;
He left the name, at which the world grew pale,
To point a moral, or adorn a tale.

*　　*　　*　　*　　*　　*

The bold Bavarian, in a luckless hour,
Tries the bold summits of Cæsarian power,
With unexpected legions bursts away,
And sees defenceless realms receive his sway :
Short sway ! fair Austria spreads her mournful charms,
The queen, the beauty, sets the world in arms ;
From hill to hill the beacon's rousing blaze
Spreads forth the hope of plunder and of praise ;
The fierce Croatian, and the wild Hussar,

With all the sons of ravage crowd the war ;
The baffled prince, in honour's flattering bloom
Of hasty greatness, finds the fatal doom ;
His foe's derision, and his subjects blame,
And steals to death, from anguish and from shame.

Vanity of Human Wishes.

WILLIAM COLLINS.

Born 1721. Died 1759.

ODE ON THE DEATH OF MR. THOMSON.[1]

In yonder grave a Druid lies,
Where slowly winds the stealing wave ;
The year's best sweets shall duteous rise
To deck its poet's sylvan grave.

In yon deep bed of whispering reeds
His airy harp shall now be laid,
That he, whose heart in sorrow bleeds,
May love through life the soothing shade.

Then maids and youths shall linger here,
And, while its sounds at distance swell,
Shall sadly seem in pity's ear
To hear the woodland pilgrim's knell.

Remembrance oft shall haunt the shore
When Thames in summer wreaths is drest,
And oft suspend the dashing oar,
To bid his gentle spirit rest !

And oft, as ease and health retire
To breezy lawn, or forest deep,
The friend shall view yon whitening spire,[2]
And mid the varied landscape weep.

But thou, who own'st that earthy bed,
Ah ! what will every dirge avail ;
Or tears, which love and pity shed,
That mourn beneath the gliding sail ?

[1] The scene of the following stanzas is supposed to lie on the Thames, near Richmond.

[2] Richmond Church, in which Thomson was buried.

Yet lives there one whose heedless eye
Shall scorn thy pale shrine glimmering near?
With him, sweet bard, may fancy die,
And joy desert the blooming year.

But thou, lorn stream, whose sullen tide
No sedge-crowned sisters now attend,
Now waft me from the green hill's side,
Whose cold turf hides the buried friend!

And see—the fairy valleys fade;
Dun night has veiled the solemn view!
Yet once again, dear parted shade,
Meek nature's child, again adieu!

The genial meads, assigned to bless
Thy life, shall mourn thy early doom;
Their hinds and shepherd girls shall dress,
With simple hands, thy rural tomb.

Long, long, thy stone and pointed clay
Shall melt the musing Briton's eyes:
O vales and wild woods! shall he say,
In yonder grave your Druid lies!

AN ODE.

WRITTEN IN THE YEAR 1746.

How sleep the brave, who sink to rest
By all their country's wishes blest!
When Spring, with dewy fingers cold,
Returns to deck their hallowed mould,
She there shall dress a sweeter sod
Than Fancy's feet have ever trod.

By fairy hands their knell is rung;
By forms unseen their dirge is sung;
There Honour comes, a pilgrim gray,
To bless the turf that wraps their clay;
And Freedom shall awhile repair,
To dwell, a weeping hermit, there!

THE PASSIONS.

When Music, heavenly maid, was young,
While yet in early Greece she sung,

The Passions oft, to hear her shell,
Thronged around her magic cell,
Exulting, trembling, raging, fainting,
Possest beyond the muse's painting :
By turns they felt the glowing mind
Disturbed, delighted, raised, refined ;
Till once, 'tis said, when all were fired,
Filled with fury, rapt, inspired,
From the supporting myrtles round
They snatched her instruments of sound ;
And, as they oft had heard apart
Sweet lessons of her forceful art,
Each (for Madness ruled the hour)
Would prove his own expressive power.
First Fear, his hand, its skill to try,
Amid the chords bewildered laid,
And back recoiled, he knew not why,
Even at the sound himself had made.
Next Anger rushed ; his eyes on fire,
In lightning owned his secret stings :
In one rude clash he struck the lyre,
And swept with hurried hands the strings.

With woful measures wan Despair
Low, sullen sounds his grief beguiled ;
A solemn, strange, and mingled air ;
'Twas sad by fits, by starts 'twas wild.

But thou, O Hope, with eyes so fair,
What was thy delighted measure?
Still it whispered promised pleasure,
And bade the lovely scenes at distance hail !
Still would her touch the strain prolong ;
And from the rocks, the woods, the vale,
She called on Echo still, through all the song ;
And, where her sweetest theme she chose,
A soft responsive voice was heard at every close,
And Hope enchanted smiled, and waved her golden hair.

And longer had she sung ;—but, with a frown,
Revenge impatient rose :
He threw his blood-stained sword, in thunder, down ;
And with a withering look,
The war-denouncing trumpet took,

And blew a blast so loud and dread,
Were ne'er prophetic sounds so full of woe !
And, ever and anon, he beat
The doubling drum, with furious heat ;
And though sometimes, each dreary pause between,
Dejected Pity, at his side,
Her soul-subduing voice applied,
Yet still he kept his wild unaltered mien,
While each strained ball of sight seemed bursting from
    his head.

Thy numbers, Jealousy, to naught were fixed ;
Sad proof of thy distressful state ;
Of differing themes the veering song was mixed ;
And now it courted love, now raving called on hate.

With eyes upraised, as one inspired,
Pale Melancholy sat retired,
And, from her wild sequestered seat,
In notes by distance made more sweet,
Poured through the mellow horn her pensive soul :
And, dashing soft from rocks around,
Bubbling runnels joined the sound ;
Through glades and glooms the mingled measure stole,
Or, o'er some haunted stream, with fond delay,
Round an holy calm diffusing,
Love of peace, and lonely musing,
In hollow murmurs died away.

But O ! how altered was its sprightlier tone,
When Cheerfulness, a nymph of healthiest hue,
Her bow across her shoulder flung,
Her buskins gemmed with morning dew,
Blew an inspiring air, that dale and thicket rung,
The hunter's call to faun and dryad known !
The oak-crowned sisters, and their chaste-eyed queen,
Satyrs and sylvan boys, were seen,
Peeping from forth their alleys green :
Brown Exercise rejoiced to hear ;
And Sport leapt up, and seized his beechen spear.

Last came Joy's ecstatic trial :
He, with viny crown advancing,

First to the lively pipe his hand addrest ;
But soon he saw the brisk awakening viol,
Whose sweet entrancing voice he loved the best ;
They would have thought who heard the strain
They saw, in Tempe's vale, her native maids,
Amidst the festal sounding shades,
To some unwearied minstrel dancing,
While, as his flying fingers kissed the strings,
Love framed with Mirth a gay fantastic round :
Loose were her tresses seen, her zone unbound ;
And he, amidst his frolic play,
As if he would the charming air repay,
Shook thousand odours from his dewy wings.
O Music ! sphere-descended maid,
Friend of pleasure, wisdom's aid !
Why, goddess ! why, to us denied,
Lay'st thou thy ancient lyre aside ?
As, in that loved Athenian bower,
You learned an all-commanding power,
Thy mimic soul, O nymph endeared,
Can well recall what then it heard ;
Where is thy native simple heart,   '
Devote to virtue, fancy, art ?
Arise, as in that elder time,
Warm, energetic, chaste, sublime !
Thy wonders, in that godlike age,
Fill thy recording sister's page—
'Tis said, and I believe the tale,
Thy humblest reed could more prevail,
Had more of strength, diviner rage,
Than all which charms this laggard age ;
E'en all at once together found,
Cecilia's mingled world of sound—
O bid our vain endeavours cease ;
Revive the just designs of Greece :
Return in all thy simple state !
Confirm the tales her sons relate !

THOMAS GRAY.

Born 1716. Died 1771.

ELEGY WRITTEN IN A COUNTRY CHURCHYARD.

THE curfew tolls the knell of parting day,
   The lowing herd winds slowly o'er the lea,
The ploughman homeward plods his weary way,
   And leaves the world to darkness and to me.

Now fades the glimmering landscape on the sight,
   And all the air a solemn stillness holds ;
Save where the beetle wheels his droning flight,
   And drowsy tinklings lull the distant folds :

Save that from yonder ivy-mantled tower,
   The moping owl does to the moon complain
Of such as, wandering near her secret bower,
   Molest her ancient solitary reign.

Beneath those rugged elms, that yew-tree's shade,
   Where heaves the turf in many a mouldering heap,
Each in his narrow cell forever laid,
   The rude forefathers of the hamlet sleep.

The breezy call of incense-breathing Morn,
   The swallow twittering from the straw-built shed,
The cock's shrill clarion, or the echoing horn,
   No more shall rouse them from their lowly bed.

For them no more the blazing hearth shall burn,
   Or busy housewife ply her evening care ;
No children run to lisp their sire's return,
   Or climb his knees the envied kiss to share.

Oft did the harvest to their sickle yield,
   Their furrow oft the stubborn glebe has broke ;
How jocund did they drive their team afield !
   How bowed the woods beneath their sturdy stroke !

Let not ambition mock their useful toil,
   Their homely joys, and destiny obscure ;
Nor grandeur here with a disdainful smile,
   The short and simple annals of the poor.

The boast of heraldry, the pomp of power,
   And all that beauty, all that wealth e'er gave,
Await alike the inevitable hour ;
   The paths of glory lead but to the grave.

Nor you, ye proud, impute to these the fault,
   If memory o'er their tomb no trophies raise,
Where through the long-drawn aisle and fretted vault
   The pealing anthem swells the note of praise.

Can storied urn, or animated bust,
   Back to its mansion call the fleeting breath ?
Can Honour's voice provoke the silent dust,
   Or flattery soothe the dull cold ear of Death ?

Perhaps in this neglected spot is laid
   Some heart once pregnant with celestial fire ;
Hands, that the rod of empire might have swayed,
   Or waked to ecstasy the living lyre.

But knowledge to their eyes her ample page,
   Rich with the spoils of time, did ne'er unroll ;
Chill penury repressed their noble rage,
   And froze the genial current of the soul.

Full many a gem of purest ray serene
   The dark unfathomed caves of ocean bear :
Full many a flower is born to blush unseen,
   And waste its sweetness on the desert air.

Some village Hampden, that with dauntless breast,
   The little tyrant of his fields withstood ;
Some mute inglorious Milton here may rest,
   Some Cromwell guiltless of his country's blood.

The applause of listening senates to command,
   The threats of pain and ruin to despise,
To scatter plenty o'er a smiling land,
   And read their history in a nation's eyes,

Their lot forbade : nor circumscribed alone
   Their growing virtues, but their crimes confined ;
Forbade to wade through slaughter to a throne,
   And shut the gates of mercy on mankind ;

The struggling pangs of conscious truth to hide,
  To quench the blushes of ingenuous shame,
Or heap the shrine of luxury and pride
  With incense kindled at the Muse's flame.

Far from the madding crowd's ignoble strife,
  Their sober wishes never learned to stray ;
Along the cool sequestered vale of life
  They kept the noiseless tenor of their way.

Yet e'en these bones from insult to protect
  Some frail memorial still erected nigh,
With uncouth rhymes and shapeless sculpture decked,
  Implores the passing tribute of a sigh.

Their names, their years, spelt by the unlettered Muse,
  The place of fame and elegy supply ;
And many a holy text around she strews,
  That teach the rustic moralist to die.

For who, to dumb forgetfulness a prey,
  This pleasing anxious being e'er resigned,
Left the warm precincts of the cheerful day,
  Nor cast one longing, lingering look behind ?

On some fond breast the parting soul relies,
  Some pious drops the closing eye requires ;
E'en from the tomb the voice of Nature cries,
  E'en in our ashes live their wonted fires.

For thee, who, mindful of the unhonoured dead,
  Dost in these lines their artless tale relate ;
If chance, by lonely Contemplation led,
  Some kindred spirit shall inquire thy fate,

Haply some hoary-headed swain may say,
  " Oft have we seen him at the peep of dawn,
Brushing with hasty steps the dews away,
  To meet the sun upon the upland lawn.

" There at the foot of yonder nodding beech,
  That wreathes its old fantastic roots so high,
His listless length at noontide would he stretch,
  And pore upon the brook that babbles by.

"Hard by yon wood, now smiling as in scorn,
   Muttering his wayward fancies he would rove ;
Now drooping woeful-wan, like one forlorn,
   Or crazed with care, or crossed in hopeless love.

"One morn I missed him on the customed hill,
   Along the heath, and near his favourite tree ;
Another came, nor yet beside the rill,
   Nor up the lawn, nor at the wood was he ;

"The next with dirges due in sad array,
   Slow through the churchway path we saw him borne
Approach and read (for thou canst read) the lay,
   Graved on the stone beneath yon aged thorn."

THE EPITAPH.

Here rests his head upon the lap of Earth
   A Youth, to Fortune and to Fame unknown :
Fair Science frowned not on his humble birth,
   And Melancholy marked him for her own.

Large was his bounty, and his soul sincere ;
   Heaven did a recompense as largely send :
He gave to misery all he had, a tear ;
   He gained from Heaven, 'twas all he wished, a frien<

No farther seek his merits to disclose,
   Or draw his frailties from their dread abode,
(There they alike in trembling hope repose,)
   The bosom of his Father and his God.

HYMN TO ADVERSITY.

DAUGHTER of Jove, relentless power,
   Thou tamer of the human breast,
Whose iron scourge, and torturing hour
   The bad affright, afflict the best !
Bound in thy adamantine chain,
The proud are taught to taste of pain,
And purple tyrants vainly groan
With pangs unfelt before, unpitied and alone.

When first thy sire to send on earth
   Virtue, his darling child, designed,

To thee he gave the heavenly birth,
   And bade to form her infant mind.
Stern rugged nurse ! thy rigid lore
With patience many a year she bore :
What sorrow was, thou bad'st her know,
And from her own she learned to melt at others' woe.

   Scared at thy frown terrific, fly
     Self-pleasing Folly's idle brood,
Wild Laughter, Noise, and thoughtless Joy,
     And leave us leisure to be good.
Light they disperse, and with them go
The summer friend, the flattering foe ;
By vain Prosperity received,
To her they vow their truth, and are again believed.

   Wisdom in sable garb arrayed,
     Immersed in rapturous thought profound,
And Melancholy, silent maid,
     With leaden eye that loves the ground,
Still on thy solemn steps attend :
Warm Charity, the general friend,
With Justice, to herself severe,
And Pity, dropping soft the sadly pleasing tear.

   O gently on thy suppliant's head,
     Dread Goddess, lay thy chastening hand !
Not in thy Gorgon terrors clad,
     Not circled with the vengeful band
(As by the impious thou art seen)
With thundering voice, and threatening mien,
With screaming Horror's funeral cry,
Despair, and fell Disease, and ghastly Poverty.

   Thy form benign, O Goddess, wear,
     Thy milder influence impart,
Thy philosophic train be there
     To soften, not to wound, my heart.
The generous spark extinct revive,
Teach me to love, and to forgive,
Exact my own defects to scan,
What others are to feel, and know myself a Man.

THE BARD.

I.

" RUIN scize thee, ruthless King !
Confusion on thy banners wait !
Though fanned by Conquest's crimson wing,
    They mock the air with idle state.
Helm, nor hauberk's [1] twisted mail,
Nor e'en thy virtues, Tyrant, shall avail
    To save thy secret soul from nightly fears,
    From Cambria's curse, from Cambria's tears !"
Such were the sounds that o'er the crested pride
    Of the first Edward scattered wild dismay,
As down the steep of Snowdon's shaggy side
    He wound with toilsome march his long array.
Stout Gloster [2] stood aghast in speechless trance :
"To arms !" cried Mortimer, [3] and couched his quiv
    lance.

I. 2.

On a rock, whose haughty brow
Frowns o'er cold Conway's foaming flood,
    Robed in the sable garb of woe,
With haggard eyes the poet stood ;
(Loose his beard, and hoary hair
Streamed, like a meteor, to the troubled air)
And with a master's hand, and prophet's fire,
Struck the deep sorrows of his lyre.
"Hark, how each giant oak, and desert cave,
    Sighs to the torrent's awful voice beneath !
O'er thee, O King ! their hundred arms they wave,
    Revenge on thee in hoarser murmurs breathe ;
Vocal no more, since Cambria's fatal day,
To high-born Hoel's harp, or soft Llewellyn's lay.

I. 3.

Cold is Cadwallo's tongue,
    That hushed the stormy main :

[1] The hauberk was a texture of steel ringlets or rings interwoven, forming of mail, that set close to the body, and adapted itself to every motion.
[2] Gilbert de Clare, surnamed the Red, Earl of Gloucester and Hertford, law to King Edward.
[3] Edmund do Mortimer, Lord of Wigmore.

Brave Urien sleeps upon his craggy bed :
  Mountains, ye mourn in vain
  Modred, whose magic song
Made huge Plinlimmon bow his cloud-topt head.
  On dreary Arvon's [1] shore they lie,
Smeared with gore, and ghastly pale :
Far, far aloof th' affrighted ravens sail ;
  The famished eagle screams, and passes by.
Dear lost companions of my tuneful art,
  Dear as the light that visits these sad eyes,
Dear as the ruddy drops that warm my heart,
  Ye died amidst your dying country's cries—
No more I weep. They do not sleep.
  On yonder cliffs, a griesly band,
I see them sit, they linger yet,
  Avengers of their native land :
With me in dreadful harmony they join,
And weave with bloody hands the tissue of thy line.

II. 1.

" Weave the warp, and weave the woof,
The winding-sheet of Edward's race :
  Give ample room, and verge enough
The characters of hell to trace.
Mark the year, and mark the night,
When Severn shall re-echo with affright   .
The shrieks of death, through Berkeley's roof that ring, [2]
Shrieks of an agonizing king !
  She-wolf of France, [3] with unrelenting fangs,
That tear'st the bowels of thy mangled mate,
  From thee be born, who o'er thy country hangs
The scourge of heaven. [4] What terrors round him wait !
Amazement in his van, with flight combined,
And sorrow's faded form, and solitude behind.

II. 2.

" Mighty victor, mighty lord !
Low on his funeral couch he lies ! [5]

'he shores of Caernarvonshire, opposite Anglesea.
Edward II., murdered in Berkeley Castle.
sabel of France, wife of Edward II.
Edward III. gained many victories in France.
Edward III., deserted on his death-bed by his children and robbed in his last
ients by his courtiers and mistress, who even drew the rings off his fingers.

No pitying heart, no eye, afford
A tear to grace his obsequies.
  Is the sable warrior [1] fled ?
Thy son is gone. He rests among the dead.
The swarm, that in thy noontide beam were born ?
Gone to salute the rising morn.
Fair laughs the morn, and soft the zephyr blows,
  While proudly riding o'er the azure realm
In gallant trim the gilded vessel goes ;
  Youth on the prow, and Pleasure at the helm !
Regardless of the sweeping whirlwind's sway,
That, hushed in grim repose, expects his evening prey.

II. 3.

" Fill high the sparkling bowl,
The rich repast prepare.
  Reft of a crown, he yet may share the feast :
Close by the regal chair
  Fell Thirst and Famine scowl
A baleful smile upon their baffled guest.
Heard ye the din of battle bray, [2]
  Lance to lance, and horse to horse ?
Long years of havoc urge their destined course,
And through the kindred squadrons mow their way.
  Ye towers of Julius, [3] London's lasting shame,
With many a foul and midnight murder fed,
  Revere his consort's faith, [4] his father's fame, [5]
And spare the meek usurper's holy head. [6]
Above, below, the rose of snow, [7]
  Twined with her blushing foe, we spread !
The bristled boar [8] in infant-gore
  Wallows beneath the thorny shade.
Now, brothers, bending o'er the accursed loom,
Stamp we our vengeance deep, and ratify his doom.

[1] The Black Prince.
[2] The wars of York and Lancaster.
[3] The Tower of London, where Henry VI., George Duke of Clarence, Edward and Richard Duke of York, were supposed to be murdered. The oldest part of structure is attributed to Julius Cæsar.
[4] Margaret of Anjou.   [5] Henry V.
[6] Henry VI., who was nearly canonized.
[7] The white and red roses, devices of York and Lancaster.
[8] Richard III. was usually known by the name of the Boar, from his device of silver boar.

III. I.

"Edward, lo! to sudden fate
(Weave we the woof. The thread is spun.)
    Half of thy heart we consecrate.[1]
(The web is wove. The work is done.)
Stay, oh stay! nor thus forlorn
Leave me unblessed, unpitied, here to mourn :
In yon bright track, that fires the western skies,
They melt, they vanish from my eyes.
But oh! what solemn scenes on Snowdon's height
    Descending slow their glittering skirts unroll?
Visions of glory, spare my aching sight!
    Ye unborn ages, crowd not on my soul!
No more our long-lost Arthur [2] we bewail.
All hail, ye genuine kings,[3] Britannia's issue, hail!

III. 2.

"Girt with many a baron bold
Sublime their starry fronts they rear ;
    And gorgeous dames, and statesmen old
In bearded majesty, appear.
In the midst a form divine!
Her eye proclaims her of the Briton-line ;
Her lion-port, her awe-commanding face,
Attempered sweet to virgin-grace.
What strings symphonious tremble in the air,
    What strains of vocal transport round her play.
Hear from the grave, great Taliessin,[4] hear ;
    They breathe a soul to animate thy clay.
Bright Rapture calls, and soaring as she sings,
Waves in the eye of heaven her many-coloured wings.

III. 3.

"The verse adorn again
    Fierce war, and faithful love,
And truth severe, by fairy diction drest.

[1] Eleanor of Castile died a few years after the conquest of Wales.
[2] It was a common belief of the Welsh nation that King Arthur was still alive in iiryland, and would return to reign over Britain.
[3] Merlin and Taliessin had prophesied that the Welsh should regain their sovergnty over the island, which prophecy seemed to be accomplished in the House of idor.
[4] Taliessin, chief of the bards, who flourished in the sixth century.

In buskined measures [1] move
Pale grief, and pleasing pain,
With horror, tyrant of the throbbing breast.
   A voice,[2] as of the cherub-choir,
Gales from blooming Eden bear ;
And distant warblings [3] lessen on my ear,
   That lost in long futurity expire.
Fond impious man, think'st thou yon sanguine cloud,
   Raised by thy breath, has quenched the orb of day ?
To-morrow he repairs the golden flood,
   And warms the nations with redoubled ray.
Enough for me ; with joy I see
   The different doom our fates assign.
Be thine despair, and sceptred care,
   To triumph, and to die, are mine."
He spoke, and headlong from the mountain's height
Deep in the roaring tide he plunged to endless night.

OLIVER GOLDSMITH.

Born 1728. Died 1774.

THE TRAVELLER.

Remote, unfriended, melancholy, slow,
Or by the lazy Scheld, or wandering Po ;
Or onward, where the rude Carinthian boor
Against the houseless stranger shuts the door ;
Or where Campania's plain forsaken lies,
A weary waste expanding to the skies ;
Where'er I roam, whatever realms I see,
My heart, untravelled, fondly turns to thee :
Still to my brother turns with ceaseless pain,
And drags at each remove a length'ning chain.
Eternal blessings crown my earliest friend,
And round his dwelling guardian saints attend ;
Blest be that spot, where cheerful guests retire
To pause from toil, and trim their evening fire ;
Blest that abode, where want and pain repair,
And every stranger finds a ready chair :

[1] Shakespeare.   [2] Milton.
[3] The succession of poets, after Milton's time.

Blest be those feasts, with simple plenty crowned,
Where all the ruddy family around
Laugh at the jests and pranks that never fail,
Or sigh with pity at some mournful tale ;
Or press the bashful stranger to his food,
And learn the luxury of doing good.
But me, not destined such delights to share,
My prime of life in wand'ring spent and care ;
Impelled with steps unceasing to pursue
Some fleeting good, that mocks me with the view ;
That like the circle bounding earth and skies,
Allures from far, yet as I follow, flies ;
My fortune leads to traverse realms alone,
And find no spot in all the world my own.

THE HAPPIEST SPOT.

But, where to find that happiest spot below,
Who can direct, when all pretend to know?
The shuddering tenant of the frigid zone
Boldly proclaims that happiest spot his own ;
Extols the treasures of his stormy seas,
And his long nights of revelry and ease :
The naked negro panting at the line,
Boasts of his golden sands and palmy wine,
Basks in the glare, or stems the tepid wave,
And thanks his gods for all the good they gave.

Such is the patriot's boast, where'er we roam,
His first, best country, ever is at home.
And yet, perhaps, if countries we compare,
And estimate the blessings which they share,
Though patriots flatter, still shall wisdom find
An equal portion dealt to all mankind ;
As different good, by art or nature given,
To different nations makes their blessings even.

From *The Traveller*.

THE VILLAGE CLERGYMAN.

Near yonder copse, where once the garden smiled,
And still where many a garden flower grows wild ;
There, where a few torn shrubs the place disclose,
The village preacher's modest mansion rose.

A man he was to all the country dear,
And passing rich with forty pounds a year ;
Remote from towns he ran his godly race,
Nor e'er had changed, nor wished to change his place ;
Unpractised he to fawn, or seek for power,
By doctrines fashioned to the varying hour,
Far other aims his heart had learned to prize,
More skilled to raise the wretched than to rise.
His house was known to all the vagrant train,
He chid their wanderings, but relieved their pain ;
The long-remembered beggar was his guest,
Whose beard descending swept his aged breast ;
The ruined spendthrift, now no longer proud,
Claimed kindred there, and had his claims allowed :
The broken soldier, kindly bade to stay,
Sat by his fire and talked the night away,
Wept o'er his wounds, or, tales of sorrow done,
Shouldered his crutch and showed how fields were wor
Pleased with his guests, the good man learned to glow,
And quite forgot their vices in their woe ;
Careless their merits or their faults to scan,
His pity gave ere charity began.

Thus to relieve the wretched was his pride,
And e'en his failings leaned to virtue's side ;
But in his duty, prompt at every call,
He watched and wept, he prayed and felt for all ;
And, as a bird each fond endearment tries
To tempt its new-fledged offspring to the skies,
He tried each art, reproved each dull delay,.
Allured to brighter worlds, and led the way.

Beside the bed where parting life was laid,
And sorrow, guilt, and pain, by turns dismayed,
The reverend champion stood.   At his control
Despair and anguish fled the struggling soul :
Comfort came down the trembling wretch to raise,
And his last faltering accents whispered praise.

At church, with meek and unaffected grace,
His looks adorned the venerable place ;
Truth from his lips prevailed with double sway,
And fools, who came to scoff, remained to pray.

The service past, around the pious man,
With steady zeal, each honest rustic ran ;
E'en children followed, with endearing wile,
And plucked his gown, to share the good man's smile,
His ready smile a parent's warmth expressed,
Their welfare pleased him, and their cares distressed ;
To them his heart, his love, his griefs were given,
But all his serious thoughts had rest in heaven.
As some tall cliff that lifts its awful form,
Swells from the vale, and midway leave sthe storm,
Though round its breast the rolling clouds are spread,
Eternal sunshine settles on its head.

From *The Deserted Village.*

STANZAS ON WOMAN.

WHEN lovely woman stoops to folly,
    And finds too late that men betray,
What charm can soothe her melancholy,
    What art can wash her guilt away ?

The only art her guilt to cover,
    To hide her shame from every eye,
To give repentance to her lover,
    And wring his bosom, is—to die.

From *The Vicar of Wakefield.*

RETALIATION.

OF old, when Scarron his companions invited,
Each guest brought his dish, and the feast was united.
If our landlord [1] supplies us with beef and with fish,
Let each guest bring himself, and he brings the best dish :
Our dean [2] shall be ven'son, just fresh from the plains ;
Our Burke [3] shall be tongue, with the garnish of brains ;
Our Will [4] shall be wild fowl, of excellent flavour ;
And Dick [5] with his pepper shall heighten the savour :
Our Cumberland's [6] sweetbread its place shall obtain ;

[1] The master of St. James's coffee-house, where the doctor and the friends he-
s characterized in the poem, occasionally dined.
[2] Dr. Barnard, Dean of Derry, in Ireland.   [3] Mr. Edmund Burke.
[4] Mr. William Burke, secretary to General Conway, and member for Bedwin.
[5] Mr. Richard Burke, collector for Granada.
[6] Mr. Richard Cumberland, author of "The West Indian," "Fashionable Lover,"
The Brothers," and other dramatic pieces.

And Douglas [1] is pudding, substantial and plain :
Our Garrick's [2] a salad ; for in him we see
Oil, vinegar, sugar, and saltness agree ;
To make out the dinner, full certain I am
That Ridge [3] is anchovy, and Reynolds [4] is lamb ;
That Hickey's [5] a capon ; and, by the same rule,
Magnanimous Goldsmith's a gooseberry fool.
At a dinner so various, at such a repast,
Who'd not be a glutton, and stick to the last ?
Here, waiter, more wine, let me sit while I'm able,
Till all my companions sink under the table ;
Then, with chaos and blunders encircling my head,
Let me ponder, and tell what I think of the dead.

   * * * * * *

Here lies our good Edmund, whose genius was such,
We scarcely can praise it, or blame it, too much ;
Who, born for the universe, narrowed his mind,
And to party gave up what was meant for mankind ;
Though fraught with all learning, yet straining his throat,
To persuade Tommy Townshend [6] to lend him a vote :
Who, too deep for his hearers, still went on refining,
And thought of convincing, while they thought of dining ;
Though equal to all things, for all things unfit,
Too nice for a statesman, too proud for a wit ;
For a patriot too cool ; for a judge disobedient ;
And too fond of the right to pursue the expedient.
In short, 'twas his fate, unemployed, or in place, sir,
To eat mutton cold, and cut blocks with a razor.

   * * * * * *

Here Douglas retires from his toils to relax,
The scourge of impostors, the terror of quacks :
Come, all ye quack bards, and ye quacking divines,
Come, and dance on the spot where your tyrant reclines :
When satire and censure encircled his throne,
I feared for your safety, I feared for my own :
But now he is gone, and we want a detector,
Our Dodds [7] shall be pious, our Kenricks [8] shall lecture ;

[1] Dr. Douglas, Bishop of Salisbury.
[2] David Garrick, Esq.   [3] Counsellor John Ridge.
[4] Sir Joshua Reynolds.   [5] An eminent attorney.
[6] Mr. T. Townshend, member for Whitchurch.
[7] Rev. Dr. Dodd.   [8] Dr. Kenrick.

Macpherson [1] write bombast, and call it a style ;
Our Townshend make speeches, and I shall compile ;
New Lauders and Bowers, the Tweed shall cross over,
No countrymen living their tricks to discover ;
Detection her taper shall quench to a spark,
And Scotchman meet Scotchman and cheat in the dark.
Here lies David Garrick, describe him who can,
And abridgment of all that is pleasant in man ;
As an actor confessed without rival to shine,
As a wit, if not first, in the very first line !
Yet, with talents like these, and an excellent heart,
The man had his failings—a dupe to his art.
Like an ill-judging beauty, his colours he spread,
And beplastered with rouge his own natural red.
On the stage he was natural, simple, affecting ;
'Twas only that when he was off he was acting.
With no reason on earth to go out of his way,
He turned and he varied, full ten times a day :
Though secure of our hearts, yet confoundedly sick
If they were not his own by finessing and trick :
He cast off his friends, as a huntsman his pack,
For he knew, when he pleased, he could whistle them back.
Of praise a mere glutton, he swallowed what came,
And the puff of a dunce, he mistook it for fame ;
Till, his relish grown callous, almost to disease,
Who peppered the highest was surest to please.
But let us be candid, and speak out our mind,
If dunces applauded, he payed them in kind.
Ye Kenricks, and Kellys [2] and Woodfalls [3] so grave,
What a commerce was yours, while you got and you gave !
How did Grub Street re-echo the shouts that you raised
While he was be-Rosciused, and you were be-praised !
But peace to his spirit, wherever it flies,
To act as an angel and mix with the skies :
Those poets who owe their best fame to his skill
Shall still be his flatterers, go where he will :
Old Shakespere receive him with praise and with love,
And Beaumont and Ben be his Kellys above.

*　　*　　*　　*　　*　　*　　*

[1] James Macpherson, Esq., who from the mere force of his style wrote down the first poet of all antiquity.
[2] Mr. Hugh Kelly, author of " False Delicacy."
[3] Mr. Woodfall, printer of the *Morning Chronicle*.

Here Reynolds is laid, and, to tell you my mind,
He has not left a wiser or better behind ;
His pencil was striking, resistless, and grand ;
His manners were gentle, complying, and bland ;
Still born to improve us in every part,
His pencil our faces, his manners our heart :
To coxcombs averse, yet most civilly steering,
When they judged without skill, he was still hard of hearing ;
When they talked of their Raphaels, Correggios, and stuff,
He shifted his trumpet,[1] and only took snuff.

WILLIAM COWPER.

Born 1731.　Died 1800.

LINES ON RECEIVING HIS MOTHER'S PICTURE.

O THAT those lips had language !　Life has passed
With me but roughly since I heard thee last.
Those lips are thine—thy own sweet smile I see,
The same that oft in childhood solaced me ;
Voice only fails, else how distinct they say,
" Grieve not, my child, chase all thy fears away !"
The meek intelligence of those dear eyes
(Blest be the art that can immortalize,
The art that baffles Time's tyrannic claim
To quench it) here shines on me still the same.
Faithful remembrancer of one so dear,
O welcome guest, though unexpected here !
Who bid'st me honour with an artless song,
Affectionate, a mother lost so long.
I will obey, not willingly alone,
But gladly, as the precept were her own :
And, while that face renews my filial grief,
Fancy shall weave a charm for my relief,
Shall steep me in Elysian reverie,
A momentary dream that thou art she.
　　My mother ! when I learned that thou wast dead,
Say, wast thou conscious of the tears I shed ?

[1] Sir Joshua Reynolds was so deaf that he was obliged to use an ear-trumpet i
company.

Hovered thy spirit o'er thy sorrowing son,
Wretch even then, life's journey just begun !
Perhaps thou gav'st me, though unfelt, a kiss ;
Perhaps a tear, if souls can weep in bliss—
Ah that maternal smile ! it answers—Yes.
I heard the bell tolled on thy burial day,
I saw the hearse that bore thee slow away,
And, turning from my nursery window, drew
A long, long sigh, and wept a last adieu !
But was it such ?—It was.—Where thou art gone,
Adieus and farewells are a sound unknown :
May I but meet thee on that peaceful shore,
The parting word shall pass my lips no more !
Thy maidens, grieved themselves at my concern,
Oft gave me promise of thy quick return.
What ardently I wished I long believed,
And, disappointed still, was still deceived.
By expectation every day beguiled.
Dupe of to-morrow even from a child.
Thus many a sad to-morrow came and went,
Till, all my stock of infant sorrow spent,
I learned at last submission to my lot ;
But, though I less deplored thee, ne'er forgot.

Where once we dwelt our name is heard no more,
Children not thine have trod my nursery floor ;
And where the gardener Robin, day by day,
Drew me to school along the public way,
Delighted with my bauble coach, and wrapped
In scarlet mantle warm, and velvet capped.
'Tis now become a history little known,
That once we called the pastoral house our own.
Short-lived possession ! but the record fair,
That memory keeps of all thy kindness there,
Still outlives many a storm, that has effaced
A thousand other themes less deeply traced.
Thy nightly visits to my chamber made,
That thou might'st know me safe and warmly laid ;
Thy morning bounties ere I left my home,
The biscuit, or confectionery plum ;
The fragrant waters on my cheeks bestowed
By thy own hand, till fresh they shone and glowed !
All this, and, more endearing still than all,
Thy constant flow of love, that knew no fall,

Ne'er roughened by those cataracts and breaks,
That humour interposed too often makes ;
All this still legible on memory's page,
And still to be so to my latest age,
Adds joy to duty, makes me glad to pay
Such honours to thee as my numbers may ;
Perhaps a frail memorial, but sincere,
Not scorned in heaven, though little noticed here.
    Could Time, his flight reversed, restore the hours,
When, playing with thy vesture's tissued flowers,
The violet, the pink, and jessamine,
I pricked them into paper with a pin,
(And thou wast happier than myself the while,
Would'st softly speak, and stroke my head, and smile),
Could those few pleasant days again appear,
Might one wish bring them, would I wish them here ?
I would not trust my heart—the dear delight
Seems so to be desired, perhaps I might.—
But no—What here we call our life is such,
So little to be loved, and thou so much,
That I should ill requite thee to constrain
Thy unbound spirit into bonds again.
    Thou, as a gallant bark from Albion's coast
(The storms all weathered and the ocean crossed)
Shoots into port at some well-havened isle,
Where spices breathe, and brighter seasons smile,
There sits quiescent on the floods, that show
Her beauteous form reflected clear below,
While airs impregnated with incense play
Around her, fanning light her streamers gay ;
So thou, with sails how swift ! hast reached the shore
"Where tempests never beat, nor billows roar." [1]
And thy loved consort on the dangerous tide
Of life long since has anchored by thy side.
But me, scarce hoping to attain that rest,
Always from port withheld, always distressed—
Me howling blasts drive devious, tempest-tossed,
Sails ripped, seams opening wide, and compass lost,
And day by day some current's thwarting force
Sets me more distant from a prosperous course.
Yet O the thought that thou art safe, and he !
That thought is joy, arrive what may to me.

[1] Garth.

My boast is not, that I deduce my birth
From loins enthroned, and rulers of the earth;
But higher far my proud pretensions rise—
The son of parents passed into the skies.
    And now, farewell—Time unrevoked has run
His wonted course, yet what I wished is done.
By contemplation's help, not sought in vain,
I seem to have lived my childhood o'er again ;
To have renewed the joys that once were mine,
Without the sin of violating thine ;
And while the wings of fancy still are free,
And I can view this mimic show of thee,
Time has but half succeeded in his theft.
Thyself removed, thy power to soothe me left.

AN EPISTLE TO JOSEPH HILL, ESQ.

DEAR Joseph,—five and twenty years ago—
Alas, how time escapes !—'Tis even so—
With frequent intercourse, and always sweet,
And always friendly, we were wont to cheat
A tedious hour—and now we never meet !
As some grave gentleman in Terence says
('Twas therefore much the same in ancient days),
Good lack, we know not what to-morrow brings—
Strange fluctuation of all human things !
True.   Changes will befall, and friends may part,
But distance only cannot change the heart :
And, were I called to prove th' assertion true,
One proof should serve—a reference to you.
Whence comes it then, that in the wane of life,
Though nothing have occurred to kindle strife,
We find the friends we fancied we had won,
Though numerous once, reduced to few or none ?
Can gold grow worthless, that has stood the touch ?
No ; gold they seemed, but they were never such.
    Horatio's servant once, with bow and cringe,
Swinging the parlour door upon its hinge,
Dreading a negative, and overawed
Lest he should trespass, begged to go abroad.
" Go, fellow!—whither ?"—turning short about—
"Nay.   Stay at home—you're always going out."
"'Tis but a step, sir, just at the street's end."
"For what ?"—" An please you, sir, to see a friend."

"A friend!"   Horatio cried, and seemed to start—
"Yea marry shalt thou, and with all my heart—
And fetch my cloak; for, though the night be raw,
I'll see him too—the first I ever saw."
  I knew the man, and knew his nature mild,
And was his plaything often when a child;
But something at that moment pinched him close,
Else he was seldom bitter or morose.
Perhaps, his confidence just then betrayed,
His grief might prompt him with the speech he made;
Perhaps 'twas mere good humour gave it birth,
The harmless play of pleasantry and mirth.
Howe'er it was, his language in my mind,
Bespoke at least a man that knew mankind.
  But not to moralize too much, and strain
To prove an evil, of which all complain,
(I hate long arguments verbosely spun,)
One story more, dear Hill, and I have done.
Once on a time an emperor, a wise man,
No matter where, in China or Japan,
Decreed, that whosoever should offend
Against the well-known duties of a friend,
Convicted once should ever after wear
But half a coat, and show his bosom bare.
The punishment importing this, do doubt,
That all was naught within, and all found out.
  O happy Britain! we have not to fear
Such hard and arbitrary measure here;
Else, could a law, like that which I relate,
Once have the sanction of our triple state,
Some few, that I have known in days of old,
Would run most dreadful risk of catching cold;
While you, my friend, whatever wind should blow,
Might traverse England safely to and fro,
An honest man, close-buttoned to the chin,
Broadcloth without, and a warm heart within.

THE CASTAWAY.

OBSCUREST night involved the sky,
  The Atlantic billows roared,
When such a destined wretch as I,
  Washed headlong from on board,

Of friends, of hope, of all bereft,
His floating home for ever left.

No braver chief could Albion boast,
   Than he, with whom he went,
Nor ever ship left Albion's coast
   With warmer wishes sent.
He loved them both, but both in vain,
Nor him beheld, nor her again.

Not long beneath the whelming brine,
   Expert to swim, he lay ;
Nor soon he felt his strength decline,
   Or courage die away ;
But waged with death a lasting strife,
Supported by despair of life.

He shouted ; nor his friends had failed
   To check the vessel's course,
But so the furious blast prevailed,
   That, pitiless perforce,
They left their outcast mate behind,
And scudded still before the wind.

Some succour yet they could afford ;
   And such as storms allow,
The cask, the coop, the floated cord,
   Delayed not to bestow.
But he, they knew, nor ship nor shore,
Whate'er they gave, should visit more.

Nor, cruel as it seemed, could he
   Their haste himself condemn,
Aware that flight, in such a sea,
   Alone could rescue them ;
Yet bitter felt it still to die
Deserted, and his friends so nigh.

He long survives, who lives an hour
   In ocean, self-upheld ;
And so long he, with unspent power,
   His destiny repelled ;
And ever, as the minutes flew,
Entreated help, or cried " Adieu !"

At length, his transient respite past,
    His comrades, who before
Had heard his voice in every blast,
    Could catch the sound no more :
For then, by toil subdued, he drank
The stifling wave, and then he sank.

No poet wept him ; but the page
    Of narrative sincere,
That tells his name, his worth, his age,
    Is wet with Anson's tear :
And tears by bards or heroes shed
Alike immortalize the dead.

I therefore purpose not, or dream,
    Descanting on his fate,
To give the melancholy theme
    A more enduring date.:
But misery still delights to trace
Its semblance in another's case.

No voice divine the storm allayed,
    No light propitious shone,
When, snatched from all effectual aid,
    We perished, each alone :
But I beneath a rougher sea,
And whelmed in deeper gulfs than he.

PROVIDENCE.

God moves in a mysterious way
    His wonders to perform ;
He plants His footsteps in the sea,
    And rides upon the storm.

Deep in unfathomable mines
    Of never-failing skill,
He treasures up His bright designs,
    And works His sovereign will.

Ye fearful saints, fresh courage take ;
    The clouds ye so much dread
Are big with mercy, and shall break
    In blessings on your head.

Judge not the Lord by feeble sense,
  But trust Him for His grace ;
Behind a frowning Providence
  He hides a smiling face.

His purposes will ripen fast,
  Unfolding every hour ;
The bud may have a bitter taste,
  But sweet will be the flower.

Blind unbelief is sure to err,
  And scan His work in vain ;
God is His own interpreter,
  And He will make it plain.

THE JOURNEY TO EMMAUS.

It happened on a solemn eventide,
Soon after He that was our Surety died,
Two bosom friends, each pensively inclined,
The scene of all those sorrows left behind,
Sought their own village, busied as they went
In musings worthy of the great event :
They spake of Him they loved, of Him whose life,
Though blameless, had incurred perpetual strife,
Whose deeds had left, in spite of hostile arts,
A deep memorial graven on their hearts.
The recollection, like a vein of ore,
The farther traced, enriched them still the more ;
They thought Him, and they justly thought Him, one
Sent to do more than he appeared t' have done ;
T' exalt a people, and to place them high
Above all else, and wondered He should die.
Ere yet they brought their journey to an end,
A stranger joined them, courteous as a friend,
And asked them with a kind engaging air
What their affliction was, and begged a share.
Informed, he gathered up the broken thread,
And, truth and wisdom gracing all he said,
Explained, illustrated, and searched so well
The tender theme, on which they chose to dwell,
That reaching home, " The night," they said, " is near,
We must not now be parted, sojourn here."

The new acquaintance soon became a guest,
And, made so welcome at their simple feast,
He blessed the bread, but vanished at the word,
And left them both exclaiming, "'Twas the Lord !
Did not our hearts feel all He deigned to say,
Did they not burn within us by the way?"

From *Conversation.*

GOD IN CREATION.

There lives and works
A soul in all things, and that soul is God.
The beauties of the wilderness are His,
That make so gay the solitary place,
Where no eye sees them ; and the fairer forms,
That cultivation glories in, are His.
He sets the bright procession on its way,
And marshals all the order of the year ;
He marks the bounds that Winter may not pass,
And blunts his pointed fury ; in its case,
Russet and rude, folds up the tender germ,
Uninjured, with inimitable art ;
And ere one flowery season fades and dies,
Designs the blooming wonders of the next.
The Lord of all, Himself through all diffused,
Sustains, and is the life of all that lives.
Nature is but a name for an effect,
Whose cause is God . . . One spirit—His,
Who wore the platted thorns with bleeding brows,
Rules universal nature. Not a flower
But shows some touch, in freckle, streak, or stain,
Of His unrivalled pencil. He inspires
Their balmy odours, and imparts their hues,
And bathes their eyes with nectar, and includes,
In grains as countless as the sea-side sands,
The forms with which He sprinkles all the earth.
Happy who walks with Him ! whom what he finds
Of flavour or of scent in fruit or flower,
Or what he views of beautiful or grand
In nature, from the broad majestic oak,
To the green blade, that twinkles in the sun,
Prompts with remembrance of a present God.

From *The Task.*

AUTOBIOGRAPHICAL.

I was a stricken deer, that left the herd
Long since ; with many an arrow deep infixed
My panting side was charged, when I withdrew
To seek a tranquil death in distant shades.
There was I found by One, who had Himself
Been hurt by the archers.   In His side he bore,
And in His hands and feet, the cruel scars.
With gentle force soliciting the darts,
He drew them forth, and healed, and bade me live.
Since then, with few associates, in remote
And silent woods I wandered, far from those
My former partners of the peopled scene ;
With few associates, and not wishing more.
Here much I ruminate, as much I may,
With other views of men and manners now
Than once, and others of a life to come.
I see that all are wanderers, gone astray
Each in his own delusions ; they are lost
In chase of fancied happiness, still woo'd
And never won.   Dream after dream ensues,
And still they dream that they shall still succeed,
And still are disappointed.   Rings the world
With the vain stir.   I sum up half mankind,
And add two thirds of the remaining half,
And find the total of their hopes and fears
Dreams, empty dreams.

                              From *The Task.*

GRACE AND THE WORLD.

"ADIEU," Vinoso cries, ere yet he sips
The purple bumper trembling at his lips,
"Adieu to all morality, if Grace
Make works a vain ingredient in the case.
My Christian hope is—Waiter, draw the cork—
If I mistake not—Blockhead ! with a fork—
Without good works, whatever some may boast,
Mere folly and delusion.—Sir, your toast.
My firm persuasion is, at least sometimes,
That Heaven will weigh man's virtues and his crimes
With nice attention, in a righteous scale,
And save or damn as these or those prevail.

I plant my foot upon this ground of trust,
And silence every fear with—God is just.
But if perchance on some dull drizzling day
A thought intrude, that says, or seems to say,
If thus the important cause is to be tried,
Suppose the beam should dip on the wrong side ;
I soon recover from these needless frights,
And God is merciful—sets all to rights.
Thus, between justice, as my prime support,
And mercy, fled to as the last resort,
I glide and steal along with heaven in view,
And—pardon me, the bottle stands with you."
    " I never will believe," the Colonel cries,
" The sanguinary schemes that some devise,
Who make the good Creator on their plan
A Being of less equity than man.
If appetite, or what divines call lust,
Which men comply with, even because they must,
Be punished with perdition, who is pure ?
Then theirs, no doubt, as well as mine, is sure.
If sentence of eternal pain belong
To every sudden slip and transient wrong,
Then Heaven enjoins the fallible and frail
A hopeless task, and damns them if they fail.
My creed (whatever some creed-makers mean
By Athanasian nonsense, or Nicene),
My creed is, he is safe that does his best,
And death's a doom sufficient for the rest,"
    " Right," says an ensign, " and for aught I see,
Your faith and mine substantially agree ;
The best of every man's performance here
Is to discharge the duties of his sphere.
A lawyer's dealing should be just and fair,
Honesty shines with great advantage there.
Fasting and prayer sit well upon a priest,
A decent caution and reserve at least.
A soldier's best is courage in the field,
With nothing here that wants to be concealed :
Manly deportment, gallant, easy, gay ;
A hand as liberal as the light of day.
The soldier thus endowed, who never shrinks
Nor closets up his thought, whate'er he thinks,

Who scorns to do an injury by stealth,
Must go to heaven—and I must drink his health.
Sir Smug," he cries (for lowest at the board,
Just made fifth chaplain of his patron lord,
His shoulders witnessing by many a shrug
How much his feelings suffered, sat Sir Smug),
" Your office is to winnow false from true ;
Come, prophet, drink, and tell us, what think you ?"
    Sighing and smiling as he takes his glass,
Which they that woo preferment rarely pass,
"Fallible man," the church-bred youth replies,
"Is still found fallible, however wise ;
And differing judgments serve but to declare
That truth lies somewhere, if we knew but where.
Of all it ever was my lot to read,
Of critics now alive, or long since dead,
The book of all the world that pleased me most
Was—well-a-day, the title-page was lost ;
The writer well remarks, a heart that knows
To take with gratitude what Heaven bestows,
With prudence always ready at our call,
To guide our use of it, is all in all.
Doubtless it is.—To which, of my own store
I superadd a few essentials more.
But these, excuse the liberty I take,
I waive just now, for conversation's sake."—
    "Spoke like an oracle !" they all exclaim,
And add Right Reverend to Smug's honoured name.

From Hope.

BOADICEA. AN ODE.

When the British warrior queen,
    Bleeding from the Roman rods,
Sought, with an indignant mien,
    Counsel of her country's gods,

Sage beneath a spreading oak
    Sat the Druid, hoary chief,
Every burning word he spoke
    Full of rage and full of grief :

" Princess ! if our aged eyes
    Weep upon thy matchless
        wrongs,

'Tis because resentment ties
    All the terrors of our tongues.

" Rome shall perish — write that
        word
    In the blood that she has
        spilt ;
Perish hopeless and abhorred,
    Deep in ruin as in guilt.

"Rome, for empire far renown-
        ed,
    Tramples on a thousand states ;

Soon her pride shall kiss the
ground,—
Hark ! the Gaul is at her gates.

"Other Romans shall arise,
Heedless of a soldier's name,
Sounds, not arms, shall win the
prize,
Harmony the path to fame.

" Then the progeny that springs
From the forests of our land,
Armed with thunder, clad with
wings,
Shall a wider world command.

" Regions Cæsar never knew
Thy posterity shall sway,

Where his eagles never flew,
None invincible as they."

Such the bard's prophetic words
Pregnant with celestial fire,
Bending as he swept the chords
Of his sweet but awful lyre.

She, with all a monarch's pride,
Felt them in her bosom glow,
Rushed to battle, fought and died
Dying, hurled them at the foe

" Ruffians, pitiless as proud,
Heaven awards the justice due
Empire is on us bestowed,
Shame and ruin wait for you !

ROBERT BURNS.

Born 1759. Died 1796.

TO A MOUNTAIN DAISY.

WEE, modest, crimson-tippèd flower,
Thou's met me in an evil hour ;
For I maun crush amang the stoure
            Thy slender stem :
To spare thee now is past my power,
            Thou bonny gem.

Alas ! it's no thy neebor sweet,
The bonny lark, companion meet
Bending thee 'mang the dewy weet
            Wi' speckled breast,
When upward-springing, blithe, to greet
            The purpling east.

Cauld blew the bitter-biting north
Upon thy early, humble birth ;
Yet cheerfully thou glinted forth
            Amid the storm ;
Scarce reared above the parent-earth
            Thy tender form.

The flaunting flowers our gardens yield,
High sheltering woods and wa's maun shield,
But thou, beneath the random bield
      O' clod, or stane,
Adorns the histie stibble-field,
      Unseen, alane.

There, in thy scanty mantle clad,
Thy snawie bosom sunward spread,
Thou lifts thy unassuming head
      In humble guise ;
But now the share uptears thy bed,
      And low thou lies !

Such is the fate of artless maid,
Sweet floweret of the rural shade !
By love's simplicity betrayed,
      And guileless trust,
Till she, like the, all soiled, is laid
      Low i' the dust.

Such is the fate of simple bard,
On life's rough ocean luckless-starred !
Unskilful he to note the card
      Of prudent lore,
Till billows rage, and gales blow hard,
      And whelm him o'er !

Such fate to suffering worth is given,
Who long with wants and woes has striven,
By human pride or cunning driven
      To misery's brink,
Till, wrenched of every stay but Heaven,
      He, ruined, sink !

Even thou who mourn'st the Daisy's fate,
That fate is thine—no distant date ;
Stern Ruin'c ploughshare drives, elate,
      Full on thy bloom,
Till crushed beneath the furrow's weight,
      Shall be thy doom !

TO A MOUSE, ON TURNING HER UP IN HER NEST, WITH THE PLOUGH.

WEE, sleekit, cowrin, tim'rous beastie,
O, what a panic's in thy breastie !
Thou need na start awa sae hasty,
              Wi' bickerin brattle [1] !
I wad be laith to rin and chase thee,
              Wi' murd'ring pattle [2] !

I'm truly sorry man's dominion
Has broken Nature's social union,
An' justifies that ill opinion,
              Which makes thee startle
At me, thy poor, earth-born companion,
              An' fellow-mortal !

I doubt na, whyles, but thou may thieve ;
What then ? poor beastie, thou maun live !
A daimen-icker [3] in a thrave
              'S a sma' request :
I'll get a blessing wi' the lave,
              And never miss't !

Thy wee bit housie, too, in ruin !
Its silly wa's the win's are strewin !
An' naething, now, to big [4] a new one,
              O' foggage green !
An' bleak December's winds ensuin,
              Baith snell [5] and keen .

Thou saw the fields laid bare an' waste,
An' weary winter comin' fast,
An' cozie here, beneath the blast,
              Thou thought to dwell,
Till, crash ! the cruel coulter past
              Out thro' thy cell.

That wee bit heap o' leaves an' stibble
Has cost thee mony a weary nibble !

[1] hurry.   [2] hand-stick for clearing the plough.
[3] An ear of corn now and then ; a thrave is twenty-four shoaves.
[4] build.   [5] bitter.

Now thou's turned out, for a' thy trouble,
But [1] house or hald, [2]
To thole [3] the winter's sleety dribble,
An' cranreuch [4] cauld !

But, Mousie, thou art no thy lane, [5]
In proving foresight may be vain :
The best-laid schemes o' mice an' men,
Gang aft agley, [6]
An' lea'e us nought but grief and pain
For promised joy.

Still thou art blest, compared wi' me !
The present only toucheth thee :
But, och ! I backward cast my e'e
On prospects drear !
An' forward, tho' I canna see,
I guess an' fear !

A BARD'S EPITAPH.

Is there a whim-inspired fool,
Owre fast for thought, owre hot for rule,
Owre blate [7] to seek, owre proud to snool [8] ?
Let him draw near ;
And owre this grassy heap sing dool,
And drap a tear.

Is there a bard of rustic song,
Who, noteless, steals the crowds among,
That weekly this arena throng ?
O, pass not by !
But, with a frater-feeling strong,
Here heave a sigh.

Is there a man whose judgment clear,
Can others teach the course to steer,
Yet runs, himself, life's mad career
Wild as the wave ?
Here pause—and, thro' the starting tear
Survey this grave.

[1] without.	[2] holding.	[3] endure.	[4] hoar-frost.
[5] thyself alone.	[6] awry.	[7] bashful.	[8] submit tamely.

The poor inhabitant below
Was quick to learn, and wise to know,
And keenly felt the friendly glow,
　　　　And softer flame ;
But thoughtless follies laid him low,
　　　　And stained his name !

Reader, attend—whether thy soul
Soars fancy's flights beyond the pole,
Or darkling grubs this earthly hole,
　　　　In low pursuit ;
Know prudent, cautious self-control
　　　　Is wisdom's root.

TO MARY IN HEAVEN.

Thou lingering star, with lessening ray,
　　That lov'st to greet the early morn,
Again thou usher'st in the day
　　My Mary from my soul was torn.
O Mary ! dear departed shade !
　　Where is thy place of blissful rest ?
Seest thou thy lover lowly laid ?
　　Hear'st thou the groans that rend his breast ?

That sacred hour can I forget ?
　　Can I forget the hallowed grove,
Where by the winding Ayr we met,
　　To live one day of parting love ?
Eternity will not efface
　　Those records dear of transports past ;
Thy image at our last embrace ;
　　Ah ! little thought we 'twas our last !

Ayr, gurgling, kissed his pebbled shore,
　　O'erhung with wild woods, thickening green,
The fragrant birch, and hawthorn hoar,
　　Twined amorous round the raptured scene.
The flowers sprang wanton to be prest,
　　The birds sang love on every spray,—
Till too, too soon, the glowing west
　　Proclaimed the speed of wingèd day.

Still o'er these scenes my memory wakes,
　　And fondly broods with miser care ;

Time but th' impression deeper makes,
  As streams their channels deeper wear.
My Mary, dear departed shade !
  Where is thy place of blissful rest?
Seest thou thy lover lowly laid?
  Hear'st thou the groans that rend his breast ?

JOHN ANDERSON, MY JO.

JOHN ANDERSON, my jo, John,
  When we were first acquent ;
Your locks were like the raven,
  Your bonnie brow was brent ; [1]
But now your brow is beld, John,
  Your locks are like the snaw ;
But blessings on your frosty pow,.
  John Anderson, my jo.

John Anderson, my jo, John,
  We clamb the hill thegether ;
And monie a canty day, John,
  We've had wi' ane anither :
Now we maun totter down, John,
  But hand in hand we'll go,
And sleep thegither at the foot,
  John Anderson, my jo.

A MAN'S A MAN FOR A' THAT.

Is there, for honest poverty,
  That hangs his head, and a' that?
The coward-slave, we pass him by,
  We dare be poor for a' that !
    For a' that, and a' that,
      Our toils obscure, and a' that ;
    The rank is but the guinea stamp ;
      The man's the gowd for a' that.

What tho' on hamely fare we dine,
  Wear hoddin-grey, [2] and a' that ;
Gie fools their silks, and knaves their wine,
  A man's a man, for a' that.

---

[1] smooth.   [2] coarse woollen cloth.

For a' that, and a' that :
    Their tinsel show, and a' that :
The honest man, tho' e'er sae poor,
    Is King o' men for a' that.

Ye see yon birkie,[1] ca'd a lord,
    Wha struts, and stares, and a' that ;
Tho' hundreds worship at his word,
    He's but a coof [2] for a' that :
      For a' that, and a' that,
        His riband, star, and a' that,
      The man of independent mind,
        He looks and laughs at a' that.

A king can mak' a belted knight,
    A marquis, duke, and a' that ;
But an honest man's aboon his might,
    Gude faith, he mauna fa' [3] that !
      For a' that, and a' that,
        Their dignities and a' that,
      The pith o' sense, and pride o' worth,
        Are higher ranks than a' that.

Then let us pray that come it may,
    As come it will for a' that ;
That sense and worth, o'er a' the earth,
    May bear the gree,[4] and a' that ;
      For a' that, and a' that,
        It's coming yet, for a' that ;
      That man to man, the world o'er,
        Shall brothers be for a' that.

BANNOCKBURN.

Scots, wha hae wi' Wallace bled,
Scots, wham Bruce has aften led ;
Welcome to your gory bed,
    Or to victorie.

Now's the day, and now's the
    hour ;
See the front o' battle lower ;

See approach proud Edward
    power—
    Chains and slaverie !

Wha will be a traitor knave ?
Wha can fill a coward's grave ?
Wha sae base as be a slave ?
    Let him turn and flee !

[1] conceited fellow.   [2] blockhead.   [3] try.   [4] pre-eminence.

Wha for Scotland's King and law
Freedom's sword will strongly draw,
Free-man stand, or free-man fa ' ?
    Let him on wi' me !

By oppression's woes and pains !
By your sons in servile chains !

We will drain our dearest veins,
    But they *shall* be free !

Lay the proud usurpers low !
Tyrants fall in every foe !
Liberty's in every blow !
    Let us do, or die !

THE MUSE OF SCOTLAND TO ROBERT BURNS.

ALL hail ! my own inspirèd Bard ?
In me thy native Muse regard !
Nor longer mourn thy fate is hard,
    Thus poorly low !
I come to give thee snch reward
    As we bestow.

Know, the great Genius of this land
Has many a light, aërial band,
Who, all beneath his high command,
    Harmoniously,
As arts or arms they understand,
    Their labours ply.

Thy Scotia's race among them share
Some fire the soldier on to dare :
Some rouse the patriot up to bare
    Corruption's heart :
Some teach the bard, a darling care,
    The tuneful art.

*   *   *   *   *   *

Some, bounded to a district-space,
Explore at large man's infant race,
To mark the embryotic trace
    Of rustic bard ;
And careful note each opening grace,
    A guide and guard.

Of these am I—Coila my name ;
And this district as mine I claim,
Where once the Campbells, chiefs of fame,
    Held ruling pow'r :
I marked thy embryo tuneful flame,
    Thy natal hour.

With future hope, I oft would gaze,
Fond, on thy little early ways,
Thy rudely-carolled chiming phrase,
        In uncouth rhymes,
Fired at the simple, artless lays
        Of other times.

I saw thee seek the sounding shore,
Delighted with the dashing roar ;
Or, when the North his fleecy store
        Drove thro' the sky,
I saw grim Nature's visage hoar
        Struck thy young eye.

Or when the deep green-mantled Earth
Warm-cherished every floweret's birth,
And joy and music pouring forth
        In every grove,
I saw thee eye the general mirth
        With boundless love.

When ripened fields, and azure skies,
Called forth the reaper's rustling noise,
I saw thee leave their evening joys,
        And lonely stalk,
To vent thy bosom's swelling rise
        In pensive walk.

When youthful Love, warm-blushing, strong,
Keen-shivering, shot thy nerves along,
Those accents, grateful to thy tongue,
        Th' adored Name,
I taught thee how to pour in song,
        To soothe thy flame.

I saw thy pulse's maddening play,
Wild send thee Pleasure's devious way,
Misled by Fancy's meteor ray,
        By Passion driven ;
But yet the light that led astray,
        Was light from Heaven.

I taught thy manners-painting strains,
Thy loves, the ways of simple swains,

Till now, o'er all my wide domains
   Thy fame extends ;
And some, the pride of Coila's plains,
   Become thy friends.

Thou canst not learn, nor can I show,
To paint with Thomson's landscape glow ;
Or wake the bosom's melting throe,
   With Shenstone's art ;
Or pour, with Gray, the moving flow
   Warm on the heart.

Yet, all beneath th' unrivalled rose,
The lowly daisy sweetly blows ;
Tho' large the forest's monarch throws
   His army shade,
Yet green the juicy hawthorn grows
   Adown the glade.

Then never murmur nor repine ;
Strive in thy humble sphere to shine ;
And trust me, not Potosi's mine,
   Nor King's regard,
Can give a bliss o'ermatching thine,
   A rustic Bard.

To give my counsels all in one,—
Thy tuneful flame still careful fan ;
Preserve the dignity of Man,
   With soul erect ;
And trust, the Universal Plan
   Will all protect.

And wear thou this—she solemn said,
And bound the Holly round my head:
The polished leaves, and berries red,
   Did rustling play ;
And, like a passing thought, she fled
   In light away.

MINOR POETS.

THOMAS TICKELL.

Born 1686. Died 1740.

TO THE EARL OF WARWICK, ON THE DEATH OF ADDISON.

Can I forget the dismal night, that gave
My soul's best part for ever to the grave !
How silent did 'his old companions tread,
By midnight lamps, the mansions of the dead,
Through breathing statues, then unheeded things,
Through rows of warriors, and through walks of kings
What awe did the slow solemn knell inspire ;
The pealing organ, and the passing choir ;
The duties by the lawn-robed prelate paid ;
And the last words, that dust to dust conveyed !
While speechless o'er thy closing grave we bend,
Accept these tears, thou dear departed friend.
Oh, gone for ever, take this last adieu ;
And sleep in peace, next thy loved Montague !
To strew fresh laurels let the task be mine,
A frequent pilgrim at thy sacred shrine ;
Mine with true sighs thy absence to bemoan,
And grave with faithful epitaphs thy stone.
If e'er from me thy loved memorial part,
May shame afflict this alienated heart ;
Of thee forgetful if I form a song,
My lyre be broken, and untuned my tongue,
My griefs be doubled, from thy image free,
And mirth a torment, unchastised by thee.
   Oft let me range the gloomy aisles alone,
Sad luxury ! to vulgar minds unknown,
Along the walls where speaking marbles show
What worthies form the hallowed mould below :
Proud names, who once the reins of empire held ;
In arms who triumphed, or in arts excelled ;
Chiefs, graced with scars, and prodigal of blood ;
Stern patriots, who for sacred freedom stood ;

¹ Addison was buried in Westminster Abbey, June, 1719.

Just men, by whom impartial laws were given ;
And saints who taught, and led, the way to heaven.
Ne'er to these chambers, where the mighty rest,
Since their foundation, came a nobler guest ;
Nor e'er was to the bowers of bliss conveyed
A fairer spirit, or more welcome shade.

CHARLES WESLEY.

Born 1708. Died 1788.

WRESTLING JACOB.

COME, O thou Traveller unknown,
  Whom still I hold, but cannot see ;
My company before is gone,
  And I am left alone with Thee ;
With Thee all night I mean to stay,
And wrestle till the break of day.

I need not tell Thee who I am,
  My misery or sin declare ;
Thyself hast called me by my name ;
  Look on Thy hands, and read it there !
But Who, I ask Thee, Who art Thou ?
Tell me thy Name, and tell me now.

In vain Thou strugglest to get free,
  I never will unloose my hold ;
Art Thou the Man that died for me ?
  The secret of Thy love unfold.
Wrestling, I will not let Thee go,
Till I thy Name, thy Nature know.

   *   *   *   *   *

Yield to me now, for I am weak,
  But confident in self-despair ;
Speak to my heart, in blessings speak,
  Be conquered by my instant prayer !
Speak, or Thou never hence shall move,
And tell me, if thy Name is Love ?

'Tis Love ! 'tis Love ! Thou diedst for me !
  I hear thy whisper in my heart !
The morning breaks, the shadows flee ;
  Pure universal Love Thou art !

To me, to all, Thy bowels move ;
Thy Nature, and thy Name, is Love !

My prayer hath power with God ; the grace
 Unspeakable I now receive ;
Through faith I see Thee face to face,
 I see Thee face to face, and live :
In vain I have not wept and strove ;
Thy Nature, and thy Name, is Love.

I know Thee, Saviour, who Thou art ;
 Jesus, the feeble sinner's Friend !
Nor wilt Thou with the night depart,
 But stay, and love me to the end !
Thy mercies never shall remove,
Thy Nature, and thy Name, is Love !

The Sun of Righteousness on me
 Hath rose, with healing in His wings ;
Withered my nature's strength, from Thee
 My soul its life and succour brings ;
My help is all laid up above ;
Thy Nature, and thy Name, is Love.

Contented now upon my thigh
 I halt, till life's short journey end ;
All helplessness, all weakness, I
 On Thee alone for strength depend ;
Nor have I power from Thee to move ;
Thy Nature, and thy Name, is Love.

Lame as I am, I take the prey,
 Hell, earth, and sin, with ease o'ercome ;
I leap for joy, pursue my way,
 And, as a bounding hart, fly home !
Through all eternity to prove,
Thy Nature, and thy Name, is Love !

CATHOLIC LOVE.

WEARY of all this wordy strife,
These notions, forms, and modes, and names,
To Thee, the Way, the Truth, the Life,
Whose love my simple heart inflames,
Divinely taught, at last I fly,
With Thee and Thine to live and die.

Forth from the midst of Babel brought,
Parties and sects I cast behind ;
Enlarged my heart, and free my thought,
Where'er the latent truth I find,
The latent truth with joy to own,
And bow to Jesu's name alone.

Redeemed by Thine almighty grace,
I taste my glorious liberty,
With open arms the world embrace,
But cleave to those who cleave to Thee ;
But only in Thy saints delight,
Who walk with God in purest white.

One with the little flock I rest,
The members sound who hold the Head ;
The chosen few, with pardon blest,
And by the anointing Spirit led
Into the mind that was in Thee,
Into the depths of Deity.

My brethren, friends, and kinsmen these,
Who do my heavenly Father's will ;
Who aim at perfect holiness,
And all Thy counsels to fulfil,
Athirst to be whate'er Thou art,
And love their God with all their heart.

For these, howe'er in flesh disjoined,
Whate'er dispersed o'er earth abroad,
Unfeigned, unbounded love I find,
And constant as the life of God ;
Fountain of life, from thence it sprung,
As pure, as even, and as strong.

Joined to the hidden church unknown
In this sure bond of perfectness,
Obscurely safe, I dwell alone,
And glory in th' uniting grace,
To me, to each believer, given,
To all Thy saints in earth and heaven.

CHARLES CHURCHILL.

Born 1731. Died 1764.

'Tis not the babbling of an idle world,
Where praise and censure are at random hurled,
That can the meanest of my thoughts control,
Or shake one settled purpose of my soul.
Free and at large might their wild curses roam
If all, if all, alas, were well at home.

THOMAS CHATTERTON.

Born 1752. Died 1770.

MINSTREL'S ROUNDELAY.

O sing unto my roundelay,
  O drop the briny tear with me,
Dance no more at holy-day,
  Like a running river be.
    My love is dead,
    Gone to his death-bed,
    All under the willow-tree.

Black his locks as the winter
    night,
  White his skin as the summer
    snow,
Red his face as the morning light,
  Cold he lies in the grave below.
    My love is dead,
    Gone to his death-bed,
    All under the willow-tree.

Sweet his tongue as the throstle's
    note,
  Quick in dance as thought can
    be,
Deft his tabor, cudgel stout,
  O he lies by the willow-tree !
    My love is dead,
    Gone to his death-bed,
    All under the willow-tree.

Hark ! the raven flaps his wing
  In the briar'd dell below ;
Hark ! the death-owl loud do
    sing,
  To the nightmares as they go
    My love is dead,
    Gone to his death-bed,
    All under the willow-tree.

See ! the white moon shines
    high :
  Whiter is my true love
    shroud ;
Whiter than the morning sky,
  Whiter than the evening clou
    My love is dead,
    Gone to his death-bed,
    All under the willow-tree.

Here upon my true love's grave
  Shall the barren flowers
    laid ;
Not one holy Saint to save
  All the coldness of a maid !
    My love is dead,
    Gone to his death-bed,
    All under the willow-tree.

With my hands I'll gird the briars
Round his holy corse to grow.
Elfin Faëry, light your fires ;
Here my body still shall bow.
My love is dead,
Gone to his death-bed,
All under the willow-tree.

Come, with acorn-cup and thorn,
Drain my heartès blood away,
Life and all its good I scorn,
Dance by night, or feast by day.
My love is dead,
Gone to his death-bed,
All under the willow-tree.

JAMES BEATTIE.

Born 1735.   Died 1803.

THE HERMIT.

At the close of the day, when the hamlet is still,
And mortals the sweets of forgetfulness prove ;
When nought but the torrent is heard on the hill,
And nought but the nightingale's song in the grove ;
'Twas thus, by the cave of the mountain afar,
While his harp rang symphonious, a hermit began ;
No more with himself, or with nature, at war,
He thought as a sage, though he felt as a man.

" Ah ! why thus abandoned to darkness and woe ?
Why, lone Philomela, that languishing fall ?
For spring shall return, and a lover bestow,
And sorrow no longer thy bosom enthrall.
But, if pity inspire thee, renew the sad lay ;
Mourn, sweetest complainer ; man calls thee to mourn.
O soothe him, whose pleasures like thine pass away ;
Full quickly they pass—but they never return.

"Now gliding remote, on the verge of the sky,
The moon half extinguished her crescent displays ;
But lately I marked, when majestic on high
She shone, and the planets were lost in her blaze.
Roll on, thou fair orb, and with gladness pursue
The path that conducts thee to splendour again :
But man's faded glory what change shall renew ?
Ah, fool ! to exult in a glory so vain !

" 'Tis night, and the landscape is lovely no more :
I mourn ; but ye woodlands, I mourn not for you ;
For morn is approaching, your charms to restore,
Perfumed with fresh fragrance and glittering with dew:

Nor yet for the ravage of winter I mourn ;
Kind nature the embryo blossom will save ;
But when shall spring visit the mouldering urn ?
O, when shall day dawn on the night of the grave ?

" 'Twas thus, by the light of false science betrayed,
That leads to bewilder, and dazzles to blind,
My thoughts wont to roam, from shade onward to shade,
Destruction before me, and sorrow behind.
' O, pity, great Father of light,' then I cried,
' Thy creature, that fain would not wander from Thee :
Lo, humbled in dust, I relinquish my pride :
From doubt and from darkness Thou only canst free ! '

" And darkness and doubt are now flying away ;
No longer I roam in conjecture forlorn :
So breaks on the traveller, faint and astray,
The bright and the balmy effulgence of morn.
See Truth, Love, and Mercy, in triumph descending,
And Nature all glowing in Eden's first bloom !
On the cold cheek of Death smiles and roses are blending,
And Beauty immortal awakes from the tomb ! "

MRS. BARBAULD.

Born 1743. Died 1825.

LIFE.

LIFE ! we've been long together,
Through pleasant and through cloudy weather ;
'Tis hard to part when friends are dear ;
Perhaps 'twill cost a sigh, a tear ;
Then steal away, give little warning,
              Choose thine own time ;
Say not " Good night," but in some brighter clime
              Bid me " Good morning."

ANONYMOUS.

About 1750.

THE LAMENT OF THE BORDER WIDOW.

My love he built me a bonnie bower,
And clad me all with lily flower ;

A braver bower you ne'er did see,
Than my true love he built for me.

There came a man, by middle day,
He spied his sport, and went his way,
And brought the king that very night,
Who broke my bower and slew my kinght.

He slew my knight to me so dear ;
He slew my knight and poined his gear ;
My servants all for life did flee,
And left me in extremitie.

I sewed his sheet, making my moan ;
I watched his corpse, myself alone ;
I watched his body, night and day ;
No living creature came that way.

I took his body on my back,
And whiles I gaed and whiles I sat ;
I digged a grave and laid him in,
And happed him with the sod so green.

But think na ye my heart was sair,
When I laid the mould on his yellow hair ?
Think na ye my heart was wae,
When turned about, away to gae ?

No living man I'll love again,
Since that my lovely knight is slain ;
With one lock of his yellow hair,
I'll bind my heart for evermair.

WILLIAM HAMILTON OF BANGOUR.

Born 1704. Died 1754.

THE BRAES OF YARROW.

A.	" Busk ye, busk ye, my bonnie, bonnie bride,
Busk ye, busk ye, my winsome marrow ;
Busk ye, busk ye, my bonnie, bonnie bride,
And think nae mair on the braes of Yarrow."

B.	" Where gat ye that bonnie, bonnie bride ?
Where gat ye that winsome marrow ?"

A.   "I gat her where I dare na weel be seen,
       Pu'ing the birks on the braes of Yarrow.

       "Weep not, weep not, my bonnie, bonnie bride,
       Weep not, weep not, my winsome marrow ;
       Nor let thy heart lament to leave
       Pu'ing the birks on the braes of Yarrow."

B.   "Why does she weep, thy bonnie, bonnie bride?
       Why does she weep, thy winsome marrow?
       And why daur ye nae mair weel be seen
       Pu'ing the birks on the braes of Yarrow ?"

A.   "Lang maun she weep, lang maun she, maun she weep,
       Lang maun she weep with dule and sorrow,
       And lang maun I nae mair weel be seen
       Pu'ing the birks on the braes of Yarrow.

       "For she has tint her lover, lover dear,
       Her lover dear, the cause of sorrow ;
       And I ha'e slain the comeliest swain
       That e'er pu'ed birks on the braes of Yarrow.

       "Why runs thy stream, O Yarrow, Yarrow, reid ?
       Why on thy braes heard the voice of sorrow ?
       And why yon melancholeous weeds,
       Hung on the bonnie birks of Yarrow !

       "What's yonder floats on the rueful, rueful flood ?
       What's yonder floats?   Oh dule and sorrow !
       Oh ! 'tis the comely swain I slew
       Upon the duleful braes of Yarrow !

       "Wash, oh, wash his wounds, his wounds in tears,
       His wounds in tears, with dule and sorrow,
       And wrap his limbs in mourning weeds,
       And lay him on the braes of Yarrow !

       "Then build, then build, ye sisters, sisters sad,
       Ye sisters sad, his tomb with sorrow,
       And weep around in waeful wise,
       His helpless fate on the braes of Yarrow.

       "Curse ye, curse ye his useless, useless shield,
       My arm that wrought the deed of sorrow,
       The fatal spear that pierced his breast,
       His comely breast, on the braes of Yarrow.

"Did I not warn thee not to love,
And warn from fight? but, to my sorrow,
O'er-rashly bold, a stronger arm
Thou met'st, and fell on the braes of Yarrow.

"Sweet smells the birk; green grows, green grows the grass,
Yellow on Yarrow's braes the gowan,
Fair hangs the apple frae the rock,
Sweet the wave of Yarrow flowan'.

"Flows Yarrow sweet? as sweet, as sweet flows Tweed,
As green its grass, its gowan yellow,
As sweet smells on its braes the birk,
The apple frae the rock as mellow.

"Fair was thy love! fair, fair indeed thy love >
In flowery bands thou him didst fetter;
Though he was fair, and well-beloved again,
Than me he never loved thee better.

"Busk ye, then, busk, my bonnie, bonnie bride,
Busk ye, busk ye, my winsome marrow;
Busk ye, and lo'e me on the banks of Tweed,
And think nae mair on the braes of Yarrow."

C.   "How can I busk, a bonnie, bonnie bride?
How can I busk, a winsome marrow?
How lo'e him on the banks of Tweed,
That slew my Love on the braes of Yarrow?

"O Yarrow fields! may never, never rain,
Nor dew thy tender blossoms cover,
For there was basely slain my Love,
My Love, as he had not been a lover!

"The boy put on his robes, his robes of green,
His purple vest, 'twas my ain sewin':
Ah, wretched me! I little, little knew
He was in these to meet his ruin.

"The boy took out his milk-white, milk-white steed,
Unheedful of my dule and sorrow;
But, ere the toofal of the night,
He lay a corpse on the braes of Yarrow.

"Much I rejoiced that waeful, waeful day,   .
I sang, my voice the woods returning;

But lang ere night the spear was flown
That slew my Love, and left me mourning.

"What can my barbarous, barbarous father do,
But with his cruel rage pursue me?
My lover's blood is on thy spear;
How canst thou, barbarous man, then woo me?

"My happy sisters may be, may be proud;
With cruel and ungentle scoffing
May bid me seek on Yarrow's braes
My lover nailèd in his coffin.

"My brother Douglas may upbraid,
And strive with threatening words to move me,
My lover's blude is on thy spear,
How canst thou ever bid me love thee?

"Yes, yes, prepare the bed, the bed of love,
With bridal-sheets my body cover;
Unbar, ye bridal maids, the door,
Let in the expected husband-lover!"

LADY ANNE LINDSAY.

Born 1750. Died 1825.

AULD ROBIN GRAY.

WHEN the sheep are in the fauld, and the kye come hame,
When a' the world to rest are gane,
The waes o' my heart fa' in showers frae my e'e,
While my gudeman lies sound by me.

Young Jamie lo'ed me weel, and sought me for his bride;
But saving a crown, he had naething else beside.
To make the crown a pound, my Jamie gaed to sea;
And the crown and the pound were baith for me.

He hadna been awa' a week but only twa,
When my father brak his arm, and the cow was stown awa'
My mother she fell sick, and my Jamie at the sea,
And auld Robin Gray came a-courtin' me.

My father couldna work, and my mother couldna spin;
I toiled day and night, but their bread I couldna win;

Auld Rob maintained them baith, and, wi' tears in his e'e,
Said, Jennie, for their sakes, oh marry me !

My heart it said nay ; I looked for Jamie back ;
But the wind it blew high, and the ship it was a wrack ;
His ship it was a wrack—why didna Jamie dee?
Or why do I live to cry, Wae's me?

My father urgit sair : my mother didna speak ;
But she looked in my face till my heart was like to break :
They gi'ed him my hand, but my heart was at the sea ;
Sae auld Robin Gray he was gudeman to me.

I hadna been a wife a week but only four,
When mournfu' as I sat on the stane at the door,
I saw my Jamie's wraith, for I couldna think it he —
Till he said, I'm come hame to marry thee.

O sair, sair did we greet, and muckle did we say ;
We took but ae kiss, and I bade him gang away :
I wish that I were dead, but I'm no like to dee ;
And why was I born to say, Wae's me !

I gang like a ghaist, and I carena to spin ;
I daurna think on Jamie, for that wad be a sin ;
But I'll do my best a gude wife aye to be,
For auld Robin Gray he is kind unto me.

LADY NAIRNE.

Born 1766. Died 1845.

THE LAND O' THE LEAL.

I'M wearin' awa', Jean,
Like snaw-wreaths in thaw, Jean,
I'm wearin' awa'
    To the land o' the leal.
There's nae sorrow there, Jean,
There's neither cauld nor care, Jean,
The day is aye fair
    In the land o' the leal.

Our bonnie bairn's there, Jean,
She was baith gude and fair, Jean,

And oh ! we grudged her sair
　　To the land o' the leal.
But sorrow's sel' wears past, Jean,
And joy's a-comin' fast, Jean,
The joy that's aye to last
　　In the land o' the leal.

Sae dear that joy was bought, Jean,
Sae free the battle fought, Jean,
That sinfu' man e'er brought
　　To the land o' the leal.
Oh ! dry your glistening e'e, Jean,
My soul langs to be free, Jean,
And angels beckon me
　　To the land o' the leal.

Oh ! haud ye leal and true, Jean,
Your day it's wearin' through, Jean,
And I'll welcome you
　　To the land o' the leal.
Now fare-ye-weel, my ain Jean,
The world's cares are vain, Jean,
We'll meet, and we'll be fain
　　In the land o' the leal.

WILLIAM BLAKE.

Born 1757.　Died 1827.

SONG.

How sweet I roamed from field to field,
And tasted all the summer's pride ;
Till I the Prince of Love beheld,
Who in the sunny beams did glide.

He showed me lilies for my hair,
And blushing roses for my brow ;
And led me through his gardens fair,
Where all his golden pleasures grow.

With sweet May-dews my wings were wet,
And Phœbus fired my vocal rage ;
He caught me in his silken net,
And shut me in his golden cage.

He loves to sit and hear me sing,
Then laughing sports and plays with me,
Then stretches out my golden wing,
And mocks my loss of liberty.

[From *Songs of Innocence.*]

INTRODUCTION.

PIPING down the valleys wild,
Piping songs of pleasant glee,
On a cloud I saw a child,
And he laughing said to me :—

"Pipe a song about a lamb :"
So I piped with merry cheer.
"Piper, pipe that song again :"
So I piped ; he wept to hear.

"Drop thy pipe, thy happy pipe,
Sing thy songs of happy cheer :"

So I sung the same again,
While he wept with joy to hear.

"Piper, sit thee down and write
In a book that all may read"—
So he vanished from my sight ;
And I pluckt a hollow reed,

And I made a rural pen,
And I stained the water clear,
And I wrote my happy songs,
Every child may joy to hear.

THE LAMB.

LITTLE lamb, who made thee?
Dost thou know who made thee
Gave thee life and bade thee feed
By the stream and o'er the mead ;
Gave thee clothing of delight,
Softest clothing, woolly, bright ;
Gave thee such a tender voice,
Making all the vales rejoice?
Little lamb, who made thee?
Dost thou know who made thee?

Little lamb, I'll tell thee ;
Little lamb, I'll tell thee.
He is callèd by thy name,
For He calls himself a Lamb.
He is meek and He is mild,
He became a little child.
I a child and thou a lamb,
We are callèd by His name.
Little lamb, God bless thee !
Little lamb, God bless thee !

THE TIGER.

TIGER, tiger, burning bright
In the forests of the night,
What immortal hand or eye
Framed thy fearful symmetry?

In what distant deeps or skies
Burnt that fire within thine eyes?
On what wings dared he aspire ?
What the hand dared seize the
    fire ?

And what shoulder, and what art,
Could twist the sinews of thy
    heart? [beat,
And when thy heart began to
What dread hand formed thy
    dread feet ?

What the hammer, what the
    chain, [brain ?
Knit thy strength and forged thy

What the anvil ?   What dread
   grasp
Dared thy deadly terrors clasp ?

When the stars threw down their
   spears,
And watered heaven with their
   tears,

Did He smile His work to see?
Did He who made the lamb, ma
   thee ?

Tiger, tiger, burning bright
In the forests of the night,
What immortal hand or eye
Framed thy fearful symmetry ?

WILLIAM WORDWSORTH.

Born 1770.   Died 1850.

MIST OPENING IN THE HILLS.

So was he lifted gently from the ground,
And with their freight homeward the shepherds moved
Through the dull mist, I following—when a step,
A single step, that freed me from the skirts
Of the blind vapour, opened to my view
Glory beyond all glory ever seen
By waking sense or by the dreaming soul !
The appearance, instantaneously disclosed,
Was of a mighty city—boldly say
A wilderness of building, sinking far
And self-withdrawn into a boundless depth
Far sinking into splendour—without end !
Fabric it seemed of diamond and of gold,
With alabaster domes, and silver spires,
And blazing terrace upon terrace, high
Uplifted ; here, serene pavilions bright,
In avenues disposed ; there, towers begirt
With battlements that on their restless fronts
Bore stars—illumination of all gems !
By earthly nature had the effect been wrought
Upon the dark materials of the storm
Now pacified : on them, and on the coves
And mountain steeps and summits, whereunto
The vapours had receded, taking there
Their station under a cerulean sky.
Oh, 'twas an unimaginable sight !
Clouds, mists, streams, watery rocks and emerald turf,
Clouds of all tincture, rocks and sapphire sky
Confused, commingled, mutually inflamed,
Molten together, and composing thus,
Each lost in each, that marvellous array
Of temple, palace, citadel, and huge
Fantastic pomp of structure without name,
In fleecy folds voluminous enwrapped.
Right in the midst, where interspace appeared

Of open court, an object like a throne
Under a shining canopy of state
Stood fixed ; and fixed resemblances were seen
To implements of ordinary use,
But vast in size, in substance glorified ;
Such as by Hebrew Prophets were beheld
In vision—forms uncouth of mightiest power
For admiration and mysterious awe.
This little Vale, a dwelling-place of Man,
Lay low beneath my feet ; 'twas visible—
I saw not, but I felt that it was there.
That which I *saw* was the revealed abode
Of Spirits in beatitude.

            From *The Excursion.*

AMONG THE MOUNTAINS.

(Greek Divinities.)

ONCE more to distant ages of the world
Let us revert, and place before our thoughts
The face which rural solitude might wear
To the unenlightened swains of pagan Greece.
—In that fair clime, the lonely herdsman, stretched
On the soft grass through half a summer's day,
With music lulled his indolent repose :
And, in some fit of weariness, if he
When his own breath was silent, chanced to hear
A distant strain, far sweeter than the sounds
Which his poor skill could make, his fancy fetched,
Even from the blazing chariot of the sun,
A beardless youth, who touched a golden lute,
And filled the illumined groves with ravishment.
The nightly hunter, lifting a bright eye
Up towards the crescent moon, with grateful heart
Called on the lovely wanderer who bestowed
That timely light, to share his joyous sport :
And hence, a beaming Goddess with her Nymphs,
Across the lawn and through the darksome grove,
Not unaccompanied with tuneful notes
By echo multiplied from rock or cave,
Swept in the storm or chase ; as moon and stars
Glance rapidly along the clouded heaven,
When winds are blowing strong. The traveller slaked
His thirst from rill or gushing fount, and thanked
The Naiad. Sunbeams, upon distant hills
Gliding apace, with shadows in their train,
Might, with small help from fancy, be transformed
Into fleet Oreads sporting visibly.
The Zephyrs fanning, as they passed, their wings,
Lacked not, for love, fair objects whom they wooed
With gentle whisper. Withered boughs grotesque,
Stripped of their leaves and twigs by hoary age,

From depth of shaggy covert peeping forth
In the low vale, or on steep mountain side ;
And, sometimes, intermixed with stirring horns
Of the live deer, or goat's depending beard,—
These were the lurking Satyrs, a wild brood
Of gamesome Deities ; or Pan himself,
The simple shepherd's awe-inspiring God !

From The Excursion.

ODE.

INTIMATIONS OF IMMORTALITY FROM RECOLLECTIONS OF EARLY CHILDHOOD.

THERE was a time when meadow, grove, and stream,
The earth, and every common sight
To me did seem
Apparelled in celestial light,
The glory and the freshness of a dream.
It is not now as it hath been of yore ;—
Turn wheresoe'er I may,
By night or day,
The things which I have seen I now can see no more.

The rainbow comes and goes,
And lovely is the rose ;
The moon doth with delight
Look round her when the heaven is bare ;
Waters on a starry night
Are beautiful and fair ;
The sunshine is a glorious birth ;
But yet I know, where'er I go,
That there hath passed away a glory from the earth.

Now, while the birds thus sing a joyous song,
And while the young lambs bound
As to the tabor's sound,
To me alone there came a thought of grief :
A timely utterance gave that thought relief,
And I again am strong :
The cataracts blow their trumpets from the steep ;
No more shall grief of mine the season wrong ;
I hear the Echoes through the mountains throng,
The Winds come to me from the fields of sleep,
And all the earth is gay ;
Land and sea
Give themselves up to jollity,
And with the heart of May
Doth every beast keep holiday ;—
Thou Child of Joy,
Shout round me, let me hear thy shouts, thou happy
Shepherd boy !

Ye blessed Creatures, I have heard the call
    Ye to each other make ; I see
The heavens laugh with you in your jubilee ;
      My heart is at your festival,
      My head hath its coronal,
The fulness of your bliss, I feel—I feel it all.
    Oh evil day ! if I were sullen
    While Earth herself is adorning,
      This sweet May morning,
    And the Children are culling
      On every side,
    In a thousand valleys far and wide,
    Fresh flowers ; while the sun shines warm,
And the Babe leaps up on his Mother's arm ;
    I hear, I hear, with joy I hear !
    —But there's a Tree, of many, one,
A single Field which I have looked upon,
Both of them speak of something that is gone :
    The Pansy at my feet
    Doth the same tale repeat :
Whither is fled the visionary gleam ?
Where is it now, the glory and the dream ?

 Our birth is but a sleep and a forgetting :
The Soul that rises with us, our life's Star
    Hath had elsewhere its setting,
      And cometh from afar :
    Not in entire forgetfulness,
    And not in utter nakedness,
But trailing clouds of glory do we come
      From God, who is our home.
Heaven lies about us in our infancy !
Shades of the prison-house begin to close
      Upon the growing Boy,
But he beholds the light, and whence it flows ;
      He sees it in his joy.
The Youth who daily farther from the east
    Must travel, still is Nature's Priest,
    And by the vision splendid
    Is on his way attended ;
At length the Man perceives it die away,
And fade into the light of common day.

Earth fills her lap with pleasures of her own
Yearnings she hath in her own natural kind,
And, even with something of a mother's mind,
      And no unworthy aim,
    The homely Nurse doth all she can
To make her Foster-child, her Innate Man,
    Forget the glories he hath known,
And that imperial palace whence he came.

Behold the Child among his new-born blisses,
A six-years' Darling of a pigmy size !
See where, 'mid work of his own hand, he lies,
Fretted by sallies of his mother's kisses,
With light upon him from his father's eyes !
See at his feet some little plan or chart,
Some fragment from his dream of human life,
Shaped by himself with newly learned art ;
 A wedding or a festival,
 A mourning or a funeral ;
  And this hath now his heart,
 And unto this he frames his song ;
  Then will he fit his tongue
To dialogues of business, love, or strife.
  But it will not be long
  Ere this be thrown aside,
  And with new joy and pride
The little Actor cons another part,
Filling from time to time his "humorous stage"
With all the Persons, down to palsied Age,
That Life brings with her in her equipage,
  As if his whole vocation
  Were endless imitation.

Thou, whose exterior semblance doth belie
  Thy Soul's immensity ;
Thou best Philosopher, who yet dost keep
Thy heritage ; thou Eye among the blind,
That, deaf and silent, read'st the eternal deep,
Haunted for ever by the eternal mind,—
  Mighty Prophet, Seer blest !
  On whom those truths do rest,
Which we are toiling all our lives to find,
In darkness lost, the darkness of the grave ;
Thou, over whom thine Immortality
Broods like the Day, a Master o'er a Slave,
A Presence which is not to be put by ;
Thou little Child, yet glorious in the might
Of heaven-born freedom on thy being's height,
Why with such earnest pains dost thou provoke
The years to bring the inevitable yoke,
Thus blindly with thy blessedness at strife?
Full soon thy Soul shall have her earthly freight,
And custom lie upon thee with a weight
Heavy as frost, and deep almost as life !

  O joy ! that in our embers
  Is something that doth live,
  That Nature yet remembers
  What was so fugitive !
The thought of our past years in me doth breed
Perpetual benediction ; not indeed

For that which is most worthy to be blest ;
Delight and liberty, the simple creed
Of Childhood, whether busy or at rest,
With new-fledged hope still fluttering in his breast :—
    Not for these I raise
    The song of thanks and praise ;
  But for those obstinate questionings
  Of sense and outward things,
  Fallings from us, vanishings,
  Blank misgivings of a Creature
Moving about in worlds not realized,
High instincts before which our mortal Nature
Did tremble like a guilty Thing surprised ;
  But for those first affections,
  Those shadowy recollections
    Which, be they what they may,
Are yet the fountain-light of all our day,
Are yet a master-light of all our seeing ;
  Uphold us, cherish, and have power to make
Our noisy years seem moments in the being
Of the eternal Silence : truths that wake
    To perish never ;
Which neither listlessness nor mad endeavor,
    Nor Man, nor Boy,
Nor all that is at enmity with joy,
Can utterly abolish or destroy !
  Hence in a season of calm weather,
    Though inland far we be,
Our souls have sight of that immortal sea,
    Which brought us hither ;
    Can in a moment travel thither,
And see the Children sport upon the shore,
And hear the mighty waters rolling evermore.

Then sing, ye Birds, sing, sing a joyous song !
    And let the young lambs bound
    As to the tabor's sound !
  We in thought will join your throng,
    Ye that pipe and ye that play,
    Ye that through your hearts to-day
    Feel the gladness of the May !
What though the radiance which was once so bright
Be now for ever taken from my sight—
Though nothing can bring back the hour
Of splendour in the grass, of glory in the flower ;
We will grieve not, rather find
Strength in what remains behind ;
In the primal sympathy,
Which having been must ever be ;
In the soothing thoughts that spring
Out of human suffering ;
In the faith that looks through death,
In years that bring the philosophic mind.

And, O ye Fountains, Meadows, Hills, and Groves,
Forebode not any severing of our loves !
Yet in my heart of hearts I feel your might ;
I only have relinquished one delight
To live beneath your more habitual sway.
I love the Brooks which down their channels fret,
Even more than when I tripped lightly as they ;
The innocent brightness of a new-born Day
          Is lovely yet ;
The Clouds that gather round the setting sun
Do take a sober colouring from an eye
That hath kept watch o'er man's mortality ;
Another race hath been, and other palms are won.
Thanks to the human heart by which we live,
Thanks to its tenderness, its joys, and fears ;
To me the meanest flower that blows can give
Thoughts that do often lie too deep for tears.

ODE TO DUTY.

STERN daughter of the Voice of God !
O Duty ! if that name thou love,
Who art a light to guide, a rod
To check the erring, and reprove ;
Thou who art victory and law
When empty terrors over-awe,
From vain temptations dost set free,
And calms't the weary strife of frail humanity !

There are who ask not if thine eye
Be on them—who, in love and truth,
Where no misgiving is, rely
Upon the genial sense of youth—
Glad Hearts ! without reproach or blot,
Who do thy work, and know it not :
Oh if through confidence misplaced
They fail, thy saving arms, dread Power ! around them cast.

Serene will be our days and bright,
And happy will our nature be,
When love is an unerring light,
And joy its own security ;
And they a blissful course may hold
Even now, who, not unwisely bold,
Live in the spirit of this creed ;
Yet seek thy firm support, according to their need.

I, loving freedom, and untried,
No sport of every random guest,
Yet, being to myself a guide,
Too blindly have reposed my trust ;
And oft, when in my heart was heard
Thy timely mandate, I deferred

The task, in smoother walks to stray ;
But thee I now would serve more strictly, if I may.

Through no disturbance of my soul,
Or strong compunction in me wrought,
I supplicate for thy control ;
But in the quietness of thought :
Me this unchartered freedom tires ;
I feel the weight of chance desires.
My hopes no more must change their name ;
I long for a repose that ever is the same.

Stern Law-giver ! yet thou dost wear
The Godhead's most benignant grace ;
Nor know we anything so fair
As is the smile upon thy face.
Flowers laugh before thee in their beds,
And fragrance in thy footing treads ;
Thou dost preserve the stars from wrong,
And the most ancient heavens through thee are fresh
    strong.

To humbler functions, awful Power !
I call thee. I myself commend
Unto thy guidance from this hour ;
Oh, let my weakness have an end !
Give unto me, made lowly wise,
The spirit of self-sacrifice ;
The confidence of reason give,
And, in the light of truth, thy Bondman let me live.

CHARACTER OF THE HAPPY WARRIOR.

Who is the happy warrior ?   Who is he
That every man in arms would wish to be?
—It is the generous Spirit, who, when brought
Among the tasks of real life, hath wrought
Upon the plan that pleased his childish thought :
Whose high endeavours are an inward light,
That make the path before him always bright :
Who, with a natural instinct to discern
What knowledge can perform, is diligent to learn ;
Abides by this resolve, and stops not there,
But makes his moral being his prime care ;
Who, doomed to go in company with Pain,
And Fear, and Bloodshed, miserable train !
Turns his necessity to glorious gain ;
In face of these doth exercise a power
Which is our human nature's highest dower ;
Controls them and subdues, transmutes, bereaves
Of their bad influence, and their good receives ;
By objects, which might force the soul to abate
Her feeling, rendered more compassionate ;

Is placable—because occasions rise
So often that demand such sacrifice ;
More skilful in self-knowledge, even more pure,
As tempted more ; more able to endure,
As more exposed to suffering and distress ;
Thence, also, more alive to tenderness.
—'Tis he whose law is reason ; who depends
Upon that law as on the best of friends ;
Whence, in a state where men are tempted still
To evil for a guard against worse ill,
And what in quality or act is best
Doth seldom on a right foundation rest,
He fixes good on good alone, and owes
To virtue every triumph that he knows :
—Who, if he rise to station of command,
Rises by open means ; and there will stand
On honourable terms, or else retire,
And in himself possess his own desire ;
Who comprehends his trust, and to the same
Keeps faithful with a singleness of aim ;
And therefore does not stoop, nor lie in wait
For wealth, or honours, or for worldly state ;
Whom they must follow ; on whose head must fall,
Like showers of manna, if they come at all :
Whose power sheds round him in the common strife,
Or mild concerns of ordinary life,
A constant influence, a peculiar grace ;
But who, if he be called upon to face
Some awful moment to which Heaven has joined
Great issues, good or bad for human kind,
Is happy as a lover ; and attired
With sudden brightness, like a man inspired ;
And, through the heat of conflict, keeps the law
In calmness made, and sees what he foresaw ;
Or, if an unexpected call succeed,
Come when it will, is equal to the need :
—He who, though thus endued as with a sense
And faculty for storm and turbulence,
Is yet a soul whose master-bias leans
To homefelt pleasures and to gentle scenes ;
Sweet images ! which, wheresoe'er they be,
Are at his heart ; and such fidelity
It is his darling passion to approve ;
More brave for this, that he hath much to love !
—'Tis, finally, the man, who, lifted high,
Conspicuous object in a Nation's eye,
Or left unthought of in obscurity,—
Who, with a toward or untoward lot,
Prosperous or adverse, to his wish or not,—
Plays, in the many games of life, that one
Where what he most doth value must be won :
Whom neither shape of danger can dismay,
Nor thought of tender happiness betray ;

Who, not content that former worth stand fast,
Looks forward, persevering to the last,
From well to better, daily self surpast.
Who, whether praise of him must walk the earth
For ever, and to noble deeds give birth,
Or he must go to dust without his fame,
And leave a dead unprofitable name—
Finds comfort in himself and in his cause ;
And, while the mortal mist is gathering, draws
His breath in confidence of Heaven's applause :
This is the happy Warrior ; this is he
That every man in arms should wish to be.

LUCY GRAY, OR SOLITUDE.

OFT I have heard of Lucy Gray :
And, when I crossed the wild,
I chanced to see at break of day
The solitary child.

No mate, no comrade Lucy knew ;
She dwelt on a wide moor,—
The sweetest thing that ever grew
Beside a human door !

You yet may spy the fawn at play,
The hare upon the green ;
But the sweet face of Lucy Gray
Will never more be seen.

"To-night will be a stormy night—
You to the town must go ;
And take a lantern, Child, to light
Your mother through the snow."

"That, Father ! will I gladly do :
'Tis scarcely afternoon—
The minster-clock has just struck two,
And yonder is the moon !"

At this the Father raised his hook,
And snapped a fagot-band ;
He plied his work ;—and Lucy took
The lantern in her hand.

Not blither is the mountain roe :
With many a wanton stroke
Her feet disperse the powdery snow,
That rises up like smoke.

The storm came on before its time,
She wandered up and down ;
And many a hill did Lucy climb,
But never reached the town.

The wretched parents all that night
Went shouting far and wide ;
But there was neither sound nor sight
To serve them for a guide.

At daybreak on a hill they stood
That overlooked the moor ;
And thence they saw the bridge of wood
A furlong from their door.

They wept—and turning homeward, cried,
" In heaven we all shall meet !"
—When in the snow the mother spied
The print of Lucy's feet.

Then downwards from the steep hill's edge
They tracked the footmarks small ;
And through the broken hawthorn hedge,
And by the long stone wall :

And then an open field they crossed ;
The marks were still the same ;
They tracked them on, nor ever lost ;
And to the bridge they came.

They followed from the snowy bank
Those footmarks, one by one,
Into the middle of the plank ;
And further there were none !

—Yet some maintain that to this day
She is a living child ;
That you may see sweet Lucy Gray
Upon the lonesome wild.

O'er rough and smooth she trips along,
And never looks behind ;
And sings a solitary song
That whistles in the wind.

THE FORCE OF PRAYER.

" WHAT is good for a bootless bene ?"
With these dark words begins my Tale ;
And their meaning is, whence can comfort spring
When Prayer is of no avail ?

" What is good for a bootless bene ?"
The Falconer to the Lady said ;
And she made answer " Endless Sorrow !"
For she knew that her son was dead.

She knew it by the Falconer's words,
And by the look in the Falconer's eye,

And by the love that was in her soul
For her youthful Romilly.

—Young Romilly through Barden woods
Is ranging high and low ;
And holds a greyhound in a leash,
To let slip on buck or doe.

The pair have reached that fearful chasm,
How tempting to bestride !
For lordly Wharf is there pent in
With rocks on either side.

The striding place is called The Strid,
A name it took of yore ;
A thousand years hath it borne that name,
And shall a thousand more.

And thither has young Romilly come,
And what may now forbid
That he, perhaps for the hundredth time,
Shall bound across the Strid ?

He sprang in glee,—for what cared he
That the river was strong, and the rocks were steep
But the greyhound in the leash hung back,
And checked him in his leap.

The Boy is in the arms of Wharf,
And strangled by a merciless force,
And never more was young Romilly seen,
Till he rose a lifeless corse.

Now there is stillness in the vale,
And sad, unspeaking sorrow :
Wharf shall be to pitying hearts,
A name more sad than Yarrow.

If for a lover the Lady wept,
A solace she might borrow
From death, and from the passion of death ;—
Old Wharf might heal her sorrow.

She weeps not for the wedding-day,
Which was to be to-morrow :
Her hope was a further-looking hope,
And hers is a mother's sorrow.

He was a tree that stood alone,
And proudly did its branches wave ;
And the root of this delightful tree
Was in her husband's grave !

Long, long, in darkness did she sit,
And her first words were, " Let there be,

In Bolton, on the field of Wharf,
A stately Priory !"'

The stately Priory was built,
And Wharf as he moved along,
To matins joined a mournful voice,
Nor failed at evensong.

And the Lady prayed in heaviness,
That looked not for relief !
But slowly did her succour come,
And a patience to her grief.

Oh, there is never sorrow of heart,
That shall lack a timely end,
If but to God we turn, and ask
Of Him to be our Friend.

SONNET.

(Composed upon Westminster Bridge, September 3, 1803.)

EARTH has not anything to show more fair ;
Dull would he be of soul who could pass by
A sight so touching in its majesty ;
This City now doth like a garment wear
The beauty of the morning ; silent, bare,
Ships, towers, domes, theatres, and temples lie
Open unto the fields, and to the sky ;
All bright and glittering in the smokeless air.
Never did sun more beautifully steep
In his first splendour valley, rock, or hill ;
Ne'er saw I, never felt, a calm so deep !
The river glideth at his own sweet will ;
Dear God ! the very houses seem asleep ;
And all that mighty heart is lying still.

THOUGHTS

SUGGESTED THE DAY AFTER SEEING THE GRAVE OF BURNS ON THE
BANKS OF NITH, NEAR THE POET'S RESIDENCE.

Too frail to keep the lofty vow
That must have followed when his brow
Was wreathed—" The Vision" tells us how—
    With holly spray,
He faltered, drifted to and fro,
    And passed away.

Well might such thoughts, dear Sister, throng
Our minds when lingering, all too long,
Over the grave of Burns we hung,
    In social grief—
Indulged as if it were a wrong
    To seek relief.

But, leaving each unquiet theme
Where gentlest judgments may misdeem,
And prompt to welcome every gleam
    Of good and fair,
Let us beside this limpid Stream
    Breathe hopeful air.

Enough of sorrow, wreck, and blight ;
Think rather of those moments bright
When to the unconsciousness of right
    His course was true,
When Wisdom prospered in his sight
    And virtue grew.

Yes, freely let our hearts expand,
Freely as in youth's season bland,
When side by side, his Book in hand,
    We wont to stray,
Our pleasure varying at command
    Of each sweet Lay.

How oft inspired must he have trode
These pathways, yon far-stretching road !
There lurks his home ; in that Abode,
    With mirth elate,
Or in his nobly pensive mood,
    The Rustic sate.

Proud thoughts that Image overawes,
Before it humbly let us pause,
And ask of Nature, from which cause
    And by what rules
She trained her Burns to win applause
    That shames the Schools.

Through busiest street and loneliest glen ·
Are felt the flashes of his pen :
He rules mid winter snows, and when
    Bees fill their hives :
Deep in the general heart of men
    His power survives.

What need of fields in some far clime   ·
Where Heroes, Sages, Bards sublime,
And all that fetched the flowing rhyme
    From genuine springs,
Shall dwell together till old Time
    Folds up his wings?

Sweet Mercy ! to the gates of Heaven
The minstrel lead, his sins forgiven ;
The rueful conflict, the heart riven
    With vain endeavour,
And memory of Earth's bitter leaven,
    Effaced for ever. ·

But why to him confine the prayer,
When kindred thoughts and yearnings bear
On the frail heart the purest share
   With all that live ?—
The best of what we do and are,
   Just God forgive !

HOOTING TO THE OWLS.

THERE was a boy ; ye knew him well, ye cliffs
And islands of Winander ! Many a time
At evening, when the earliest stars began
To move along the edges of the hills,
Rising or setting, would he stand alone,
Beneath the trees or by the glimmering lake,
And there, with fingers interwoven, both hands
Pressed closely palm to palm and to his mouth
Uplifted, he, as through an instrument, —
Blew mimic hootings to the silent owls,
That they might answer him.—And they would shout
Across the watery vale, and shout again,
Responsive to his call, with quivering peals,
And long halloos, and screams, and echoes loud
Redoubled and redoubled ; concourse wild
Of jocund mirth and din ! And when it chanced
That pauses of deep silence mocked his skill :
Then sometimes in that silence, while he hung
Listening, a gentle shock of mild surprise
Has carried far into his heart the voice
Of mountain torrents ; or the visible scene
Would enter unawares into his mind
With all its solemn imagery, its rocks,
Its woods, and that uncertain heaven received
Into the bosom of the steady lake.

This boy was taken from his mates, and died
In childhood, ere he was full twelve years old.
Fair is the spot, most beautiful the vale
Where he was born and bred : the churchyard hangs
Upon a slope above the village school :
And through that churchyard when my way has led
At evening, I believe that often-times
A long half-hour together I have stood
Mute, looking at the grave in which he lies.

YEW-TREES.

THERE is a Yew-tree, pride of Lorton Vale,
Which to this day stands single, in the midst
Of its own darkness, as it stood of yore :
Not loth to furnish weapons for the bands
Of Umfraville and Percy ere they marched
To Scotland's heaths ; or those that crossed the sea

And drew their sounding bows at Azincour,
Perhaps at earlier Crecy, or Poictiers.
Of vast circumference and gloom profound
This solitary Tree ! a living thing
Produced too slowly ever to decay ;
Of form and aspect too magnificent
To be destroyed.   But worthier still of note
Are those fraternal Four of Borrowdale,
Joined in one solemn and capacious grove ;
Huge trunks ! and each particular trunk a growth
Of intertwisted fibres serpentine
Upcoiling, and inveterately convolved ;
Not uninformed with Phantasy, and looks
That threaten the profane ;—a pillared shade
Upon whose grassless floor of red-brown hue
By sheddings from the pining umbrage tinged
Perennially—beneath whose sable roof
Of boughs, as if for festal purpose, decked
With unrejoicing berries,—ghostly Shapes
May meet at noon-tide ;—Fear and trembling Hope,
Silence and Foresight ; Death the Skeleton,
And Time the Shadow ;—there to celebrate,
As in a natural temple scattered o'er
With altars undisturbed of mossy stone,
United worship ; or in mute repose
To lie, and listen to the mountain flood
Murmuring from Glaramara's inmost caves.

DAFFODILS.

I WANDERED lonely as a cloud
    That floats on high o'er vales and hills,
When all at once I saw a crowd,
    A host of golden daffodils,
Beside the lake, beneath the trees,
Fluttering and dancing in the breeze.

Continuous as the stars that shine
    And twinkle on the milky way,
They stretched in never-ending line
    Along the margin of a bay ;
Ten thousand saw I at a glance,
Tossing their heads in sprightly dance.

The waves beside them danced, but they
    Outdid the sparkling waves in glee :
A poet could not but be gay
    In such a jocund company ;
I gazed, and gazed, but little thought
What wealth the show to me had brought :

For oft, when on my couch I lie
    In vacant or in pensive mood,

They flash upon that inward eye
  Which is the bliss of solitude ;
And then my heart with pleasure fills,
And dances with the daffodils.

LUCY.

She dwelt among the untrodden ways
  Beside the springs of Dove ;
A maid whom there were none to praise,
  And very few to love.

A violet by a mossy stone,
  Half-hidden from the eye !
—Fair as a star, when only one
  Is shining in the sky.

She lived unknown, and few could know
  When Lucy ceased to be ;
But she is in her grave, and oh !
  The difference to me !

SONNETS.

MILTON.

Milton ! thou shouldst be living at this hour :
England hath need of thee ; she is a fen
Of stagnant waters ; altar, sword, and pen,
Fireside, the heroic wealth of hall and bower,
Have forfeited their ancient English dower
Of inward happiness.   We are selfish men ;
Oh raise us up, return to us again,
And give us manners, virtue, freedom, power.
Thy soul was like a Star, and dwelt apart.
Thou hadst a voice whose sound was like the sea—
Pure as the naked heavens, majestic, free ;
So didst thou travel on life's common way
In cheerful godliness ; and yet thy heart
The lowliest duties on herself did lay.

THE WORLD AND NATURE.

The world is too much with us ; late and soon,
Getting and spending, we lay waste our powers :
Little we see in Nature that is ours ;
We have given our hearts away, a sordid boon !
This Sea that bears her bosom to the moon ;
The winds that will be howling at all hours,
And are up-gathered now like sleeping flowers ;
For this, for everything, we are out of tune ;
It moves us not.—Great God ! I'd rather be
A Pagan suckled in a creed outworn ;

So might I, standing on this pleasant lea,
Have glimpses that would make me less forlorn ;
Have sight of Proteus rising from the sea,
Or hear old Triton blow his wreathèd horn.

THE WILD DUCK'S NEST.

THE imperial Consort of the Fairy-king
Owns not a sylvan bower, or gorgeous cell
With emerald floored, and with purpureal shell
Ceiling'd and roofed, that is so fair a thing
As this low structure, for the tasks of Spring,
Prepared by one who loves the buoyant swell
Of the brisk waves, yet here consents to dwell ;
And spreads in steadfast peace her brooding wing.
Words cannot paint the o'ershadowing yew-tree bough,
And dimly-gleaming nest—a hollow crown
Of golden leaves inlaid with silver down,
Fine as the mother's softest plumes allow :
I gazed—and, self-accused while gazing, sighed
For human kind, weak slaves of cumbrous pride !

SAMUEL TAYLOR COLERIDGE.

Born 1772. Died 1834.

SEVERED FRIENDSHIP.

ALAS ! they had been friends in youth,
But whispering tongues can poison truth ;
And constancy lives in realms above ;
And life is thorny ; and youth is vain ;
And to be wroth with one we love,
Doth work like madness in the brain.
And thus it chanced, as I divine,
With Roland and Sir Leoline.
Each spake words of high disdain
And insult to his heart's best brother :
They parted—ne'er to meet again !
But never either found another
To free the hollow heart from paining—
They stood aloof, the scars remaining,
Like cliffs which had been rent asunder ;
A dreary sea now flows between ;
But neither heat, nor frost, nor thunder,
Shall wholly do away, I ween,
The marks of that which once hath been.

From *Christabel*

LOVE.

ALL thoughts, all passions, all delights,
Whatever stirs this mortal frame,
All are but ministers of Love,
    And feed his sacred flame.

Oft in my waking dreams do I
Live o'er again that happy hour,
When midway on the mount I lay,
    Beside the ruined tower.

The moonshine, stealing o'er the scene,
Had blended with the lights of eve ;
And she was there, my hope, my joy,
    My own dear Genevieve !

She leaned against the armèd man,
The statue of the armèd knight ;
She stood and listened to my lay,
    Amid the lingering light.

Few sorrows hath she of her own,
My hope ! my joy ! my Genevieve !
She loves me best whene'er I sing
    The songs that make her grieve.

I played a soft and doleful air,
I sang an old moving story—
An old rude song, that suited well
    That ruin wild and hoary.

She listened with a flitting blush,
With downcast eyes, and modest grace ;
For well she knew, I could not choose
    But gaze upon her face.

I told her of the Knight that wore
Upon his shield a burning brand ;
And that for ten long years he wooed
    The Lady of the Land.

I told her how he pined : and ah !
The deep, the low, the pleading tone
With which I sang another's love,
    Interpreted my own.

She listened with a flitting blush,
With downcast eyes, and modest grace ;
And she forgave me that I gazed
    Too fondly on her face.

But when I told the cruel scorn
That crazed that bold and lovely Knight.

And that he crossed the mountain-woods,
    Nor rested day nor night ;

That sometimes from the savage den,
And sometimes from the darksome shade,
And sometimes starting up at once
    In green and sunny glade,—

There came and looked him in the face
An angel beautiful and bright ;
And that he knew it was a fiend,
    This miserable Knight !

And that, unknowing what he did,
He leaped amid a murderous band,
And saved from outrage worse than death
    The Lady of the Land ;—

And how she wept, and clasped his knees,
And how she tended him in vain ;
And ever strove to expiate
    The scorn that crazed his brain ;—

And that she nursed him in a cave ;
And how his madness went away,
When on the yellow forest-leaves
    A dying man he lay ;—

His dying words—but when I reached
That tenderest strain of all the ditty,
My faltering voice and pausing harp
    Disturbed her soul with pity !

All impulses of soul and sense
Had thrilled my guileless Genevieve ;
The music and the doleful tale,
    The rich and balmy eve ;

And hopes, and fears that kindle hope,
An undistinguishable throng,
And gentle wishes long subdued,
    Subdued and cherished long !

She wept with pity and delight,
She blushed with love and virgin shame ;
And like the murmur of a dream,
    I heard her breathe my name.

Her bosom heaved—she stept aside,
As conscious of my look she stept—
Then suddenly, with timorous eye,
    She fled to me and wept.

She half enclosed me with her arms,
She pressed me with a meek embrace ;

And bending back her head, looked up,
And gazed upon my face.

'Twas partly love, and partly fear,
And partly 'twas a bashful art,
That I might rather feel, than see,
  The swelling of her heart.

I calmed her fears, and she was calm,
And told her love with virgin pride ;
And so I won my Genevieve,
  My bright and beauteous Bride.

HYMN BEFORE SUNRISE, IN THE VALE OF CHAMOUNI.

HAST thou a charm to stay the morning star
In his steep course ? So long he seems to pause
On thy bald awful head, O sovran Blanc! !
The Arvé and Arveiron at thy base
Rave ceaselessly ; but thou, most awful Form
Risest from forth thy silent sea of pines,
How silently ! Around thee and above
Deep is the air, and dark, substantial, black,
An ebon mass : methinks thou piercest it
As with a wedge ! But when I looked again,
It is thine own calm home, thy crystal shrine,
Thy habitation from eternity !
O dread and silent Mount ! I gazed upon thee,
Till thou, still present to the bodily sense,
Didst vanish from my thought : entranced in prayer
I worshipped the Invisible alone.
    Yet, like some sweet beguiling melody,
So sweet, we know not we are listening to it,
Thou, the meanwhile, wast blending with my thought,
Yea, with my life and life's own secret joy,
Till the dilating soul, enrapt, transfused,
Into the mighty vision passing—there,
As in her natural form, swelled vast to Heaven !
    Awake, my soul ! not only passive praise
Thou owest ! not alone these swelling tears,
Mute thanks, and secret ecstasy ! Awake,
Voice of sweet song ! Awake, my Heart, awake !
Green vales and icy cliffs, all join my Hymn.
    Thou first and chief, sole sovran of the Vale,
Oh, struggling with the darkness all the night,
And visited all night by troops of stars,
Or when they climb the sky, or when they sink :
Companion of the morning star at dawn,
Thyself Earth's rosy star, and of the dawn
Co-herald : wake, oh wake, and utter praise !
Who sank thy sunless pillars deep in earth ?
Who filled thy countenance with rosy light ?
Who made thee parent of perpetual streams ?

And you, ye five wild torrents, fiercely glad !
Who called you forth from night and utter death,
From dark and icy caverns called you forth,
Down those precipitous, black, jagged rocks,
For ever shattered and the same for ever?
Who gave you your invulnerable life,
Your strength, your speed, your fury, and your joy,
Unceasing thunder and eternal foam ?
And who commanded (and the silence came),
Here let the billows stiffen and have rest ?
　　Ye ice-falls ! ye that from the mountain's brow
Adown enormous ravines slope amain—
Torrents, methinks, that heard a mighty voice,
And stopped at once amid their maddest plunge !
Motionless torrents ! silent cataracts !
Who made you glorious as the gates of Heaven
Beneath the keen full moon ? Who bade the sun
Clothe you with rainbows ? Who, with living flowers
Of loveliest blue, spread garlands at your feet ?—
God ! let the torrents, like a shout of nations,
Answer ! and let the ice-plains echo, God !
God ! sing, ye meadow-streams, with gladsome voice !
Ye pine-groves, with your soft and soul-like sounds !
And they too have a voice, yon piles of snow,
And in their perilous fall shall thunder, God !
　　Ye living flowers that skirt the eternal frost !
Ye wild goats sporting round the eagle's nest !
Ye eagles, playmates of the mountain-storm !
Ye lightnings, the dread arrows of the clouds !
Ye signs and wonders of the elements,
Utter forth God, and fill the hills with praise !
　　Thou, too, hoar Mount ! with thy sky-pointing peaks,
Oft from whose feet the avalanche, unheard,
Shoots downward, glittering through the pure serene,
Into the depth of clouds that veil thy breast—
Thou too again, stupendous Mountain ! thou,
That as I raise my head, awhile bowed low
In adoration, upward from thy base
Slow travelling with dim eyes suffused with tears,
Solemnly seemest, like a vapoury cloud,
To rise before me—Rise, oh, ever rise,
Rise like a cloud of incense from the earth !
Thou kingly Spirit throned among the hills,
Thou dread ambassador from Earth to Heaven,
Great hierarch ! tell thou the silent sky,
And tell the stars, and tell yon rising sun,
Earth, with her thousand voices, praises God.

ROBERT SOUTHEY.

Born 1774.   Died 1843.

A PRAYER.

IMITATED FROM THE PERSIAN.

LORD! who art merciful as well as just,
Incline Thine ear to me, a child of dust!
Not what I would, O Lord! I offer Thee,
 Alas! but what I can.
Father Almighty, who hast made me man,
And bade me look to heaven, for Thou art there,
Accept my sacrifice and humble prayer.
Four things which are not in Thy treasury,
I lay before Thee, Lord, with this petition:
 My nothingness, my wants,
 My sins, and my contrition.

THE LIBRARY.

My days among the Dead are past;
 Around me I behold,
Where'er these casual eyes are cast,
 The mighty minds of old;
My never failing friends are they,
With whom I converse day by day.

With them I take delight in weal,
 And seek relief in woe;
And while I understand and feel
 How much to them I owe,
My cheeks have often been bedewed
With tears of thoughtful gratitude.

My thoughts are with the Dead, with them
 I live in long past years,
Their virtues love, their faults condemn,
 Partake their hopes and fears,
And from their lessons seek and find
Instruction with a humble mind.

My hopes are with the Dead, anon
 With them my place shall be;
And I with them shall travel on
 Through all Futurity;
Yet leaving here a name, I trust,
Which will not perish in the dust.

THE MAGIC THREAD.

THE thread she spun it gleamed like gold
    In the light of the odorous fire,
    Yet was it so wondrously thin,
That, save when it shone in the light,
You might look for it closely in vain.
    The youth sat watching it,
    And she observed his wonder,
    And then again she spake,
    And still her speech was song ;
"Now twine it round thy hands, I say,
Now twine it round thy hands, I pray !
My thread is small, my thread is fine,
        But he must be
        A stronger than thee,
Who can break this thread of mine !"

And up she raised her bright blue eyes,
    And sweetly she smiled on him,
        And he conceived no ill ;
And round and round his right hand,
    And round and round his left,
    He wound the thread so fine.
And then again the woman spake,
    And still her speech was song,
"Now thy strength, O stranger, strain !
Now then break the slender chain."

        Thalaba strove, but the thread
        By magic hands was spun,
And in his cheek the flush of shame
    Arose, commixt with fear.
    She beheld and laughed at him,
    And then again she sung,
"My thread is small, my thread is fine,
        But he must be
        A stronger than thee,
Who can break this thread of mine !"

And up she raised her bright blue eyes,
    And fiercely she smiled on him :
"I thank thee, I thank thee, Hodeirah's son !
I thank thee for doing what can't be undone,
For binding thyself in the chain I have spun !"
    Then from his head she wrenched
        A lock of his raven hair,
        And cast it in the fire,
        And cried aloud as it burnt,
    "Sister ! Sister ! hear my voice !
    Sister ! Sister ! come and rejoice !
        The thread is spun,
        The prize is won,

The work is done,
For I have made captive Hodeirah's son."
From *Thalaba*.

SIR WALTER SCOTT

Born 1771. Died 1836.

NELSON, PITT, AND FOX.

DEEP graved in every British heart,
O never let those names depart :
Say to your sons—Lo here his grave,
Who victor died on Gadite wave ;
To him, as to the burning levin,
Short, bright, resistless course was given.
  Where'er his country's foes were found
Was heard the fated thunder's sound,
Till burst the bolt on yonder shore,
Rolled, blazed, destroyed,—and was no more.

Nor mourn ye less his perished worth,
Who bade the conqueror go forth,
And launched that thunderbolt of war
On Egypt, Hafnia, Trafalgar ;
Who, born to guide such high emprize,
For Britain's weal was early wise :
Alas ! to whom the Almighty gave,
For Britain's sins, an early grave !
His worth, who, in his mightiest hour,
A bauble held the pride of power,
Spurned at the sordid lust of pelf,
And served his Albion for herself ;
Who, when the frantic crowd amain
Strained at subjection's bursting rein,
O'er their wild mood full conquest gained,
The pride, he would not crush, restrained,
Showed their fierce zeal a worthier cause,
And brought the freeman's arm to aid the freeman's laws.

Hadst thou but lived, though stripped of power,
A watchman on the lonely tower,
Thy thrilling trump had roused the land,
When fraud or danger were at hand ;
By thee, as by the beacon-light,
Our pilots had kept course aright ;
As some proud column, though alone,
Thy strength had propped the tottering throne.
Now is the stately column broke,
The beacon-light is quenched in smoke,
The trumpets silver sound is still,
The warder silent on the hill !

Oh, think, how to his latest day,
When Death, just hovering, claimed his prey,
With Palinure's unaltered mood,
Firm at his dangerous post he stood ;
Each call for needful rest repelled,
With dying hand the rudder held,
Till, in his fall, with fateful sway,
The steerage of the realm gave way !
Then, while on Britain's thousand plains,
One unpolluted church remains,
Whose peaceful bells ne'er sent around
The bloody tocsin's maddening sound,
But still, upon the hallowed day,
Convoke the swains to praise and pray ;
While faith and civil peace are dear,
Grace this cold marble with a tear,—
He, who preserved them, PITT, lies here !

Nor yet suppress the generous sigh,
Because his Rival slumbers nigh ;
Nor be thy *requiescat* dumb,
Lest it be said o'er Fox's tomb.
For talents mourn, untimely lost,
When best employed, and wanted most ;
Mourn genius high, and lore profound,
And wit that loved to play, not wound ;
And all the reasoning powers divine,
To penetrate, resolve, combine ;
And feelings keen, and fancy's glow,—
They sleep with him who sleeps below ;
And, if thou mourn'st they could not save
From error him who owns this grave,
Be every harsher thought suppressed,
And sacred be the last long rest !
Here, where the end of earthly things
Lays heroes, patriots, bards and kings ;
Where stiff the hand, and still the tongue,
Of those who fought, and spoke and sung ;
Here, where the fretted aisles prolong
The distant notes of holy song,
As if some angel spoke agen,
All peace on earth, good-will to men ;
If ever from an English heart,
Oh *here* let prejudice depart,
And, partial feeling cast aside,
Record that Fox a Briton died !
When Europe crouched to France's yoke,
And Austria bent, and Prussia broke,
And the firm Russian's purpose brave
Was bartered by a timorous slave,
Even then dishonour's peace he spurned,
The sullied olive-branch returned,
Stood for his country's glory fast,
And nailed her colours to the mast.

Heaven, to reward his firmness, gave
A portion in this honoured grave ;
And ne'er held marble in its trust
Of two such wondrous men the dust.

With more than mortal powers endowed,
How high they soared above the crowd !
Theirs was no common party race,
Jostling by dark intrigue for place ;
Like fabled gods, their mighty war
Shook realms and nations in its jar ;
Beneath each banner proud to stand,
Looked up the noblest of the land,
Till through the British world were known
The names of Pitt and Fox alone.
Spells of such force no wizard grave
E'er framed in dark Thessalian cave,
Though he could drain the ocean dry,
And force the planets from the sky.
These spells are spent, and spent with these,
The wine of life is on the lees.
Genius, and taste, and talent gone,
For ever tombed beneath the stone,
Where—taming thought to human pride !—
The mighty chiefs sleep side by side.
Drop upon Fox's grave the tear
'Twill trickle to his rival's bier ;
O'er Pitt's the mournful requiem sound
And Fox's shall the notes rebound.
The solemn echo seems to cry,—
" Here let their discord with them die ;
Speak not for those a separate doom
Whom Fate made brothers in the tomb,
But search the land of living men,
Where will you find their like agen ?"

                From *Marmion.*

MARMION'S DEFIANCE OF THE DOUGLAS.

Not far advanced was morning day,
When Marmion did his troop array
    To Surrey's camp to ride ;
He had safe conduct for his band,
Beneath the royal seal and hand,
    And Douglas gave a guide :
The ancient Earl, with stately grace,
Would Clara on her palfrey place,
And whispered, in an undertone,
" Let the hawk stoop, his prey is flown."
The train from out the castle drew ;
But Marmion stopped to bid adieu :
" Though something I might plain," he said,

"Of cold respect to stranger guest,
Sent hither by your king's behest,
While in Tantallon's towers I stayed ;
Part we in friendship from your land,
And, noble Earl, receive my hand."
But Douglas round him drew his cloak,
Folded his arms, and thus he spoke :—
"My manors, halls, and bowers, shall still
Be open to my sovereign's will,
To each one whom he lists, howe'er
Unmeet to be the owner's peer.
My castles are my king's alone,
From turret to foundation-stone—
The hand of Douglas is his own :
And never shall in friendly grasp
The hand of such as Marmion clasp."

Burned Marmion's swarthy cheek like fire,
And shook his very frame for ire,
And—"This to me !" he said,
"An 'twere not for thy hoary beard,
Such hand as Marmion's had not spared
      To cleave the Douglas' head !
And, first I tell thee, haughty Peer,
He, who does England's message here,
Although the meanest in her state,
May well, proud Angus, be thy mate :
And, Douglas, more I tell thee here,
      Even in thy pitch of pride,
Here in thy hold, thy vassals near,
(Nay, never look upon your lord,
And lay your hands upon his sword,)
      I tell thee, thou'rt defied !
And if thou said'st, I am not peer
To any lord in Scotland here,
Lowland or Highland, far or near,
      Lord Angus, thou hast lied !"
On the Earl's cheek the flush of rage
O'ercame the ashen hue of age :
Fierce he broke forth—"And darest thou then
To beard the lion in his den,
      The Douglas in his hall ?
And hopest thou hence unscathed to go?
No, by Saint Bryde of Bothwell, no !—
Up drawbridge, grooms—what Warder, ho !
      Let the portcullis fall."

Lord Marmion turned,—well was his need,
And dashed the rowels in his steed,
Like arrow through the archway sprung,
The ponderous gate behind him rung :
To pass there was such scanty room,
The bars, descending, razed his plume.

The steed along the drawbridge flies,
Just as it trembled on the rise ;
Not lighter does the swallow skim
Along the smooth lake's level brim :
And when Lord Marmion reached his band,
He halts, and turns with clenchèd hand,
And shout of loud defiance pours,
And shook his gauntlet at the towers.
"Horse ! horse !" the Douglas cried, "and chase !"
But soon he reined his fury's pace :
" A royal messenger he came,
Though most unworthy of the name.
A letter forged ! .Saint Jude to speed !
Did ever knight so foul a deed !
At first in heart it liked me ill,
When the king praised his clerkly skill.
Thanks to Saint Bothan, son of mine,
Save Gawain, ne'er could pen a line :
So swore I, and I swear it still,
Let my boy-bishop fret his fill.
Saint Mary mend my fiery mood !
Old age ne'er cools the Douglas blood,
" I thought to slay him where he stood.—
'Tis pity of him too,'' he cried ;
"Bold can he speak, and fairly ride,
I warrant him a warrior tried."
With this his mandate he recalls,
And slowly seeks his castle halls.

From Marmion.

THE CHASE.

I.

THE stag at eve had drunk his fill,
Where danced the moon on Monan's rill,
And deep his midnight lair had made
In lone Glenartney's hazel shade ;
But when the sun his beacon red
Had kindled on Benvoirlich's head,
The deep-mouthed bloodhound's heavy bay
Resounded up the rocky way,
And faint, from farther distance borne,
Were heard the clanging hoof and horn.

II.

As chief who hears his warder call,
" To arms ! the foemen storm the wall,"
The antlered monarch of the waste
Sprung from his heathery couch in haste.
But, ere his fleet career he took,
The dew-drops from his flanks he shook ;
Like crested leader proud and high,
Tossed his beamed frontlet to the sky ;

A moment gazed adown the dale,
A moment snuffed the tainted gale,
A moment listened to the cry,
That thickened as the chase drew nigh ,
Then, as the headmost foes appeared,
With one brave bound the copse he cleared
And stretching forward free and far,
Sought the wild heaths of Uam-Var.

III.

Yelled on the view the opening pack,
Rock, glen, and cavern paid them back ;
To many a mingled sound at once
The awakened mountain gave response.
A hundred dogs bayed deep and strong,
Clattered a hundred steeds along,
Their peal the merry horns rang out,
A hundred voices joined the shout ;
With hark and whoop and wild halloo,
No rest Benvoirlich's echoes knew.·
Far from the tumult fled the roe,
Close in her covert cowered the doe,
The falcon from her cairn on high,
Cast on the rout a wondering eye,
Till far beyond her piercing ken
The hurricane had swept the glen.
Faint, and more faint, its failing din
Returned from cavern, cliff and linn,
And silence settled, wide and still,
On the lone wood and mighty hill.

IV.

Less loud the sounds of sylvan war
Disturbed the heights of Uam-Var,
And roused the cavern, where, 'tis told,
A giant made his den of old ;
For ere that steep ascent was won,
High in his pathway hung the sun,
And many a gallant, stayed perforce,
Was fain to breathe his faltering horse ;
And of the trackers of the deer
Scarce half the lessening pack was near ;
So shrewdly, on the mountain-side,
Had the bold burst their mettle tried.

V.

The noble stag was pausing now
Upon the mountain's southern brow,
Where broad extended, far beneath,
The varied realms of fair Menteith.

With anxious eye he wandered o'er
Mountain and meadow, moss and moor,
And pondered refuge from his toil,
By far Lochard or Aberfoyle.
But nearer was the copsewood grey,
That waved and wept on Loch Achray,
And mingled with the pine-trees blue
On the bold cliffs of Ben-venue.
Fresh vigour with the hope returned,
With flying foot the heath he spurned,
Held westward with unwearied race,
And left behind the panting chase.

VI.

'Twere long to tell what steeds gave o'er,
As swept the hunt through Cambus more,
What reins were tightened in despair,
When rose Benledi's ridge in air ;
Who flagged upon Bochastle's heath,
Who shunned to stem the flooded Teith,
For twice that day, from shore to shore,
The gallant stag swam stoutly o'er.
Few were the stragglers, following far,
That reached the lake of Vennachar ;
And when the Brigg of Turk was won,
The headmost horseman rode alone.

VII.

Alone, but with unabated zeal,
That horseman plied the scourge and steel ;
For, jaded now, and spent with toil,
Embossed with foam, and dark with soil,
While every gasp with sobs he drew,
The laboring stag strained full in view.
Two dogs of black St. Hubert's breed,
Unmatched for courage, breath, and speed,
Fast on his flying traces came,
And all but won that desperate game ;
For, scarce a spear's length from his haunch,
Vindictive toiled the bloodhounds stanch ;
Nor nearer might the dogs attain,
Nor farther might the quarry strain,
Thus up the margin of the lake,
Between the precipice and brake,
O'er stock and rock their race they take.

VIII.

The hunter marked that mountain high,
The lone lake's western boundary,
And deemed the stag must turn to bay,
Where that huge rampart barred the way ;

Already glorying in the prize,
Measured his antlers with his eyes ;
For the death-wound, and death halloo,
Mustered his breath, his whinyard drew,
But, thundering as he came prepared,
With ready arm and weapon bared,
The wily quarry shunned the shock,
And turned him from the opposing rock ;
Then, dashing down a darksome glen,
Soon lost to hound and hunter's ken,
In the deep Trosach's wildest nook
His solitary refuge took.
There, while close couched, the thicket shed
Cold dews and wild flowers on his head,
He heard the baffled dogs in vain
Rave through the hollow pass amain,
Chiding the rocks that yelled again.

IX.

Close on the hounds the hunter came,
To cheer them on the vanished game ;
But, stumbling in the rugged dell,
The gallant horse exhausted fell.
The impatient rider strove in vain
To rouse him with the spur and rein,
For the good steed, his labours o'er,
Stretched his stiff limbs, to rise no more ;
Then, touched with pity and remorse,
He sorrowed o'er the expiring horse.
" I little thought, when first thy rein
I slacked upon the banks of Seine,
That Highland eagle e'er should feed
On thy fleet limbs, my matchless steed !
Woe worth the chase, woe worth the day,
That cost thy life, my gallant gray !"

X.

Then through the dell his horn resounds,
From vain pursuit to call the hounds.
Back limped, with slow and crippled pace,
The sulky leaders of the chase ;
Close to their master's side they pressed,
With drooping tail and humbled crest ;
But still the dingle's hollow throat
Prolonged the swelling bugle-note.
The owlets started from their dream,
The eagles answered with their scream,
Round and around the sounds were cast,
Till echo seemed an answering blast ;
And on the hunter hied his way,
To join some comrades of the day ;

Yet often paused, so strange the road,
So wondrous were the scenes it showed.

From *The Lady of the Lake.*

LOCH KATRINE.

THE summer dawn's reflected hue
To purple changed Loch Katrine blue ;
Mildly and soft the western breeze
Just kissed the lake, just stirred the trees,
And the pleased lake, like maiden coy,
Trembled, but dimpled not for joy ;
The mountain-shadows on her breast
Were neither broken nor at rest ;
In bright uncertainty they lie,
Like future joys to Fancy's eye.
The water-lily to the light
Her chalice reared of silver bright ;
The doe awoke, and to the lawn,
Begemmed with dewdrops, led her fawn ;
The grey mist left the mountain side,
The torrent showed its glistening pride ;
Invisible in fleckèd sky,
The lark sent down her revelry ;
The blackbird and the speckled thrush
Good-morrow gave from brake and bush ;
In answer cooed the cushat dove,
Her notes of peace, and rest, and love.

From *The Lady of the Lake.*

THE LAY OF ROSABELLE.

OH listen, listen, ladies gay !
No haughty feat of arms I tell ;
Soft is the note, and sad the lay,
That mourns the lovely Rosabelle.

—"Moor, moor the barge, ye gallant crew !
And, gentle ladye, deign to stay !
Rest thee in Castle Ravensheuch,
Nor tempt the stormy firth to-day.

" The blackening wave is edged with white ;
To inch and rock the sea-mews fly ;
The fishers have heard the Water Sprite,
Whose screams forebode that wreck is nigh.

"Last night the gifted Seer did view
A wet shroud swathed round ladye gay ;
Then stay thee, Fair, in Ravensheuch ;
Why cross the gloomy firth to-day ?"

"'Tis not because Lord Lindesay's heir
To-night at Roslin leads the ball,

But that my ladye mother there
Sits lonely in her castle-hall.

" 'Tis not because the ring they ride,
And Lindesay at the ring rides well,
But that my sire the wine will chide,
If 'tis not filled by Rosabelle."—

O'er Roslin all that dreary night
A wondrous blaze was seen to gleam ;
'Twas broader than the watch-fire's light,
And redder than the bright moon-beam.

It glared on Roslin's castled rock,
It ruddied all the copse-wood glen ;
'Twas seen from Dryden's groves of oak,
And seen from caverned Hawthorned.

Seemed all on fire that chapel proud,
Where Roslin's chiefs uncoffined lie ;
Each Baron, for a sable shroud,
Sheathed in his iron panoply.

Seemed all on fire, within, around,
Deep sacristy and altars pale ;
Shone every pillar foliage-bound,
And glimmered all the dead men's mail.

Blazed battlement and pinnet high,
Blazed every rose-carved buttress fair—
So still they blaze, when fate is nigh
The lordly line of high St. Clair.

There are twenty of Roslin's barons bold
Lie buried within that proud chapelle ;
Each one the holy vault doth hold—
But the sea holds lovely Rosabelle !

And each St. Clair was buried there,
With candle, with book, and with knell ;
But the sea-caves rung, and the wild winds sung,
The dirge of lovely Rosabelle.

From The Lay of the Last Minstrel.

LOCHINVAR.

Oh, young Lochinvar is come out of the west ;
Through all the wide Border his steed was the best,
And save his good broadsword he weapons had none ;
He rode all unarmed, and he rode all alone.
So faithful in love, and so dauntless in war,
There never was knight like the young Lochinvar.

He stayed not for brake, and he stopped not for stone,
He swam the Eske river where ford there was none ;

But ere he alighted at Netherby gate,
The bride had consented, the gallant came late :
For a laggard in love, and a dastard in war,
Was to wed the fair Ellen of brave Lochinvar.

So boldly he entered the Netherby hall,
Among bridesmen and kinsmen, and brothers and all :
Then spoke the bride's father, his hand on his sword,
(For the poor craven bridegroom said never a word),
"O come ye in peace here, or come ye in war,
Or to dance at our bridal, young Lord Lochinvar?"

"I long wooed your daughter, my suit you denied ;
Love swells like the Solway, but ebbs like its tide—
And now I am come, with this lost love of mine,
To lead but one measure, drink one cup of wine.
There are maidens in Scotland more lovely by far,
That would gladly be bride to the young Lochinvar."

The bride kissed the goblet, the knight took it up,
He quaffed off the wine, and he threw down the cup,
She looked down to blush, and she looked up to sigh,
With a smile on her lips and a tear in her eye.
He took her soft hand ere her mother could bar,—
"Now tread we a measure!" said young Lochinvar.

So stately his form, and so lovely her face,
That never a hall such a galliard did grace ;
While her mother did fret, and her father did fume,
And the bridegroom stood dangling his bonnet and plume ;
And the bridemaidens whispered, " 'Twere better by far
To have matched our fair cousin with young Lochinvar."

One touch to her hand, and one word in her ear,
When they reached the hall door, and the charger stood near ;
So light to the croupe the fair lady he swung,
So light to the saddle before her he sprung !—
"She is won ! we are gone, over bank, bush, and scaur ;
They'll have fleet steeds that follow," quoth young Lochinvar.

There was mounting 'mong Graemes of the Netherby clan ;
Forsters, Fenwicks, and Musgraves, they rode and they ran :
There was racing, and chasing, on Cannobie Lee,
But the lost bride of Netherby ne'er did they see.
So daring in love, and so dauntless in war,
Have ye e'er heard of gallant like young Lochinvar?

From Marmion.

COUNTY GUY.

Ah ! County Guy, the hour in nigh,
  The sun has left the lea ;
The orange flower perfumes the bower,
  The breeze is on the sea.

The lark, his lay who thrilled all day,
  Sits hushed his partner nigh ;
Breeze, bird, and flower, confess the hour,
  But where is County Guy?

The village maid steals through the shade,
  Her shepherd's suit to hear ;
To beauty shy, by lattice high,
  Sings high-born Cavalier.
The star of Love, all stars above,
  Now reigns o'er earth and sky ;
And high and low the influence know—
  But where is County Guy?

THE SUN UPON THE WEIRDLAW HILL.

THE sun upon the Weirdlaw Hill,
  In Ettrick's vale, is sinking sweet ;
The westland wind is husht and still,
  The lake lies sleeping at my feet.
Yet not the landscape to mine eye
  Bears those bright hues that once it bore ;
Though evening, with her richest dye,
  Flames o'er the hills of Ettrick's shore.

With listless look along the plain,
  I see Tweed's silver current glide,
And coldly mark the holy fane
  Of Melrose rise in ruined pride.
The quiet lake, the balmy air,
  The hill, the stream, the tower, the tree,—
Are they still such as once they were?
  Or is the dreary change in me?

Alas, the warped and broken board,
  How can it bear the painter's dye !
The harp of strained and tuneless chord,
  How to the minstrel's skill reply !
To aching eyes each landscape lowers,
  To feverish pulse each gale blows chill ;
And Araby's or Eden's bowers
  Were barren as this moorland hill.

JAMES HOGG.

Born 1770. Died 1835.

KILMENY.

BONNY Kilmeny gaed up the glen ;
But it wasna to meet Duneira's men,

Nor the rosy monk of the isle to see,
For Kilmeny was pure as pure could be.
It was only to hear the Yorlin sing,
And pu' the cress flower round the spring—
The scarlet hypp, and the hind-berry,
And the nut that hung frae the hazel-tree ;
For Kilmeny was pure as pure could be.
But lang may her minny look over the wa',
And lang may she seek i' the greenwood shaw ;
Lang the laird of Duneira blame,
And lang, lang greet ere Kilmeny come hame.

When many a day had come and fled,
When grief grew calm, and hope was dead,
When mass for Kilmeny's soul had been sung,
When the bedesman had prayed, and the dead-bell rung,
Late, late in a gloamin', when all was still,
When the fringe was red on the westlin bill ;
The wood was sere, the moon i' the wane,
The reek o' the cot hung over the plain—
Like a little wee cloud in the world its lane—
When the ingle low'd with an eiry leme,
Late, late in the gloamin' Kilmeny came hame !

"Kilmeny, Kilmeny, where have you been ?
Long hae we sought both holt and den—
By linn, by ford, and green-wood tree ;
Yet you are halesome and fair to see.
Where got you that joup o' the lily sheen ?
That bonny snood o' the birk sae green?
And these roses, the fairest that ever was seen ?
Kilmeny, Kilmeny, where have you been ?"

Kilmeny looked up with a lovely grace,
But nae smile was seen on Kilmeny's face :
As still was her look, and as still was her e'e,
As the stillness that lay on the emerant lee,
Or the mist that sleeps on the waveless sea.
For Kilmeny had been she knew not where,
And Kilmeny had seen what she could not declare ;
Kilmeny had been where the cock never crew,
Where the rain never fell, and the wind never blew ;
But it seemed as the harp of the sky had rung,
And the airs of heaven played round her tongue,
When she spake of the lovely forms she had seen,
And a land where sin had never been—
A land of love, and a land of light,
Withouten sun, or moon, or night ;
Where the river swa'd a living stream,
And the light a pure celestial beam :
The land of vision it would seem,
A still, an everlasting dream.

In yon greenwood there is a waik,
And in that waik there is a wene,
And in that wene there is a maike,
That neither has flesh, blood, nor bane ;
And down in yon green wood he walks his lane.

In that green wood Kilmeny lay,
Her bosom happed wi' the flowerets gay ;
But the air was soft, and the silence deep,
And bonny Kilmeny fell sound asleep ;
She kenned nae mair, nor opened her e'e,
Till waked by the hymns of a far countrye.

        *   *   *   *   *

They bore her away, she wist not how,
For she felt not arm, not rest below ;
But so swift they wained her through the light,
'Twas like the motion of sound or sight ;
They seemed to split the gales of air,
And yet nor gale nor breeze was there.
Unnumbered groves below them grew ;
They came, they past, and backward flew,
Like floods of blossoms gliding on,
In moment seen, in moment gone.
O, never vales to mortal view
Appeared like those o'er which they flew ;
That land to human spirits given,
The lowermost vales of the storied heaven ;
From whence they view the worlds below,
And heaven's blue gate with sapphires glow—
More glory yet unmeet to know.

        *   *   *   *   *

Then Kilmeny begged again to see
The friends she had left in her own countrye,
To tell of the place where she had been,
And the glories in the land unseen ;
To warn the living maidens fair,
The loved of Heaven, the spirit's care,
That all whose minds unmeled remain.
Shall bloom in beauty when Time is gane.

With distant music soft and deep,
They lulled Kilmeny sound asleep ;
And when she wakened, she lay her lane,
All happed wi' flowers in the greenwood wene.
When seven long years had come and fled ;
When grief was calm, and hope was dead ;
When scarce was remembered Kilmeny's name,
Late, late in the gloamin' Kilmeny came hame !
And oh, her beauty was fair to see,
But still and steadfast was her e'e !
Such beauty bard might ne'er declare,
For there was no pride nor passion there ;

And the soft desire of maiden's e'en,
In that mild face could never be seen.
Her seymar was the lily flower,
And her cheek the moss-rose in the shower ;
And her voice like the distant melodye
That floats along the twilight sea.
But she loved to raike the lonely glen,
And keepèd afar frae the haunts of men ;
Her holy hymns unheard to sing,
To suck the flowers, and drink the spring.
But wherever her peaceful form appeared,
The wild beasts of the hill were cheered ;
The wolf played blithely round the field,
The lordly bison lowed and kneeled ;
The dun deer woed wi' manner bland,
And cowered aneath her lily hand.
And when at even the woodlands rung,
When hymns of other worlds she sung,
In ecstasy of sweet devotion,
O, then the glen was all in motion !
The wild beasts of the forest came,
Broke from their bughts and faulds the tame,
And goved around, charmed and amazed ;
Even the dull cattle crooned and gazed,
And murmured and looked with anxious pain,
For something, the mystery to explain.
The buzzard came with the throstle-cock,
The corby left her houf in the rock ;
The blackbird along wi' the eagle flew ;
The hind came tripping o'er the dew ;
The wolf and the kid their raike began ;
And the tod, and the lamb, and the leveret ran ;
The hawk and the hern attour them hung,
And the merl and the mavis forhooyed their young ;
And all in a peaceful ring where hurled ;
It was like an eve in a sinless world !

When a month and a day had come and gane,
Kilmeny sought the greenwood wene ;
There laid her down on the leaves sae green,
And Kilmeny on earth was never mair seen.
But oh, the words that fell from her mouth
Were words of wonder, and words of truth !
But all the land were in fear and dread,
For they kenned na whether she was living or dead.
It wasna her hame, and she couldna remain ;
She left this world of sorrow and pain,
And returned to the land of thought again.

A BOY'S SONG.

WHERE the pools are bright and deep,
Where the grey trout lies asleep,

Up the river and o'er the lea,
That's the way for Billy and me.

Where the blackbird sings the latest,
Where the hawthorn blooms the sweetest,
Where the nestlings chirp and flee,
That's the way for Billy and me.

Where the mowers mow the cleanest,
Where the hay lies thick and greenest ;
There to trace the homeward bee,
That's the way for Billy and me.

Where the hazel bank is steepest,
Where the shadow lies the deepest,
Where the clustering nuts fall free,
That's the way for Billy and me.

Why the boys should drive away
Little maidens from their play,
Or love to banter and fight so well,
That's the thing I never could tell.

But this I know, I love to play,
Through the meadow, along the hay ;
Up the water and o'er the lea,
That's the way for Billy and me.

LORD BYRON.

Born 1788. Died 1824.

FROM "THE BRIDE OF ABYDOS."

Know ye the land where the cypress and myrtle
Are emblems of deeds that are done in their clime?
Where the rage of the vulture, the love of the turtle,
Now melt into sorrow, now madden to crime!
Know ye the land of the cedar and vine,
Where the flowers ever blossom, the beams ever shine ;
Where the light wings of Zephyr, oppressed with perfume
Wax faint o'er the gardens of Gúl in her bloom ;
Where the citron and olive are fairest of fruit,
And the voice of the nightingale never is mute ;
Where the tints of the earth, and the hues of the sky,
In colour though varied, in beauty may vie,
And the purple of ocean is deepest in dye ;
Where the virgins are soft as the roses they twine,
And all, save the spirit of man, is divine?
'Tis the clime of the East ; 'tis the land of the sun—
Can he smile on such deeds as his children have done?

Oh ! wild as the accents of lover's farewell
Are the hearts which they bear, and the tales which they tell.

STANZAS FOR MUSIC.

THERE's not a joy the world can give like that it takes away,
When the glow of early youth declines in feeling's dull decay :
'Tis not on youth's smooth cheek the blush alone, which fades so fast,
But the tender bloom of heart is gone, ere youth itself be past.

Then the few whose spirits float above the wreck of happiness,
Are driven o'er the shoals of guilt or ocean of excess :
The magnet of their course is gone, or only points in vain
The shore to which their shivered sail shall never stretch again.

Then the mortal coldness of the soul till death itself comes down ;
It cannot feel for others' woes, it dare not dream its own ;
That heavy chill has frozen o'er the fountain of our tears,
And though the eye may sparkle still, 'tis where the ice appears.

Though wit may flash from fluent lips, and mirth distract the breast,
Through midnight hours that yield no more their former hope of rest ;
'Tis but as ivy leaves around the ruined turret wreath,
All green and wildly fresh without, but worn and grey beneath.

Oh could I feel as I have felt—or be what I have been,
Or weep as I could once have wept o'er many a vanished scene ;
As springs in deserts found seem sweet, all brackish though they be,
So, midst the withered waste of life, those tears would flow to me.

THE OCEAN.

THERE is a pleasure in the pathless woods,
There is a rapture on the lonely shore,
There is society, where none intrudes,
By the deep Sea, and music in its roar :
I love not Man the less, but Nature more,
From these our interviews, in which I steal
From all I may be, or have been before.
To mingle with the Universe, and feel
What I can ne'er express, yet cannot all conceal.

Roll on, thou deep and dark blue Ocean—roll !
Ten thousand fleets sweep over thee in vain ;
Man marks the earth with ruin—his control
Stops with the shore ; upon the watery plain
The wrecks are all thy deed, nor doth remain
A shadow of man's ravage, save his own,
When, in a moment, like a drop of rain,
He sinks into thy depths with bubbling groan,
Without a grave, unknelled, uncoffined, and unknown.

His steps are not upon thy paths,—thy fields
Are not a spoil for him,—thou dost arise

And shake him from thee : the vile strength he wields
For earth's destruction thou dost all despise,
Spurning him from thy bosom to the skies,
And send'st him, shivering in thy playful spray
And howling, to his Gods, where haply lies
His pretty hope in some near port or bay,
And dashest him again to earth :—there let him lay.

The armaments which thunderstrike the walls
Of rock-built cities, bidding nations quake,
And monarchs tremble in their capitals,
The oak leviathans, whose huge ribs make
Their clay creator the vain title take
Of lord of thee, and arbiter of war—
These are thy toys, and, as the snowy flake,
They melt into thy yeast of waves, which mar
Alike the Armada's pride or spoils of Trafalgar.

Thy shores are empires, changed in all save thee—
Assyria, Greece, Rome, Carthage, what are they?
Thy waters washed them power while they were free,
And many a tyrant since ; their shores obey
The stranger, slave, or savage ; their decay
Has dried up realms to deserts :—not so thou ;—
Unchangeable, save to thy wild waves' play,
Time writes no wrinkle on thine azure brow :
Such as creation's dawn beheld, thou rollest now.

Thou glorious mirror, where the Almighty's form
Glasses itself in tempests ; in all time,—
Calm or convulsed, in breeze, or gale, or storm,
Icing the pole, or in the torrid clime
Dark-heaving—boundless, endless, and sublime,
The image of eternity, the throne
Of the invisible ; even from out thy slime
The monsters of the deep are made ; each zone
Obeys thee ; thou goest forth, dread, fathomless, alone.

And I have loved thee, Ocean ! and my joy
Of youthful sports was on thy breast to be
Borne, like thy bubbles, onward : from a boy
I wantoned with thy breakers—they to me
Were a delight ; and if the freshening sea
Made them a terror—'twas a pleasing fear,
For I was as it were a child of thee,
And trusted to thy billows far and near,
And laid my hand upon thy mane—as I do here.
                              From *Childe Harold.*

BEFORE THE BATTLE OF WATERLOO.

There was a sound of revelry by night,
And Belgium's capital had gathered then

Her beauty and her chivalry, and bright
The lamps shone o'er fair women and bravo men ;
A thousand hearts beat happily ; and when
Music arose with its voluptuous swell,
Soft eyes looked love to eyes which spake again,
And all went merry as a marriage bell ;
But hush ! hark ! a deep sound strikes like a rising knell !

Did ye not hear it?—no ; 'twas but the wind,
Or the car rattling o'er the stony street ;
On with the dance ! let joy be unconfined ;
No sleep till morn, when youth and pleasure meet
To chase the glowing hours with flying feet—
But, hark !—that heavy sound breaks in once moro,
As if the clouds its echo would repeat ;
And nearer, clearer, deadlier than before !
Arm ! arm ! it is—it is—the cannon's opening roar !

Within a windowed niche of that high hall
Sate Brunswick's fated chieftain ; he did hear
That sound the first amid the festival,
And caught its tone with death's prophetic ear ;
And when they smiled because he deemed it near,
His heart more truly knew that peal too well
Which stretched his father on a bloody bier,
And roused the vengeance blood alone could quell :
He rushed into the field, and foremost, fighting, fell.

Ah ! then and there was hurrying to and fro,
And gathering tears, and tremblings of distress,
And cheeks all pale, which, but an hour ago,
Blushed at the praise of their own loveliness ;
And there were sudden partings, such as press
The life from out young hearts, and choking sighs
Which ne'er might be repeated : who would guess
If ever more should meet those mutual eyes,
Since upon night so sweet such awful morn could rise ?

And there was mounting in hot haste : the steed,
The mustering squadron, and the clattering car,
Went pouring forward with impetuous speed,
And swiftly forming in the ranks of war ;
And the deep thunder peal on peal afar ;
And near, the beat of the alarming drum,
Roused up the soldier ere the morning star ;
While thronged the citizens, with terror dumb,
Or whispering, with white lips—"The foe ! They come ! they
    come !"

And wild and high the "Camerons' Gathering" rose,
The war-note of Lochiel, which Albyn's hills
Have heard ; and heard, too, have her Saxon foes :—
How in the noon of night that pibroch thrills,
Savage and shrill ! But, with the breath which fills

Their mountain pipe, so fill the mountaineers
With the fierce native daring which instils
The stirring memory of a thousand years,
And Evan's, Donald's fame rings in each clansman's ears.

*   *   *   *   *   *   *

Last noon beheld them full of lusty life,
Last eve in beauty's circle proudly gay,
The midnight brought the signal-sound of strife,
The morn the marshalling in arms—the day
Battle's magnificently stern array !
The thunder clouds close o'er it, which when rent,
The earth is covered thick with other clay,
Which her own clay shall cover, heaped and pent,
Rider and horse,—friend, foe,—in one red burial blent !

From *Childe Harold.*

THE DEATH OF HENRY KIRKE WHITE.

UNHAPPY White ! while life was in its spring,
And thy young muse just waved its joyous wing,
The spoiler came ; and all thy promise fair
Has sought the grave, to sleep for ever there,
Oh ! what a noble heart was here undone,
When Science' self destroyed her favourite son !
Yes, she too much indulged thy fond pursuit,
She sowed the seeds, but Death has reaped the fruit.
'Twas thine own genius gave the fatal blow,
And helped to plant the wound that laid thee low :
So the struck eagle, stretched upon the plain,
No more through rolling clouds to soar again,
Viewed his own feather on the fatal dart,
And winged the shaft that quivered in his heart ;
Keen were his pangs, but keener far to feel,
He nursed the pinion which impelled the steel ;
While the same plumage that had warmed his nest,
Drank the last life-drop of his bleeding breast.

From *English Bards and Scotch Reviewers.*

THE ISLES OF GREECE.

THE isles of Greece ! The isles of Greece !
   Where burning Sappho loved and sung,
Where grew the arts of war and peace,
   Where Delos rose, and Phœbus sprung !
Eternal summer gilds them yet,
But all, except their sun, is set.

The Scian and the Teian muse,
   The hero's harp, the lover's lute,
Have found the fame your shores refuse :
   Their place of birth alone is mute
To sounds which echo further west
Than your sires' "Islands of the Blest."

The mountains look on Marathon—
   And Marathon looks on the sea ;
And musing there an hour alone,
   I dreamed that Greece might still be free ;
For standing on the Perians' grave,
I could not deem myself a slave.

A king sate on the rocky brow
   Which looks o'er sea-born Salamis ;
And ships, by thousands, lay below,
   And men in nations ;—all were his !
He counted them at break of day—
And when the sun set, where were they ?

And where are they ? and where art thou,
   My country ? On thy voiceless shore
The heroic lay is tuneless now—
   The heroic bosom beats no more !
And must thy lyre, so long divine,
Degenerate into hands like mine ?

'Tis something, in the dearth of fame,
   Though linked among a fettered race,
To feel at least a patriot's shame,
   Even as I sing, suffuse my face ;
For what is left the poet here ?
For Greeks a blush—for Greece a tear.

Must *we* but weep o'er days more blest ?
   Must *we* but blush ?—Our fathers bled.
Earth ! render back from out thy breast
   A remnant of our Spartan dead !
Of the three hundred grant but three,
To make a new Thermopylæ !

What, silent still ? and silent all ?
   Ah ! no :—the voices of the dead
Sound like a distant torrent's fall,
   And answer, " Let one living head,
But one arise—we come, we come !"
'Tis but the living who are dumb.

In vain—in vain : strike other chords ;
   Fill high the cup with Samian wine !
Leave battles to the Turkish hordes,
   And shed the blood of Scio's vine !
Hark ! rising to the ignoble call,
How answers each bold Bacchanal !

You have the Pyrrhic dance as yet ;
   Where is the Pyrrhic phalanx gone ?
Of two such lessons, why forget
   The nobler and the manlier one !
You have the letters Cadmus gave—
Think ye he meant them for a slave ?

Fill high the bowl with Samian wine !
　We will not think of themes like these !
It made Anacreon's song divine :
　He served—but served Polycrates—
A tyrant : but our masters then
Were still, at least, our countrymen.

The tyrant of the Chersonese
　Was freedom's best and bravest friend ;
That tyrant was Militiades !
　Oh ! that the present hour would lend
Another despot of the kind !
Such chains as his were sure to bind.

Fill high the bowl with Samian wine !
　On Suli's rock and Parga's shore
Exists the remnant of a line
　Such as the Doric mothers bore ;
And there, perhaps, some seed is sown,
The Heracleidan blood might own.

Trust not for freedom to the Franks—
　They have a king who buys and sells ;
In native swords, and native ranks,
　The only hope of courage dwells :
But Turkish force, and Latin fraud,
Would break your shield, however broad.

Fill high the bowl with Samian wine !
　Our virgins dance beneath the shade—
I see their glorious black eyes shine ;
　But, gazing on each glowing maid,
My own the burning tear-drop laves,
To think such breasts must suckle slaves.

Place me on Sunium's marbled steep,
　Where nothing, save the waves and I,
May here our mutual murmurs sweep ;
　There, swan-like, let me sing and die :
A land of slaves shall ne'er be mine—
Dash down yon cup of Samian wine !

ON THE DAY I COMPLETE MY THIRTY-SIXTH YEAR.

'Tis time this heart should be unmoved,
　Since others it hath ceased to move :
Yet, though I cannot be beloved,
　　Still let me love !

My days are in the yellow leaf ;
　The flowers, the fruits of love are gone ;
The worm, the canker, and the grief
　　Are mine alone !

The fire that on my bosom preys
    Is lone as some volcanic isle ;
No torch is kindled at its blaze—
        A funeral pile.

The hope, the fear, the jealous care,
    The exalted portion of the pain
And power of love, I cannot share,
        But wear the chain.

But 'tis not *thus*—and 'tis not *here*—
    Such thoughts should shake my soul, nor *now*
Where glory decks the hero's bier,
        Or binds his brow.

The sword, the banner, and the field,
    Glory and Greece, around me see !
The Spartan, borne upon his shield,
        Was not more free.

Awake ! (not Greece—she *is* awake !)
    Awake, my spirit ! Think through *whom*
Thy life-blood tracks its parent lake,
        And then strike home !

Tread those reviving passions down,
    Unworthy manhood !—unto thee
Indifferent should the smile or frown
        Of beauty be.

If thou regret'st thy youth, *why live ?*
    The land of honourable death
Is here :—up to the field, and give
        Away thy breath !

Seek out—less often sought than found—
    A soldier's grave, for thee the best ;
Then look around, and choose thy ground,
        And take thy rest.

THOMAS MOORE.

Born 1779. Died 1852.

MY BIRTHDAY.

" My birthday !"—what a different sound
    That word had in my youthful ears !
And now, each time the day comes round,
    Less and less white its mark appears !

When first our scanty years are told,
It seems like pastime to grow old ;
And, as Youth counts the shining links
    That Time around him binds so fast,
Pleased with the task, he little thinks
    How hard that chain will press at last !
Vain was the man, and false as vain,
    Who said—" Were he ordained to run
His long career of life again,
    He would do all that he *had* done.[1]
Ah ! tis not thus the voice that dwells
    In sober birthdays speaks to me ;
Far otherwise—of time it tells
    Lavished unwisely, carelessly—
Of counsel mocked—of talents, made
    Haply for high and pure designs,
But oft, like Israel's incense, laid
    Upon unholy, earthly shrines !
Of nursing many a wrong desire ;
    Of wandering after Love too far,
And taking every meteor fire,
    That crossed my pathway, for his star.—
All this it tells, and, could I trace
    The imperfect picture o'er again,
With power to add, retouch, efface
    The lights and shades, the joy and pain,
How little of the past would stay !
How quickly all should melt away—
All, but that Freedom of the Mind
    Which hath been more than wealth to me,—
Those friendships in my boyhood twined,
    And kept till now unchangingly ;
And that dear home, that saving ark,
    Where Love's true light at last I found,
Cheering within, when all grows dark,
    And comfortless, and stormy round !

DEAR HARP OF MY COUNTRY.

Dear Harp of my Country ! in darkness I found thee,
    The cold chain of silence had hung o'er thee long,
When proudly, my own Island Harp, I unbound thee,
    And gave all thy chords to light ! freedom, and song !

The warm lay of love and the light note of gladness
    Have wakened thy fondest, thy liveliest thrill ;
But, so oft hast thou echoed the deep sigh of sadness,
    That even in thy mirth it will steal from thee still.

Dear Harp of my Country ! farewell to thy numbers,
    This sweet wreath of song is the last we shall twine !

[1] Fontenelle : "Si je recomençais ma carrière, je ferai tout ce que j'ai fait."

Go, sleep with the sunshine of Fame on thy slumbers,
    Till touched by some hand less unworthy than mine.

If the pulse of the patriot, soldier, or lover,
    Have throbb'd at our lay, 'tis thy glory alone ;
I was but as the wind, passing heedlessly over,
    And all the wild sweetness I wak'd was thy own.

THIS WORLD IS ALL A FLEETING SHOW.

THIS world is all a fleeting show,
    For man's illusion given ;
The smiles of Joy, the tears of Woe,
Deceitful shine, deceitful flow,—
    There's nothing true but heaven !

And false the light on Glory's plume,
    As fading hues of Even ;
And Love, and Hope, and Beauty's bloom,
Are blossoms gathered for the tomb,—
    There's nothing bright but Heaven !

Poor wanderers of a stormy day,
    From wave to wave we're driven,
And Fancy's flash, and Reason's ray,
Serve but to light the troubled way,—
    There's nothing calm but Heaven !

THE HARP THAT ONCE THROUGH TARA'S HALLS.

THE harp that once through Tara's halls
    The soul of music shed,
Now hangs as mute on Tara's walls,
    As if that soul were fled.

So sleeps the pride of former days,
    So glory's thrill is o'er,
And hearts, that once beat high for praise,
    Now feel that pulse no more.

No more to chiefs and ladies bright
    The harp of Tara swells ;
The chord alone, that breaks at night,
    Its tale of ruin tells.

Thus Freedom now so seldom wakes,
    The only throb she gives,
Is when some heart indignant breaks,
    To show that still she lives.

THE MINSTREL-BOY.

THE Minstrel-boy to the war is gone,
    In the ranks of death you'll find him ;

His father's sword he has girded on,
  And his wild harp slung behind him.—
" Land of song ! " said the warrior bard,
  " Though all the world betrays thee,
One sword, at least, thy right shall guard,
  One faithful harp shall praise thee ! "

The Minstrel fell !—but the foeman's chain
  Could not bring his proud soul under :
The harp he loved ne'er spoke again,
  For he tore its chords asunder ;
And said, " No chains shall sully thee,
  Thou soul of love and bravery !
Thy songs were made for the brave and free,—
  They shall never sound in slavery ! "

THE MEETING OF THE WATERS.

THERE's not in the wide world a valley so sweet,
As that vale in whose bosom the bright waters meet ;
Oh ! the last rays of feeling and life must depart,
Ere the bloom of that valley shall fade from my heart !

Yet it was not that Nature had shed o'er the scene
Her purest of crystal and brightest of green ;
'Twas not her soft magic of streamlet or hill,
Oh ! no—it was something more exquisite still.

'Twas that friends, the beloved of my bosom, were near,
Who made every dear scene of enchantment more dear,
And who felt how the best charms of Nature improve,
When we see them reflected from looks that we love.

Sweet vale of Avoca ! how calm could I rest
In thy bosom of shade, with the friends I love best,
Where the storms that we feel in this cold world should
And our hearts, like thy waters, be mingled in peace.

CHARLES LAMB.

Born 1775. Died 1834.

LINES WRITTEN IN MY OWN ALBUM.

FRESH clad from heaven in robes of white,
A young probationer of light,
Thou wert, my soul, an album bright,

A spotless leaf ; but thought, and care,
And friend and foe, in foul and fair,
Have " written strange defeatures " there ;

And Time with heaviest hand of all,
Like that fierce writing on the wall,
Hath stamped sad dates—he can't recall.

And error, gilding worst designs—
Like speckled snake that strays and shines—
Betrays his path by crooked lines ;

And vice hath left his ugly blot ;
And good resolves, a moment hot,
Fairly begun—but finished not ;

And fruitless late remorse doth trace—
Like Hebrew lore a backward pace—
Her irrecoverable race.

Disjointed numbers ; sense unknit ;
Huge reams of folly ; shreds of wit ;
Compose the mingled mass of it.

My scalded eyes no longer brook
Upon this ink-blurred thing to look—
Go, shut the leaves, and clasp the book.

OLD FAMILIAR FACES.

I HAVE had playmates, I have had companions,
In my days of childhood, in my joyful school days ;
All, all are gone, the old familiar faces.

I have been laughing, I have been carousing,
Drinking late, sitting late, with my bosom cronies ;
All, all are gone, the old familiar faces.

I loved a love once, fairest among women ;
Closed are her doors on me, I must not see her—
All, all are gone, the old familiar faces.

I have a friend, a kinder friend has no man ;
Like an ingrate, I left my friend abruptly ;—
Left him, to muse on the old familiar faces.

Ghost-like I paced round the haunts of my childhood ;
Earth seemed a desert I was bound to traverse,
Seeking to find the old familiar faces.

Friend of my bosom, thou more than a brother,
Why wert not thou born in my father's dwelling?
So might we talk of the old familiar faces ;—

How some they have died, and some they have left me,
And some are taken from me ; all are departed ;
All, all are gone, the old familiar faces.

LEIGH HUNT.

Born 1784.   Died 1859.

THE FISH, THE MAN, AND THE SPIRIT.

The Man to the Fish.

You strange, astonished-looking, angle-faced,
Dreary-mouthed, gaping wretches of the sea,
Gulping salt-water everlastingly,
Cold-blooded, though with red your blood be graced,
And mute, though dwellers in the roaring waste ;
And you all shapes beside that fishy be,—
Some round, some flat, some long, all devilry,
Legless, unloving, infamously chaste :—
O scaly, slippery, wet, swift, staring wights,
What is't you do ? what life lead ? eh, dull goggles ?
How do ye vary your dull days and nights ?
How pass your Sundays ? Are ye still but joggles,
In ceaseless wash ?   Still nought but gapes, and bites,
And drinks, and stares, diversified with boggles ?

A Fish answers.

Amazing monster ! that, for aught I know,
With the first sight of thee didst make our race
For ever stare ! O, flat and shocking face,
Grimly divided from the breast below !
Thou that on dry land horribly dost go,
With a split body, and most ridiculous pace,
Prong after prong, disgracer of all grace,
Long-useless-finned, haired, upright, unwet, slow.

O breather of unbreathable, swordsharp air,
How canst exist ? how bear thyself, thou dry
And dreary sloth ! What particle canst share
Of the only blessed life,—the watery ?
I sometimes see of ye an actual *pair*
Go by, linked fin by fin ! most odiously.

The Fish turns into a Man, and then into a Spirit, and again speaks.

Indulge thy smiling scorn, if smiling still,
O man ! and loathe, but with a sort of love :
For difference must its use by difference prove,
And, in sweet clang, the spheres with music fill.
One of the spirits am I, that at his will
Live in whatever has life,—fish, eagle, dove,—
No hate, no pride, beneath nought, nor above,
A visitor of the rounds of God's sweet skill.

Man's life is warm, glad, sad, twixt loves and graves,
Boundless in hope, honoured with pangs austere,

Heaven-gazing ; and his angel-wings ho craves ;—
The fish is swift, small-needing, vague yet clear,
A cold, sweet, silver life, wrapt in round waves,
Quickened with touches of transporting fear.

ABOU BEN ADHEM AND THE ANGEL.

Abou Ben Adhem (may his tribe increase !)
Awoke one night from a deep dream of peace,
And saw, within the moonlight in his room,
Making it rich, and like a lily bloom,
An Angel, writing in a book of gold :—
Exceeding peace had made Ben Adhem bold,
And to the Presence in the room he said,
"What writest thou ?"—the Vision raised its head,
And, with a look made of all sweet accord,
Answered, "The names of those that love the Lord."
"And is mine one?" said Abou. "Nay, not so,"
Replied the Angel. Abou spoke more low,
But cheerly still ; and said, "I pray thee, then,
Write me as one that loves his fellow-men."
The Angel wrote, and vanished. The next night
It came again with a great wakening light,
And showed the names of those whom love of God had
     blessed,
And lo ! Ben Adhem's name led all the rest.

TO T. L. H., SIX YEARS OLD, DURING A SICKNESS.

Sleep breathes at last from out
     thee,
My little patient boy ;
And balmy rest about thee
Smooths off the day's annoy.
I sit me down and think
Of all thy winning ways ;
Yet almost wish, with sudden
     shrink,
That I had less to praise.

Thy sidelong pillowed meekness,
Thy thanks to all that aid,
Thy heart, in pain and weakness,
Of fancied faults afraid ;
The little trembling hand
That wipes thy quiet tears,
These, these are things that may
     demand
Dread memories for years.

Sorrows, I've had severe ones,
I will not think of now ;

And calmly 'midst my dear ones,
Have wasted with dry brow ;
But when thy fingers press
And pat my stooping head,
I cannot bear the gentleness—
The tears are in their bed.

Ah, first-born of thy mother,
When life and hope were new ;
Kind playmate of thy brother,
Thy sister, father, too ;.
My light where'er I go,
My bird when prison-bound,
My hand-in-hand companion—no,
My prayers shall hold thee
     round.

To say—"he has departed"—
"His voice—his face—is gone !"
To feel impatient-hearted,
Yet feel we must bear on
Ah, I could not endure
To whisper of such woe,

Unless I felt this sleep ensure
  That it will not be so.

Yet still he's fixed and sleeping,
  This silence too, the while—
Its very hush and creeping

Seems whispering as a smile :
Something divine and dim
Seems going by one's ear,
Like parting wings of Cherubim
Who say, "We've finished
  here."

JOHN KEATS.

Born 1795. Died 1821.

MADELINE IN HER CHAMBER.

A CASEMENT high and triple-arched there was,
All garlanded with carven imageries
Of fruits, and flowers, and bunches of knot-grass,
And diamonded with panes of quaint device,
Innumerable of stains and splendid dyes,
As are the tiger-moth's deep damasked wings ;
And in the midst, 'mong thousand heraldries,
And twilight saints, and dim emblazonings,
A shielded scutcheon blushed with blood of queens and kings

Full on this casement shone the wintry moon,
And threw warm gules on Madeline's fair breast,
As down she knelt for heaven's grace and boon ;
Rose-bloom fell on her hands, together prest,
And on her silver cross fair amethyst,
And on her hair a glory, like a saint :
She seemed a splendid angel, newly drest,
Save wings, for heaven :—Porphyro grew faint :
She knelt, so pure a thing, so free from mortal taint.

Anon his heart revives : her vespers done,
Of all its wreathed pearls her hair she frees ;
Unclasps her warmèd jewels one by one ;
Loosens her fragrant boddice ; by degrees
Her rich attire creeps rustling to her knees :
Half-hidden, like a mermaid in sea-weed.
Pensive awhile she dreams awake, and sees,
In fancy, fair St. Agnes in her bed,
But dares not look behind, or all the charm is fled.

Soon, trembling in her soft and chilly nest,
In sort of wakeful swoon, perplexed she lay,
Until the poppied warmth of sleep oppressed
Her soothed limbs, and soul fatigued away ;
Flown, like a thought, until the morrow-day ;
Blissfully havened both from joy and pain ;
Clasped like a missal where swart Paynims pray ;
Blinded alike from sunshine and from rain,
As though a rose should shut, and be a bud again.

From *The Eve of St. Agnes.*

HYPERION'S GLOOM.

But horrors, portioned to a giant nerve,
Oft made Hyperion ache. His palace bright,
Bastioned with pyramids of glowing gold,
And touched with shade of bronzed obelisks,
Glared a blood red through all its thousand courts,
Arches, and domes, and fiery galleries ;
And all its curtains of Aurorian clouds
Flushed angerly ; while sometimes eagles' wings,
Unseen before by Gods or wondering men,
Darkened the place ; and neighing steeds were heard,
Not heard before by Gods or wondering men.
Also, when he would taste the spicy wreaths
Of incense, breathed aloft from sacred hills,
Instead of sweets, his ample palate took
Savour of poisonous brass and metal sick :
And so, when harboured in the sleepy west,
After the full completion of fair day,
For rest divine upon exalted couch,
And slumber in the arms of melody,
He paced away the pleasant hours of ease
With stride colossal, on from hall to hall ;
While far within each aisle and deep recess,
His winged minions in close clusters stood,
Amazed and full of fear ; like anxious men
Who on wide plains gather in panting troops,
When earthquakes jar their battlements and towers.
Even now, while Saturn, roused from icy trance,
Went step for step with Thea through the woods,
Hyperion, leaving twilight in the rear,
Came slope upon the threshold of the west :
Then, as was wont, his palace-door flew ope
In smoothed silence, save what solemn tubes,
Blown by the serious zephyrs, gave of sweet
And wandering sounds, slow-breathed melodies ;
And like a rose in vermeil tint and shape,
In fragrance soft, and coolness to the eye,
That inlet to severe magnificence
Stood full blown, for the God to enter in.
    He entered, but he entered full of wrath ;
His flaming robes streamed out beyond his heels,
And gave a roar, as if of earthly fire,
That scared away the meek ethereal Hours
And made their dove-wings tremble. On he flared,
From stately nave to nave, from vault to vault,
Through bowers of fragrant and enwreathed light,
And diamond-paved lustrous long arcades,
Until he reached the great main cupola ;
There standing fierce beneath, he stampt his foot,
And from the basements deep to the high towers
Jarred his own golden region ; and before
The quavering thunder thereupon had ceased,

His voice leapt out, despite of godlike curb,
To this result : "O dreams of day and night !
O monstrous forms ! O effigies of pain !
O spectres busy in a cold, cold gloom !
O lank-eared Phantoms of black-weeded pools !
Why do I know ye ? why have I seen ye ? why
Is my eternal essence thus distraught
To see and to behold these horrors new?
Saturn is fallen, am I too to fall ?
Am I to leave this haven of my rest,
This cradle of my glory, this soft clime,
This calm luxuriance of blissful light,   -
These crystalline pavilions, and pure fanes,
Of all my lucent empire?   It is left
Deserted, void, nor any haunt of mine.
The blaze, the splendour, and the symmetry,
I cannot see—but darkness, death and darkness.
Even here, into my centre of repose,
The shady visions come to domineer,
Insult, and blind, and stifle up my pomp—
Fall!—No, by Tellus and her briny robes !
Over the fiery frontier of my realms
I will advance a terrible right arm
Shall scare that infant thunderer, rebel Jove,
And bid old Saturn take his throne again."

From Hyperion.

THE TITANS.

ALL eyes were on Enceladus's face,
And they beheld, while still Hyperion's name
Flew from his lips up to the vaulted rocks,
A pallid gleam across his features stern :
Not savage, for he saw full many a God
Wroth as himself.   He looked upon them all,
And in each face he saw a gleam of light,
But splendider in Saturn's, whose hoar locks
Shone like the bubbling foam about a keel
When the prow sweeps into a midnight cove.
In pale and silver silence they remained,
Till suddenly a splendour, like the morn,
Pervaded all the beetling gloomy steeps,
All the sad spaces of oblivion,
And every gulf, and every chasm old,
And every height, and every sullen depth,
Voiceless, or hoarse with loud tormented streams :
And all the everlasting cataracts,
And all the headlong torrents far and near,
Mantled before in darkness and huge shade,
Now saw the light and made it terrible.
It was Hyperion :—a granite peak
His bright feet touched, and there he staid to view
The misery his brilliance had betrayed

To the most hateful seeing of itself.
Golden his hair of short Numidian curl,
Regal his shape majestic, a vast shade
In midst of his own brightness, like the bulk
Of Memnon's image at the set of sun
To one who travels from the dusking East :
Sighs, too, as mournful as that Memnon's harp,
He uttered, while his hands, contemplative,
He pressed together, and in silence stood.
Despondence seized again the fallen Gods
At sight of the dejected King of Day,
And many hid their faces from the light :
But fierce Enceladus sent forth his eyes
Among the brotherhood ; and, at their glare,
Uprose Iäpetus, and Creüs too,
And Phorcus, sea-born, and together strode
To where he towered on his eminence.
There those four shouted forth old Saturn's name ;
Hyperion from the peak loud answered, "Saturn !"
Saturn sat near the Mother of the Gods,
In whose face was no joy, though all the Gods
Gave from their hollow throats the name of "Saturn !"

From Hyperion.

APOLLO.

Chief isle of the embowered Cyclades,
Rejoice, O Delos, with thine olives green,
And poplars, and lawn-shading palms, and beech,
In which the zephyr breathes the loudest song,
And hazels thick, dark-stemmed beneath the shade :
Apollo is once more the golden theme !
Where was he, when the Giant of the Sun
Stood bright, amid the sorrow of his peers?
Together had he left his mother fair
And his twin-sister sleeping in their bower,
And in the morning twilight wandered forth
Beside the osiers of a rivulet,
Full ankle-deep in lilies of the vale.
The nightingale had ceased, and a few stars
Were lingering in the heavens, while the thrush
Began calm-throated.   Throughout all the isle
There was no covert, no retired cave
Unhaunted by the murmurous noise of waves,
Though scarcely heard in many a green recess.
He listened, and he wept, and his bright tears
Went trickling down the golden bow he held.—
Thus with half-shut suffused eyes he stood,
While from beneath some cumbrous boughs hard by
With solemn step an awful Goddess came,
And there was purport in her looks for him,
Which he with eager guess began to read
Perplexed, the while melodiously he said :
" How camest thou over the unfooted sea ?

Or bath that antique mien and robed form
Moved in these vales invisible till now?
Sure I have heard those vestments sweeping o'er
The fallen leaves, when I have sat alone
In cool mid forest. Surely I have traced
The rustle of those ample skirts about
These grassy solitudes, and seen the flowers
Lift up their heads, as still the whisper passed.
Goddess ! I have beheld those eyes before,
And their eternal calm, and all that face,
Or I have dreamed."—"Yes," said the supreme shape.

From Hyperion.

LA BELLE DAME SANS MERCY.

Ah, what can ail thee, wretched wight,
   Alone and palely loitering?
The sedge is withered from the lake,
   And no birds sing.

Ah, what can ail thee, wretched wight,
   So haggard and so woe-begone?
The squirrel's granary is full,
   And the harvest's done.

I see a lily on thy brow,
   With anguish moist and fever-dew;
And on thy cheek a fading rose
   Fast withereth too.

I met a Lady in the meads,
   Full beautiful, a fairy's child;
Her hair was long, her foot was light,
   And her eyes were wild.

I set her on my pacing steed,
   And nothing else saw all day long;
For sideways would she lean, and sing
   A fairy's song.

I made a garland for her head,
   And bracelets too, and fragrant zone:
She looked at me as she did love,
   And made sweet moan.

She found me roots of relish sweet,
   And honey wild, and manna dew;
And sure in language strange she said,
   "I love thee true."

She took me to her elfin grot,
   And there she gazed and sighèd deep,
And there I shut her wild sad eyes—
   So kissed to sleep.

And there we slumbered on the moss,
 And there I dreamed, ah, woe betide,
The latest I had ever dreamed
 On the cold hill-side.

I saw pale kings, and princes too,
 Pale warriors, death-pale were they all,
Who cried, "La belle dame sans mercy
 Hath thee in thrall!"

I saw their starved lips in the gloom
 With horrid warning gapèd wide,
And I awoke and found me here,
 On the cold hill-side.

And this is why I sojourn here,
 Alone and palely loitering,
Though the sedge is withered from the lake,
 And no birds sing.

ON FIRST LOOKING INTO CHAPMAN'S HOMER.

Much have I travelled in the realms of gold,
And many goodly states and kingdoms seen:
Round many western islands have I been
Which bards in fealty to Apollo hold.
Oft of one wide expanse had I been told
That deep-browed Homer ruled as his demesne;
Yet did I never breathe its pure serene
Till I heard Chapman speak out loud and bold:
Then felt I like some watcher of the skies
When a new planet swims into his ken;
Or like stout Cortez when with eagle eyes
He stared at the Pacific—and all his men
Looked at each other with a wild surmise—
Silent, upon a peak in Darien.

ON LEAVING SOME FRIENDS AT AN EARLY HOUR.

Give me a golden pen, and let me lean
On heaped-up flowers, in regions clear, and far;
Bring me a tablet whiter than a star,
Or hand of hymning angel, when 'tis seen
The silver strings of heavenly harp atween:
And let there glide by many a pearly car,
Pink robes, and wavy hair, and diamond jar,
And half discovered wings, and glances keen.
The while let music wander round my ears,
And as it reaches each delicious ending,
Let me write down a line of glorious tone,
And full of many wonders of the spheres:
For what a height my spirit is contending!
'Tis not content to be so soon alone.

PERCY BYSSHE SHELLEY.

Born 1792. Died 1822.

THE POET.

There was a Poet whose untimely tomb
No human hand with pious reverence reared,
But the charmed eddies of autumnal winds
Built o'er his mouldering bones a pyramid
Of mouldering leaves in the waste wilderness.
A lovely youth, no mourning maiden decked
With weeping flowers or votive cypress-wreath
The lone couch of his everlasting sleep :
Gentle and brave and generous, no lorn bard
Breathed o'er his dark fate one melodious sigh :
He lived, he died, he sang, in solitude.
Strangers have wept to hear his passionate notes ;
And virgins, as unknown he passed, have pined
And wasted for fond love of his wild eyes.
The fire of those soft orbs has ceased to burn,
And Silence, too enamoured of that voice,
Locks its mute music in her rugged cell.

By solemn vision and bright silver dream
His infancy was nurtured.   Every sight
And sound from the vast earth and ambient air
Sent to his heart its choicest impulses.
The fountains of divine philosophy
Fled not his thirsting lips : and all of great
Or good or lovely which the sacred past
In truth or fable consecrates he felt
And knew.   When early youth had passed, he left
His cold fireside and alienated home,
To seek strange truths in undiscovered lands.
Many a wide waste and tangled wilderness
Had lured his fearless steps ; and he has brought
With his sweet voice and eyes, from savage men,
His rest and food.   Nature's most secret steps
He like her shadow has pursued, where'er
The red volcano overcanopies
Its fields of snow, and pinnacles of ice
With burning smoke ; or where bitumen-lakes
On black bare pointed islets ever beat
With sluggish surge ; or where the secret caves
Rugged and dark, winding among the springs
Of fire and poison, inaccessible
To avarice or pride, their starry domes
Of diamond and of gold expand above
Numberless and immeasurable halls,
Frequent with crystal column, and clear shrines

Of pearl, and thrones radiant with chrysolite.
Nor had that scene of ampler majesty
Than gems or gold, the varying roof of heaven
And the green earth, lost in his heart its claims
To love and wonder. He would linger long
In lonesome vales, making the wild his home ;
Until the doves and squirrels would partake
From his innocuous hand his bloodless food,
Lured by the gentle meaning of his looks,—
And the wild antelope, that starts whene'er
The dry leaf rustles in the brake, suspend
Her timid steps, to gaze upon a form
More graceful than her own.
                              His wandering step,
Obedient to high thoughts, has visited
The awful ruins of the days of old
Athens and Tyre, and Balbec, and the wate
Where stood Jerusalem, the fallen towers
Of Babylon, the eternal pyramids,
Memphis and Thebes, and whatsoe'er of strange,
Sculptured on alabaster obelisk,
Or jasper tomb, or mutilated sphinx,   ·
Dark Ethiopia on her desert hills
Conceals. Among the ruined temples there,
Stupendous columns, and wild images
Of more than man, where marble demons watch
The zodiac's brazen mystery, and dead men
Hang their mute thoughts on the mute walls around,
He lingered, poring on memorials
Of the world's youth ; through the long burning day
Gazed on those speechless shapes ; nor when the moon
Filled the mysterious halls with floating shades,
Suspended he that task, but ever gazed
And gazed, till meaning on his vacant mind
Flashed like strong inspiration, and he saw
The thrilling secrets of the birth of time.
                    From *Alastor, or the Spirit of Solitude.*

ADONIAS ; AN ELEGY ON THE DEATH OF JOHN KEATS.

I.

I WEEP for Adonais—he is dead !
Oh weep for Adonais ! though our tears
Thaw not the frost which binds so dear a head !
And thou, sad Hour selected from all years
To mourn our loss, roused thy obscure compeers,
And teach them thine own sorrow ! Say, "With me
Died Adonais ! Till our future dares
Forget the past, his fate and fame shall be
An echo and a light unto eternity.

II.

Where wert thou, mighty Mother, when he lay,
When thy son lay, pierced by the shaft which flies
In darkness? Where was lorn Urania
When Adonais died? With veilèd eyes,
Mid listening Echoes. in her paradise
She sate, while one with soft enamoured breath,
Rekindled all the fading melodies
With which, like flowers that mock the corse beneath,
He had adorned and hid the coming bulk of Death.

III.

Oh weep for Adonais—he is dead !
Wake, melancholy Mother, wake and weep !—
Yet wherefore ? Quench within their burning bed
Thy fiery tears, and let thy loud heart keep,
Like his, a mute and uncomplaining sleep ;
For he is gone where all things wise and fair
Descend.   Oh dream not that the amorous deep
Will yet restore him to the vital air ;
Death feeds on his mute voice, and laughs at our despair.

*   *   *   *   *   *

XXII.

He will awake no more, oh never more !
"Wake thou," cried Misery, " childless Mother ! Rise
Out of thy sleep, and slake in thy heart's core
A wound more fierce than his, with tears and sighs."
And all the Dreams that watched Urania's eyes,
And all the Echoes whom their Sister's song
Had held in holy silence, cried "Arise ;"
Swift as a thought by the snake Memory stung,
From her ambrosial rest the fading Splendour sprung.

XXIII.

She rose like an autumnal Night that springs
Out of the east, and follows wild and drear
The golden Day, which on eternal wings
Even as a ghost abandoning a bier,
Has left the Earth a corpse.   Sorrow and fear
So struck, so roused, so rapt, Urania ;
So saddened round her like an atmosphere
Of stormy mist ; so swept her on her way,
Even to the mournful place where Adonais lay.

XXIV.

Out of her secret paradise she sped,
Through camps and cities rough with stone and steel
And human hearts, which to her aery tread
Yielding not, wounded the invisible

Palms of her tender feet where'er they fell.
And barbèd tongues, and thoughts more sharp than they,
Rent the soft form they never could repel,
Whose sacred blood, like the young flowers of May,
Paved with eternal flowers that undeserving way.

XXV.

In the death-chamber for a moment Death,
Shamed by the presence of that living Might,
Blushed to annihilation, and the breath
Revisited those lips, and life's pale light
Flashed through those limbs so late her dear delight.
" Leave me not wild and drear and comfortless,
As silent lightning leaves the starless night !
Leave me not !" cried Urania. Her distress
Roused Death : Death rose and smiled, and met her vain
    caress.

XXVI.

" Stay yet awhile ! speak to me once again !
Kiss me, so long but as a kiss may live !
And in my heartless breast and burning brain
That word, that kiss, shall all thoughts else survive,
With food of saddest memory kept alive,
Now thou art dead, as if it were a part
Of thee, my Adonais ! I would give
All that I am, to be as now thou art :—
But I am chained to Time, and cannot thence depart.

XXVII.

" O gentle child, beautiful as thou wert,
Why didst thou leave the trodden paths of men
Too soon, and with weak hands though mighty heart
Dare the unpastured dragon in his den ?
Defenceless as thou wert, oh where was then
Wisdom the mirrored shield, or Scorn the spear ?—
Or, hadst thou waited the full cycle when
Thy spirit should have filled its crescent sphere,
The monsters of life's waste had fled from thee like deer.

XXVIII.

" The herded wolves bold only to pursue ;
The obscene ravens clamorous o'er the dead ;
The vultures to the conqueror's banner true,
Who feed where Desolation first has fed,
And whose wings rain contagion,—how they fled
When, like Apollo from his golden bow,
The Pythian of the age one arrow sped
And smiled !—The spoilers tempt no second blow,
They fawn on the proud feet that spurn them lying low.

XXIX.

"The sun comes forth, and many reptiles spawn ;
He sets, and each ephemeral insect then
Is gathered into death without a dawn,
And the immortal stars awake again.
So is it in the world of living men :
A godlike mind soars forth, in its delight
Making earth bare and veiling heaven ; and when
It sinks, the swarms that dimmed or shared its light
Leave to its kindred lamps the spirit's awful night."

XXX.

Thus ceased she : and the Mountain shepherds [1] came,
Their garland's sere, their magic mantles rent ;
The Pilgrim of Eternity, whose fame
Over his living head like heaven is bent,
An early but enduring monument ;
Came, veiling all the lightnings of his song
In sorrow.   From her wilds Ierne sent
The sweetest lyrist of her saddest wrong,
And love taught grief to fall like music from his tongue.

XXXI.

Midst others of less note came one frail form,
A phantom among men, companionless
As the last cloud of an expiring storm,
Whose thunder is its knell.   He, as I guess,
Had gazed on Nature's naked loveliness
Actæon-like ; and now he fled astray
With feeble steps o'er the world's wilderness,
And his own thoughts along that rugged way
Pursued like raging hounds their father and their prey.

XXXII.

A pard-like Spirit beautiful and swift—
A love in desolation masked—a power
Girt round with weakness ; it can scarce uplift
The weight of the superincumbent hour.
It is a dying lamp, a falling shower,
A breaking billow ;—even whilst we speak
Is it not broken?   On the withering flower
The killing sun shines brightly ; on a cheek
The life can burn in blood even while the heart may bre

XXXIII.

His head was bound with pansies overblown,
And faded violets, white and pied and blue ;
And a light spear topped with a cypress-cone,
Round whose rude shaft dark ivy-tresses grew

[1] The poets referred to in stanzas xxx.-xxxiv. are Byron, Moore, and Sh himself.

Yet dripping with the forest's noonday dew,
Vibrated, as the ever-beating heart
Shook the weak hand that grasped it. Of that crew
He came the last, neglected and apart ;
A herd-abandoned deer struck by the hunter's dart.

XXXIV.

All stood aloof, and at his partial moan
Smiled through their tears. Well knew that gentle band
Who in another's fate now wept his own ;
As in the accents of an unknown land
He sang new sorrow, sad Urania scanned
The stranger's mien, and murmured "Who art thou?"
He answered not, but with a sudden hand
Made bare his branded and ensanguined brow,
Which was like Cain's or Christ's—oh that it should be so !

*　　*　　*　　*　　*　　*

XXXIX.

Peace, Peace ! he is not dead, he doth not sleep !
He hath awakened from the dream of life.
'Tis we who, lost in stormy visions, keep
With phantoms an unprofitable strife,
And in mad trance strike with our spirit's knife
Invulnerable nothings. *We* decay
Like corpses in a charnel ; fear and grief
Convulse us and consume us day by day,
And cold hopes swarm like worms within our living clay.

XL.

He has outsoared the shadow of our night ;
Envy and calumny and hate and pain,
And that unrest which men miscall delight,
Can touch him not and torture not again ;
From the contagion of the world's slow stain
He is secure ; and now can never mourn
A heart grown cold, a head grown grey, in vain—
Nor, when the spirit's self has ceased to burn,
With sparkless ashes load an unlamented urn.

XLI.

He lives, he wakes—'tis Death is dead, not he ;
Mourn not for Adonais.—Thou young Dawn,
Turn all thy dew to splendour, for from thee
The spirit thou lamentest is not gone !
Ye caverns and ye forests, cease to moan !
Cease, ye faint flowers and fountains ! and, thou Air
Which like a mourning-veil thy scarf hadst thrown
O'er the abandoned Earth, now leave it bare
Even to the joyous stars which smile on its despair.

XLII.

He is made one with Nature. There is heard
His voice in all her music ; from the moan
Of thunder, to the song of night's sweet bird.
He is a presence to be felt and known
In darkness and in light, from herb and stone,—
Spreading itself where'er that power may move
Which has withdrawn his being to its own,
Which wields the World with never-wearied love,
Sustains it from beneath, and kindles it above.

XLIII.

He is a portion of the loveliness
Which once he made more lovely. He doth bear
His part, while the One Spirit's plastic stress
Sweeps through the dull dense world ; compelling there
All new successions to the forms they wear ;
Torturing the unwilling dross, that checks its flight,
To its own likeness, as each mass may bear ;
And bursting in its beauty and its might
From trees and beasts and men into the heavens light.

XLIV.

The splendours of the firmament of time
May be eclipsed, but are extinguished not ;
Like stars to their appointed height thy climb,
And death is a low mist which cannot blot
The brightness it may veil. When lofty thought
Lifts a young heart above its mortal lair,
And love and life contend in it for what
Shall be its earthly doom, the dead live there,
And move like winds of light on dark and stormy air.

XLV.

The inheritors of unfulfilled renown
Rose from their thrones, built beyond mortal thought
Far in the unapparent.   Chatterton
Rose pale, his solemn agony had not
Yet faded from him : Sidney as he fought,
And as he fell, and as he lived and loved,
Sublimely mild, a spirit without spot,
Arose ; and Lucan by his death approved ;—
Oblivion as they rose shrank like a thing reproved.

XLVI.

And many more, whose names on earth are dark,
But whose transmitted effluence cannot die
So long as fire outlives the parent spark,
Rose, robed in dazzling immortality.
"Thou art become as one of us," they cry ;
"It was for thee you kingless sphere has long
Swung blind in unascending majesty,

Silent alone amid an heaven of song.
Assume thy wingèd throne, thou Vesper of our throng!"

* * * * * * *

LII.

The One remains, the many change and pass ;
Heaven's light for ever shines, earth's shadows fly ;
Life, like a dome of many-coloured glass,
Stains the white radiance of eternity,
Until Death tramples it to fragments.—Die,
If thou wouldst be with that which thou dost seek !
Follow where all is fled !—Rome's azure sky,
Flowers, ruins, statues, music, words, are weak
The glory they transfuse with fitting truth to speak.

LIII.

Why linger, why turn back, why shrink, my heart ?
Thy hopes are gone before : from all things here
They have departed ; thou shouldst now depart.
A light is past from the revolving year,
And man and woman ; and what still is dear
Attracts to crush, repels to make thee wither.
The soft sky smiles, the low wind whispers near :
'Tis Adonais calls ! Oh hasten thither !
No more let life divide what death can join together.

LIV.

That light whose smile kindles the universe,
That beauty in which all things work and move,
That benediction which the eclipsing curse
Of birth can quench not, that sustaining Love
Which, through the web of being blindly wove
By man and beast and earth and air and sea,
Burns bright or dim, as each are mirrors of
The fire for which all thirst, now beams on me,
Consuming the last clouds of cold mortality.

LV.

The breath whose might I have invoked in song
Descends on me ; my spirit's bark is driven
Far from.the shore, far from the trembling throng
Whose sails were never to the tempest given.
The massy earth and spherèd skies are riven !
I am borne darkly, fearfully afar !
Whilst, burning through the inmost veil of heaven,
The soul of Adonais, like a star,
Beacons from the abode where the Eternal are.

THE CLOUD.

I.

I BRING fresh showers for the thirsting flowers
    From the seas and the streams ;
I bear light shade for the leaves when laid
    In their noonday dreams.
From my wings are shaken the dews that waken
    The sweet buds every one,
When rocked to rest on their Mother's breast,
    As she dances about in the sun.
I wield the flail of the lashing hail,
    And whiten the green plains under ;
And then again I dissolve it in rain,
    And laugh as I pass in thunder.

II.

I sift the snow on the mountains below,
    And their great pines groan aghast ;
And all the night 'tis my pillow white,
    While I sleep in the arms of the Blast.
Sublime on the towers of my skiey bowers
    Lightning my pilot sits ;
In a cavern under is fettered the Thunder,
    It struggles and howls at fits.
Over earth and ocean with gentle motion
    This pilot is guiding me,
Lured by the love of the Genii that move
    In the depths of the purple sea ;
Over the rills and the crags and the hills,
    Over the lakes and the plains,
Wherever he dream under mountain or stream
    The Spirit he loves remains ;
And I all the while bask in heaven's blue smile,
    Whilst he is dissolving in rains.

III.

The sanguine Sunrise, with his meteor eyes,
    And his burning plumes outspread,
Leaps on the back of my sailing rack,
    When the morning star shines dead.
As on the jag of a mountain-crag
    Which an earthquake rocks and swings
As eagle alit one moment may sit
    In the light of its golden wings.
And, when Sunset may breathe, from the lit sea beneath,
    Its ardours of rest and of love,
And the crimson pall of eve may fall
    From the depth of heaven above,
With wings folded I rest on mine airy nest,
    As still as a brooding dove.

IV.

That orbèd maiden with white fire laden,
  Whom mortals call the Moon,
Glides glimmering o'er my fleece-like floor
  By the midnight breezes strewn ;
And wherever the beat of her unseen feet,
  Which only the angels hear,
May have broken the woof of my tent's thin roof,
  The Stars peep behind her and peer.
And I laugh to see them whirl and flee
  Like a swarm of golden bees,
When I widen the rent in my wind-built tent,—
  Till the calm rivers, lakes, and seas,
Like strips of the sky fallen through me on high,
  Are each paved with the moon and these.

V.

I bind the Sun's throne with a burning zone,
  And the Moon's with a girdle of pearl ;
The volcanoes are dim, and the Stars reel and swim,
  When the Whirlwinds my banner unfurl.
From cape to cape, with a bridge-like shape,
  Over a torrent sea,
Sunbeam-proof, I hang like a roof ;
  The mountains its columns be.
The triumphal arch through which I march,
  With hurricane, fire, and snow,
When the Powers of the air are chained to my chair,
  In the million-coloured bow ;
The sphere-fire above its soft colours wove,
  While the moist Earth was laughing below.

VI.

I am the daughter of Earth and Water,
  And the nursling of the Sky ;
I pass through the pores of the ocean and shores ;
  I change, but I cannot die.
For after the rain, when with never a stain
  The pavilion of heaven is bare,
And the winds and sunbeams with their convex gleams
  Build up the blue dome of air,
I silently laugh at my own cenotaph—
  And out of the caverns of rain,
Like a child from the womb, like a ghost from the tomb,
  I rise, and unbuild it again.

ODE TO THE WEST WIND.

O WILD West Wind, thou breath of Autumn's being,
Thou, from whose unseen presence the leaves dead
Are driven, like ghosts from an enchanter fleeing,
Yellow, and black, and pale, and hectic red,

Pestilence-stricken multitudes ! O thou,
Who chariotest to their dark wintry bed
The wingèd seeds, where they lie cold and low,
Each like a corpse within its grave, until
Thine azure sister of the Spring shall blow
Her clarion o'er the dreaming earth, and fill
(Driving sweet buds like flocks to feed in air)
With living hues and odours plain and hill :
Wild Spirit, which art moving everywhere ;
Destroyer and Preserver ; hear, O hear !

*   *   *   *   *   *

Thou who didst waken from his summer-dreams
The blue Mediterranean, where he lay,
Lulled by the coil of his crystalline streams,
Beside a pumice isle in Baiæ's bay,
And saw in sleep old palaces and towers
Quivering within the wave's intenser day,
All overgrown with azure moss and flowers
So sweet, the sense faints picturing them ! Thou
For whose path the Atlantic's level powers
Cleave themselves into chasms, while far below
The sea-blooms and the oozy woods which wear
The sapless foliage of the ocean, know
Thy voice, and suddenly grow gray with fear,
And tremble and despoil themselves : O hear !

If I were a dead leaf thou mightest bear ;
If I were a swift cloud to fly with thee ;
A wave to pant beneath thy power, and share
The impulse of thy strength, only less free
Than thou, O uncontrollable ! If even
I were as in my boyhood, and could be
The comrade of thy wanderings over heaven,
As then, when to outstrip the skyey speed
Scarce seemed a vision,—I would ne'er have striven
As thus with thee in prayer in my sore need.
Oh ! lift me as a wave, a leaf, a cloud !
I fall upon the thorns of life ! I bleed !
A heavy weight of hours has chained and bowed
One too like thee :—tameless, and swift, and proud.

Make me thy lyre, even as the forest is :
What if my leaves are falling like its own ?
The tumult of thy mighty harmonies
Will take from both a deep autumnal tone,
Sweet though in sadness. Be thou, Spirit fierce,
My spirit ! Be thou me, impetuous one !
Drive my dead thoughts over the universe
Like withered leaves to quicken a new birth ·
And, by the incantation of this verse,
Scatter, as from an unextinguished hearth

Ashes and sparks, my words among mankind !
Be through my lips to unawakened earth
The trumpet of a prophecy ! O Wind,
If Winter comes, can Spring be far behind ?

STANZAS WRITTEN IN DEJECTION NEAR NAPLES.

THE sun is warm, the sky is clear,
    The waves are dancing fast and bright,
Blue isles and snowy mountains wear
    The purple noon's transparent light :
The breath of the moist air is light
    Around its unexpanded buds ;
Like many a voice of one delight,
    The winds, the birds, the ocean-floods,
The City's voice itself is soft like Solitude's.

I see the Deep's untrampled floor
    With green and purple sea-weeds strown ;
I see the waves upon the shore,
    Like light dissolved in star-showers, thrown :
I sit upon the sands alone ;
    The lightning of the noontide ocean
Is flashing round me, and a tone
    Arises from its measured motion—
How sweet ! did any heart now share in my emotion.

Alas ! I have nor hope nor health,
    Nor peace within nor calm around,
Nor that content, surpassing wealth,
    The sage in meditation found,
And walked with inward glory crowned—
    Nor fame, nor power, nor love, nor leisure ;
Others I see whom these surround—
    Smiling they live, and call life pleasure ;—
To me that cup has been dealt in another measure.

Yet now despair itself is mild,
    Even as the winds and waters are ;
I could lie down like a tired child,
    And weep away the life of care
Which I have borne, and yet must bear,
    Till death like sleep might steal on me,
And I might feel in the warm air
    My cheek grow cold, and hear the sea
Breathe o'er my dying brain its last monotony.

Some might lament that I were cold,
    As I when this sweet day is gone,
Which my lost heart, too soon grown old,
    Insults with this untimely moan ;
They might lament—for I am one
    Whom men love not,—and yet regret ;
Unlike this day, which, when the sun
    Shall on its stainless glory set,
Will linger, though enjoyed, like joy in memory yet.

TO ——

Music, when soft voices die,
Vibrates in the memory ;
Odours, when sweet violets sicken,
Live within the sense they quicken ;

Rose-leaves, when the rose is dead,
Are heaped for the belovèd's bed ;
And so thy thoughts, when thou art gone,
Love itself shall slumber on.

FELICIA HEMANS.

Born 1793. Died 1835.

A BALLAD OF RONCESVALLES.

Thou hast not been with the festal throng
  At the pouring of the wine,
Men bear not from the hall of song
  So dark a mien as thine !
    There's blood upon thy shield,
    There's dust upon thy plume,
'Thou that hast brought from some disastrous field
    That brow of wrath and gloom.''

''And is there blood upon my shield !
  Maiden, it well may be !
We have sent the streams from our battle-field
  All darkened to the sea !
    We have given the founts a stain
    Midst our woods of ancient pine ;
And the ground is wet—but not with rain,
    Deep dyed—but not with wine.

''The ground is wet—but not with rain ;
  We have been in war array,
And the noblest blood of Christian Spain
  Hath bathed her soil to-day.
    I have seen the strong man die,
    And the stripling meet his fate,
Where the mountain winds go sounding by
    In the Roncesvalles' Strait.

''In the gloomy Roncesvalles' Strait
  There are helms and lances cleft ;
And they that moved at morn elate
  On a bed of heath are left !-

There's many a fair young face
  Which the war-steed hath gone o'er ;
At many a board there is kept a place
  For those those that come no more !"

" Alas for love, for woman's breast,
  If woe like this must be !
Hast thou seen a youth with an eagle crest
  And a white plume waving free ?
    With his proud quick-flashing eye,
      And his mien of kingly state,
Doth he come from where the swords flashed high
  In the Roncesvalles' Strait?"

"In the gloomy Roncesvalles' Strait
  I saw, and marked him well ;
For nobly on his steed he sate
  When the pride of manhood fell.
    But it is not youth that turns
      From the field of spears again;
For the boy's high heart too wildly burns
  Till it rests among the slain."

" Thou canst not say that *he* lies low,
  The lovely and the brave ?
Oh none could look on his joyous brow
  And think upon his grave !
    Dark, dark perchance the day
      Hath been with valour's fate ;
But he is on his homeward way
  From the Roncesvalles' Strait.

" There is dust upon his joyous brow,
  And o'er his graceful head,
And the war-horse will not wake him now,
  Though it browse his greensward bed.
    I have seen the stripling die,
      And the strong man meet his fate, ·
Where the mountain winds go sounding by,
  In the Roncesvalles' Strait."

THE HOMES OF ENGLAND.

THE stately homes of England,
  How beautiful they stand,
Amidst their tall ancestral trees,
  O'er all the pleasant land !
The deer across their greensward bound
  Through shade and sunny gleam,
And the swan glides past them with the sound
  Of some rejoicing stream.

The merry homes of England—
  Around their hearths by night,

What gladsome looks of household love
 Meet in the ruddy light !
There woman's voice flows forth in song
 Or childhood's tale is told ;
And lips move tunefully along
 Some glorious page of old.

The blessed homes of England,
 How softly on their bowers
Is laid the holy quietness
 That breathes from Sabbath hours !
Solemn, yet sweet, the church bells' chime
 Floats through their woods at morn,
All other sounds in that still time
 Of breeze and leaf are born.

The cottage homes of England !
 By thousands on her plains,
They are smiling o'er the silvery brooks,
 And round the hamlet fanes.
Through glowing orchards forth they peep,
 Each from its nook of leaves,
And fearless there the lowly sleep,
 As the bird beneath their eaves.

The free fair homes of England !
 Long, long to hut and hall,
May hearts of native proof be reared
 To guard each hallowed wall.
And green for ever be her groves,
 And bright the flowery sod,
Where first the child's glad spirit loves
 Its country and its God.

A DIRGE.

CALM on the bosom of thy God,
 Fair spirit, rest thee now !
E'en while with ours thy footsteps trod
 His seal was on thy brow.

Dust, to its narrow house beneath !
 Soul, to its place on high !
They that have seen thy look in death
 No more may fear to die.

THE GRAVES OF A HOUSEHOLD.

THEY grew in beauty side by side,
 They filled one home with glee !
Their graves are severed far and wide,
 By mountain, stream, and sea.

The same fond mother bent at night
  O'er each fair sleeping brow :
She had each folded flower in sight—
  Where are those dreamers now ?

One 'midst the forests of the west,
  By a dark stream is laid—
The Indian knows his place of rest,
  Far in the cedar shade.

The sea, the blue lone sea, hath one—
  He lies where pearls lie deep :
He was the loved of all, yet none
  O'er his low bed may weep.

One sleeps where southern vines are drest
  Above the noble slain !
He wrapt his colours round his breast
  On a blood-red field of Spain.

And one—o'er *her* the myrtle showers
  Its leaves, by soft winds fanned ;.
She faded 'midst Italian flowers—
  The last of that bright band.

And parted thus they rest who played
  Beneath the same green tree ;
Whose voices mingled as they prayed
  Around one parent knee !

They that with smiles lit up the hall,
  And cheered with song the hearth'!—
Alas, for love ! if *thou* wert all,
  And naught beyond, O earth !

CASABIANCA.

THE boy stood on the burning deck,
  Whence all but he had fled ;
The flame that lit the battle's wreck,
  Shone round him o'er the dead.
Yet beautiful and bright he stood,
  As born to rule the storm ;
A creature of heroic blood,
  A proud, though child-like form !

The flames rolled on—he would not go
  Without his father's word ;—
That father, faint in death below,
  His voice no longer heard.
He called aloud : "Say, father, say
  If yet my task is done !"—
He knew not that the chieftain lay
  Unconscious of his son.

"Speak, father!" once again he cried,
    "If I may yet be gone !"
And but the booming shots replied,
    And fast the flames rolled on.
Upon his brow he felt their breath,
    And in his waving hair,
And looked from that lone post of death,
    In still yet brave despair ;

And shouted but once more aloud,
    "My father ! must I stay ?"
While o'er him fast, through sail and shroud,
    The wreathing fires made way.
They wrapt the ship in splendour wild,
    They caught the flag on high,
And streamed above the gallant child,
    Like banners in the sky.

There came a burst of thunder sound,—
    The boy !—oh, where was he ?
Ask of the winds, that far around
    With fragments strewed the sea,—
With mast, and helm, and pennon fair,
    That well had borne their part ;
But the noblest thing that perished there,
    Was that young faithful heart !

THOMAS CAMPBELL.

Born 1777. Died 1844.

YE MARINERS OF ENGLAND.

Ye mariners of England !
    That guard our native seas,
Whose flag has braved a thousand years
    The battle and the breeze !
Your glorious standard launch again
    To match another foe,
And sweep through the deep,
    While the stormy winds do blow ;
While the battle rages loud and long,
    And the stormy winds do blow.

The spirits of your fathers
    Shall start from every wave !—
For the deck it was their field of fame,
    And Ocean was their grave :
Where Blake and mighty Nelson fell
    Your manly hearts shall glow,

As ye sweep through the deep,
  While the stormy winds do blow,
While the battle rages loud and long,
  And the stormy winds do blow.

Britannia needs no bulwark,
  No towers along the steep :
Her march is o' er the mountain waves,
  Her home is on the deep.
With thunders from her native oak
  She quells the floods below—
As they roar on the shore,
  When the stormy winds do blow ;
When the battle rages loud and long,
  And the stormy winds do blow.

The meteor flag of England
  Shall yet terrific burn,
Till danger's troubled night depart
  And the star of peace return.
Till then, ye ocean-warriors !
  Our song and feast shall flow
To the fame of your name,
  When the storm has ceased to blow ;
When the fiery fight is heard no more,
  And the storm has ceased to blow.

THE BATTLE OF THE BALTIC.

Of Nelson and the North
Sing the glorious day's renown,
When to battle fierce came forth
All the might of Denmark's crown,
And her arms along the deep proudly shone :
By each gun the lighted brand
In a bold determined hand,
And the Prince of all the land
Led them on.

Like leviathans afloat
Lay their bulwarks on the brine,
While the sign of battle flew
On the lofty British line ;
It was ten of April morn by the chime ;
As they drifted on their path,
There was silence deep as death,
And the boldest held his breath
For a time.

But the might of England flushed
To anticipate the scene ;
And her van the fleeter rushed
O'er the deadly space between.—
" Hearts of oak !" our captain cried ; when each gun
From its adamantine lips

Spread a death-shade round the ships,
Like the hurricane eclipse
Of the sun.

Again ! again ! again !
And the havoc did not slack,
Till a feeble cheer the Dane
To our cheering sent us back ;—
Their shots along the deep slowly boom : —
Then ceased—and all is wail,
As they strike the shattered sail,
Or, in conflagration pale,
Light the gloom.

Out spoke the victor then,
As he hailed them o'er the wave ;
" Ye are brothers ! ye are men !
And we conquer but to save ;
So peace instead of death let us bring :
But yield, proud foe, thy fleet
With the crews at England's feet,
And make submission meet
To our King."

Then Denmark blest our chief,
That he gave her wounds repose ;
And the sounds of joy and grief
From her people wildly rose,
As death withdrew his shades from the day ;
While the sun looked smiling bright
O'er a wide and woeful sight,
Where the fires of funeral light
Died away.

Now joy, old England, raise
For the tidings of thy might,
By the festal cities' blaze,
While the wine cup shines in light ;
And yet amid that joy and uproar,
Let us think of them that sleep,
Full many a fathom deep,
By thy wild and stormy steep,
Elsinore !

Brave hearts ! to Britain's pride
Once so faithful and so true,
On the deck of fame that died,
With the gallant good Riou,—
Soft sigh the winds of heaven o'er their grave !
While the billow mournful rolls,
And the mermaid's song condoles,
Singing glory to the souls
Of the brave !

HOHENLINDEN.

On Linden, when the sun was low,
All bloodless lay the untrodden snow ;
And dark as winter was the flow
    Of Iser, rolling rapidly.

But Linden saw another sight,
When the drum beat at dead of night,
Commanding fires of death to light
    The darkness of her scenery.

By torch and trumpet fast arrayed,
Each horseman drew his battle-blade,
And furious every charger neighed
    To join the dreadful revelry.

Then shook the hills, with thunder riven :
Then rushed the steed, to battle driven ;
And, louder than the bolts of Heaven,
    Far flashed the red artillery.

But redder yet that light shall glow
On Linden's hills of crimsoned snow,
And bloodier yet the torrent flow
    Of Iser, rolling rapidly.

'Tis morn ; but scarce yon level sun
Can pierce the war-clouds, rolling dun,
Where furious Frank and fiery Hun
    Shout in their sulphurous canopy.

The combat deepens. On, ye brave,
Who rush to glory, or the grave !
Wave, Munich, all thy banners wave,
    And charge with all thy chivalry !

Few, few shall part, where many meet ;
The snow shall be their winding-sheet ;
And every turf beneath their feet
    Shall be a soldier's sepulchre.

THE SOLDIER'S DREAM.

Our bugles sang truce, for the night-cloud had lowered
And the sentinel stars set their watch in the sky ;
And thousands had sunk on the ground overpowered,
The weary to sleep, and the wounded to die.

When reposing that night on my pallet of straw,
By the wolf-scaring fagot that guarded the slain,
At the dead of the night a sweet vision I saw,
And thrice ere the morning I dreamed it again.

Methought from the battle-field's dreadful array
Far, far I had roamed on a desolate track :
'Twas Autumn—and sunshine arose on the way
To the home of my fathers, that welcomed me back.

I flew to the pleasant fields traversed so oft
In life's morning march, when my bosom was young ;
I heard my own mountain goats bleating aloft,
And knew the sweet strain that the corn-reapers sung.

Then pledged we the wine-cup, and fondly I swore
From my home and my weeping friends never to part ;
My little ones kissed me a thousand times o'er,
And my wife sobbed aloud in her fulness of heart.

"Stay, stay with us,—rest ; thou art weary and worn !"
And fain was their war-broken soldier to stay ;—
But sorrow returned with the dawning of morn,
And the voice in my dreaming ear melted away.

THOMAS HOOD.

Born 1799. Died 1845.

THE DEATHBED.

WE watched her breathing through the night,
  Her breathing soft and low,
As in her breast the wave of life
  Kept heaving to and fro.

So silently we seemed to speak,
  So slowly moved about,
As we had lent her half our powers,
  To eke her being out.

Our very hopes belied our fears,
  Our fears our hopes belied ;
We thought her dying when she slept,
  And sleeping when she died.

For when the morn came dim and sad,
  And chill with early showers,
Her quiet eyelids closed—she had
  Another morn than ours.

THE BRIDGE OF SIGHS.

ONE more Unfortunate,
Weary of breath,
Rashly importunate,
Gone to her death !

Take her up tenderly,
Lift her with care ;
Fashioned so slenderly,
Young, and so fair !

Look at her garments,
Clinging like cerements ;
Whilst the wave constantly
Drips from her clothing ;
Take her up instantly,
Loving, not loathing.—

Touch her not scornfully ;
Think of her mournfully,

Gently and humanly ;
Not of the stains of her,
All that remains of her
Now is pure womanly.

Make no deep scrutiny
Into her mutiny,
Rash and undutiful :
Past all dishonour,
Death has left on her
Only the beautiful.

Still, for all slips of hers,
One of Eve's family—
Wipe those poor lips of hers
Oozing so clammily.

Loop up her tresses
Escaped from the comb,
Her fair auburn tresses ;
Whilst wonderment guesses
Where was her home ?

Who was her father ?
Who was her mother ?
Had she a sister ?
Had she a brother ?
Or was there a dearer one
Still, and a nearer one
Yet, than all other ?

Alas ! for the rarity
Of Christian charity
Under the sun !
Oh ! it was pitiful !
Near a whole city full,
Home she had none.

Sisterly, brotherly,
Fatherly, motherly
Feelings had changed ;
Love, by harsh evidence,
Thrown from its eminence ;
Even God's providence
Seeming estranged.

Where the lamps quiver
So far in the river,
With many a light
From window and casement,
From garret to basement,
She stood, with amazement,
Houseless by night.

The bleak wind of March
Made her tremble and shiver ;
But not the dark arch,
Or the black flowing river :
Mad from life's history,
Glad to death's mystery,
Swift to be hurled—
Anywhere, anywhere
Out of the world !

In she plunged boldly,
No matter how coldly
The rough river ran,—
Over the brink of it,
Picture it—think of it,
Dissolute Man !
Lave in it, drink of it,
Then, if you can !

Take her up tenderly,
Lift her with care ;
Fashioned so slenderly,
Young, and so fair !

Ere her limbs frigidly
Stiffen too rigidly,
Decently,—kindly,—
Smooth, and compose them ;
And her eyes, close them,
Staring so blindly !

Dreadfully staring
Thro' muddy impurity,
As when with the daring
Last look of despairing
Fixed on futurity.

Perishing gloomily,
Spurred by contumely,
Cold inhumanity,
Burning insanity,
Into her rest.—
Cross her hands humbly
As if praying dumbly,
Over her breast !

Owning her weakness,
Her evil behaviour,
And leaving, with meekness,
Her sins to her Saviour !

SAMUEL ROGERS.

Born 1762. Died 1855.

HUMAN LIFE.

The lark has sung his carol in the sky,
The bees have hummed their noontide lullaby ;
Still in the vale the village bells ring round,
Still in Llewellyn hall the jests resound ;
For now the candle-cup is circling there,
Now, glad at heart, the gossips breathe their prayer,
And, crowding, stop the cradle to admire
The babe, the sleeping image of his sire.
A few short years, and then these sounds shall hail
The day again, and gladness fill the vale ;
So soon the child a youth, the youth a man,
Eager to run the race his fathers ran.
Then the huge ox shall yield the broad sirloin ;
The ale, now brewed, in floods of amber shine ;
And, basking in the chimney's ample blaze,
'Mid many a tale told of his boyish days,
The nurse shall cry, of all her ills beguiled,
" 'Twas on her knees he sat so oft and smiled."
　　And soon again shall music swell the breeze,
Soon, issuing forth, shall glitter through the trees
Vestures of nuptial white ; and hymns be sung,
And violets scattered round ; and old and young,
In every cottage porch with garlands green,
Stand still to gaze, and gazing, bless the scene,
While, her dark eyes declining, by his side,
Moves in her virgin veil the gentle bride.
　　And once alas ! nor in a distant hour,
Another voice shall come from yonder tower ;
While in dim chambers long black weeds are seen,
And weeping heard where joy has only been ;
When, by his children borne, and from his door,
Slowly departing to return no more,
He rests in holy earth with them that went before.
　　And such is human life ; so gliding on,
It glimmers like a meteor and is gone !
Yet is the tale, brief though it be, as strange,
As full, methinks, of wild and wondrous change,
As any, that the wandering tribes require,
Stretched in the desert round their evening fire ;
As any sung of old, in hall or bower,
To minstrel harps at midnight's witching hour !

A MOTHER'S LOVE.

HER, by her smile, how soon the stranger knows ;
How soon by his the glad discovery shows,
As to her lips she lifts the lovely boy,
What answering looks of sympathy and joy !
He walks, he speaks.   In many a broken word,
His wants, his wishes, and his griefs are heard.
And ever, ever to her lap he flies,
When rosy sleep comes on with sweet surprise.
Locked in her arms, his arms across her flung
(That name most dear for ever on his tongue),
As with soft accents round her neck he clings,
And, cheek to cheek, her lulling songs she sings,
How blest to feel the beatings of his heart :
Breathe his sweet breath, and bliss for bliss impart ;
Watch o'er his slumbers like the brooding dove,
And, if she can, exhaust a mother's love !

But soon a nobler task enjoins her care.
Apart she joins his little hands in prayer,
Telling of Him who sees in secret there !
And now the volume on her knee has caught
His wandering eye— now many a written thought
Never to die, with many a lisping sweet,
His moving, murmuring lips endeavour to repeat.

ELIZABETH BARRETT BROWNING.

Born 1801. Died 1861.

THE SLEEP.

OF all the thoughts of God that are
Borne inward into souls afar,
    Along the Psalmist's music deep,
Now tell me if that any is,
For gift or grace, surpassing this—
    "He giveth His belovèd, sleep?"

What would we give to our beloved ?
The hero's heart to be unmoved,
    The poet's star-tuned harp to sweep,
The patriot's voice to teach and rouse,
The monarch's crown to light the brows ? —
    He giveth his belovèd, sleep.

What do we give to our beloved ?
A little faith all undisproved,

A little dust to overweep,
And bitter memories to make
  The whole earth blasted for our sake :
    He giveth His belovèd, sleep.

"Sleep soft, beloved !" we sometimes say,
Who have no tune to charm away
  Sad dreams that through the eyelids creep :
But never doleful dream again
Shall break the happy slumber, when
    He giveth His belovèd, sleep.

O earth, so full of dreary noises !
O men, with wailing in your voices !
  O delvèd gold, the wailers' heap !
O strife, O curse, that o'er it fall !
God strikes a silence through you all,
    And giveth His belovèd, sleep.

His dews drop mutely on the hill,
His cloud above it faileth still,
  Though on its slope men sow and reap :
More softly than the dew is shed,
Or cloud is floated overhead,
    He giveth His belovèd, sleep.

Ay, men may wonder while they scan
A living, thinking, feeling man,
  Confirmed in such a rest to keep ;
But angels say, and through the word
I think their happy smile is *heard,*—
    "He giveth his belovèd, sleep."

For me, my heart that erst did go
Most like a tired child at a show,
  Seeing through tears the jugglers leap—
Would fain its wearied vision close,
And childlike on His love repose,
    Who "giveth His belovèd, sleep."

And Friends—dear Friends—when it shall be
That this low breath is gone from me,—
  When round my bier ye come to weep ;
Let one, most loving of you all,
Say, "Not a tear must o'er her fall,
    He giveth His belovèd, sleep."

COWPER'S GRAVE.

It is a place where poets crowned may feel the heart's decaying ;
It is a place where happy saints may weep amid their praying :
Yet let the grief and humbleness as low as silence languish :
Earth surely now may give her calm to whom she gave her anguish.

O poets, from a maniac's tongue was poured the deathless singing !
O Christians, at your cross of hope a hopeless hand was clinging !
O men, this man in brotherhood your weary paths beguiling,
Groaned inly while he taught you peace, and died while ye were smil-
    ing !

And now, what time ye all may read through dimming tears his story,
How discord on the music fell, and darkness on the glory,
And how when, one by one, sweet sounds and wandering lights
    departed,
He wore no less a loving face because so broken-hearted—

He shall be strong to sanctify the poet's high vocation,
And bow the meekest Christian down in meeker adoration ;
Nor ever shall he be, in praise, by wise or good forsaken,
Named softly as the household name of one whom God hath taken.

With quiet sadness and no gloom I learn to think upon him,
With meekness that is gratefulness to God whose heaven hath won
    him,
Who suffered once the madness cloud to his own love to blind him,
But gently led the blind along where breath and bird could find him.

And wrought within his shattered brain such quick poetic senses
As hills have language for, and stars, harmonious influences :
The pulse of dew within the grass kept his within its number,
And silent shadows from the trees refreshed him like a slumber.

Wild timid hares were drawn from woods to share his home-caresses,
Uplooking to his human eyes with sylvan tendernesses :
The very world, by God's constraint, from falsehood's ways removing,
Its women and its men became, beside him, true and loving.

And though, in blindness, he remained unconscious of that guiding,
And things provided came without the sweet sense of providing,
He testified this solemn truth, while frenzy desolated,
—Nor man nor nature satisfies whom only God created.

Like a sick child that knoweth not his mother while she blesses
And drops upon his burning brow the coolness of her kisses,—
Then turns his fevered eyes around —" My mother ! where's my
    mother ?"—
As if such tender words and deeds could come from any other !—

The fever gone, with leaps of heart he sees her bending o'er him,
Her face all pale with watchful love, the unwary love she bore him !—
Thus woke the poet from the dream his life's long fever gave him,
Beneath those deep pathetic Eyes which closed in death to save him.

Thus? oh, not *thus?* no type of earth can image that awaking,
Wherein he scarcely heard the chant of seraphs round him breaking,
Or felt the new immortal throb of soul from body parted,
But felt those Eyes alone, and knew, " *My* Saviour ! *not* deserted !"

Deserted ! Who hath dreamt that when the cross in darkness rested,
Upon the Victim's hidden face no love was manifested?
What frantic hands outstretched have e'er the atoning drops averted
What tears have washed them from the soul, that *one* should b
    deserted ?

Deserted ! God could separate from His own essence rather ;
And Adam's sins have swept between the righteous Son and Father
Yea, once, Immanuel's orphaned cry His universe hath shaken—
It went up single, echoless, "My God, I am forsaken !"

It went up from the Holy's lips amid His lost creation,
That, of the lost, no son should use those words of desolation !
That earth's worst phrenzies, marring hope, should mar not hope
    fruition,
And I, on Cowper's grave, should see his rapture in a vision.

A CHILD ASLEEP.

How he sleepeth, having drunken
    Weary childhood's mandragore !
From his pretty eyes have sunken
    Pleasures to make room for more :
Sleeping near the withered nosegay which he pulled the day before.

Nosegays ! leave them for the waking ;
    Throw them earthward where they grew ;
Dim are such beside the breaking
    Amaranths he looks unto :
Folded eyes see brighter colours than the open ever do.

Vision unto vision calleth
    While the young child dreameth on :
Fair, O dreamer, thee befalleth
    With the glory thou has won !
Darker wast thou in the garden yestermorn by summer sun.

We should see the spirits ringing
    Round thee, were the clouds away ;
'Tis the child-heart draws them, singing
    In the silent-seeming clay—
Singing ! stars that seem the mutest go in music all the way.

*   *   *   *   *

Speak not ! he is consecrated ;
    Breathe no breath across his eyes :
Lifted up and separated
    On the hand of God he lies
In a sweetness beyond touching, held in cloistral sanctities.

Could ye bless him, father—mother,
    Bless the dimple in his cheek?
Dare ye look at one another
    And the benediction speak?
Would ye not break out in weeping and confess yourselves too weak

He is harmless, ye are sinful ;
    Ye are troubled, he at ease :
From his slumber, virtue winful
    Floweth onward with increase.
Dare not bless him ! but be blessèd by his peace, and go in peace.

THE CRY OF THE CHILDREN.

Do ye hear the children weeping, O my brothers,
    Ere the sorrow comes with years?
They are leaning their young heads against their mother's,
    And *that* cannot stop their tears.
The young lambs are bleating in the meadows,
    The young birds are chirping in the nest,
The young fawns are playing with the shadows,
    The young flowers are blowing towards the west—
But the young, young children, O my brothers,
    They are weeping bitterly !
They are weeping in the play-time of the others,
    In the country of the free.

Do not question the young children in the sorrow
    Why their tears are falling so?
The old man may weep for his to-morrow
    Which is lost in Long Ago ;
The old tree is leafless in the forest,
    The old year is ending in the frost,
The old wound, if stricken, is the sorest,
    The old hope is hardest to be lost :
But the young, young children, O my brothers,
    Do you ask them why they stand
Weeping sore before the bosom of their mothers,
    In our happy Fatherland ?

They look up with their pale and sunken faces,
    And their looks are sad to see,
For the man's hoary anguish draws and presses
    Down the cheeks of infancy ;
"Your old earth," they say, " is very dreary,
    Our young feet," they say, " are very weak ;
Few paces have we taken, yet are weary—
    The grave rest is very far to seek :—
Ask the aged why they weep, and not the children,
    For the outside earth is cold,
And we young ones stand without, in our bewildering,
    And the graves are for the old.

" True," say the children, " it may happen
    That we die before our time :
Little Alice died last year, her grave is shapen
    Like a snowball, in the rime.
We looked into the pit prepared to take her :
    Was no room for any work in the close clay !—
From the sleep wherein she lieth none will wake her,
    Crying, ' Get up, little Alice ! it is day.'

If you listen by that grave, in sun or shower,
  With your ear down, little Alice never cries ;
Could we see her face, be sure we should not know her,
  For the smile has time for growing in her eyes :
And merry go her moments, lulled and stilled in
      The shroud by the kirk-chime.
It is good when it happens," say the children,
    "That we die before our time."

Alas, alas, the children ! they are seeking
    Death in life, as best to have :
They are binding up their hearts away from breaking,
    With a cerement from the grave.
Go out, children, from the mine and from the city,
  Sing out, children, as the little thrushes do ;
Pluck your handfuls of the meadow cowslips pretty,
  Laugh aloud, to feel your fingers let them through !
But they answer, " Are your cowslips of the meadows
    Like our weeds anear the mine ?
Leave us quiet in the dark of our coal shadows,
    From your pleasures fair and fine !

" For oh," say the children, " we are weary,
    And we cannot run or leap ;
If we cared for any meadows, it were merely
    To drop down in them and sleep.
Our knees tremble sorely in the stooping,
  We fall upon our faces, trying to go ;
And, underneath our heavy eyelids drooping,
  The reddest flower would look as pale as snow.
For, all day we drag our burden tiring,
    Through the coal-dark underground ;
Or, all day, we drive the wheels of iron
    In the factories round and round.

" For all day, the wheels are droning, turning,
    Their wind comes in our faces,
Till our hearts turn, our heads with pulses burning,
    And the walls turn in their places.
Turns the sky in the high window blank and reeling,
  Turns the long light that drops adown the wall,
Turn the black flies that crawl along the ceiling,
  All are turning, all the day, and we with all.
And all day, the iron wheels are droning,
    And sometimes we could pray,
' O ye wheels' (breaking out in a mad moaning),
    ' Stop ! be silent for to-day !' "

Ay, be silent ! Let them hear each other breathing
    For a moment, mouth to mouth !
Let them touch each other's hands, in a fresh wreathing
    Of their tender human youth !

Let them feel, that this cold metallic motion
    Is not all the life God fashions or reveals ;
Let them prove their living souls against the motion
    That they live in you, or under you, O wheels !
Still, all day, the iron wheels go onward,
        Grinding life down from its mark ;
And the children's souls, which God is calling sunward,
        Spin on blindly in the dark.

Now tell the poor young children, O my brothers,
        To look up to Him, and pray ;
So the blessed One who blesseth all the others,
    Will bless them another day.
They answer, "Who is God that He should hear us,
    While the rushing of the iron wheels is stirred ?
When we sob aloud, the human creatures near us
    Pass by, hearing not, or answer not a word.
And we hear not (for the wheels in their resounding)
        Strangers speaking at the door :
Is it likely God, with angels singing round Him,
        Hears our weeping any more ?

" Two words, indeed, of praying, we remember,
        And at midnight's hour of harm,
' Our Father,' looking upward in the chamber,
        We say softly for a charm.
We know no other words except ' Our Father,'
    And we think that, in some pause of angels' song,
God may pluck them with the silence sweet to gather,
    And hold both within His right hand which is strong.
' Our Father,' if he heard us, He would surely
        (For they call Him good and mild)
Answer, smiling down the steep world very purely,
        ' Come and rest with me, my child !'

" But no," say the children, weeping faster,
        " He is speechless as a stone :
And they tell us, of His image is the master
        Who commands us to work on.
Go to !" say the children, —" up in Heaven,
    Dark, wheel-like, turning clouds are all we find.
Do not mock us ; grief has made us unbelieving ;
    We look up for God, but tears have made us blind."
Do you hear the children weeping and disproving,
        O my brothers, what ye preach ?
For God's possible is taught by His world's loving,
        And the children doubt of each.

And well may the children weep before you !
        They are weary ere they run ;
They have never seen the sunshine, nor the glory
        Which is brighter than the sun.

They know the grief of man, without its wisdom,
    They sink in man's despair, without its calm ;
Are slaves, without the liberty in Christdom,
    Are martyrs, by the pang without the palm :
Are worn as if with age, yet unretrievingly
        The harvest of its memories cannot reap,—
Are orphans of the earthly love and heavenly.
        Let them weep ! Let them weep !

They look up with their pale and sunken faces,
        And their look is dread to see,
For they mind you of their angels in high places,
        With eyes turned on Deity.
" How long," they say, " how long, O cruel nation,
    Will you stand, to move the world, on a child's heart,—
Stifle down, with a mailed heel its palpitation,
    And tread onward, to your throne amid the mart ?
Our blood splashes upward, O gold-heaper,
        And your purple shows your path !
But the child's sob in the silence curses deeper,
        Than the strong man in his wrath.''

ARTHUR HUGH CLOUGH.

Born 1819. Died 1861.

COME BACK !

Come back, come back, behold with straining mast,
And swelling sail, behold her steaming fast ;
With one new sun to see her voyage o'er,
With morning light to touch her native shore.
        Come back, come back !

Come back, come back, while westward labouring by,
With sail-less yards, a bare black hulk we fly.
See how the gale we fight with, sweeps her back,
To her lost home, on our forsaken track.
        Come back, come back !

Come back, come back, across the flying foam,
We hear faint far-off voices call us home.
Come back, ye seem to say ; ye seek in vain ;
We went, we sought, and homeward turned again.
        Come back, come back !

Come back, come back ; and whither back or why ?
To fan quenched hopes, forsaken schemes to try ;
Walk the old fields ; pace the familiar street ;
Dream with the idlers, with the bards compete.
        Come back, come back !

Come back ; come back, and whither and for what ?
To finger idly some old Gordian knot,
Unskilled to sunder, and too weak to cleave,
And with much toil attain to half-believe.
      Come back, come back !

Come back, come back ; yea back, indeed, do go
Sighs panting thick, and tears that want to flow ;
Fond fluttering hopes upraise their useless wings,
And wishes idly struggle in the strings ;
      Come back, come back ?

Come back, come back ; more eager than the breeze,
The flying fancies sweep across the seas,
And lighter far than ocean's flying foam,
The heart's fond message hurries to its home.
      Come back, come back !

      Come back, come back !
Back hies the foam ; the hoisted flag streams back ;
The long smoke wavers on the homeward track,
Back fly with winds things which the winds obey,
The strong ship follows its appointed way.

WITH WHOM IS NO VARIABLENESS, NEITHER SHADOW OF TURNING."

It fortifies my soul to know
That, though I perish, Truth is so :
That, howsoe'er I stray and range,
Whate'er I do, Thou dost not change.
I steadier step when I recall
That, if I slip, Thou dost not fall.

SAY NOT, THE STRUGGLE NOUGHT AVAILETH.

Say not, the struggle nought availeth,
    The labour and the wounds are vain,
The enemy faints not, nor faileth,
    And as things have been they remain.

If hopes were dupes, fears may be liars ;
    It may be, in yon smoke concealed,
Your comrades chase e'en now the fliers,
    And, but for you, possess the field.

For while the tired waves, vainly breaking,
    Seem here no painful inch to gain,
Far back, through creeks and inlets making,
    Comes silent, flooding in, the main,

And not by eastern windows only,
    When daylight comes, comes in the light,
In front, the sun climbs slow, how slowly,
    But westward, look, the land is bright.

COME HOME, COME HOME.

Come home, come home, and where is home for me,
Whose ship is driving o'er the trackless sea?
To the frail bark here plunging on its way,
To the wild waters, shall I turn and say
To the plunging bark, or to the salt sea foam,
　　　　　You are my home?

Fields once I walked in, faces once I knew,
Familiar things so old my heart believed them true,
These far, far back, behind me lie, before
The dark clouds mutter, and the deep seas roar,
And speak to them that 'neath and o'er them roam
　　　　　No words of home.

Beyond the clouds, beyond the waves that roar,
There may indeed, or may not be, a shore,
Where fields as green, and hands and hearts as true,
The old forgotten semblance may renew,
And offer exiles driven far o'er the salt sea foam
　　　　　Another home.

But toil and pain must wear out many a day,
And days bear weeks, and weeks bear months away,
Ere, if at all, the weary traveller hear,
With accents whispered in his wayworn ear,
A voice he dares to listen to, say, Come
　　　　　To thy true home.

Come home, come home! And where a home hath he
Whose ship is driving o'er the driving sea?
Through clouds that mutter, and o'er waves that roar,
Say, shall we find, or shall we not, a shore
That is, as is not ship or ocean foam,
　　　　　Indeed our home?

QUA CURSUM VENTUS.

As ships, becalmed at eve, that lay
　　With canvas drooping, side by side,
Two towers of sail at dawn of day
　　Are scarce long leagues apart descried;

When fell the night, upsprung the breeze,
　　And all the darkling hours they plied,
Nor dreamt but each the self-same seas
　　By each was cleaving, side by side:

E'en so—but why the tale reveal
　　Of those, whom year by year unchanged,
Brief absence joined anew to feel,
　　Astounded, soul from soul estranged?

At dead of night their sails were filled,
  And onward each rejoicing steered—
Ah, neither blame, for neither willed,
  Or wist, what first with dawn appeared !

To veer, how vain ! On, onward strain,
  Brave barks ! In light, in darkness too,
Through winds and tides one compass guides—
  To that, and your own selves, be true.

But O blithe breeze ! and O great seas,
  Though ne'er, that earliest parting past,
On your wide plain they join again,
  Together lead them home at last.

One port, methought, alike they sought,
  One purpose hold where'er they fare,
O bounding breeze, O rushing seas !
  At last, at last, unite them there !

"WHAT WENT YE OUT FOR TO SEE?"

ACROSS the sea, along the shore,
In numbers ever more and more,
From lonely hut and busy town,
The valley through, the mountain down,
What was it ye went out to see,
Ye silly folk of Galilee ?
The reed that in the wind doth shake ?
The weed that washes in the lake ?
The reeds that waver, the weeds that float ?—
" A young man preaching in a boat."

What was it ye went out to hear,
By sea and land, from far and near ?
A teacher ? Rather seek the feet
Of those who sit in Moses' seat,
Go humbly seek, and bow to them,
Far off in great Jerusalem.
From them that in her courts ye saw,
Her perfect doctors of the law,
What is it came ye here to note ?—
" A young man preaching in a boat."

A prophet ! Boys and women weak !
  Declare, or cease to rave ;
Whence is it he hath learned to speak ?
  Say, who his doctrine gave ?
A prophet ? Prophet wherefore he
  Of all in Israel tribes ?—
He teacheth with authority,
  And not as do the Scribes.

WHERE ARE THE GREAT, WHOM THOU WOULDST WISH TO PRAISE THEE?

WHERE are the great, whom thou wouldst wish to praise thee ?
Where are the pure, whom thou wouldst choose to love thee?
Where are the brave, to stand supreme above thee,
Whose high commands would cheer, whose chiding raise thee ?
   Seek, seeker, in thyself ; submit to find
   In the stones, bread, and life in the blank mind.

CHARLES KINGSLEY.

Born 1819. Died 1875.

THE SANDS OF DEE.

" O MARY, go and call the cattle home,
   And call the cattle home,
   And call the cattle home,
   Across the sands o' Dee ;''
The western wind was wild and dank wi' foam,
   And all alone went she.

The creeping tide crept up along the sand,
   And o'er and o'er the sand,
   And round and round the sand,
   As far as eye could see.
The blinding mist came down, and hid the land—
   And never home came she.

"Oh ! is it weed, or fish, or floating hair—
   A tress o' golden hair,
   O' drownèd maiden's hair,
   Above the nets at sea ?
Was never salmon yet that shone so fair
   Among the stakes on Dee."

A FAREWELL.

My fairest child, I have no song to give you ;
   No lark could pipe to skies so dull and gray :
Yet, ere we part, one lesson I can leave you,
   For every day.

I'll teach you how to sing a clearer carol
   Than lark's, who hails the dawn o'er breezy down,
To earn yourself a purer poet's laurel
   Than Shakespeare's crown.

Be good, sweet maid, and let who can be clever ;
  Do noble things, not dream them, all day long :
And so make Life, Death, and that vast For-Ever
  One grand, sweet song.

LORRAINE.

"Are you ready _or your steeple-chase, Lorraine, Lorraine, Lorrèe ?
Barum, Barum, Barum, Barum, Barum, Barum, Baree.
You're booked to ride your capping race to-day at Coulterlee,
You're booked to ride Vindictive, for all the world to see,
To keep him straight, and keep him first, and win the run for me."
Barum, Barum, Barum, Barum, Barum, Barum, Baree.

She clasped her new-born baby, poor Lorraine, Lorraine, Lorrèe,
Barum, Barum, Barum, Barum, Barum, Barum, Baree.
"I cannot ride Vindictive, as any man might see,
And I will not ride Vindictive, with this baby on my knee,
He's killed a boy, he's killed a man, and why should he kill me ?"

"Unless you ride Vindictive, Lorraine, Lorraine, Lorrèe,
Unless you ride Vindictive, to-day at Coulterlee,
And land him safe across the brook, and win the blank for me,
It's you may keep your baby, for you'll get no keep from me."

"That husbands could be cruel," said Lorraine Lorraine, Lorrèe,
"That husbands could be cruel, I have known for seasons three ;
But oh ! to ride Vindictive, while a baby cries for me,
And be killed across a fence at last for all the world to see !"

She mastered young Vindictive,—oh ! the gallant lass was she !
And kept him straight, and won the race, as near as near could be ;
But he killed her at the brook against a pollard willow tree,
Oh, he killed her at the brook, the brute, for all the world to see,—
And no one but the baby cried for poor Lorraine, Lorrèe.

MINOR POETS.

HENRY KIRKE WHITE.

Born 1785. Died 1806.

TO AN EARLY PRIMROSE.

MILD offspring of a dark and sullen sire !
Whose modest form, so delicately fine,
  Was nursed in whirling storms,
  And cradled in the winds.

Thee, when young Spring first questioned Winter's sway,
And dared the sturdy blusterer to the fight,
    Thee on this bank he threw
    To mark his victory.

In this low vale, the promise of the year,
Serene, thou openest to the nipping gale,
    Unnoticed and alone,
    Thy tender elegance.

So virtue blooms, brought forth amid the storms
Of chill adversity ; in some lone walk
    Of life she rears her head,
    Obscure and unobserved ;

While every bleaching breeze that on her blows,
Chastens her spotless purity of breast,
    And hardens her to bear
    Serene the ills of life.

CHARLES WOLFE.

Born 1791. Died 1823.

THE BURIAL OF SIR JOHN MOORE.

Not a drum was heard, not a funeral note,
As his corse to the rampart we hurried ;
Not a soldier discharged his farewell shot
O'er the grave where our hero we buried.

We buried him darkly at dead of night,
The sods with our bayonets turning ;
By the struggling moonbeam's misty light,
And the lantern dimly burning.

No useless coffin enclosed his breast,
Not in sheet nor in shroud we wound him :
But he lay like a warrior taking his rest,
With his martial cloak around him.

Few and short were the prayers we said,
And we spoke not a word of sorrow ;
But we steadfastly gazed on the face that was dead,
And we bitterly thought of the morrow.

We thought, as we hollowed his narrow bed,
And smoothed down his lonely pillow,
That the foe and the stranger would tread o'er his head,
And we far away on the billow !

Lightly they'll talk of the spirit that's gone,
And o'er his cold ashes upbraid him,—
But little he'll reck, if they let him sleep on
In the grave where a Briton has laid him.

But half of our heavy task was done,
When the clock struck the hour for retiring ;
And we heard the distant and random gun
That the foe was sullenly firing.

Slowly and sadly we laid him down,
From the field of his fame fresh and gory ;
We carved not a line, and we raised not a stone—
But we left him alone with his glory.

BISHOP HEBER.

Born 1783.   Died 1826.

HYMN TO THE SEASONS.

WHEN Spring unlocks the flowers to paint the laughing soil ;
When Summer's balmy showers refresh the mower's toil ;
When Winter binds in frosty chains the fallow and the flood ; —
In God the earth rejoiceth still, and owns his Maker good.

The birds that wake the morning, and those that love the shade ;
The winds that sweep the mountain, or lull the drowsy glade ;
The sun that from his amber bower rejoiceth on his way,
The moon and stars, their Master's name in silent pomp display.

Shall Man, the lord of Nature, expectant of the sky,
Shall man, alone unthankful, his little praise deny?
No ; let the year forsake his course, the seasons cease to be,
Thee, Master, must we always love, and, Saviour, honour Thee.

The flowers of Spring may wither, the hope of Summer fade,
The Autumn droop in Winter, the birds forsake the shade ;
The winds be lulled, the sun and moon forget their old decree,—
But we, in Nature's latest hour, O Lord ! will cling to Thee.

FROM BISHOP HEBER'S JOURNAL.

If thou wert by my side, my love,
  How fast would evening fail
In green Bengala's palmy grove,
  Listening the nightingale !

If thou, my love, wert by my side,
  My babies at my knee,
How gaily would our pinnace glide
  O'er Gunga's mimic sea !

I miss thee at the dawing gray,
    When on our deck reclined,
In careless ease my limbs I lay,
    And woo the cooler wind.

I miss thee when by Gunga's stream
    My twilight steps I guide,
But most beneath the lamp's pale beam
    I miss thee from my side.

I spread my books, my pencil try,
    The lingering noon to cheer,
Bnt miss thy kind approving eye,
    Thy meek attentive ear.

But when of morn or eve the star
    Beholds me on my knee,
I feel, though thou art distant far,
    Thy prayers ascend for me.

Then on ! then on ! where duty leads,
    My course be onward still ;
O'er broad Hindostan's sultry meads,
    O'er bleak Almorah's hill.

That course, nor Delhi's kingly gates,
    Nor wild Malwah detain :
For sweet the bliss us both awaits
    By yonder western main.

Thy towers, Bombay, gleam bright, they say.
    Across the dark-blue sea ;
But ne'er were hearts so light and gay
    As then shall meet in thee !

EPIPHANY.

BRIGHTEST and best of the sons of the morning !
    Dawn on our darkness, and lend us Thine aid,
Star of the East, the horizon adorning,
    Guide where our Infant Redeemer is laid !

Cold on His cradle the dewdrops are shining,
    Low lies His head with the beasts of the stall :
Angels adore Him in slumber reclining—
    Maker, and Monarch, and Saviour of all !

Say, shall we yield Him, in costly devotion,
    Odours of Edom, and offerings divine—
Gems of the mountain, and pearls of the ocean,
    Myrrh from the forest, and gold from the mine?

Vainly we offer each ample oblation,
    Vainly with gifts would His favour secure,
Richer by far is the heart's adoration,
    Dearer to God are the prayers of the poor.

Brightest and best of the sons of the morning!
Dawn on our darkness, and lend us Thine aid,
Star of the East, the horizon adorning,
Guide where our infant Redeemer is laid!

BLANCO WHITE.

Born 1773. Died 1840.

NIGHT AND DEATH.

Mysterious Night! when our first parent knew
Thee from report divine, and heard thy name,
Did he not tremble for this lovely frame,
This glorious canopy of light and blue?
Yet, 'neath a curtain of translucent dew,
Bathed in the rays of the great setting flame,
Hesperus with the host of heaven came,
And lo! creation widened in man's view.
Who could have thought such darkness lay concealed
Within thy beams, O sun! or who could find,
Whilst fly, and leaf, and insect stood revealed,
That to such countless orbs thou mad'st us blind!
Why do we then shun death with anxious strife?
If light can thus deceive, wherefore not life?

ALLAN CUNNINGHAM.

Born 1784. Died 1842.

A WET SHEET AND A FLOWING SEA.

A wet sheet and a flowing sea,
    A wind that follows fast,
And fills the white and rustling sail,
    And bends the gallant mast.

HARTLEY COLERIDGE.

Born 1796. Died 1849.

ON THE BLANK LEAF OF A BIBLE.

When I received this volume small,
    My years were barely seventeen;
When it was hoped I should be all,
    Which once, alas! I might have been.

And now my years are thirty-five,
  And every mother hopes her lamb,
And every happy child alive,
  Will never be what now I am.

But yet should any chance to look
  On the strange medley scribbled here,
I charge thee, tell them, little book,
  I am not vile as I appear.

Oh tell them though my purpose lame
  In fortune's race was still behind,—
Though earthly blots defiled my name,
  They ne'er abused my better mind.

Of what men are, and why they are,
  So weak, so woefully beguiled,
Much have I learned, but better far,
  I know my soul is reconciled.

MARY MAGDALENE.

SHE sat and wept beside His feet ; the weight
Of sin oppressed her heart : for all the blame,
And the poor malice of the worldly shame,
To her were past, extinct, and out of date ;
Only the sin remained—the leprous state.
She would be melted by the heat of love,
By fires far fiercer than are blown to prove,
And purge the silver ore adulterate.
She sat and wept, and with her untressed hair,
Still wiped the feet she was so blest to touch,
And He wiped off the soiling of despair
From her sweet soul, because she loved so much.
I am a sinner full of doubts and fears,
Make me a humble thing of love and tears.

JAMES MONTGOMERY.

Born 1771. Died 1854.

THE COMMON LOT.

ONCE, in the flight of ages past,
  There lived a Man :—and WHO WAS HE ?—
Mortal ! howe'er thy lot be cast,
  That Man resembled thee.

Unknown the region of his birth,
  The land in which he died unknown :
His name has perished from the earth ;
  This truth survives alone :—

That joy and grief, and hope and fear,
  Alternate triumphed in his breast ;
His bliss and woe,—a smile, a tear !—
  Oblivion hides the rest.

The bounding pulse, the languid limb,
  The changing spirit's rise and fall,
We know that these were felt by him,
  For these are felt by all.

He suffered,—but his pangs are o'er ;
  Enjoyed,—but his delights are fled ;
Had friends,—his friends are now no more ;
  And foes,—his foes are dead.

He loved,—but whom he loved, the grave
  Hath lost in its unconscious womb :
Oh she was fair !—but nought could save
  Her beauty from the tomb.

He saw whatever thou hast seen ;
  Encountered all that troubles thee :
He was—whatever thou hast been ;
  He is—what thou shalt be.

The rolling seasons, day and night,
  Sun, moon, and stars, the earth and main,
Erewhile his portion, life, and light,
  To him exist in vain.

The clouds and sunbeams, o'er his eye
  That once their shades and glory threw,
Have left in yonder silent sky
  No vestige where they flew.

The annals of the human race,
  Their ruins since the world began,
Of him afford no other trace
  Than this,—THERE LIVED A MAN !

JOHN WILSON.

Born 1788. Died 1854.

THE EVENING CLOUD.

A CLOUD lay cradled near the setting sun,
A gleam of crimson tinged its braided snow :
Long had I watched the glory moving on
O'er the still radiance of the lake below.

Tranquil its spirit seemed, and floated slow !
Even in its very motion there was rest ;
While every breath of eve that chanced to blow
Wafted the traveller to the beauteous West.
Emblem, methought, of the departed soul !
To whose white robe the gleam of bliss is given :
And by the breath of mercy made to roll
Right onwards to the golden gates of Heaven,
Where, to the eye of faith, it peaceful lies,
And tells to man his glorious destinies.

THOMAS BABINGTON MACAULAY.

Born 1800.   Died 1859.

THE SPEECH OF ICILIUS.

Now, by your children's cradles, now by your father's graves,
Be men to-day, Quirites, or be for ever slaves !
For this did Servius give us laws?   For this did Lucrece bleed?
For this was the great vengeance wrought on Tarquin's evil seed?
For this did those false sons make red the axes of their sire?
For this did Scævola's right hand hiss in the Tuscan fire?
Shall the vile fox-earth awe the race that stormed the lion's den ?
Shall we, who could not brook one lord, crouch to the wicked Ten
Oh for that ancient spirit which curbed the Senate's will !
Oh for the tents which in old time whitened the Sacred Hill !
In those brave days our fathers stood firmly side by side ;
They faced the Marcian fury ; they tamed the Fabian pride ;
They drove the fiercest Quinctius an outcast forth from Rome :
They sent the haughtiest Claudius with shivered fasces home.
But what their care bequeathed us our madness flung away :
All the ripe fruit of threescore years was blighted in a day.
Exult, ye proud Patricians !   The hard-fought fight is o'er.
We strove for honours—'twas in vain : for freedom—'tis no more.
No crier to the polling summons the eager throng ;
No tribune breathes the word of might that guards the weak fro1
   wrong.
Our very hearts, that were so high, sink down beneath your will.
Riches, and lands, and power, and state—ye have them :—kee
   them still.'
Still keep the holy fillets ; still keep the purple gown,
The axes, and the curule chair, the car, and laurel crown :
Still press us for your cohorts, and, when the fight is done,
Still fill your garners from the soil which our good swords hav
   won.
Still, like a spreading ulcer, which leech-craft may not cure,
Let your foul usance eat away the substance of the poor.
Still let your haggard debtors bear all their fathers bore ;
Still let your dens of torment be noisome as of yore ;
No fire when Tiber freezes ; no air in dog-star heat ;
And store of rods for free-born backs, and holes for free-born fee

Heap heavier still the fetters ; bar closer still the grate,
Patient as sheep we yield us up unto your cruel hate.
But, by the shades beneath us, and by the Gods above,
Add not unto your cruel hate your yet more cruel love !
Have ye not graceful ladies, whose spotless lineage springs
From Consuls, and High Pontiffs, and ancient Alban kings ?
Ladies, who deign not on our paths to set their tender feet,
Who from their cars look down with scorn upon the wondering
    street,
Who in Carinthian mirrors their own proud smiles behold,
And breathe of Capuan odours, and shine with Spanish gold ?
Then leave the poor Plebeian his single tie to life—
The sweet, sweet love of daughter, of sister, and of wife,
The gentle speech, the balm for all that his vexed soul endures,
The kiss, in which he half forgets even such a yoke as yours.
Still let the maiden's beauty swell the father's breast with pride ;
Still let the bridegroom's arms enfold an unpolluted bride.
Spare us the inexpiable wrong, the unutterable shame,
That turns the coward's heart to steel, the sluggard's blood to
    flame,
Lest, when our latest hope is fled, ye taste of our despair,
And learn by proof, in some wild hour, how much the wretched
    dare.

                     From *Lays of Ancient Rome.*

LINES WRITTEN AFTER HIS DEFEAT AT THE EDINBURGH ELECTION. JUNE 30, 1847.

THE day of tumult, strife, defeat was o'er,
    Worn out with toil and noise and scorn and spleen,
I slumbered, and in slumber saw once more
    A room in an old mansion, long unseen.

That room, methought, was curtained from the light,
    Yet through the curtain shone the moon's cold ray,
Full on a cradle, where, in linen white,
    Sleeping life's first soft sleep, an infant lay.

And lo! the fairy queens, who rule our birth,
    Drew nigh to bless that new-born baby's doom.
With noiseless steps that left no trace on earth,
    From gloom they came, to vanish into gloom.

Scarce deigning on the boy a glance to cast,
    Swept careless by the gorgeous queen of Gain.
More careless still the queen of Fashion passed,
    With mincing gait, and sneer of cold disdain.

The queen of Power tossed high her jewelled head,
    And o'er her shoulder threw a wrathful frown.
The queen of Pleasure on the pillow shed
    Scarce one stray rose-leaf from her fragrant crown.

Still fay in long procession followed fay,
 And still the little couch remained unblest.
But when those wayward sprites had passed away,
 Came one, the last, the loveliest and the best.

Oh, lovely lady, with the eyes of light,
 And laurels clustering round thy lofty brow,
Who by the cradle's side didst watch that night,
 Warbling a low sweet music, who wast thou?

"Yes, darling, let them go," so ran the strain,
 "Yes, let them go, Youth, Pleasure, Fashion, Power,
And all the busy elves to whose domain
 Belong the nether aim, the fleeting hour.

"Without one envious sigh, one anxious scheme
 The nether aim, the fleeting hour resign ;
Mine is the world of thought, the world of dream,
 Mine all the past, and all the future mine.

"In the dark hour of shame I deigned to stand
 Beside the frowning peers at Bacon's side ;
On a far shore I smoothed with tender hand,
 Through months of pain, the sleepless bed of Hyde ;

"I brought the wise and good of ancient days
 To cheer the cell where Raleigh pined alone ;
I lightened Milton's darkness with the blaze
 Of the bright ranks that guard the eternal throne.

"And even so, my child, it is my pleasure
 That thou not *then* alone shouldst feel me nigh,
When in domestic bliss or studious leisure
 The weeks uncounted go, uncounted fly.

"No when on restless night dawns cheerless morrow,
 When weary soul, and wasting body pine,
Thine am I still, in sickness and in sorrow,
 In conflict, obloquy, want, exile, thine.

"Thine when on mountain heights the snowbirds scream,
 When more than Thulè's winter barbs the breeze,
When scarce through low'ring clouds one sickly beam
 Lights the drear May-day of Antarctic seas.

"Thine when around thy litter's track all day
 White sandhills shall reflect the blinding glare ;
Or, when through forests, breathing death, thy way
 All night shall wind by many a tiger's lair.

"Thine most, when friends turn pale and traitors fly,
. When, hard beset, thy spirit justly proud,
For truth, peace, freedom, mercy, dares defy
 A sullen priesthood, or a raging crowd.

"Amidst the din of all things fell and vile,
   Hate's yell, and Envy's hiss, and Folly's bray,
Remember me, and with an untaught smile,
   See riches, baubles, flatterers, pass away.

"Yes; they will pass away! nor deem it strange;
   They come and go, as comes and goes the sea;
And let them come and go; thou, through all change,
   Fix thy firm gaze on virtue, and on me."

EPITAPH ON A JACOBITE.

To my true king I offered free from stain
Courage and faith; vain faith, and courage vain.
For him, I threw lands, honours, wealth, away,
And one dear hope, that was more prized than they.
For him I languished in a foreign clime,
Grey-haired with sorrow in my manhood's prime;
Heard on Lavernia Scargill's whispering trees,
And pined by Arno for my lovelier Tees;
Beheld each night my home in fevered sleep,
Each morning started from the dream to weep;
Till God, who saw me tried too sorely, gave
The resting-place I asked, an early grave.
Oh thou, whom chance leads to this nameless stone,
From that proud country which was once mine own,
By those white cliffs I never more must see,
By that dear language which I spake like thee,
Forget all feuds, and shed one English tear
O'er English dust. A broken heart lies here.

WALTER SAVAGE LANDOR.

Born 1775. Died 1864.

SWEET SCENTS.

               WHEN hath wind or rain
Borne hard upon weak plants that wanted me,
And I (however they might bluster round)
Walkt off? 'Twere most ungrateful: for sweet scents
Are the swift vehicles of still sweeter thoughts,
And nurse and pillow the dull memory
That would let drop without them her best stores,
They bring me tales of youth and tones of love,
And 'tis and ever was my wish and way
To let all flowers live freely, and all die
(Whene'er their Genius bids their souls depart)
Among their kindred in their native place.
I never pluck the rose; the violet's head

Hath shaken with my breath upon its bank
And not reproacht it ; the ever sacred cup
Of the pure lily hath between my hands
Felt safe, unsoiled, nor lost one grain of gold.

THE SHELL.

I HAVE sinuous shells of pearly hue
Within, and they that lustre have imbibed
In the Sun's palace porch, where when unyoked
His chariot-wheel stands midway in the wave :
Shake one and it awakens, then apply
Its polished lips to your attentive ear,
And it remembers its august abodes,
And murmurs as the ocean murmurs there.

From *Gebir*.

ROSE AYLMER.

Oh what avails the sceptred race,
Oh what the form divine !
What every virtue, every grace !
Rose Aylmer, all were thine.

Rose Aylmer whom these wakeful eyes
May weep, but never see,
A night of memories and of sighs
I consecrate to thee.

ON HIS SEVENTY-FIFTH BIRTHDAY.

I STROVE with none, for none was worth my strife,
Nature I loved, and next to nature, Art ;
I warmed both hands before the fire of life,
It sinks, and I am ready to depart.

ADELAIDE ANNE PROCTER.

Born 1835. Died 1864.

A LOST CHORD.

SEATED one day at the Organ,
I was weary and ill at ease,
And my fingers wandered idly
Over the noisy keys.

I do not know what I was playing,
Or what I was dreaming then ;
But I struck one chord of music,
Like the sound of a great Amen.

It flooded the crimson twilight
  Like the close of an Angel's Psalm,
And it lay on my fevered spirit
  With a touch of infinite calm.

It quieted pain and sorrow,
  Like love overcoming strife ;
It seemed the harmonious echo
  From our discordant life.

It linked all perplexed meanings
  Into one perfect peace,
And trembled away into silence,
  As if it were loth to cease.

I have sought, but I seek it vainly,
  That one lost chord divine,
Which came from the soul of the Organ,
  And entered into mine.

It may be that Death's bright angel
  Will speak in that chord again,—
It may be that only in Heaven
  I shall hear that grand Amen.

JOHN KEBLE.

Born 1792. Died 1866.

FIRST SUNDAY AFTER EPIPHANY.

LESSONS sweet of spring returning,
  Welcome to the thoughtful heart !
May I call ye sense or learning,
  Instinct pure, or Heaven-taught art?
Be your title what it may,
  Sweet the lengthening April day,
While with you the soul is free,
Ranging wild o'er hill and lea.

Soft as Memnon's harp at morning,
  To the inward ear devout,
Touched by light, with heavenly warning
  Your transporting chords ring out.
Every leaf in every nook,
Every wave in every brook,
Chanting with a solemn voice,
Minds us of our better choice.

Needs no show of mountain hoary,
  Winding shore or deepening glen,
Where the landscape in its glory
  Teaches truth to wandering men :

Give true hearts but earth and sky,
  And some flowers to bloom and die,—
Homely scenes and simple views
Lowly thoughts may best infuse.

See the soft green willow springing
  Where the waters gently pass,
Every way her free arms flinging
  O'er the moist and reedy grass.
Long ere winter blasts are fled,
See her tipped with vernal red,
And her kindly flower displayed
Ere her leaf can cast a shade.

Though the rudest hand assail her,
  Patiently she droops awhile,
But when showers and breezes hail her,
  Wears again her willing smile
Thus I learn Contentment's power
From the slighted willow bower,
Ready to give thanks and live
On the least that Heaven may give.

If, the quiet brooklet leaving,
  Up the stony vale I wind,
Haply half in fancy grieving
  For the shades I leave behind,
By the dusty wayside drear,
Nightingales with joyous cheer
Sing, my sadness to reprove,
Gladlier than in cultured grove.

Where the thickest boughs are twining
  Of the greenest darkest tree,
There they plunge, the light declining—
  All may hear, but none may see.
Fearless of the passing hoof,
Hardly will they fleet aloof ;
So they live in modest ways,
Trust entire, and ceaseless praise.

SECOND SUNDAY AFTER EASTER.

O for a sculptor's hand,
  That thou might'st take thy stand,
Thy wild hair floating on the eastern breeze,
  Thy tranced yet open gaze
  Fixed on the desert haze,
As one who deep in heaven some airy pageant sees.

  In outline dim and vast
  Their fearful shadows cast
The giant forms of empires on their way
  To ruin : one by one
  They tower and they are gone,
Yet in the Prophet's soul the dreams of avarice stay.

No sun or star so bright
In all the world of light
That they should draw to Heaven his downward eye :
He hears th' Almighty's word,
He sees the angel's sword,
Yet low upon the earth his heart and treasure lie.

Lo ! from yon argent field,
To him and us revealed,
One gentle Star glides down, on earth to dwell.
Chained as they are below
Our eyes may see it glow,
And as it mounts again, may track its brightness well.

To him it glared afar,
A token of wild war,
The banner of his Lord's victorious wrath :
But close to us it gleams,
Its soothing lustre streams
Around our home's green walls, and on our church-way path.

We in the tents abide
Which he at distance eyed
Like goodly cedars by the waters spread,
While seven red altar-fires
Rose up in wavy spires,
Where on the mount he watched his sorceries dark and dread.

He watched till morning's ray
On lake and meadow lay,
And willow-shaded streams, that silent sweep
Around the bannered lines,
Where by their several signs
The desert-wearied tribes in sight of Canaan sleep.

He watched till knowledge came
Upon his soul like flame,
Not of those magic fires at random caught :
But true prophetic light
Flashed o'er him, high and bright,
Flashed once, and died away, and left his darkened thought.

And can he choose but fear,
Who feels his God so near,
That when he fain would curse, his powerless tongue
In blessing only moves ?—
Alas ! the world he loves
Too close around his heart her tangling veil hath flung.

Sceptre and Star divine,
Who in Thine inmost shrine
Hast made us worshippers, O claim Thine own ;
More than Thy seers we know—
O teach our love to grow
Up to Thy heavenly light, and reap what Thou hast sown.

EDWARD, LORD LYTTON.

Born 1805.   Died 1872.

THE DESIRE OF FAME.

I DO confess that I have wished to give
  My land the gift of no ignoble name,
And in that holier air have sought to live,
  Sunned with the hope of fame.

Do I lament that I have seen the bays
  Denied my own, not worthier brows above,
Foes quick to scoff, and friends afraid to praise,—
  More active hate than love?

Do I lament that roseate youth has flown
  In the hard labour grudged its niggard meed,
And cull from far and juster lands alone
  Few flowers from many a seed?

No! for whoever with an earnest soul
  Strives for some end from this low world afar,
Still upward travels, though he miss the goal,
  And strays—but towards a star.

Better than fame is still the wish for fame,
  The constant training for a glorious strife:
The athlete nurtured for the Olympian Game,
  Gains strength at least for life.

The wish for Fame is faith in holy things
  That soothe the life, and shall outlive the tomb—
A reverent listening for some angel wings
  That cower above the gloom.

To gladden earth with beauty, or men's lives
  To serve with action, or their souls with truth,—
These are the ends for which the hope survives
  The ignobler thirsts of youth.

No, I lament not, though these leaves may fall
  From the sered branches on the desert plain,
Mocked by the idle wings that waft; and all
  Life's blooms, its last, in vain!

If vain for others, not in vain for me,—
  Who builds an altar let him worship there;
What needs the crowd? though lone the shrine may be,
  Not hallowed less the prayer.

Enough if haply in the after days,
   When by the altar sleeps the funeral stone,
When gone the mists our human passions raise,
   And Truth is seen alone :

When causeless Hate can wound its prey no more,
   And fawns its late repentance o'er the dead,
If gentler footsteps from some kindlier shore
   Pause by the narrow bed.

Or if yon children, whose young souls of glee
   Float to mine ear, the evening gales along,
Recall some echo, in their years to be,
   Of not all-perished song !

Taking some spark to glad the hearth, or light
   The student lamp, from now neglected fires,—
And one sad memory in the sons requite
   What—I forgive the sires.

ALEXANDER SMITH.

Born 1830. Died 1867.

FORGETFULNESS.

I HID my face awhile, then cried aloud,
"No one can give forgetfulness ; not one.
No one can tell me who can give it me.
I asked of Joy, as he went laughing past,
Crushing a bunch of grapes against his lips,
And suddenly the light forsook his face,
His orbs were blind with tears—*he* could not tell.
I asked of Grief, as with red eyes he came
From a sweet infant's bier ; and at the sound
He started, shook his head, with quick hand drew
His mantle o'er his face, and turned away
'Mong the blue twilight-mists."   Sleep did not raise
His heavy lids, but in a drowsy voice,
Like murmur of a leafy sycamore
When bees are swarming in the glimmering leaves,
Said, "I've a younger brother, very wise,
Silent and still, who ever dwells alone—
His name is Death : seek him, and he may know."
I cried, "O angel, is there no one else?"
But Sleep stood silent, and his eyes were closed.

Methought, when I awoke, "We have two lives ;
The soul of man is like the rolling world,
One half in day, the other dipt in night,
The one has music and the flying cloud,

The other, silence and the wakeful stars."
I drew my window-curtains, and instead
Of the used yesterday, there laughing stood
A new-born morning from the Infinite
Before my very face : my heart leaped up,
Inexorable Labour called me forth ;
And as I hurried through the busy streets,
There was a sense of envy in my heart
Of lazy lengths of rivers in the sun,
Larks soaring up the ever-soaring sky,
And mild kine couched in fields of uncrushed dew.

From Horton.

A DREAM.

Fair lady, in my dream
Methought I was a weak and lonely bird,
In search of summer, wandered on the sea,
Toiling through mists, drenched by the arrowy rain,
Struck by the heartless winds : at last, methought
I came upon an isle in whose sweet air
I dried my feathers, smoothed my ruffled breast,
And skimmed delight from off the waving woods.
Thy coming, lady, reads this dream of mine :
I am the swallow, thou the summer land.

From A Life Drama.

THE DYING KING.

A grim old king,
Whose blood leapt madly when the trumpets brayed
To joyous battle 'mid a storm of steeds,
Won a rich kingdom on a battle-day ;
But in the sunset he was ebbing fast,
Ringed by his weeping lords. His left hand held
His white steed, to the belly splashed with blood,
That seemed to mourn him with his drooping head ;
His right, his broken brand ; and in his ear
His old victorious banners flap the winds.
He called his faithful herald to his side,—
" Go ! tell the dead I come !" With a proud smile,
The warrior with a stab let out his soul,
Which fled and shrieked through all the other world,
"Ye dead ! My master comes !" And there was pause
Till the great shade should enter.

From A Life Drama.

DUTY AND FAME.

My life was a long dream ; when I awoke,
Duty stood like an angel in my path,
And seemed so terrible, I could have turned
Into my yesterdays, and wandered back
To distant childhood, and gone out to God
By the gate of birth, not death. Lift, lift me up

By thy sweet inspiration, as the tide
Lifts up a stranded boat upon the beach.
I will go forth 'mong men, not mailed in scorn,
But in the armour of a pure intent.
Great duties are before me and great songs,
And whether crowned or crownless when I fall
It matters not, so as God's work is done.
I've learned to prize the quiet lightning-deed,
Not the applauding thunder at its heels
Which men call Fame.

From *A Life Drama.*

THOMAS CARLYLE.

Born 1795. Died 1881.

TO-DAY.

So here hath been dawning
Another blue day :
Think wilt thou let it
Slip useless away.

Out of Eternity
This new Day is born ;
Into Eternity,
At night, will return.

Behold it aforetime
No eye ever did ;
So soon it for ever
From all eyes is hid.

Here hath been dawning
Another blue Day :
Think wilt thou let it
Slip useless away.

ADIEU.

LET time and chance combine,
        combine,
  Let time and chance combine ;
The fairest love from heaven
        above,
  That love of yours was mine,
                My dear,
  That love of yours was mine.

The past is fled and gone, and
        gone,
  The past is fled and gone ;
If nought but pain to me remain,
  I'll fare in memory on,
                My dear,
  I'll fare in memory on.

The saddest tears must fall, must
        fall,
  The saddest tears must fall ;

In weal or woe, in this world be-
        low,
  I love you ever and all,
                My dear,
  I love you ever and all.

A long road full of pain, of pain,
  A long road full of pain ;
One soul, one heart, sworn ne'er
        to part,—
  We ne'er can meet again,
                My dear,
  We ne'er can meet again.

Hard fate will not allow, allow,
  Hard fate will not allow ;
We blessed were as the angels
        are,—
  Adieu for ever now,
                My dear,
  Adieu for ever now.

ARTHUR PENRHYN STANLEY.

Born 1815.   Died 1881.

ASH WEDNESDAY.

(Written on the anniversary of the deaths of his mother and wife.)

O DAY of Ashes !—twice for me
  Thy mournful title hast thou earned,
For twice my life of life by thee
  Has been to dust and ashes turned.
No need, dark day, that thou shouldst borrow
The trappings of a formal sorrow ;
In thee are cherished fresh and deep
Long memories that cannot sleep.

My Mother—on that fatal day,
  O'er seas and deserts far apart,
The guardian genius passed away
  That nursed my very mind and heart—
The oracle that never failed,
The faith serene that never quailed,
The kindred soul that knew my thought
Before its speech or form was wrought.

My Wife—when closed that fatal night,
  My being turned once more to stone,
I watched her spirit take its flight,
  And found myself again alone.
The sunshine of the heart was dead,
The glory of the home was fled,
The smile that made the dark world bright,
The love that made all duty light.

Now that those scenes of bliss are gone,
  Now that the long years roll away,
The two Ash Wednesdays blend in one,
  One sad yet almost festal day :
The emblem of that union blest,
Where lofty souls together rest,
Star differing each from star in glory,
Yet telling each its own high story.

When this day bids us from within
  Look out on human strifes and storms :
The worst man's hope, the best man's sin,
  The world's base arts, Faith's hollow forms—
One answer comes in accents dear,
Yet as the piercing sunbeam clear,
The secret of the better life
Read by my Mother and my Wife.

THE UNTRAVELLED TRAVELLER.

(Lines written on the recovery of Prince Leopold.)

"When brothers part for manhood's race,"
  And gladly seek from year to year,
From scene to scene, from place to place,
  The wonders of each opening sphere,
Is there no venturous path in store,
To undiscovered haunt or shore,
For him whom Fate forbade to roam,
The untravelled traveller at home?

Yes, gallant youth! What though to thee
  Nor Egypt's sands, nor Russia's snows,
Nor Grecian isle, nor tropic sea,
  Nor Western worlds, their wealth disclose;
Thy wanderings have been vaster far
Than midnight sun or southern star;
And thou, too, hast thy trophies won,
Of toils achieved and exploits done.

For thrice thy weary feet have trod
  The pathway to the realms of Death;
And leaning on the hand of God,
  With halting step and panting breath,
Thrice from the edge of that dread bourn,
From which no travellers return,
Thou hast, like him who rose at Nain,
Come back to life and light again.

Each winding of that mournful way,
  Each inlet of that shadowy shore,
Through restless night and tedious day
  'Twas thine to fathom and explore;
Through hairbreath scapes and shocks as rude
As e'er are met in fire or flood,
Thou, in thy solitary strife,
Hast borne aloft thy charmèd life.

Yet in this pilgrimage of ill
  Sweet tracts and isles of peace were thine—
Dear watchful friends, strong gentle skill,
  Consoling words of Love Divine,
A Royal mother's ceaseless care,
A nation's sympathizing prayer,
The everlasting Arms beneath
That lightened even the load of death.

Those long descents, that upward climb,
  Shall give an inward strength and force,
Breathed as by Alpine heights sublime
  Through all thy dark and perilous course.

Not Afric's swamps nor Biscay's wave
Demand a heart more firm and brave,
Than may for thee be born and bred,
Even on thy sick and lonely bed.

And still as months and years roll by,
　A world-wide prospect shall unfold—
The realm of art, the poet's sky,
　The land of wisdom's purest gold.
These shalt thou traverse to and fro,
In search of these thy heart shall glow,
And many a straggler shall be led
To follow in thine onward tread.

"Hast Thou, O Father, dear and true,
　One blessing only—none for me?
Bless, O my Father, bless me too,
　Out of Thy boundless charity."
Rest, troubled spirit, calmly rest;
He blesses, and thou shalt be blest;
And from thy hard-wrought happiness
Thou wilt the world around thee bless.

GEORGE ELIOT.

Born 1820.　Died 1881.

On, may I join the choir invisible
Of those immortal dead who live again
In minds made better by their presence : live
In pulses stirred to generosity,
In deeds of daring rectitude, in scorn
For miserable aims that end with self,
In thoughts sublime that pierce the night like stars,
And with their mild persistence urge man's search
To vaster issues.
　　　　　So to live is heaven :
To make undying music in the world,
Breathing as beauteous order that controls
With growing sway the growing life of man.
So we inherit that sweet purity
For which we struggled, failed, and agonized
With widening retrospect that bred despair.
Rebellious flesh that would not be subdued,
A vicious parent shaming still its child,
Poor anxious penitence, is quick dissolved ;
Its discords, quenched by meeting harmonies,
Die in the large and charitable air.
And all our rarer, better, truer self,
That sobbed religiously in yearning song,

That watched to ease the burthen of the world,
Laboriously tracing what must be,
And what may yet be better—saw within
A worthier image for the sanctuary,
And shaped it forth before the multitude
Divinely human, raising worship so
To higher reverence more mixed with love—
That better self shall live till human Time
Shall fold its eyelids, and the human sky
Be gathered like a scroll within the tomb
Unread for ever.
        This is life to come,
Which martyred men have made more glorious
For us who strive to follow. May I reach
That purest heaven, be to other souls
The cup of strength in some great agony,
Enkindle generous ardour, feed pure love,
Beget the smiles that have no cruelty—
Be the sweet presence of a good diffused,
And in diffusion ever more intense.
So shall I join the choir invisible
Whose music is the gladness of the world.

ANNA LÆTITIA WARING.

About 1850.

THY WILL BE DONE.

FATHER, I know that all my life
  Is portioned out for me,
And the changes that are sure to come
  I do not fear to see ;
But I ask Thee for a present mind,
  Intent on pleasing Thee.

I ask Thee for a thoughtful love,
  Through constant watching wise,
To meet the glad with joyful smiles
  And to wipe the weeping eyes :
And a heart at leisure from itself,
  To soothe and sympathize.

I would not have the restless will
  That hurries to and fro ;
Seeking for some great thing to do,
  A secret thing to know :
I would be treated as a child,
  And guided where I go.

Wherever in the world I am,
　In whatsoe'er estate,
I have a fellowship with men
　To keep and cultivate,
And a work of lowly love to do,
　For the Lord on whom I wait.

So I ask Thee for the daily strength,
　To none that ask denied,
And a mind to blend with outward strife
　While keeping at Thy side ;
Content to fill a little space,
　So Thou be glorified.

And if some things I do not ask
　In my cup of blessing be,
I would have my spirit filled the more
　With grateful love to Thee ;
And careful, less to serve Thee much,
　Than to please Thee perfectly.

There are briers besetting every path
　That call for patient care ;
There is a cross in every lot,
　And an earnest need for prayer ;
But a lowly heart, that leans on Thee,
　Is happy anywhere.

In a service which Thy will appoints,
　There are no bonds for me ;
For my inmost heart is taught the truth
　That makes Thy children free :
And a life of self-renouncing love
　Is a life of liberty.

ANONYMOUS.

THE NIGHTMARE.

I.

I come in gleams from the land of dreams,
　Wrapped round in the midnight's pall ;
Ye may hear my groan in the night-wind's moan,
　When the tapestry flaps on the wall.
I come from my rest in the death-owl's nest,
　When she screams in fear and pain,
And my wings gleam bright in the wild moonlight,
　As it whirls round the madman's brain,
And down sweeps my car like a falling star,
　When the winds have hushed their breath,
When ye feel in the air from the cold sepulchre,
　The damp sad smell of death.

II.

My vigil I keep by the murderer's sleep,
    When dreams round his senses spin,
And ride on his breast, and trouble his rest,
    In the shape of his deadliest sin ;
And hollow and low is his groan of woe,
    In the depth of his strangling pain,
And his cold black eye rolls in agony,
    And faintly rattles his chain ;
The sweat-drops fall on the dark prison wall,
    He wakes with a deep-drawn sigh ;
He hears my tread as I pass from his bed,
    And he calls on the saints on high.

III.

I fly to the bed where the weary head
    Of the poet its rest must seek,
And with false dreams of fame I kindle the flame
    Of joy on his pallid cheek.
No thought does he take of the world awake
    And its cold and heartless pleasure,
The holy fire of his own loved lyre,
    Is his best and dearest treasure ;
But neglect's foul sting that cheek must bring
    To a darker and deadlier hue ;—
The last dear token his lyre is broken,
    And his heart is broken too.

IV.

When the maiden asleep for her lover may weep
    Afar on the boundless sea,
And she dreams he is pressed to her welcome breast,
    Returned from his dangers free ;
I come in the form of a wave of the storm,
    And sweep him away from her heart,
And then in her dream she starts with a scream,
    To think that in death they part ;
And still in the light of her tear-bound sight,
    The images whirl and dance,
Till my swift elision dispels the vision,
    And she wakes as from a trance.

V.

When the clouds first born of the breezy morn
    In the western chambers roam,
I glide away in the twilight gray,
    To rest in my shadowy home ;
And darkness and sleep to their kingdoms sweep,
    And dreams rustle by like a storm,
But where I dwell no man can tell,
    Who has seen my hideous form,

Whether it be in the caves of the sea,
　When the rolling breakers go,
Or the crystal sphere of the upper air,
　Or the Stygian depths below.

A RIPPLE ON THE LAKE.

THERE was a ripple on the water's face,
A ripple on the waters of Loch Fyne.
Bright fell the sunshine, with a sportive grace,
Sweet sang the throstle from her island shrine.
"Save me, God! save me!" but a moment past
Uprose the shriek of frenzied agony ;
From the clear wave, a dying youth aghast
Glared round and upwards as he breathed that cry ;
Then sank, slow drifting through the unfathomed space,
Down to the dark burial 'mid the wild weeds' twine.
So came that ripple on the water's face,
That ripple on the waters Loch Fyne.